MIST C

They went deviously ho
no warmth from the pale sun and no plea
from their talk. The woman's malice had been too plain; and Margery remembered unhappily that this Redfern had been wife to a servant whose master had died at Chester one fateful Candle mas. Now the woman dwelt on the Nutter land, for which she surely gave obedience to the Rough Lee. Margery remembered again the dark eyes that had gleamed so coldly in that house not an hour ago; and remembering them, she felt a sudden dread. Soon and somehow she might expect the mud to stir in these Pendle undercurrents, and when it stirred it would surely disturb what seemed a present happiness. Happiness, she now thought, was a quality that did not flourish in the lee of Pendle Hill.

Also available from A. G. (Northern) Ltd

The Lancashire Witches by
Harrison Ainsworth

Robert Neill

MIST OVER PENDLE

Arrow Books Limited
20 Vauxhall Bridge Road, London SW1V 2SA

An imprint of Random House UK Ltd

London Melbourne Sydney Auckland
Wellington Johannesburg and agencies
throughout the world

Special edition for A. G. (Northern) Ltd,
Farnworth, Lancashire BL4 9NE, 1992

Printed in Great Britain
by Cox & Wyman Ltd, Reading, Berks

ISBN 0 09 929451 6

To the

Dusty Memory

of

MASTER THOMAS POTTS

Sometime Clerk to the Judges in
The Circuit of the North Parts

Who in November, 1612, at his Lodging
in Chancery Lane, wrote of the

Late

WONDERFUL DISCOVERIE OF WITCHES

in the
Countie of Lancaster

De veniam Ignoto non displicuisse meretur
Festinat studiis qui placuisse tibi

Contents

1	The Cuckoo Child	9
2	The Country Gentleman	18
3	The Brooding Hill	30
4	Candle Light	39
5	The Rough Lee	46
6	The Puritan	56
7	The Demdike Brood	66
8	Dark Elegance	78
9	The King's Justice	87
10	Undercurrents	97
11	The Chapel-of-Ease	106
12	The Mill at Wheathead	113
13	The Miller's Daughter	122
14	The Fates are Three	132
15	The Eve of All Hallows	142
16	The English Mission	152
17	The Lady Bountiful	160
18	Ambition's Track	171

19	Martinmas	180
20	The Gentleman from Lathom	188
21	The Scent of Evil	198
22	The Dark House of Nutter	207
23	Clouds over Wheathead	216
24	The Breaking Storm	226
25	Aftermath	237
26	Taffeta and Velvet	248
27	The Traveller by Night	258
28	'To Drive Away Sorrow'	268
29	The Secret Cold	277
30	East Wind in Pendle	286
31	Candlemas	296
32	Cold Comforts	304
33	The Bitterness of Death	312
34	The Stricken Pedlar	324
35	Easter Duties	338
36	Charity and Silence	350
37	Moon-Kissed	361
38	The Steward's Room	374

1

The Cuckoo Child

In December 1595 died Dr. William Whitaker, Master of St. John's College and Regius Professor of Divinity in the University of Cambridge. He left to his widow some books, some sermons, and the care of eight children, the youngest not a week old. And since he had been a poor man, he left her very little else.

It soon appeared that she might expect little help from his College, for he had been more esteemed out of it than in it. He had been too stern a Calvinist to please the Fellows, who would have liked him better, as one of them had said, if they had found in him more of sweet England and less of sour Geneva. He had been known, too, for a habit which has never won liking for any man, a habit of being sorry for himself, of complaining that his preferment had never matched his deserts; and the Fellows thought this assertion a slight upon the worth of their Mastership. Nor had he mended matters by a vain attempt, some two years before, to leave St. John's for the more lucrative Mastership of Trinity, which had then been vacant. So when he was gone, his widow, who had always echoed his sentiments with a tart and busy tongue, did not find the Fellows more generous than they had a duty to be.

Mistress Whitaker therefore withdrew from Cambridge and conveyed herself and her children to London, where she might hope to find more generous friends. For Dr. Whitaker had not been her only husband. She had married him when she was already the widow of that Dudley Fenner whom all Kent knew and honoured as a puritan divine, and whose *Short And Profitable Treatise Of Lawful And Un-*

lawful Recreation had crossed every frontier in Europe. She had, indeed, borne Dr. Fenner two children, and this, she supposed, might now commend her to his family and to such others as might still honour his name.

As she supposed, so it proved. She found his family and his friends, and she laid them under contribution. She extracted a little from the Fellows of St. John's. She extracted rather more from Dr. Whitaker's benefactor and uncle, the aged Alexander Nowell who was Dean of St. Paul's and author of those famous catechisms of which the smallest still largely survives in the Book of Common Prayer. And thus provided she set up a modest home near Lambeth, where she felt herself securely within the aura of the Church. Here, in the years that followed, she devoted herself to the care of her children, and especially to that of the lately born infant. This youngest was a girl named Margery.

These were lean years and hard, for her means were small for what was to be done. But by perseverance and economy, by expedient and denial, she contrived to bring them all through the years of dependence; and as each came to a proper age she appealed to their father's family for what was needed as a start in life. This, or as little of it as might suffice, each in turn received, for the Whitakers were not ungenerous. They were a family of some substance, holding a good estate at Holme in the County of Lancaster, and they gave to each a portion which, if it seemed little, did in fact suffice. One by one, therefore, Mistress Whitaker sent her children out into the world: Alexander, the eldest, to Cambridge and a Fellowship of Trinity; Richard to a bookseller's trade in Holborn; Prudence as housekeeper to Richard; Laurence into Holy Orders; Sarah and Elizabeth into parsonages as the wives and helps of divines.

Matters were so disposed, all but Margery having gone from home, when in May of 1611 Mistress Whitaker, exhausted by her long exertions, went into a distemper and shortly died.

When she had been decorously laid to rest and the funeral sermon gravely preached, the elders of her family met in Richard's house above the bookshop in Holborn to discuss what has to be discussed at such a time; and when they had dined and some lesser matters had been settled,

Prudence brought them to the greater one: what, she demanded, was to be done with Margery?

They looked at one another unhappily, for this had been in all their thoughts. Alexander coughed and tried to put it aside. The girl, he said, was young, the matter not urgent; it could properly wait till they met again. He was airy about it, and he was moving on when Richard stopped him. By his leave, said Richard, the matter *was* urgent; it could by no means wait till they met again.

Alexander flushed angrily. He was the eldest, and he was not used to being contradicted like that; but Prudence and Richard were of one mind about this, and they spoke that mind firmly. The young Margery had been their guest and ward for some days now, and they had cause to know it. Richard could recall no time when his apprentices had been so turbulent and so disposed to dream at their duties, and Prudence had been asking bitterly how she was to order her house and contrive for her guests when it was one woman's full work to keep an eye on Margery. So she and Richard spoke with one voice: something must be done with Margery, and would Alexander please say what?

If Margery had been at all like her sisters there would have been no problem, for she was now approaching her sixteenth birthday and might therefore be accounted almost of marriageable age; if she had been like her sisters the family's name and repute would have tempted more than one good curate to contract for such a wife to grace his parsonage, bear his children, and support him through the ills of life. The trouble was, as her family had long since ceased to conceal from themselves, that Margery was not in the least like her sisters, in body or in mind. They were dark of hair and thin of face as their mother had been; devout of mind and sober of speech as their father had been; fitting wives for any divine. But this Margery was of another mould. She was lithe of limb and firm of muscle, and if she was not truly beautiful she at least caught and held attention—especially, said her sisters, masculine attention. She had a firmly moulded chin, a lean and humorous mouth, and eyebrows that lifted easily to point the meanings of her impertinences; her whole face, indeed, was eloquent, and it gave expression to a variety of sentiments—some of them, according to her sisters, being sentiments that a girl of her age ought not to have, let alone express. Her eyes, too, although they mirrored beyond mistake a quick and questioning intelligence, could yet hold a ripple of humour and a twinkle of mischief; and this they did, as her family thought, a great deal too often, and sometimes at scandalously ill-chosen moments. Her hair, also, set her apart in the family, for it was of an unusual brown; a brown a little darker than golden, but having in it an odd streak of red which lurked in the depths and gave a sudden glint when the sunlight caught it. Margery, in short, was the cuckoo in the nest, and how such a girl had been born into such a family none could tell. It was well indeed for Mistress Whitaker that she moved among divines; folk of another sort might have wondered shamefully.

Of Margery's talents and accomplishments there was less complaint to be made. It had to be admitted that the girl had put her quick wits to some good uses. The arts of reading and writing, which her sisters had gained slowly and with labour, had come to her easily and without need of compulsion. She added to them some rudiments of Latin, earnestly instilled into her by an eccentric divine who had fancied that they would make her a closer companion for the curate she would surely wed. In manners and deportment she was well instructed. She had as much of needlework and the household arts as might properly be expected of one who had not yet ruled an establishment. She could do household accounts fairly and decently. And from a friendly neighbour, who was a Huguenot out of France and by trade a riding-master, she had learned something of the management of a horse.

She had, too, some other learning which her family had not noticed. In a house so frequented by the puritan clergy and their friends there had been no lack of talk—talk for the most part of theology and its many controversies; and for many an hour she had sat composed and silent while her quick mind took in more than the talkers dreamed of. If she had had a mind to, which she most assuredly had not, she could have expounded as well as any of them the doctrines of that John Calvin whose *Institutio*, it seemed, had dwarfed and superseded *De Civitate Dei*; she could have rehearsed the points in which this Calvin had been so impertinently criticised by the Dutchman Hermanns, whom they latinised into Arminius; she could have spoken of that Erastus whose *Explicatio* lent support to the claims of the civil power; and she could have added her private belief that all three of them had expended a vast deal of words upon a trifling particle of matter. But this belief, along with some others, she found it prudent to keep to herself.

Yet had this been all, the matter might have been arranged. Her admitted accomplishments and the worth of her family might have been set against that impertinent and disconcerting glance, and a husband might have been found, strong enough in arm and mind to keep her in a decent order. But it was not all. For it could hardly be denied that the girl's interests were by no means where they should be. Though her face could remain impassive and dutiful when she so wished, it could also break quickly into an easy smile, which went with a flicker of the eye and an odd crinkle of the forehead; a combination, it was noted, which she seldom bestowed on members of her family. It was a charm, so her sisters said, which the girl reserved for men, and young men at that; and upon them it had been seen to have the most undesirable effects. Her family had not yet forgotten that dreadful Sunday, not six months gone, when, the sermon being but half done and the young visiting preacher just turning his hour-glass, this graceless girl had suddenly turned that smile and crinkle full upon him, so that he stumbled in his discourse, forgot his text, and seemed unable, through the whole of his second hour, to turn his eyes to any other pew. Nor, even after that scandal, had the girl shown any disposition to mend her ways and turn her thoughts to a devout and sober life. All that could be devised for her improvement had been tried. She had been instructed and admonished; she had been scolded and coaxed; she had been prayed for, and prayed with; she had been tenderly exhorted and soundly whipped; and all to no effect. She remained as she had always been: composed, inscrutable and deplorable, a menace to the peace and good name of her family.

This, then, was the problem that her unhappy brothers and sisters had now to face. What was to be done with Margery? Where, indeed, *was* Margery?

It was Alexander who asked that, and they looked at one another with surprise. Nobody, it seemed, had thought of that. Her presence had not been thought necessary, and now she had to be hastily summoned while Alexander fidgeted impatiently. But for once she was not hard to find; and she came in quickly and walked to the table, graceful and alert in spite of the faded black of her kirtle and the prim severity of her thin white collar. Her young face was impassive as she stood quietly in front of Alexander, demurely waiting for him to speak. He was a big florid fellow, grave in the bands and black of a divine, and his podgy fingers tapped importantly as he spoke.

'How,' he demanded, 'may such a girl as you, undutiful and undevout, be wedded to a godly man?'

The girl dropped her eyes and said nothing. He looked her over coldly.

'By your own conduct you are in a way to destroy yourself. What man who has the Grace within him would wed with such as you?'

Again he had no answer. The girl stood silent, hands clasped and eyes cast down. Alexander raised his voice.

'Do you hear me speak?'

'Yes brother.' Her quiet voice was clear and musical.

'Then why do you not answer?'

'In truth brother, I know not what to answer.'

'That I believe. And you should blush for it. Are you not ashamed to be our sister?'

'Yes brother.'

Prudence stirred suddenly, and Margery pressed her lips. She was wondering whether she had let that answer ring too true. She had no fear that Alexander would notice it. Alexander never noticed any of her subtleties. But Prudence was different, and Margery had learned to watch her eldest sister warily. Prudence, she thought, knew her and her ways a deal too well.

But Alexander was speaking again. With his head flung back and his fingers drumming, he boomed resonantly. How, he asked, could they marry this girl to any man they knew, esteemed, and wished to be connected with? Yet, that being barred, what else could be done with her? Were they to maintain her in an idle spinsterhood? *He* certainly was not. Alexander snorted at the prospect and rounded on Margery to tell her that she was an idle, insolent, godless baggage, the pride of the Devil and the shame of her family.

He was vicious over it, and Margery flushed as she heard it. She felt her clasped fingers grow moist, but she held her poise and told herself she must make no answer. There was indeed no answer she could have made which would not have been accounted insolence, and Alexander had a short way with insolence. Since their mother's death, authority resided with Alexander, and he had already let Margery know it. He had been in the house only two days, but she had already fallen foul of him by an incautious answer to one of his heavy rebukes. He had mended her manners with a supple hazel stick, and she was not disposed to take any more risks. So she held her peace and stood in silence while Richard remarked that since she could not be married to a divine she must needs be married to a fellow of lesser sort.

But Alexander snorted again. Such a fellow, he said, would set little store by the family's worth, and would certainly require a proper portion to go with the girl. And who would find her such a portion? Assuredly *he* would not. Nor, it seemed, would the Whitakers of Holme, who had let it be understood that they had done as much as they cared to do. The suggestion was idle, and Richard should have known better than to make it.

Richard glared and relapsed into silence. It was Prudence, of the practical mind, who made answer instead. Somehow, she declared, a portion must be found. Without one there would be no husband, and they would have the girl on their hands for ever. With one there might even be a goodly husband, since even a divine might well look past a fault or two for a portion that would furnish out his parsonage; and when Alexander reared his head at this slur on his cloth, Prudence swept that aside with a sniff. What, she demanded, did he mean to do about it?

It was at this moment that Richard had his inspiration. It set him bubbling with excited speech till Prudence asked him acidly if he thought this was Pentecost. Then he sobered and began to explain himself. Their grandmother, he reminded them, had been Elizabeth Nowell of Read, who had married Thomas Whitaker of Holme. Her younger brother had been Alexander Nowell, the Dean; and Roger Nowell, her eldest brother, had inherited his father's estate in Lancashire—at Read, where the Calder river touches the Forest of Pendle.

Richard paused impressively, pleased to have them mystified. Then, ponderously, he went on. This Roger's grandson, another Roger Nowell, now owned and ruled at Read —and surely there was kinship there?

Kinship? They looked at one another doubtfully, and Richard, more pleased than ever, said it all over again. He had another word to say before he would let them speak. Richard, as even Prudence agreed, was an excellent bookseller, and he had used his Lancashire connections to extend his trade. More than one Lancashire gentleman ordered books from Richard, and only last month, he told them, he had sent to this Roger Nowell a copy of the King's great work, the *Demonology*—though why a country gentleman should want that erudite and expensive tome Richard could not tell. But that was no matter. What concerned them was that Richard's account, which included some generous charges for carriage, had been paid promptly and without quibbling; they might suppose, therefore, that Roger Nowell was not short of money. He was, said Richard, a man of fifty, with his wife dead these many years and his children now grown and gone into the world; in these days he dwelt alone at Read, and Richard had been told that he stood in no fair repute with neighbours, who found him an arrogant fellow of bitter tongue and peremptory manners. But that again was no matter; what concerned them was the kinship.

Richard ended, and Prudence was heard to say that kinship there certainly was; it might not be too much to say that Margery was this Roger's cousin.

'Cousin?' Alexander stroked his nose and brooded on that. 'Our grandmother being his grandfather's sister, she should be . . .'

'Cousin,' said Richard firmly. 'Any kinsman may be called cousin among gentlefolk.'

'It could be.' Alexander stroked his nose again, and Margery, still standing in front of him, stirred slightly as her quick wits perceived that a marriage-portion, even if it could be had, might be a doubtful blessing. It would attract a husband, no doubt—and Alexander would choose the husband. Margery's nose wrinkled at the thought.

'Cousin or no cousin,' said Alexander suddenly, 'why suppose he'll find a portion for Margery? Why should he? He's never seen the girl.'

'That's the core of it,' said Richard.

'Do you speak in riddles?'

'Not so. He'd be even less likely to find for her if he *had* seen her.'

'That at least is true.' Alexander snorted again.

Then, for the first time, Laurence spoke. He was younger than the other two, a quiet scholarly man whose thoughts stayed in his study with the *Disputatio de Sacra Scriptura contra hujus temporis Haereticos* which he was writing as a counterblast to the deplorable Arminius. It is to be suspected that he found this talk of marriage-portions tedious.

'Whether this Roger Nowell will call Margery cousin and find her a portion, or whether he won't,' said Laurence, 'is best ascertained by asking him. There's nothing lost by that. At worst he can but say no.'

'It's worth trying,' said Prudence firmly, and even Alexander could hardly deny that. But he would by no means consent to Richard's writing the letter. That, he said, belonged to him as the eldest. He would write directly. And since these were days of vacation, when he need not be in Cambridge, he would continue as Richard's guest until an answer should be received.

Prudence sighed wearily.

2

The Country Gentleman

So promptly did Alexander write his letter, and so speedy were the carriers, that an answer came back from Roger Nowell in no more than a month; and it was not a happy month for Margery.

She did indeed get some walks abroad, and once she got as far as Whitehall, where there were some very fine gentlemen sauntering in the sunshine and dallying with their ladies. But for the most part she was kept fast to the house and made to work. Prudence declared that her young sister was in much need of discipline. Already, said Prudence, the girl's head was stuffed with dreams; dreams of airs and graces, of clothes and horses and fine young gentlemen; dreams, in short, of every vapid vanity. What the girl needed was work, and now was the time to see she got it. So Margery was haled into the kitchen and set to seethe and bake; when that was done she was set to iron the linen or scrub the floor; and if she had an idle hour she was sent to the parlour and set to needlework. Prudence was ruthless about it, and Margery submitted because she had to; she knew well enough where authority lay. But under it she was mutinous, for this was by no means her notion of a proper life. She knew all about that crinkling smile and the glint of red in her hair; she knew she had quicker wits and a cooler head than most; and the thought was steady in her that if she were once set among proper men she might put those talents to a proper use. And here she was, grunting in a kitchen that she might learn to cook more succulently for some podgy brother-chosen brute! She was almost in tears when she thought about it. Nor was she much happier in her cooler moments, for then she brooded anxiously on the letter that had been sent to Roger Nowell. If he refused her a portion, it seemed that she must stay here and sport with apprentices—when she could evade Prudence. If he found her a portion she might expect to be quickly married, and she had no illusions about the sort of husband she would have to take and the sort of life she would have to lead. There would be no place then for high hopes and a crinkling smile.

Then came the answer from Roger Nowell, and it was not the answer that Alexander had expected. His voice was swelling with indignation as he read it to them:

'Send the girl straightway to me that I may view her and use her by her deserts. If her blood be red of Nowell she may stay by me and have fair provision. If it be whey she shall return whence she came, and at my charges. These for her journey.

Roger Nowell.'

And 'these' were silver crowns, twenty of them, done in a silken bag; it was tied and sealed, and the seal had the arms of Nowell, three cups sable on a field of argent.

It was a letter that pleased them not at all. Alexander grew heated at its brevity, Richard grumbled at its arrogance, and Prudence declared that it would puff the girl's vanity even further, but if it was short it was also plain, and its very shortness suggested that Roger Nowell was not a man to be argued with, not a man from whom anything might be had unless he were given his own way. They talked it round through the heat of a July afternoon, and their talk ended as might have been foreseen. Margery was summoned before Alexander and curtly bidden to prepare herself for a journey to the North Parts.

It did not occur to Alexander to ask what Margery's thoughts might be on this, and Margery, as usual, kept them to herself. She stayed impassive and inscrutable, but behind it she was excited; and if she was a little frightened she was at least not displeased. Nor was she indignant; if Roger Nowell wanted to look at her, Margery could see nothing against that; she had a growing belief that she was worth looking at, and she was disposed to think well of a man who wanted to look at her. Her quick mind had already seen the possibilities. At the best, 'stay by me and have fair provision' might mean a dream come true. At the worst there would be some exciting travels, and also, if Roger Nowell's crowns were well expended, some new clothes; and of these Margery thought she stood in much need. So she stayed grave and placid, and she even assented dutifully when she was told that Prudence would take her shopping the next week.

She did her best to be dutiful when they came to it, though this she found difficult. She and Prudence had markedly different ideas as to what was to be done. To Prudence it was obvious that Margery must be equipped with such grave and sober clothing as would befit a daughter of their house, whereas Margery's tastes did not run at all to the grave and sober. They came to argument at once. Margery said that since she was going into the country she must have a riding-habit, and she pressed for it earnestly. But Prudence would have none of such fripperies, and since she had the authority, Margery had to submit; yet Prudence, within the limits of her tastes, was both shrewd and determined, and even Margery had to admit that she did the work well. She took the twenty crowns that had been sent, she extracted another twenty from her brothers and she saw to it that Margery was soundly and decently furnished. There was a fine new kirtle of twilled woollen saye, all in black except for a white lace collar that spread widely about the shoulders; and there was a little ruff of starched linen that could be worn instead of the collar on a great occasion. There were two gowns, a day-gown of flowered sarcenet, loose in the sleeves and open at the front for wearing over the kirtle; and a night-gown of puke, dyed in the wool to dark mulberry and made warm and full for wear by the fireside of an evening. There were the three petticoats that would give fullness to the kirtle, two of saye and the third of silk sarcenet because it was meant to be displayed when the kirtle was lifted in walking. There were smocks of white Holland, to be worn under the kirtle by day and as sleeping-wear in bed. There were two pairs of pumps to wear in the house, one of fine leather and one of tufted taffeta; and a pair of cork-soled pantofles to wear over the pumps when out of doors. And as a grudging concession to a new fashion there were some little squares of white cambric, meant to be carried in the hand to give an air of daintiness; these were called hand kerchiefs.

They all but quarrelled when they came to the buying of hats, and it was the unseen Roger Nowell who rescued Margery from that. Prudence had a taste in hats that made Margery shudder. She took it for granted that any woman indoors would wear the small laced hood called a coif, and out of doors the small black rimless cap that every merchant's wife wore. Margery, who had no wish at all to look like a merchant's wife, wanted a copintank, the tall round-brimmed hat with the steeple-crown that every gentleman wore; it was, she said, now the fashion for ladies to wear them too, and she wanted one. Prudence sniffed audibly, and Margery had to submit to the buying of coifs she did not intend to wear and hats which she contemptuously called porringers—which, since Prudence was at that moment wearing one, did not put them on happier terms. They were both red and angry as they walked home in the afternoon heat, Margery sullen to the point of mutiny and Prudence saying bitter things about ungrateful girls. Margery thought nervously about her brother's hazel stick, and went cautiously with tight-pressed lips. And then, suddenly, everything changed. For on the doorstep they met an apprentice bearing a small canvas packet which his master, a goldsmith, had just received from the merchant who was his agent in Preston; it was directed to Mistress Margery Whitaker, and the seal had the arms of Nowell.

Margery had it in her hand before Prudence could so much as speak, and then she took the stair at a run. Once in her bedchamber she ripped it open and found a single sheet of paper and a silken bag, tied and sealed as before; it dropped to the table and clinked. Then, with her fingers trembling with excitement, she opened the paper and read the bold and level script:

Being come to Preston, take a lodging at the Angel *in the Friargate, telling the host thereof you seek me, your kinsman. I will take order for all else. These for your own self, to do with as you will, none overseeing you.*

Roger Nowell.

And the contents of the silken bag were silver crowns, twenty of them as before.

That was enough for Margery. She went for supper with a bright cheek and a sparkling eye, and all thoughts of quarrels were forgotten. She had only one thing in her thoughts now, and that was the riding-habit she had been pining for since her journey had first been mooted. It was within her grasp now, and she could have hugged Roger Nowell. True, she would have to be careful; twenty crowns made only a hundred shillings, and she would have to spread them thinly; it would have to be mockado instead of velvet, and the hat would have to be felt instead of beaver fur, but the thing was within her grasp and she would seek it as she had been told to do—none overseeing her.

She slipped away in the morning as soon as breakfast was done, and with the persistence of a nosing dog she went from mercer to mercer, asking prices and feeling mockados with a fine disregard of everything but her own needs; and at the ninth shop, where she stayed as usual until her welcome had grown thin, she was offered a riding-habit that had been made for a lady who in the end had not taken it. Margery took one look at it and then fell to haggling like a Lombard money-changer. There was a doublet cut like a man's, and of orange-tawny mockado pinked with silver tinsel; it was cut in the new style, buttoning in the front and needing no stomacher, and the sleeves were of the new style too, plainly shaped and tight-fitting. There was the long and extravagantly pleated riding-skirt called a safeguard, also of the orange-tawny, and lined, like the doublet, with orange sarcenet; and to complete it there was a riding-cloak, long and full, from a warm russet frieze of the fine Penistone weave.

She got all that for thirteen crowns, and the afternoon saw her out again, apparently impervious to dust and heat. She began with an hour spent trying hats, and she enjoyed that more than the milliner did. In the end she picked on a good black felt, pinked like the doublet with silver tinsel; she could trim it for herself, and at least it was a proper copintank and not a porringer. For another fifteen shillings she had a pair of long boots in a good Spanish leather, soft and unpolished. Then she had a pair of gloves in brown doeskin, with silver lace at the cuffs of the gauntlets; she bought orange feathers for the crown of the hat, and orange ribbons for its brim; and then, with only two shillings left, she spent them on a pound of the famous yellow starch which Mistress Turner had made so fashionable for ruffs.

She came home penniless and triumphant, and laid all the things gleefully on her bed; and Prudence, coming to see what foolishness those silver crowns had led her young sister into, gazed icily at the array and sniffed again; they were, she said, fit only for a Whitehall fly-by-night, which Margery seemed in a fair way to becoming. She went out with a bang of the door, and Margery put her tongue out at it; it was not for sisterly approval that she had chosen the orange-tawny.

Nothing could disturb her calm in the week that remained. She even kept her composure and spoke polite thanks when Richard produced a book which brother Alexander had sent from Cambridge as his parting gift to her; it was Alexander Nowell's *Homily On The Justice Of God,* and Margery looked at it gravely and as gravely said that she would be sure to make good use of it. Then all was ready, and when August was a week old they took her to St. Paul's Cross, where a wagon waited; it had come from Kendal with a load of Westmorland wool, and the wagoner, having no load to carry back, had been glad to agree for four passengers at a modest charge; and as the other three were a divine and his wife and daughter, it could not be doubted that Margery was travelling within the proprieties.

Farewells were said, and Margery climbed into the wagon. She was wearing her oldest and shabbiest kirtle, for this was not to be travel in luxury; if the wagoner's charges had been modest, the comfort he provided was modest too; all he had been able to do for his passengers was to spread some straw within the wagon, and it was insufficient provision, as Margery realised as soon as the thick-set horses began their steady walk. The springless wagon banged and jolted, and the passengers suffered with what fortitude they could summon. The stout wooden floor, besides being as hard as granite, was dark and oily from numberless loads of wool, and from the same source it had acquired a scent that would never leave it; to add to these discomforts, there were countless wool-combings mixed with the straw, and if anything more was needed to teach Margery what travelling meant, she found it in a growing suspicion which was amply confirmed before the day was out; there were fleas in the wool.

The wagoner was a cheerful fellow—too cheerful, they thought when they complained of the fleas and he roared with laughter; there were always fleas in wool, he said. But he swept the wagon that night, and then he swilled it clean before putting in fresh straw; and the next day, if they were a little damp, they were at least unbitten. But nothing the wagoner could do could make them comfortable. The boards and the jolts, the smells of oil and wool, the choking dust and the scorching sun: these remained.

But if the rutted roads were hot and dusty, at least they were not muddy. The heavy wheels banged and bounced, but they turned; there was never any danger of being bogged, and so swiftly was the journey accomplished that it lasted scarcely three weeks. On the second day of September, in the heat of a shining afternoon, they came down a gentle grassy slope and saw at its foot the river Ribble, placid in its bordering meadows. Beyond it, clean and grey in the summer light, was the little town of Preston, and in less than an hour they had crossed the stream and entered the town. They found it busy, for this was a market-day and the streets were a press of men, townsmen in gowns and doublets, and yeomen in homespuns and riding-boots; and here where the press was thickest, in the street called the Friargate, Margery alighted and sought the *Angel*.

The clear cool light of the next morning found her sitting on the low linen-covered seat that ran under the window of her chamber in the *Angel*; she had set the lattice wide, and she was savouring the clean freshness of the air as she watched the wakening bustle in the Friargate below. From time to time she leaned out to see more clearly, and such passers-by as then chanced to look up had a glimpse of a fresh young face set against orange-tawny; and some of them, she noted, showed a disposition to look again. That was as it should be, and Margery nodded with satisfaction; she was beginning to like this County of Lancaster.

So indeed she might, for the *Angel* had given her of its best. The first mention of her cousin's name had worked wonders with the landlord; porters had gone scurrying to fetch her baggage while his wife conducted her to her chamber above stair, and he himself had instantly despatched a lad to Read with word of her coming. She had supped well, and slept well, and while she breakfasted the landlord had been with her again to say that the lad was back from Read. Master Nowell sent his felicitations; he would ride when he had breakfasted, and he might be expected in Preston before eleven. All was therefore very well, and but for one gnawing thought Margery would have had perfect content.

The gnawing thought, of course, was of Roger Nowell. Margery was far too clear-sighted not to know that she might need all her wits, and more, in the weeks to come. She thought she might fairly judge from his letters that Roger Nowell was peremptory, perceptive, and not ungenerous; but what else he might be, those short letters could not show. He might be a gloomy bigot or a genial roisterer, a kindly scholar or a swaggering rake; there was nothing to show. But whatever he was, he might enforce himself on her with what harshness he chose, and there would be none to say him nay; that, at least, was certain, and she would have no more protection than her own wits could furnish.

She shivered a little at her thoughts, and withdrew her eyes from the street. But the cheer of the sunlit room and the glow of the orange-tawny heartened her, and she ran across to peer into the little steel mirror that hung on the opposite wall. That heartened her further. In any event, she told herself, it was too late now for such broodings. All was set, and the issue hung on the one thing she could not yet know—on the manner of man it was who was riding in from Read.

She seated herself by the window once more, and again she glanced thoughtfully round the room, asking herself anxiously whether all was as it should be in readiness for his coming. She nodded approval of what she saw. All was very tidy and decent; the canvas travelling-bags, packed and tied, waited by the door; near them, on the side-table, were hat and gloves, and the russet cloak placed carelessly to display exactly the right amount of its orange lining. And, some six feet from where she sat, a wisp of thread lay on the floor, white against the dark boards. This was not an accident.

It had to do with that streak of redness in her hair. Margery had a strong suspicion that this lurking redness was a potent charm, and she had every intention of making the most of it in the encounter she now awaited. But she also knew, having looked into the matter with some care, that this redness needed full sunlight to bring it out fully. Herein lay the difficulty. For the window was low, and the shaft of incoming sunlight was therefore low also; and she had discovered by careful trial that the sunlight would be below her hair when she stood to greet her cousin. Wherefore, something must be contrived, and Margery had contrived it with a fine simplicity. Since she could not bring the sunlight up to her hair, she must bring her hair down to the sunlight, and a formal curtsey would do this admirably. It was, moreover, a thing very proper to the occasion, and she knew that she could perform it with a most becoming grace. All that was needed, therefore, was to ensure that when she made her curtsey her hair should sink exactly into that narrow shaft of sunlight. Hence that wisp of thread. It marked the exact spot where she must point her toe to begin the curtsey. She had placed it precisely, after some careful trials.

She looked out into the Friargate again, marking the growing bustle and the occasional upward glance of burgher or apprentice. But the sun was rising higher, and more and more her eyes turned to that distant end of the street whence, very soon now, she might see a horseman ride. She wanted some warning of his coming, and more and more her eyes sought in the press for the rider who should seek the *Angel*.

Yet in the end she missed his coming. For chancing to look into the room she saw with sudden alarm that the sunlight had moved from the wisp of thread. She was at first angry, and then amused that she should have thought the sun stayed still. But she had to try the curtsey again, three separate times, before she was satisfied; and as she rose after placing the thread again, there was a clatter of horses in the arch below, a shouting and a running of feet, and the landlord's voice raised in a greeting to Master Nowell.

She felt her heart pounding as she hurried to her place and stood to face the door. She made swiftly sure that she stood correctly, feet together, back hollowed, head erect and hands clasped. Then, with her face a little pale and her breath a little fast, she waited, very straight and still, and heard the ring of boots on the stair and in the passage—a brisk confident tread, with a firm drop of heel and a pleasant jingle of spurs. Then the hinges creaked, and there was a man in the doorway.

He halted, stiff and impassive, and considered her gravely; a big man, full six feet of him, broad of shoulder and slim of hip, with an alert vigour that belied the flecks of grey in his beard. There was something sombre in this sun-browned face with the thick eyebrows and the big jutting nose; yet it seemed to Margery that here too was something friendly, something even of humour in the lines of his forehead. Then, while she looked, he swept his beaver off; and the breath caught in her throat as she saw the glint of red in his brown hair.

She steadied herself, and as he came towards her she gave him her best curtsey. It was deftly done, and as she had planned. And as her head sank into the shaft of sunlight, his advance stopped abruptly, and he stood staring.

'God's Grace!' he said softly. 'God's Grace!'

Deliberately she did not rise. She knew she was set to advantage; there would be nothing lost by waiting. So, for a moment, they stayed, he looking down at her and she looking up at him. Then he flung hat and whip to the window-seat and began peeling off his gloves.

'Get up, little cousin.'

His voice was bantering, and of a sudden he broke into a smile that lit his face and changed his whole aspect; and it was Margery's turn to stare as she saw the odd crinkle of the forehead that came with the smile.

'You *are* little cousin, not a doubt of it. How do they call you?'

'Margery Whitaker, by your leave sir.'

He flung his gloves after his hat.

'If you'd said Margery Nowell, you'd still have had my leave—or any man's. None would deny it you while you look so. However . . .'

His smile came again, and it was infectious. It called hers out in response, and she felt her forehead crinkle. He stopped short in the act of loosening his cloak.

'God's Grace!' he said again. 'None indeed! And I had thought to see . . .'

He broke off, and his face grew thoughtful as he walked to the window.

Margery, watching in silence, asked herself why this man stood so far apart from other men. That he did stand apart was clear; why, was not so clear. Certainly it was not his clothes. His leather jerkin, serge breeches, and cloak of russet frieze were homely enough, and his beaver was almost shabby. There was nothing to distinguish him from the yeomen she had seen in the street except the bright steel sword-hilt in the folds of his cloak—that, and his eyes. And then she understood. For in this man's eyes, unmistakably and in full measure, was that nameless force which in all times and places has been authority; and Margery, who had never seen it before, knew it on the instant for what it was.

He was smiling again now, and curiosity was raging in Margery. She decided to risk it.

'Pray sir,' she said, 'what was it that you thought to see? Or whom?'

'That? Why, nothing at all . . .' But his smile was broadening, and something impish was creeping into it. 'Nay, if you will have it, I thought to see some pudding-faced wench, with hair free from curl, and flanks like a Flemish mare.'

Margery nearly choked. She was not used to this sort of thing. It flouted all she had been taught; and because it delighted her, it lured her into archness. She made her curtsey again, most formally and deliberately, and she looked up at her cousin with lifting eyebrows and a smile that had an inviting touch of impudence.

'Must I then regret it, sir, that I do not match your expectations?'

She was still sunk in her curtsey, poised gracefully and delicately; she was pleased with that riposte, and her eyes showed it as she waited for his answer. It came instantly, and it was not what she had expected. He had slipped his cloak from his shoulders, and it was hanging loosely from his arm; now, with a speed that gave no warning, he swung it by the collar, and its fast-moving folds, sweeping low across the floor, took her by the ankles; her delicate balance broke at once, and she went down with an undignified thump.

'Here's impudence!' said Roger Nowell. And Margery, sitting on the floor and looking ruefully up at him, saw his grin and went helplessly into laughter.

3

The Brooding Hill

Half an hour later, after he had shown what a sharp-set man can do to beef and ale, and Margery had shown what a healthy girl can do in emulation, they were in the saddle. He had mounted her on a lively grey mare and was beside her on a big chestnut. Her bags followed on a pack-horse led by a mounted servant.

It was high noon when they came from the inn yard into the Friargate, and Margery gave thanks to Fortune as they trotted the length of the street. She had waited for this moment since she had first set eyes on the orange-tawny, and here she was in the glittering sunlight, mounted as she had never thought to be mounted, and squired by a cousin who had already made himself a lodestone for her thoughts. The grey mare seemed happy to be away, and Margery was happy with her.

But soon, when they had cleared the town and put its cobbled streets a mile or two behind them, she began to have some different thoughts. They were descending a long steep slope to an arm of the Ribble which flowed southward at its foot. The track was rough and getting rougher; the mare was lively and getting livelier, and was not at all like the placid palfrey she had once ridden with her Huguenot instructor. Soon she was asking herself whether a side-saddle was a safe seat on such a mount and on such a track; nor did the heavy and extravagantly pleated safeguard seem quite so desirable now as it had done in the *Angel* an hour before. She became anxious, and from being anxious she became acutely fearful lest at any moment she leave the saddle altogether. She was grateful when the watchful Roger saw her troubles and leaned over to reduce both horses to a walk. So they came without mishap to the river, crossed it, and began to climb the opposite slope. Margery's confidence was returning, and soon she was able to look about her with interest.

'Salmesbury,' said Roger suddenly, waving to his left. 'Home of Southworth, the recusant.'

'Recusant?'

'Aye. Old Sir John, I mean, though he's dead now. The recusant of all recusants. Do you have papists in your ken at home?'

'Papists!' Margery was startled, for papists, as she had always heard, were vile treacherous rogues, false to God and King alike; and recusants were the worst and stiffest-necked of papists.

'Aye, papists,' said Roger again. 'Do you have none at your home?'

'Why no, sir. Not within my knowing.'

'They'll be within your knowing here. We've good store of them in this County.' He spoke casually, as if this were no great matter, and Margery stared in astonishment.

'But surely, sir, the Justices . . .'

Her cousin laughed heartily.

'The Justices, Not they! And I speak with knowledge, for I'm one myself.'

'You!' She almost lost her saddle in the shock of that. 'You sir? A papist?'

'God's Grace no!' He was shaking with laughter. 'Not a papist, little cousin. Merely one of the King's Justices within this County.' Then suddenly his laughter died and he spoke more gravely. 'From whom did you learn of papists?'

'Why sir, from my brothers, and my mother. And from some others too.'

'Aye.' He nodded as though understanding had come to him. 'I'd some letters from your brothers . . .'

He lapsed into silence as the horses went slowly up the long ascent, and Margery was glad enough to be silent while she gave her mind to this. She had not known that he was a Justice, but she did know that that was a dignity coveted by many country gentlemen and achieved by very few; there must be some, and in high places, who held him in esteem if he were in the Commission. And then she came back to what perplexed her.

'Touching these papists sir . . .'

'Oh, the papists?' His light humour returned instantly. 'Touching these papists, little cousin, they're men and women like the rest of us, and are therefore good, bad and indifferent—mostly indifferent. And for us Justices, we have duties enough without scenting a Jesuit behind every chimney-breast. If we truly scented treason, we'd truly serve the King—even Scotch Jimmy. But as it is . . .'

He broke off with a shrug of his shoulders. But Margery was not satisfied.

'Aye sir,' she answered. 'As it is. But *how* is it?'

She was at a loss, and she genuinely wanted to know. Roger seemed to sense this, for he answered her soberly.

'If my neighbour be an honest gentleman,' he said, 'then, papist or no papist, I'm not the man to harry him for the sport of it. There are houses here where a priest or two may verily be behind a chimney. But what of it? Who's harmed?'

Margery brooded. These were not at all the views that her brothers had held. Soon she came to it again.

'But—six years ago sir, when the powder was placed . . .'

'Oh that? Catesby and his crew? The man was mad. But our papists here are not such as he. They're country gentlemen, concerned with their pigs and their corn and the worth of their October.'

'October?'

'Ale, little cousin—the gift of God.'

He seemed to dismiss the matter, and while Margery groped for an answer, it happened. She had foreseen it and she had forgotten it; and now it happened. The grey mare slipped and recovered. Margery slipped and did not recover. She slipped wholly from the saddle, down the mare's flanks, and into the long dry grass that fringed the track. And for the second time that day she sat looking ruefully upwards at a laughing cousin.

Then he dismounted in one unbroken movement. Gloved hands came behind her shoulders and pulled her easily to her feet. He brushed dry grass from her back, and helped her to mount. Thereafter they went at a cautious walk.

They came to a fork of the road and he bore to the left, remarking that this was their road for Whalley. It seemed to rouse him from his thoughts, and there was a suspicious crinkle in his forehead as he looked across at Margery.

'Little cousin!'

His tone warned her that the impish mood had him again, and she watched him warily. But he was stroking his horse's neck and seemed in no hurry.

'In the days of my youth,' he said at length, 'when I was young and lewd, a wench had two legs like the rest of us. No doubt she still has?'

Margery gasped. She had not learned to answer men who talked like this.

'Why yes, sir.' There seemed nothing else to say.

'Then why,' asked Roger airily, 'why the Devil can't she put them one each side a horse like the rest of us?'

Margery crushed surprise and sought for an answer. Something warned her that this, or at least the manner of it, was meant to test her. If so, it would be proper to show a seemly confusion. But then, as she groped for words, some deep instinct warned her against dissembling. For this man, only the truth was fitting. So she decided on truth, but truth clothed in his own short phrases.

'As to wenches in general,' she said, 'they fear to be unseemly. As to this wench in particular, she at least fears to be thought unseemly.'

He looked sharply at her.

'You distinguish nicely. But why?'

His tone was not unfriendly, and Margery decided to stick to the truth.

'It's the girl who's thought unseemly who's punished.'

'Rather than the one who truly is? You see sharply for your youth. It is even so.' He looked her in the eyes, and then he nodded thoughtfully. 'It's as I suppose, little cousin. You've been bred a puritan.'

'Why—why yes sir. I think I have.'

Again he was silent as the horses ambled on; and now, as they traversed the ups and downs of the undulating road, something new caught her eye. She began to see, from each rise of the road, a great broad-backed hill which ran across the sky before them, a sweep of green set against the blue. She looked at it idly, then with interest, and at last searchingly; she began to feel under a compulsion to look at it—almost *its* compulsion. There was something odd about this hill, something not to be defined, something she could almost fancy to be disturbing. Disturbing or not, this hill compelled attention.

'Little cousin . . .'

Margery's mind left the hill at once; she was learning that this form of address usually presaged something that needed full attention. He was looking directly at her.

'Were you bred a puritan, or bred among puritans? Which?'

She stared back, puzzled, and he explained himself.

'Are you in truth and heart a puritan? Or did they fail in that?'

'Why sir, I . . .' She hesitated, and then decided for the truth again. 'Indeed sir, I fear they found me an exceeding disappointment.'

'Well answered, little cousin. It runs not with the blood of Nowell.'

He went back into his thoughts, and the hill came back into hers. It was looming larger now, and she could see brown patches in the green of it, patches, no doubt, where Autumn had turned the bracken. Here and there white dots suggested sheep. Margery's forehead puckered as she stared. This hill fascinated her. If a hill could have an indwelling Spirit, then surely this one had—and it might not be the most friendly of Spirits. There was some brooding quality about this hill, as though it were sentient and knew more than it chose to tell. She told herself not to be foolish, but the fancy persisted. This hill seemed different from other hills, as though it possessed something—or even, perhaps, as though something possessed *it*. Margery became almost uneasy, and she was glad to hear Roger's voice when he spoke again. He had turned in his saddle to face her, and she could see that he was in earnest.

'Since you've come into this County,' he said, 'you'd best know how the wind sets. We've papists here, as I've said. That's no matter. They run a decent course and make civil neighbours. But here also we've puritans, a noisy crew of them, hot against the Devil and a deal hotter against the papists. Wherefore they give much time to urging it on Nick Banister and me that we bestir ourselves in the harrying of papists—which Nick and I, who have to hold the peace, are by no means disposed to do. We are therefore much murmured against and looked at sideways, and we have at times given answers that have not mended tempers—and puritans, as I've noted, have commonly very sour tempers.'

'Aye sir.' Margery knew all about the tempers of puritans, and she was by no means sorry to hear her cousin speak in such terms. 'But may I know who this Master Banister is, whom you speak of?'

'He's from Altham, to the sou'west there. He and I are the Justices in these parts. Nick's of the Quorum too.'

'The Quorum, sir?'

'Those Justices who are set apart as knowing more of law than the rest of us. *Quorum unum esse volumus*, as the statutes say.'

Margery nodded; she was scholar enough to follow that. And then he had more to say.

'In short, little cousin, the set of the wind is that your cousin here is on mighty poor terms with some. And that's a wind that may cool you also.'

'I'll not be disturbed by that,' she retorted. 'It's been so with me since I can remember.'

'You also? Graceless girl!'

But there was pleasure in his brown face, and Margery thought she might risk another question.

'You speak of papists sir, and puritans. But do all your folk lean those ways?'

'The most of our folk lean to the ale-bench only. They attend church as the law commands, and they backslide when they can. And those few that are earnest lean, as you put it, the one way or the other—Rome or Geneva.'

He lapsed into silence again, and it occurred to Margery that she might do well to take warning. This man put things crisply. He had wits sharp as her own, and she thought it might be prudent to remember that. She had been accustomed of late to hatch her schemes on the supposition that her brothers were slow-witted—that they would perceive none of her sharper subtleties. That, she now thought, might have its dangers if practised on cousin Roger.

They dropped steeply to a clear and gurgling river, and turned across a low stone bridge into Whalley town. Roger made no halt. In the town's centre he turned away up another steep ascent, and as he did so he gestured over his shoulder at the grey stone church that stood by the parting of the roads.

'Touching the way a girl should sit a horse,' he said suddenly, 'I did not speak wholly in jest. I would not indeed have you ride this road otherwise than aside. The wives of Whalley can clack their tongues as loudly as other wives, and that's their sport of Sundays at the church yonder. But it's another matter in the Forest, where tracks are rough and there's none of consequence to note how you ride nor where. On those tracks a fallen rider may linger long, and you'll be wise to consider what's safe, not what's thought seemly.'

'Aye sir.' She was doubtful of his meaning. 'But pray, what do others do in this Forest?'

'Meaning the women? For the most part they go not in the Forest, or if they do, they ride pillion behind husband or brother.'

He laughed at Margery's wry face.

'Aye aye, little cousin,' he said. 'I'm with you there. Sit your own horse and I'll think the better of you for it. There are folk enough who dismount when tracks grow rough.'

And Margery, finding a compliment in that, was suddenly aware that the esteem of this man, whom she had met but six hours before, had become of consequence to her. She felt herself colour and to cover that she plunged into a question.

'Tell me, sir,' she said, 'what is this Forest of which you speak?'

'It's not known to you?' He waved broadly to his left. 'Yonder is Pendle Hill, a vast thing and running to the nor'west. Once round this sou'west corner we shall be at Read. And if you follow beyond Read, going to the nor'east beside the Hill, that's Pendle Forest—and a raw rough place it is. Hill and clough, rock and stream, grass and bracken, scrub and woodland. There's a church and a mill and some hamlets of the grey stone. There's all of that in the Forest—aye, and the Devil knows what besides.'

'A church, sir? In a forest?'

'Aye. For it's not that sort of forest—not a place where trees have been since time began. It's the other sort of forest, the hunting demesne. Have you heard of one in the south, below Winchester?'

'The one called New, though it's old?'

'That one. And after that manner is Pendle, though it's wilder and it's rougher. It was the hunting forest of the Lacys up at Clitheroe yonder. They came with Norman William, and for four hundred years they held it and they hunted it. Therefore the hamlets—booths, we call them. They were for the foresters and verderers. Therefore also the church. The monks at Whalley saw to that. But the monks are gone now, and the Lacys, too, and we who stay put the place to what use we can. But it's still a wild uncomely place where it's better to be wise than seemly.'

The steep road swung to the left and grew narrower and steeper. At its top it turned sharply, and soon they were dropping down a gradient that set the horses stumbling and scraping. It brought them to a narrow stream which splashed noisily in a stony bed.

'Sabden brook,' said Roger. 'You'll come to know it better.'

The horses toiled up the killing slope beyond, and when at last they gained its summit there was rolling parkland to their right. Roger halted at a simple gate.

'We'll save a mile and ride in here,' he said.

Margery heard him with relief. She had had more than enough of the saddle for one day. But this day was not yet done, and her cousin had yet a surprise for her. Now, at journey's end, he showed her yet another of his moods. He turned his back on the gate, and deliberately walked his horse up the slope on the other side of the road. Margery followed, wondering what this portended; and when she came up with him he was sitting his horse in silence and staring across a steep valley to Pendle Hill beyond.

Neither of them spoke, and Margery, catching his mood, stared also at the scene. The sun was just sinking, and to her left the western sky was a blaze of gold, streaked with silver cloud. Before her, the great hill, green no longer, was a soft smoking blue, deeper where the gullies were; at its foot the trees were black. And as she watched, while the sun slipped lower and the silver clouds turned red, a deep purple crept out of the gullies and spread itself over all. It crept up to meet the sky. It crept down to engulf the trees. It spread, and it deepened, till all the hill was one vast brooding thing.

Roger spoke softly.

'Our country folk have at times a happy trick of speech. Daylight Gate, they call this hour. And surely it is a thing from God.'

Then his horse stamped and whinnied, and at once he was on earth again.

'Come!' he said. 'The mist's rising. We'll be better within doors.'

4

Candle Light

Margery came down the stair in some trepidation. She had made what haste she could. There had been a country girl waiting in her bedchamber, a girl who had named herself Anne Sowerbutts and professed herself at Mistress Whitaker's service. There had been, too, another proof of somebody's thought—a great tub of steaming water, a rare luxury, and a welcome one after three such weeks of travelling. And now Margery, refreshed and refurbished, was coming down the stair, very trim and neat in her new kirtle of saye and her flowered sarcenet gown. Yet she had a doubt, She remembered her cousin's homely clothes, his leather jerkin and his serge breeches, and she was asking herself anxiously whether he wore such homespun of an evening. She had heard that many country gentlemen did, and if so she would feel overdressed and out of place; but there was no help for it, and certainly she had nothing else that she could fittingly wear. So she tilted her chin, steadied her breath, and marched boldly into the room he had called his parlour.

Her fear of being overdressed ended at the first glance. At the end of the long oak-panelled room a fire sizzled on a stone hearth. Above the hearth, on the wide shelf of stone, candles burned, two at either end; between them, clear in their warm light, was a slowly ticking clock, done in black with the base of it set in silver; and leaning against the chimney-breast, gazing pensively at the clock, was Roger Nowell—but a different Roger Nowell. He was in wine-red velvet, with arabesques of gold on his doublet-front; cloth-of-gold made his girdle and shone in the slashings of his sleeves. He wore no gown, but stood slim and strong in the glow of the candles and the flicker of the fire. In his hand was a tall-stemmed glass, deep and sparkling, and the red wine matched his velvet.

He turned to greet her, correct, elegant, and very sure of himself. Then, when she was come half way down the room, he grew very straight and erect; and lifting his glass almost to his eyes, he smiled at her across the wine. At that she stopped, and sensing a salutation she sank into a full curtsey.

He sipped his wine. But as she rose he looked very searchingly at her, from her head to her feet; and she stood very still, knowing that he was appraising her clothes.

The smile flickered across his face again, and he nodded as though pleased.

'Of a puritan severity,' was his comment. 'But within that good.'

It was Margery's turn to smile, as much from relief as from pleasure.

'Of your own choice?' he asked.

'Not wholly. My sister . . .'

'I guessed as much. But the habit you wore today?'

She nodded.

'That was . . .' She stopped; then coloured a little as she changed the word she had meant to use.

'That was ours,' she amended it. 'It is of my choice and of your kindness. For which, sir, my grateful thanks.'

'Say not so. I've had daughters. But let's not linger on this. It's more than time we supped.'

He led her from the parlour and thence to a room much larger, and this was a pool of shadow with only the centre bright; but here was candle light on oak, and set on the oak was silver of a sort she had never seen. The candles and the flowers were set in silver; the salt and the spices were in silver; the spoons and skewers were of silver; and every piece was so wrought and chased that even she, all unversed in such matters, knew it to be the work of no common craftsman. Servants in blue and white placed their chairs, and when she was seated she looked again across the gleaming oak to the wonderful silver and to her cousin in his red and gold; and seeing all this, she found herself wondering at the contrast from the rough simplicity of his riding-clothes. Then he caught her thought and smiled.

'In these days,' he explained, 'I'm so much among the country folk by day that by nightfall I'm almost rustic. Which is why, for an hour or two, I make it my business to be otherwise. There are gentlemen enough who forget the need for that.'

A roast of mutton appeared, and the plates were set before them. There was nothing rustic in his eating, she noted; for he used only knife and skewer, and never set fingers to his meat. Then, while she was attentive to match his manners, he spoke again.

'You chose your riding-habit with a pretty taste,' he told her. 'It will serve you excellent well to the church on Sundays. Indeed, little cousin . . .'

He stopped to look across at her, his forehead crinkling with amusement.

'Indeed, sir?'

'It may bring some green faces among the proud wives of Whalley—and I'll not promise they'll like you the better for that.'

But her smile was as mischievous as his.

'I'll not forgo it for that, sir, since it seems that you approve it.'

'I approve it well—for Whalley. Not so well for the Forest. You'll be safer there in rustics.'

They finished with the mutton, and the plates were taken. Margery looked next for the usual beans and cabbage, but instead she found a thing like a great mis-shapen egg with a pale brown skin. She stared blankly at it, and Roger burst out laughing.

'Never fear, little cousin! It's no more than a vegetable. Try eating it!'

'But how? And what is it?'

'As to how, with knife and skewer. As to what, it's from a plant of Virginia, this being the root of it. The name of it, potato. I brought the seed home myself, and it grows tolerably in the garden here.'

Margery prodded the thing doubtfully, then cut it and dutifully tasted the queer stuff. Roger watched with amusement. But later, when the tarts and cheesecakes had come and gone, he took her back to the parlour and poured wine for her; then, taking from the ingle shelf a thick brown book, he handed it to her without comment. She opened it and found it to be called a Herbal, being a book that told curious things of curious plants; and while Roger busied himself further at the ingle shelf, she turned to its title-page and learned that it had been written by one John Gerard a dozen years before; and on this page, besides his name, there was a portrait engraved of this Master Gerard holding out a plant that had flowers above and these potato things below.

She looked up from the book, and at once her interest was transferred to her cousin; for he had taken from the shelf a tiny bowl of white clay with a long curving tube leaving it at one side; and now, with this tube put in his mouth, he had taken a flaming brand from the fire and was holding it to the bowl. Smoke rose, and a strange fragrance; and Margery, watching intently, remembered that her brothers had spoken much against a habit called the drinking of tobacco. They had said that it was spreading in the town; and no doubt this was it.

'Another plant from Virginia,' said Roger, as he saw her interest. 'You'll get to know it if you stay by me. But have you read all in the book that touches the potato plant?'

She had not, and she applied herself to the Herbal again. There was more about the potato than the engraving, for she found some pages where were set out the nature and habits of this odd plant, which, it seemed, Master Gerard had made shift to grow for himself in his garden at Holborn. Margery read with interest.

'Little cousin!'

She looked up with a start, and found Roger watching her with a smile and crinkle that in herself would have presaged mischief. She put the book down on her knee and faced him.

'This potato has an odd taste. Myself, I find it pleasing, but others do not. That may be true of more out of Holborn than potato.'

She coloured a little as she caught the double meaning. She had just come from Holborn. But at once he reassured her.

'I've said I find the taste pleasing. It's the others who do not, and it's with them I'm concerned just now.

He took some sheets of paper from the press behind his chair.

'All in all, I'd three letters concerning you,' he said. 'The first, from a brother Alexander, announced your being of this world. That was when I desired to see you. The second, from a brother Richard, announced your coming. It spoke somewhat in your praise, but more in the praise of a sister Prudence who was to oversee your buyings. That was when I supposed you'd be glad to buy without her if I sent you the means.'

He put down the two letters and flicked the sheets of a third. Margery sat tense and alert. She had not known there had been a third.

'Both of those spoke in your praise. But this last does not.' He held it up. 'It's again from this brother Richard. It was written after you had left, and it passed you on the road. He thought, no doubt, that when you were away and beyond knowledge, he might more safely speak his mind. So you'd best know what his mind is.'

Margery looked at him, flushed and unhappy. This was mean of Richard.

'He writes that you are wilful and of a great conceit, that you are impatient of counsel, disobedient and insolent to your elders. He adds that you stand in much need of a round curbing, and he hopes that I'll supply it. And for that work he gives me the approval and authority of your brothers—which I'm no doubt to suppose kind of him.'

Margery sat silent, hating Richard. Nothing in this letter could be wholly denied; everything in it could poison her cousin's esteem of her. She had thought that Richard could be paltry; she had known he could be vicious. But this exceeded anything she had supposed of him.

'The little rat!'

Roger's low mutter burst into her thoughts like a thunderclap; and then this unbelievable cousin of hers rose from his chair, swept up all the sheets, and deliberately thrust them into the fire. He stood in silence, watching as they burned; and when nothing remained of them but some grey flakes, he turned and looked her in the eye.

'To have written such a tale at the outset would have been honest,' he said. 'Not to have written it at all would have been generous. But to write it when you had started . . .'

He shrugged in disgust.

'You'll note that I've not questioned its truth,' he went on. 'I verily believe you have all those faults. Is it not so?'

Margery hung her head in embarrassment.

'It . . . it may be so,' she said slowly.

'It is surely so,' came the swift answer. 'Because, little cousin . . .'

An incisive ring had come into his voice, and Margery looked up nervously.

'Because, little cousin, it's the exact tale, word by word and fault by fault, that has ever been told of me.'

'Oh!' She gasped with relief.

'So we'll not quarrel over that. It's others that are like to do the quarrelling, and it's for us to stand together. And indeed I think we're too much akin to quarrel. You, too, may perhaps find odd tastes pleasing.'

Margery gaped at him. Then she laughed a little wildly, and suddenly burst into tears.

He showed some wisdom at that. He left her alone, and sat at his ease with his wine and tobacco. But when she had recovered herself and was able to smile ruefully at him, he put down his glass and pipe and came across to her chair. He took both her hands and drew her to her feet.

'You've had a deal of travelling,' he said. 'And this has been a day both long and trying. Sleep's your best medicine. So get you to bed and seek it.'

He pulled at a bell-cord.

'I have an ill repute with some,' he told her, 'and I foresee that you will have the same. But that's no matter so long as you have esteem of those you do esteem.'

He put down her hands and spoke more lightly.

'Meantime, you're my cousin and my guest, and as both I make you welcome.'

He led her to the foot of the stair, and himself lit her small carrying-candle from the tall ones that burned there. He handed it to her gravely.

'God's Grace to you, little cousin!'

'And . . . and to you!'

She ran quickly up the stair until a warm splash from the flickering candle warned her to be careful. She turned and saw him still where he had been, at the foot of the stair; and as she looked, he nodded and turned away.

In her bedchamber, candles were already lit, and Anne Sowerbutts, warned by the bell, was waiting. Margery let the girl help her from her kirtle and into the warm night-gown of puke; and then, pleasant though it was to have this attendance, she sent the girl away. At this moment she wanted to be alone.

Being alone, she looked round her at the big four-poster with the carved oak tester and the rose-red curtains, at the carved and panelled tiring-table, and at the crystal mirror beyond it; no steel circle, this, but a tall sheet of glass backed by a shining surface. Then she lit more candles, so that six of them burned; and these she placed so that all their light fell to the front of the crystal mirror. And with that she slipped out of the long gown and stood only in her smock. This she grasped, and gathered it tightly round her; and stood so, in the light before the mirror, turning this way and that, until she was reassured. She was not like a Flemish mare.

She pulled the warm gown round her again, and sitting by the tiring-table she drew a pair of candles close to the glass; then she brought her face against it, looked long and searchingly, and again was reassured. Certainly she was not pudding-faced.

Then, because she remembered all that he had said, she grew busy, sitting there before the mirror. A full quarter-hour slipped by before she rose, drew three of the bed-curtains, and blew all the candles but one. And when she had said her prayers, blown the last candle and drawn the last curtain, and was wriggling between the scented cambric sheets of the great bed, she spared a kindly thought for her great-uncle Alexander, whose *Homily* made such excellent curling-papers.

5

The Rough Lee

She was still sunk in sleep when Anne Sowerbutts drew back the bed-curtains and let in a flood of sunlight that picked a glint from her tousled hair and turned the dust into a glittering mist. It heartened her, and when she had yawned and stretched, and at last climbed out of bed, she told Anne to give her the orange-tawny again. Stiff though she was from yesterday, the brightness of the morning set her hoping for another ride this day.

She was not disappointed. When she was down the stair she found Roger already in his homely riding-clothes and addressing himself to a breakfast of cold bacon, wheaten bread, and frothing brown ale. He waved to her to do likewise.

'Riding,' he observed, as she seated herself delicately, 'is apt to work such mischief. You'll forget it when you're warm. Could you sit a horse again today?'

She grimaced at him and wriggled in her chair, but she nodded assent.

'That's well,' he said. 'There's some trouble up the Forest and I must look to it. So you may ride with me, if you're of that mind, and see people and places, and perhaps the trouble too.'

'Aye, sir.' She was already helping herself to bacon and feeling appreciative of this easy household. 'May I know what the trouble is?'

'That's what we're to learn.' He pushed back his chair and filled his ale-mug afresh. 'All I know is that Wilsey—he's our Constable—sent word, a half-hour gone, of a man dead at a place called the Rough Lee. And some people, it seems, are asking why. Which is a nuisance. I was due at Altham today. Are you finished?'

'I . . . I think so.'

He looked her in the eye, and burst out laughing.

'That's an answer more of manners than of stomach. I'd forgotten your youth. Get you to it! Mitton won't mind waiting.'

He began to charge his tobacco pipe while Margery, nothing loath, attacked the bacon again and helped herself to more ale. The frugality of her mother's housekeeping had taught her to take chances when they came.

'This ale,' she said happily. 'Do you call it small ale here?'

'Mostly.' Roger's eyebrows had taken a sardonic lift. 'You find it none so small?'

'It's better than our best. As for our small . . .'

'I know it. I know your London ale—and a poor-weak-sinner's brew it is! You must try our October . . .'

He put fire to his pipe while Margery cut at the bacon for a third time. She ate steadily until curiosity woke in her. Then she looked up at Roger.

'This Mitton, sir, who won't mind waiting. May I know who he is?'

'He isn't. He's dead. That's why he won't mind waiting.'

'Oh!'

And Margery, who had been contemplating a fourth attack on the bacon, suddenly decided not to. Instead she told Roger she had finished.

'You're sure?' He looked hard at her. 'To horse then in ten minutes' time.'

She was out of the house in less than that, and on the gravel by the great door she found the horses, held by the man who had led the pack-horse yesterday. He handed her a packet done in white cloth.

'Bread and cheese,' he explained. 'Master Nowell said it should be in your saddle-bag.'

She took it with a surprise which he must have noticed.

'Said you'd not had much breakfast,' he added, 'and maybe you'd be sharp set before we're back.'

Margery saw no sense in contradicting this, so she took the packet and stuffed it into her saddle-bag. Then she turned to look at him more carefully. She saw a small stocky fellow, thick-set and strong, with fair hair, unwavering blue eyes, and a nose that looked as if it had once been broken. She found herself smiling at him, and he smiled back with a display of startlingly white teeth in a face so brown and creased that she wondered where, and under what suns, he had been. Margery's smile broadened. She thought she liked this man.

Then Roger came out of the house to join them, pulling on his gloves as he walked.

'So you've met,' he said. 'That's well. You should know Tom Peyton, little cousin. We've been together many a year, and he's my old and trusty friend.'

And Margery knew from his tone that he meant it. She turned to Tom Peyton again.

'I hope you'll be in some sort my friend too,' she told him. 'I'm a stranger here and have need of friends.'

His smile broadened into a grin.

'Do my best ma'am. Command me.'

Roger nodded approval and then swung lightly into his saddle. Tom Peyton held Margery's stirrup.

They went away at a brisk trot, and soon Margery was staring at the contrast between this country and the Kentish fields she had known. She could not, indeed, see it as fully as she could have wished, for much of the road lay between banks that cut the view; but she was soon aware that they were climbing to a bleak and undulating moorland, a place of rock and bracken, of tufted grass and scattered trees.

Roger waved his gloved hand to the left.

'The great hill's yonder,' he explained, 'and it runs, as I told you, to the nor'east. This side, there's a great broad face of it that dips to the valley where runs the Sabden brook...'

'Which we crossed last night?'

'That one. And this side of the brook the ground sweeps up again to this ridge, which marches with the hill. We're on the outer face of the ridge just now, which is why there's no good view of the hill. But look to your right!'

He waved at the broad prospect that had opened below them. For a couple of miles the ground fell smoothly to where a sunlit river shone silver. Beyond it the hills rose again.

'That's the Calder,' he said. 'And those few dwellings beyond it make Burnley.'

Margery considered it observantly. This, she thought, was farmland, but not the farmland she had known in Kent. This was a rougher land, with the cattle lean and the trees in scattered clumps. Stubble fields seen here and there suggested lighter crops than the Kentish farmers cut.

Roger saw her thought.

'These are no wheat lands,' he said. 'We contrive a little of it for our own tables, but the most of our folk must needs make shift with barley—and little enough of that.'

'And is barley all your people's living?'

'No. There's pasture too, as you may see, and it's better than you'd suppose. Even in the Lacys' time there were vaccaries here.'

'Vaccaries?'

'Cow pastures. What else? But here's the open ground. Now see!'

They had ended the climb at last, and now to their left the ground fell steeply to a silver thread which she guessed to be the Sabden brook. Beyond it was the great hill, bare and stark in the sunlight.

'What's on the hill?' he asked.

Margery looked keenly, and at once she saw what he meant. The hill was in full light, and from the one end to the other its great flank was dotted with white specks which could only be grazing sheep.

'There's our true living,' said Roger. 'There they graze. There's wool to be clipped and carded and spun, and cloth to be wove and dyed. And beyond all that, there's flesh to be roasted and boiled, and there's milk and cheese for some. God's chosen animal, the sheep.'

Margery gurgled with amusement. This, as a theological pronouncement, was new to her.

'And is it a good living, sir, that this chosen animal gives?'

Roger frowned at that.

'No,' he answered shortly, 'not for all. It's very well for us who are the owners. It's well enough for the yeomen, who in their way are owners too. But for the common sort it's not nearly so well. Sheep give less work than wheat, and there are folk in plenty here who eke out their barley bread with stolen mutton. How say you, Tom?'

'I'd say less, sir, if they'd let their thieving stop at mutton.'

'I'll not gainsay you. That place yonder is Fence.'

They had dropped from the crest of the ridge now, and were riding along its outer face with a grey stone hamlet in view below them.

'Fence? That's an odd name sir?'

'There was store of deer there once, kept safe behind a fence.'

Margery nodded. She was admiring the sweep of this sunlit valley, with its green and silver set against the blue and white of the sky.

'And those are the Hoarstones,' said Tom Peyton.

He was pointing at some tall stones rising out of the ground to their right, and Margery grew curious; but for once, Roger did not know the answer.

'Ask me not,' he said. 'We call them so, and none knows how they came, nor whence.'

'The country folk,' said Tom Peyton, 'have a tale that the Devil sits among the stones on certain nights, and the fairies on the other nights.'

'Fairies?' Margery smiled. 'You keep fairies here?'

Roger grunted.

'I'll not vouch for the fairies,' he said, 'but we've certainly got the Devil.'

They had a minute's silence, and then Margery was at it again.

'This Rough Lee to which we go,' she said. 'Is that where this Mitton lived?'

'Aye indeed, and as house steward!' Roger laughed aloud. 'God's Grace! House steward in a yeoman's home, as though Dick Nutter were a belted earl! It's a woman's madness!'

Margery looked at him inquiringly, and he explained it patiently.

'I mean Mistress Nutter,' he said. 'Mistress Nutter of the Rough Lee—known through the Forest as Our Alice. She came here out of Trawden some twenty years agone, and she came as the wife of plain Dick Nutter. Then she took airs, and would have herself the wife of Master Richard Nutter—though he's Dick to all Pendle. And of late she's so puffed that none doubts she means to end as the wife of Richard Nutter of the Rough Lee, Esquire—if God do but give her land enough.'

'God, is it?'

Tom Peyton flung the question quickly, and Roger turned sharply at it. For a moment Margery expected trouble, thinking her cousin might resent this as an impertinence. Then she saw that she was wrong, and at once she guessed why. These two had been many a year together, and no doubt Tom Peyton was privileged to speak his mind. Roger, she saw, was smiling.

'Again I'll not gainsay you, Tom. We'll say, if the Devil should find for his own.'

Then he seemed to remember Margery again.

'But of your question, this Mitton was her house steward in these last years—him that used to be the pig man! And now he's dead. And I don't yet know what's thought odd in that.'

They had crossed to the inner face of the ridge again, and soon the great hill was in full view to the left. Another mile brought them to a turning, and the road dipped steeply down to the inner valley. At the bottom were crossroads, and Roger stopped and pointed.

'You see the four roads meet? Opposite, the road comes from Barley, which is a mile or two beyond in a cleft of the hill. To the right of the Barley road, the high ground is called Wheathead. What's to the left we call Goldshaw. And in Goldshaw . . .'

He pointed away to his left, where the ground rose steeply, and Margery, following that, saw a cluster of buildings, all in the grey stone and perched high on the naked hill.

'I told you we'd a church within the Forest,' he went on. 'There it is, and we call it the Newchurch, though it's been there many a year. Do you see it there, below the road?'

'Aye sir. With the road running past it?'

'Just so. Past it and above it. Had we been for Barley or for Wheathead, we might have used that road.'

He pointed down to the crossroads far below them.

'Do you mark the water there?'

Margery had already seen it, a shining stream that ran by the Barley road and seemed to come from the great hill behind. At the crossroads it turned sharply and then followed the road that ran to the right.

'It's the Pendle Water,' said Roger. 'We must drop to the crossroads and thence follow the Water to the right there.

A mile downstream from that, and we shall be at the Rough Lee.'

'Being a house, sir?'

'Being mainly a house, but with a cottage or two lying near. That's to be expected, since these Nutters are folk of substance. As yeomen go, Dick Nutter is the wealthiest in Pendle.'

He put his horse to a cautious walk down the hill to the crossroads. The others followed.

'I'm told,' he went on, 'that we shall not see Alice this day. She's away at Lathom, she and her precious son.'

'Lathom sir?'

'Aye, Lathom House—by Ormskirk, to the west beyond Preston. Where lives the Earl of Derby, the Lieutenant of this County. Alice has a kinsman who's some secretary or clerk in milord's Household, and it's this fellow she visits—she and Miles.'

'Miles?'

'That's her son—a slender reed of some twenty summers. The fellow at Lathom's not much more than that. What's his plaguey name? I can never hold it. How's he named, Tom?'

'Potter sir. Matthew Potter.'

'Aye, Potter it is. And what's the kinship? Is he cousin to Alice, or what is he?'

'Depends where you ask it sir.' Tom Peyton had a broad grin.

'How?'

'At the Rough Lee they says nephew. At the alehouse they says bastard. You take your choice.'

'Thanks. I've made mine and I'll not ask yours.'

They were down the steep slope at last, and there, by the side of the clear and bubbling stream, a horseman waited. Roger waved an arm in greeting, and the man returned it with a cheerful flourish of his hat. Margery scanned him with interest as they came to the water and let the horses pick their careful way across. She saw a tall ungainly fellow, with big hands and feet and unruly hair; his cheerful grin and happy untidiness gave him a friendly look as he pulled his hat at Roger.

'Glad to see you Jim.' Roger sounded as though he liked the man.

'Thank you sir.' Wilsey's voice was as cheerful as the rest of him. 'Sorry there's this trouble, but I thought I'd best call you.'

'It's no fault of yours. But what *is* the trouble?'

'It's Baldwin sir.'

'Baldwin?' Roger did not sound pleased. 'I thought it was Mitton.'

'Oh aye sir. It's Mitton that's dead, but it's Baldwin that's the trouble, if you take me.'

'Baldwin usually *is* the trouble I've noticed. What is it this time?'

'What you might guess, sir. Thinks the Devil's had Harry.'

Roger's eyebrows lifted sardonically.

'The Devil, is it? That's what Baldwin would think. And who's His Hellship's agent this time?'

Wilsey had a grin that split his face.

'The Demdike sir.'

'Again what I might guess. If we're to believe Baldwin, that woman's the Devil's agent-general for these parts.'

The sunlight came dappling through the trees as they rode down the wooded banks of the stream. Roger had lapsed into a thoughtful silence, and Margery had a chance to consider what she had heard. Its general meaning was plain enough. Somebody called Baldwin thought that somebody called Demdike had bewitched this Mitton, and Margery found no cause for surprise in that. She had heard talk enough at home about witchcraft, about the tales that ran, and the books and pamphlets that tumbled from the presses. Roger too, she noted, had shown no surprise; and with that there came to her a sudden memory of her brother Richard asking why a country gentleman should wish to buy the King's great book about the witches. Then, while she asked herself what this portended, Roger's voice disturbed her thoughts.

'Here's the Rough Lee,' he said suddenly.

They had come to a substantial stone house, large and well proportioned, and set back from the road in a proper dignity. As they dismounted, a slight and sandy-haired man with a shuffling walk and an unhappy look came to greet them; in a yeoman's jerkin he might have looked at ease, but he had a laced doublet of green which somehow gave him the air of a lackey flaunting it in his master's second-best. Roger, however, greeted him heartily.

'Good day to you Dick!' he called, and Margery guessed that this must be the Dick Nutter he had spoken of.

'Good day to you, Master Nowell!' It sounded like a forced imitation of Roger's heartiness. 'Though it's no very good day for us here.'

'So I'm told. What's this of Harry Mitton?'

'He's dead this morning.' The man shuffled awkwardly. 'And the Demdike woman's been here, and her infernal granddaughter with her. But Baldwin can tell you more of that.'

'Baldwin? Is he here now?'

'Aye—and waiting for you.'

'The Devil he is!' Roger handed his horse to a fellow who had come out for it. 'Then we'll go in. But I'm forgetting—here's Mistress Whitaker, who's my cousin and guest. Cousin, this is Master Richard Nutter—though he's Dick to all Pendle.'

Dick Nutter made a leg at her, shyly and awkwardly, and Margery acknowledged it with a friendly smile. She thought there was something to like in Dick Nutter, and perhaps something to pity too. She wondered what his wife was really like, and whether the green doublet had been her choice rather than his.

He took them in and led them to what Margery judged to be the Steward's room, a simple place which was part parlour and part pantry; and Roger, who had remained covered, swept off his hat to the dead man stretched on the table there.

Margery looked without emotion. Death, after all, was a common sight, and she had seen it many times. Harry Mitton, when all was said, had merely gone the way so many had gone; and it was no great matter.

She looked at him observantly. He had been a big man, and older than most. She thought he might have been something past sixty, so he had had more than his share of life. She could imagine him, portly, pompous, and red of face, working to impress the stranger with his own importance; even in death he looked that kind of man. But if death had not changed him in that, it had changed him in something else. There was an odd look about him as he lay there, still and quiet on the long oak table; and as Margery considered him, asking herself what it was, there came to her the memory of another death like this. There had been an innkeeper at Lambeth, just such a red and portly man, who had worked himself into a heat, moving wine casks under an August sun, until he had collapsed among them with arm and leg drawn tight and his face pulled awry. He had muttered thickly and had died within the hour; and in death he had looked as Harry Mitton now looked.

There was a stir behind the door, and a man who had been sitting there rose quietly to his feet, slipping under his arm the book he had been reading. He was a sturdy and finely made man of some fifty years, wiry and strong, and with a brown and sunburned face which in repose might have been friendly but now looked tense and strained. Margery, curious as ever, looked at the book he had been reading and saw it was a Psalter. She looked from that to his brown leather jerkin and plain falling band, to his close-cropped hair and burning eyes, to the hard lines of his brow and jaw. Then she stiffened warily; she had learned to know a puritan when she saw one.

6

The Puritan

'God's Grace to you!'

'And to you, Master Nowell!' His voice was as firm and resonant as Roger's. 'And may it be upon us all, since we all have need of it.'

'Amen to that!' Roger nodded shortly. 'What's to do here?'

The man with the Psalter looked him in the eye.

'It's a foul tale,' he said, 'and best not told in this presence. We'll be sweeter in the air.'

Roger nodded assent, and then followed silently as Dick Nutter led them through the house and into a formal walled garden behind. He did not stop there, but led them through a gate in the garden wall and so to a sloping pasture beyond. In silence they followed him across its green turf till they came to a grey stone dairy, set where the pasture ended and the ground swept steeply up to a commanding ridge. Here they halted, and the puritan eyed them grimly.

'Here,' he said, 'it was. Here it came upon him.'

Roger looked about him attentively, and in so doing he caught Margery's eye.

'Faith, little cousin! I'd all but forgotten you.' There was a flicker of amusement in his eye as he made his tone formal. 'Give me leave to present Master Richard Baldwin. Master Baldwin, my cousin, Mistress Whitaker.'

The man turned to Margery and seemed to become aware of her for the first time. He looked her slowly up and down, noting the gay orange-tawny, the slashed and buttoned doublet, the plumed copintank and the laced gloves. His lips pressed together and his eyes grew hard as pebbles. In silence he made the slightest of bows.

Margery stood stiffly under his scrutiny, tense and alert and with her mind racing. She knew precisely what Richard Baldwin was thinking. Puritan disapproval was not new to her, and she drew now on her experience of it. This man seemed to count for something here, and to stand well with him might help her to stand well with cousin Roger; and since to do that had become important to her, she was in no mood now to stand on niceties. She must soften this Richard Baldwin, and she was seeking the way of it when he spoke.

'I don't remember you as a neighbour, mistress. You'll be from further parts?'

That gave her a chance, and she took it on the wing.

'I was born in Cambridge,' she told him, 'where my father professed Divinity. And I was bred in Lambeth, where my brothers were ordained.'

The Psalter moved between his fingers and a shade of doubt came into his eyes. The watchful Margery missed nothing.

'Lambeth?' he said slowly. 'I've heard of that as a godly place.'

'I've known it as that,' came the solemn answer.

'Aye, Lambeth,' he repeated. He seemed less sure of himself now. 'Then you'll have heard the Archbishop? You'll have heard him preach?'

That was easy.

'By Dr. Bancroft I was baptised, and later heard many of his sermons.'

'Aye—Bancroft.' The voice was harder again. 'But what of His Grace that now is? What of him, mistress?'

She was in no doubt about the meaning of this. Bancroft had been something of a High Churchman and hence suspect among the puritans; but George Abbot, enthroned at Canterbury hardly a year ago, was as stout a puritan as any. Margery smiled gravely.

'I've sat beneath Dr. Abbot many times,' she said. She was pleased with that, it had the right puritan tang. 'And,' she added hastily, 'I've more than once heard him discourse at his own table where we sat at meat.'

This was true. Her father's name had stood high, and his

writings against the Jesuit Bellarmino had found favour enough to win for his family some notice from both Archbishops.

'At his own table?' Baldwin spoke musingly. 'That's a goodly place. And yet . . .'

He broke off as his eye lit again upon the orange-tawny. Then Roger came to her help.

'Richard! Richard!' he said. 'Of your charity, let's leave Archbishops till we've done with Harry Mitton. Get to your tale, man, and let's be done!'

Margery, well satisfied, retired into silence. Her cousin had sounded pleased and Master Baldwin had sounded interested; and that, she thought, was the work half done. It was her turn now to listen.

Richard Baldwin told his tale simply and without artifice. He stood in the sunlight, bare-headed and cloakless as he had come, and his strong resonant tones came easily above the sighing of the wind and the rustle of the grass.

'We'd been busy at the mill since first light,' he said. 'I'd a word to put to Dick here about the grain I'm working for him, and the lads being all busied I bade my girl ride over. And here's her tale. Wishing to know Dick's whereabouts, she came to this place, where Mitton then was. He was here, just where we are now and with him in talk was the Demdike crone.'

'The old one?' This came from Roger, sharply.

'Aye, the old beldame—the grandmother. But a half-score paces back was the young whelp, the granddaughter.'

'Alizon?'

'She. My girl hadn't a doubt that the old crone was begging and Mitton refusing, for as she drew close she heard him bid the woman be off.'

'And then?'

'Aye—then. Mark it well. Demdike drew off, cursing like a soldier's drab; and twice she stopped to spit. Harry Mitton took a pace or two after her. Whereat the whelp Alizon stoops, picks a fistful of cow-dung, wet and fresh as it lies, and flings it in Mitton's face. And him turned sixty, mark you—and a churchwarden.'

'I mark.' Roger's voice was quiet. 'And then?'

'She runs up the slope, and Mitton after her—being justly angered.'

Richard Baldwin paused, and his level gaze swept round the circle of his listeners. He seemed to address himself to them all, and his voice came slowly and deliberately.

'Harry Mitton had not run a score of paces up that hill when some power struck him down. He fell on his face, and he lay there, grovelling and twitching—for my lass to look on.'

'And then?' Roger's voice was without expression.

'Then? Why, Grace screamed at what she saw, and the whelp Alizon ran as though she'd the Devil at her. Then out comes Dick Nutter here—and of what followed he may speak himself.'

'And what says he?'

Dick Nutter fidgeted unhappily as they all turned to him, but he did his best with the tale.

'There's little more to tell,' he said. 'Richard's lass screamed, and I ran out and saw it—just as Richard's said. There was Harry on his face and the girl Alizon running like a mad thing.'

'What of the Demdike?'

'I heeded her nothing, nor she me. There was a gardener came out too, and a cowman, and between us we got Harry in—and a rare sweating job we had of it, with his weight and this ground. But we got him in and laid him as you saw.'

'He still living?'

'Aye, and twitching. Then I sent a lad to bid Richard come fetch his daughter, she being in no fit state to go alone.'

'No doubt.' Roger seemed deep in thought. 'And then?'

But it was Richard Baldwin who took up the tale again, and there was a tremor in his voice now, as though he were deeply stirred.

'I'd Dick's message,' he said, 'and I guessed poor Harry as good as dead. I bade the lad ride on to summon Wilsey, and I nigh foundered my horse getting down here. I prayed God as I rode that it might please Him to spare Harry Mitton. But it pleased Him not, and before I came the man was gone.'

'Aye, gone he was.' Dick Nutter spoke again. 'There was naught we could do. He lay there and snored, jerking and twitching, and his face red as a cornfield poppy. Betimes he tried to speak, or so it seemed, for we never kenned a word. And then, of a sudden, he was dead. And that's all there's to it.'

'All?' Richard Baldwin's voice rose passionately. 'All, d'ye say? All?' He turned from Dick Nutter and spoke directly to Roger. 'When I'd seen poor Harry dead and quiet, I came out here in great unease of spirit. And there on this hillside, not twenty roods away, were two damned witches squatting like gorged crows—Demdike and her squinting bastard.'

'Who?' Wilsey spoke for the first time. 'Which of them? Alizon? Or Squinting Lizzie?'

'In human pity, tell us a plain tale!' Roger sounded exasperated. 'I grow giddy between this brood of women. Whom do you speak of now?'

Baldwin explained carefully, speaking clearly and with a slow patience.

'There are but three to think of,' he said. 'There's Demdike, the old beldame who began the whole damned brood. There's her daughter whom she names Elizabeth and who takes second name Device from a fool she says married her. And . . .'

'Is that Squinting Lizzie?'

'So Wilsey says. And surely she's afflicted of the eyes . . . Beyond that, there's the third generation, this whelp Alizon, who's daughter to this Elizabeth Device and hence granddaughter to the Demdike.'

'Yet first you said . . .'

'I said that first there were Demdike and the whelp Alizon. And so there were. But the whelp ran off, and her mother must have took her place, for it was her I saw.'

'The grandmother remaining? I see.' Roger's face had the faintest of smiles. 'Then the matter, as you see it, stands how?'

'Is there need to say how?' Baldwin sounded impatient. 'They're known reputed witches, all of them. The whelp flings dung. Mitton makes at her, and the old one strikes him down. Then, her own power not sufficing, she calls Device, her daughter, to help make an end of him. Is it not enough?'

Roger looked slowly round the circle from one to another, as though searching out their thoughts.

'It would be enough,' he said quietly, 'if I were sure that any power had struck him.'

'If you were sure?' Richard Baldwin's stern voice shook with fury. 'What meaning has sure if this be not it?'

Roger chose to answer him indirectly.

'This Mitton,' he said, 'to be more just than courteous, might be called stout of girth. And none so young. It's ill work for such a one to run up hills in the sun.'

'You doubt. You doubt all things.' Baldwin was flaming in accusation. 'You doubt that this killed Mitton. You doubt all power of witches. You set aside the Holy Writ. You set aside what the King has writ. And you doubt! I tell you, whoever doubts the Devil's power will doubt God's power before he's done. I have said to you before . . .'

'And you'd best not say it again.'

Margery jerked to attention. There had been a note in Roger's voice which she had never heard in any voice before. It cut Baldwin short in the height of his fury, and he stopped, his hard breathing noisy in the silence.

For a moment there was open hostility. But both men kept their tempers, and Roger broke the tension with a sudden smile.

'We'd best not quarrel, Richard,' he said. 'That's how the Devil wins.'

But Richard Baldwin was harder to appease. He turned aside and spoke bitterly.

'Thou makest us to be rebuked of our neighbours,' he recited. 'To be laughed to scorn and had in derision of them that are round about us.'

Margery picked up her scattered thoughts. She had sat in churches and at family prayers too often to miss the quotation, and suddenly she dared an intervention.

'The forty-fourth Psalm, is it not?' she said. 'But Master Baldwin, is there not also a word in the eighty-ninth?'

She knew how to talk to puritans. He whipped round as though he had been stung, and she saw him groping for it. Then, before he had found it, she gave it him.

'What man is he that liveth and shall not see death?' She looked him straight in the eye. 'I take that to mean, sir, that death is natural to men.'

A faint nod from Roger showed his approval. Baldwin turned from Margery to Roger. Then, still in silence, he turned back to Margery, and once again there was doubt in his eyes. The others stood in watchful silence.

'You've been well schooled, mistress,' he said slowly.

Then Roger spoke crisply.

'It's matter of my duty as a Justice, Richard. Granting that a witch has power and may strike a man, I nevertheless can't commit till I've determined that she's in fact done so. Wherefore my duty here is plain. I must see these women. Where shall they be sought?'

Richard Baldwin had recovered his poise. He looked Roger very straight in the eye.

'If I've misjudged this, I'll be sorry for that,' he said simply.

'Thanks for that, Richard. Since we're of a mind on it, we may seek the Demdike brood.'

Then Jim Wilsey cut in with a cheerful heartiness that helped to ease the tension.

'That's good,' he said. 'Then we'd best get us to the Malkin Tower. It's home to them all, and they'll be back there by now.'

'Like enough!' said Dick Nutter, and led them back through the garden to the house.

They mounted, all six of them, and took to the road again, riding now beyond the Rough Lee and with the Pendle Water still splashing beside them. Wilsey was riding with Roger, and seeing them deep in talk, Margery fell back. To her surprise, Richard Baldwin came alongside her. As usual, he spoke his mind without prelude.

'You'll know more of Holy Writ than the Psalms, mistress?'

'I trust so, indeed.' She was watchful, and wondering what was coming.

'Tell me, then, what's commanded for a witch in the Book of the Exodus?'

Margery felt more at ease. She knew this with certainty. Every puritan used this text, and she answered easily.

'In the twenty-second chapter? Thou shalt not suffer a witch to live?'

He nodded approvingly.

'Just so. And is not that enough?'

Margery sought evasions, that she might neither contradict this man nor range herself with him against Roger. And while she hesitated he pressed her again.

'And of this woman and her daughter and her daughter's daughter, the three of them damned alike—what's declared of such as they?'

Margery thought quickly and as quickly found the answer, thankful that these puritans all leaned on the same texts; and again she quoted it easily.

'The twentieth chapter? "I the Lord thy God am a jealous God, visiting the iniquity of the fathers upon the children unto the third and fourth generation of them that hate me." Is that it, Master Baldwin?'

It was, and Master Baldwin plainly wanted to discuss it further, but Margery would have none of it. She knew that look in a puritan's eye, and she knew the sort of talk it presaged, and at this moment she felt that she could not bear with it. Her mind was on present matters, and she wanted to know where they were, where and what this Malkin Tower might be, and some more about this woman called Demdike. She was curious, too, about this man, and about the Grace he had called his daughter. So she asked him quickly where they were.

If he was disappointed, he hid it well. There was, as she was coming to perceive, a natural courtesy in Richard Baldwin, and it was not always over-ridden by his puritan bluntness. He looked about him shrewdly. They had come a couple of miles from the Rough Lee, and the Pendle Water had swept to the right and was now far from the road; he pointed to the curve of it.

'You see,' he said. 'The Water's gone from the road. It turns back on itself and goes to join the Calder. But see you now.'

They had topped a short steep slope, and before them the prospect had changed abruptly. In front of them was a long and grassy valley, rising and curving into the far distance; and here their road swung to the right, and then seemed to swing left again behind a grassy hill, as though it followed the shoulder of this valley. To their left a stony track led down to the bottom of the valley, and Margery could see its white streak as it wound up the slope beyond.

'That's for Wheathead,' he told her. 'It would bring you to the mill where I have my home and work. And one day, mistress, if you'll take that ride, I'll be glad indeed to greet you there.'

He looked across at her with a touch of shyness that sat oddly on him. Margery was in haste to answer.

'That, sir, I'll surely do, and soon. My thanks for those words.'

She was both pleased and flattered. Clearly she was on the way to having his liking. Besides, she was as curious as ever, and she wanted to see his home and daughter. She would certainly visit this mill at Wheathead—but not, she thought, in orange-tawny and a plumed copintank.

A moment's halt was enough for Roger, and then he led them off the road, so that they were riding on the bare grass and climbing obliquely out of the valley. Again it was Richard Baldwin who explained.

'You saw the road go round the hill? We may join it again this way. We do but shorten corners. It's the Gisburn road and it runs along the crest of the valley.'

His meaning was plain when they had topped the crest. Here was a windy moorland with the thin road crossing it, straight and stark.

'And what more do you see?'

Richard Baldwin spoke quietly, and Margery had no doubt of his meaning. Set by the road, lonely and desolate, was another of the grey stone houses, but this time a mere cottage. It stood alone, far from the life of the Forest. No outbuildings ringed it. No animals, not a cow, nor a sheep, not even a chicken, seemed to belong to it. Its only sign of life was a wisp of smoke flattening into the wind from its single chimney. It stood alone and desolate, an outcast from the dwellings of men.

'So!' Richard Baldwin spoke with menace in his voice. 'The Malkin Tower.'

They were riding swiftly now, down the bare slope of the grass. The awful cottage drew nearer, and Margery could soon see that its desolation was not of position only. It was decayed, ramshackle, desperate. There were holes in the thatch and cracks in the walls; the bounding fence was torn into crazy gaps. But for the smoke, she would have supposed the place derelict and abandoned these twenty years. If this was a human habitation, it surely ought not to be.

Under the horses' feet a hare sprang from nowhere and

went bounding and leaping over the tufted grass. Roger turned in his saddle.

'You saw it?' he called.

'The hare?'

'What our country folk would call a malkin. And here we are! The Malkin Tower!'

7

The Demdike Brood

They hitched their horses to what was left of the fence and Jim Wilsey led them to the door. This was his privilege as Constable, and Roger followed behind him. Margery, in the rear, had time to note the pitiful ruin of the place, the split and battered door, the broken windows, the litter of filth on the ground about. Whatever these Demdikes might be, the Malkin Tower was testimony to their poverty and squalor.

Wilsey kicked sharply on the door and set the crazy thing shivering. He waited, kicked again, and looked inquiringly at Roger. Margery guessed why. Wilsey, as Constable, was an officer elected of the parish; but the King's peace lay on the crazy door, and only the King's Justice might give leave to force it. But so much was not needed. A bolt screeched, and the door swung slowly open to disclose a man—or the semblance of one.

Margery looked in surprise. She had expected a woman, and even if she had expected a man she would hardly have expected such a man as this. He was a tall thin fellow, in shirt and tattered breeches, and with sacking tied about his shirt in the place of a jerkin; and shirt, sacking and breeches alike were slimy with dirt. His head rolled above a long thin neck, and his eyes rolled in his head till they showed their whites. His dirt, his fantastic dress, and his idiot looks made it hard to fix his age, though he was obviously young. Margery guessed that he might be about twenty. And no sooner had he opened the door than he loosed a great whooping laugh; then his mouth dropped open, and he stood gaping.

Wilsey wanted no more invitation. He marched in, Roger after him, and shouldered the fellow aside. One by one the others followed, and all the men stayed covered.

The dark low room was as foul and ruinous as the rest of the place. A heavy rough-hewn table filled most of the mud floor. To the left of it, set against the wall, was a long wooden chest. Beyond, on the back wall, a low bench covered with rags and straw looked as if it served someone as a bed. To the right of the table a peat fire smoked on a cracked stone hearth. By this hearth, sunk in the shadows, sat three women.

Margery had heard endless talk of witches. She had read of them in books and in many a lurid broadsheet. Once she had been in the crowd to see one hanged. But she had never seen a living witch at close quarters, and she stared now with undisguised interest at these three women. Unquestionably they were the three generations Baldwin had spoken of. One was pitiful in extreme old age; one was in vigorous middle life; and the third was a young girl whose age might have matched Margery's. This, no doubt, was the 'whelp' of Baldwin's tale.

A crackling word from Wilsey brought all three women to their feet, while the fellow who had let them in moved to the window. Tom Peyton hooked one of the stools from the hearth and set it at the table's end for Roger, who moved slowly to it. Wilsey, as Constable, stood to his right, Tom Peyton to his left. Baldwin and Nutter hovered behind him. Margery moved to the chest by the wall, thinking it would serve her as a seat; but before she reached it there was an interruption.

Roger, in settling himself, pushed his long legs under the table. At once there came a quick squeal and a rustling in the straw. Then, from the other end of the table, a child shot out, rushed wildly at the door, and ran head down into Margery.

Margery grunted, and held on to the frightened child. Roger jumped to his feet, and the gaping fellow by the window loosed his idiot laugh again. For a moment there was confusion. Then Roger seated himself again. Tom Peyton silenced the laughter with a vicious jab in the stomach, and in another moment Margery was sufficiently recovered to look curiously at her capture.

The child was very young, a girl who could have been no more than eight, and something in her won Margery's sympathy at once. It was not only her pitiful state of fright, not only her unkempt neglect, not only the coarse rough smock that clothed her; beyond all these, this child was attractive. She had a strong, cleanly cut little face, clear grey eyes, and hair that might have been golden without its dirt; and though she looked pinched and underfed, she was nevertheless well limbed and of good proportions. She pulled and struggled for a moment. Then she gave it up and buried herself in Margery's cloak. Margery pulled her out of it and tilted the little face towards her own.

'What is it, child?' she asked. 'You needn't fear. There's none here will do you any hurt.'

The child clung to Margery with both her grubby hands and looked about her nervously. Then she looked up again and seemed to take courage. Margery patted her shoulder.

'That's better,' she said. 'Now come and sit with me.'

She led to the chest by the wall, and seated herself; and after a little hesitation the child sat beside her and nestled against her. Margery pulled the fold of her cloak round the thin body and patted the child reassuringly.

'Which being ordered,' said Roger, 'we'll proceed.'

He gave a slight nod of approval to Margery and cast a steady glance at the child; and suddenly, as his eyes held hers, the crinkly smile lit his face, and Margery felt the child gasp with pleasure.

'You're well seated, little maid,' said Roger. And then his face turned grave and he gave attention to the three women by the hearth.

'Which first, sir?' asked Wilsey. 'Demdike, is it?'

Roger nodded.

'If that's her true name. I've heard it's not.'

'Stand out, old one!' said Wilsey sharply. 'You other two can stand back. Now, tell Master Nowell how you're named.'

The old woman by the hearth moved slowly forward, leaning on a stick that tapped as she came. She was old far beyond what was common. Margery, scanning her keenly as she came from the shadows, thought she be far beyond the threescore years and ten. She was as bedraggled as the rest, and had a ragged kirtle from which age and filth had removed the last trace of colour. She moved unsteadily, and groped with her stick as if her sight were all but gone. Yet she was not wholly blind, and the little deep-set eyes shone brightly in the seamed brown face.

'You're asked how you're named,' said Wilsey again.

In a flat toneless voice she gave her name as Elizabeth Sowtherns.

'Sowtherns? Or Demdike? Which?' asked Wilsey sharply.

'Which you please,' came the venomous answer.

There was a stir by the hearth, and the middle-aged woman suddenly spat, as though to show approval of this. Tom Peyton sprang forward indignantly, and then stopped abruptly as Roger's hand slapped the table imperiously. Margery, glancing sideways, saw Roger with his head thrown back, his nostrils dilated and his eyebrows drawn down. He looked steadily at the offender. Then he spoke in a voice that gave Margery little shivers.

'You're to learn your manners,' he said. 'If you give me cause again, you'll go outside and have the lesson applied to your back.'

The silence of a frozen night fell on the room. The woman turned white and kept silence. Margery held her breath. Then Richard Baldwin's whip broke the silence, slapping gently against his boot, and Margery saw that his face matched Roger's. This she noted without surprise; she knew something of puritan hardness.

Then the tension relaxed. Roger nodded as though satisfied. He turned again to the old woman.

'I've known you as Demdike,' he said, 'and Demdike you'll remain. You'll need to tell me now what passed between you and Harry Mitton when the sun was new this day. Now loosen your tongue.'

Demdike looked round her nervously, from the one side to the other, and drew no comfort from it. She spoke in her toneless quavering voice and kept her eyes down, on the floor, on the table, on the hearth—anywhere but on Roger's face.

'Nowt passed of any weight,' she said. 'I'm old and poor, and none to find for me, and there's been no bite in the house since yestere'en, and the cold's colder when your belly clings. And this day, being blind when it's bright, I had my gran'daughter, ugly lump that she is, lead me down to the Rough Lee, where I'd thought to have blue milk if nowt better. And seeing Harry Mitton there, it came to me to ask of him a penny for the buying of meat.'

She paused and stood silent, looking down at her twisting hands.

'And then?' asked Roger steadily. 'What did Mitton say?'

'Called me a ditch drab and bade me be off.'

'I'll not ask what you called him. But what followed?'

Demdike looked about her again, hesitant and uneasy.

'I trudged up the hill,' came the answer at last.

'And Mitton?' Roger's voice was ominously quiet.

There was another pause. Behind Roger's back, Richard Baldwin stirred impatiently.

'I saw nowt,' she answered sullenly, 'so I can tell nowt.'

Roger slapped the table again, and the woman stepped back hurriedly.

'You'll be wise,' he told her, 'not to suppose I'm to be treated as a fool. What happened to Mitton?'

There was an edge in his voice now, and Demdike had evidently heard it.

'He ran at my gran'daughter,' she said slowly, 'and something felled him.'

'Something? What was it? You?'

That came sharply enough, but Demdike's answer came as sharply.

'I know nowt of it. I saw him on his belly, and that's all.'

'All, was it? How came he to run at your granddaughter?'

'Don't know. She'd best tell of that.'

'She shall. Meantime, stand back. I'll want you again.' He turned sharply to the middle-aged woman. 'Now you,' he said, 'come out here, and have a thought to your manners.'

She slouched forward sullenly. It was the first time she had been out of the shadows, and Margery drew breath sharply at sight of her. She was a woman of perhaps forty, big-boned, angular and of powerful build. She had lank black hair and uneven teeth that were almost as black; and between hair and teeth were two dark rolling eyes which showed the most preposterous squint Margery had ever seen. The left eye looked down, the right eye up, so that however she stood she could show the pupil of no more than one; of the other, only the rolling white could be seen.

Margery saw and shuddered. It was not only the hideous

squint. The lines of this woman's face, the set of her chin and the drooping twist of her mouth, all joined in a picture of malice and savage temper. The girl who clung to Margery suddenly buried her head in testimony to her fear of the woman who stood slouching there, quelled by a threat and silent only from fear.

'Name?' asked Wilsey sharply.

'Elizabeth Device.' There was a rumble of anger in the deep voice.

'Condition?'

'Widow.'

'Whose?'

'John Device.'

Roger's foot tapped the floor, and Wilsey abandoned his formal questions abruptly. Roger leaned forward.

'How came you to join your mother behind the Rough Lee this morning?'

'Walked.'

Roger's eyebrows puckered ominously.

'You'd best not be pert. Who called you there?'

'None.'

'Then why did you go?'

'The old 'un hadn't come back.'

'So you went to fetch her? Then why did you not fetch her?'

'I did.'

'You did not. You sat on the hill with her. Doing what?'

'Doing nowt. Just sitting.'

Roger sat back and viewed her steadily. His foot tapped the floor again.

'Stand back and wait. You, also, will be wanted again. Now, the youngest.'

Elizabeth Device returned his stare venomously, but she did as she was ordered and stepped back in silence. In the same silence the girl by the hearth stepped forward to the table.

Again Margery peered keenly, and her first impression was confirmed. This girl must have been of her own age, or at most not a year older. There the resemblance ended. This girl followed her mother; neither her youth nor the absence of the squint could conceal the likeness. She was slimmer and smaller, though time might alter that; but she had the black hair and the dark eyes, the droop at the corners of the mouth, and the same mute suggestion of malice and evil temper. If she differed from her mother it was in lacking her mother's fierce courage, though the sly darting of her eyes hinted at a cunning that might serve her instead.

She came forward nervously, plainly frightened and ill at ease. Roger spoke at once, not waiting for Wilsey this time.

'Your name?'

'Alizon Device, sir.'

'Her daughter?' Roger jerked his head towards the sullen Elizabeth.

'If it please you, sir.'

'It doesn't.'

'No, sir.'

She suddenly clasped her hands behind her back and stood waiting in silence. Margery watched with complete understanding. The girl had offended, and knew it; and now she hoped to soften judgment by showing the best manners she had. Margery had done exactly that too often not to recognise it. But sympathy did not go with recognition; she had already decided that she had no liking for Alizon Device.

'What passed between you and Harry Mitton?'

Roger's question came sharply, and the girl moved uneasily, her mouth twitching.

'Nothing, sir,' she said at last. 'Not a word at all.'

'That's possibly true—as to the word. But what else?'

'Nothing else, sir. Nothing at all.'

'What fool do you take me for?' The edge was back in Roger's voice. 'What did you do?'

The girl looked sullen, her shifty eyes everywhere but on her questioner.

'I'm told you flung a fistful of dung at Harry Mitton. Did you so?'

There was silence again—a silence sharply shattered by the idiot laugh from the window.

'Hey! Hey! Hey!' came a shrill high voice. 'Dung for the old—ugh!'

Tom Peyton's fist had dug into the fellow's stomach, and he went sprawling on his back, whooping like a croup-stricken child.

'Who the Devil's that?' asked Roger curtly. 'And what ails the fellow?'

Wilsey answered him.

'It's young Jemmy, sir—another of 'em.'

'Jemmy? Meaning James?'

'Yessir. James Device. He's another of hers.' Wilsey signed at the squinting Elizabeth.

'Oh? Your brother, is it?' This to Alizon.

'Yes sir, if it please you.'

'Again it does not. What ails him?'

Once more Wilsey gave the answer.

'He's moon-kissed, sir. Wanting. Always has been. He's well known for it.'

'I don't doubt it.' Roger watched not unsympathetically as Tom Peyton hauled the lad to his feet. Then he turned briskly to Alizon Device again.

'Now, of this dung you're said to have thrown at Mitton. What's your tale?'

'I didn't, sir. Never at all, sir. Not a thing like that, sir. No, sir.'

Roger stared at her.

'Never?' he asked coldly.

'Never, sir. I'll swear by—by . . .'

'Spare your perjuries. You were seen to throw dung at Harry Mitton, and seen by one whose word is beyond doubting.'

'No, sir.'

'You're still denying it?'

'Yes, sir. And if there's only one against me . . .'

She broke off and stood silent, her mouth twisting in a sly smile.

Roger turned slowly to the men behind him.

'You see her meaning, Richard?'

'I see she's an impudent liar, and much that's worse besides.' There was anger in Baldwin's voice.

'I nothing doubt it. But you see her meaning? She's made it very clear. With only one witness I may neither commit to Sessions nor deal summarily. It's to be deplored, but you see it?'

Roger's voice was airy. The girl's shifty smile grew broader while Baldwin stood speechless in his anger.

'Ye-es.' Roger was positively drawling, and Margery

watched carefully. It had occurred to her that if she were in Alizon's place she would not trust this blandness.

'I think, Richard, that this flinging of dung is not a matter for the law. Could it be matter for the Church?'

'The Church?'

Baldwin sounded puzzled and suspicious, and Margery thought he suspected blasphemy. Puritans often did, she had noticed. But Roger stayed placid.

'Aye, the Church. Or if not the Church, at least the churchwarden. Which is to say, it's left to you. I'm told you've some force in your arm.'

Baldwin understood. So did Alizon. There was no smile left on her twitching pallid face as Richard Baldwin slipped round beside the table.

'I want the grandmother again.' Roger's voice came curtly. 'Demdike—where is she?'

Tom Peyton pushed her forward, and then flung the door open as Baldwin gripped Alizon by the neck and hustled her out. Margery heard his whip crack before the door was shut, and the girl's shrill screaming came steadily as Roger probed again into old Demdike's tale. Margery hardly listened. She was considering this Alizon, and what a fool the girl must be to have supposed she could match her slyness against Roger. Margery nodded her approval. Alizon was certainly being dealt with roundly, and Margery thought that proper. One could not have a world in which girls were free to fling dung at churchwardens.

The door creaked open, and a sobbing whimpering girl was thrust in and left to sprawl painfully on the mud floor. Richard Baldwin followed, and Margery scanned his hard face shrewdly. It was as she had expected. She had seen that pitiless chill in puritans before.

Roger's quiet questioning went on. Alizon faded into near silence, and Margery began to lose interest. Then suddenly her attention moved to the child at her side. She had seemed to be asleep and had certainly taken no interest in what had gone on; but now she was sitting up, neither sleepy nor nervous. From the straw that littered the room, she had picked a stalk of barley that seemed to have an ear or two of grain left in it; and she was now busily engaged in rubbing out these ears and eating them, raw and filthy as they were. Margery looked, and was a little shocked. But then she remembered what Demdike had said of a house without food since yesterday. If that were so, the child must be ravenous, and as Margery thought of that she remembered the bread and cheese that Tom Peyton had given her for her saddle-bags.

She glanced at Roger again, and with an apologetic smile to him, she rose to her feet, beckoned to the child to follow, and tiptoed to the door. She passed out into the sunlight, and the child followed obediently.

The saddle-bag yielded its treasure, and Margery, who had herself some reputation for appetite, watched a performance that surprised her. The child went at the food like a starving dog; she ate noisily and hurriedly, with an evident determination to miss no crumb; and as she ate she clung tenaciously to what remained, as though she feared it might yet be snatched from her. Margery watched intently, happy to have fed the child and angered that there should have been such need for it.

The child made an end; then she burrowed in the grass in search of lost crumbs, and at length lay on her back with a satisfied grunt. Margery watched with a smile. She was finding it pleasant here in the soft wind and the high sun of noon.

'Is that better, little maid?' she asked.

The child nodded and sighed happily. Margery sat on the grass at her side.

'And what do they call you?'

'Jennet.'

'Jennet what?'

'Jennet Device.'

'Device?' Margery tried to take this in. 'Do you mean that . . . that your mother . . . that we saw your mother inside there?'

The child nodded again, and Margery tried to make sense of this. This child was perhaps seven or eight years old. Alizon was at most ten years older. So the squinting Elizabeth must be this child's mother, and Alizon her sister. But . . .

'Is Alizon your sister then?'

Another nod.

'Oh!' Margery looked again at this shapely child with the fair hair and the clear eyes, and mentally compared her with

Alizon's dark shifty cunning. Then she saw a possible explanation. Alizon and Jennet might have the same mother, but it by no means followed, especially with such a mother, that they had the same father.

Jennet sat up suddenly and began to take stock of Margery. Her shrewd young eyes roved up and down from the plumed hat to the fine soft boots, and at last settled into a steady stare at Margery's face.

'Who are you?' asked Jennet bluntly.

Margery gravely told her, adding that she was come on a visit to Master Nowell.

'Why?'

This was difficult. Margery could think of no very good answer. 'Because Master Nowell wished to see me,' was the best she could do. But it seemed to satisfy Jennet, who nodded gravely.

'Me too,' she said. And Margery took this to mean that she had Jennet's approval.

'I like you,' added Jennet suddenly; and Margery, who had disconcerted many, was for once disconcerted herself.

Then voices by the door brought her quickly to her feet as Jennet dived through the crazy fence like a startled rabbit. Roger had come out, and was walking slowly to the horses. Richard Baldwin, at his side, seemed to be expostulating with him, and Roger was having none of it.

'There's no profit in complaint,' he was saying. 'You know full well that when there's no confession I can't commit for witchcraft without two witnesses at the least. And here there's only one, even if she is your daughter. No doubt it's to be deplored, but I can't mend it. And nor can you, Richard.'

'Confession could have been had.' Baldwin's voice was almost savage. 'There are ways of having it, if you'd but use them.'

'Ways? Aye, ways enough!' Roger had stopped in his walk. 'I know such ways and I know what they end in. But I'm a Justice of the Peace in this County of Lancaster, not a Spaniard turned loose in the Low Countries. Let that be held in mind.'

But Richard Baldwin was not quelled.

'In all matters else, I'd say amen,' he answered. 'But here's sin against God, and the wrath of God shall be on us if we give it breeding ground. It stinks before the Lord, and it's to be cut out, root and branch. In God's name, I say, shrink not from some small severities when there's His work to do.'

Roger shook his head slowly.

'It's not my way, Richard, and I'll not do it.'

Richard Baldwin found his stirrup and swung into his saddle.

'On your head be it!' he retorted. 'But I much fear it may be on all our heads.'

He turned to Margery and suddenly swept his hat off to her. For a moment he waited, sitting rigid on his horse, while the bright sun lit his sober clothes and gave a tint of bronze to a face that was still and hard as granite. Then, without another word, he turned his horse and rode away.

Roger turned slowly to Margery.

'The fear of God,' he said, 'is the root of some evils. It's a way fear has.'

8

Dark Elegance

'Parsons,' said Roger gloomily, 'change with the times, and not always for the better.'

He said it on Sunday morning as they were riding to the church at Whalley, and Margery looked across hopefully. She was beginning to know this fine sardonic tone of his.

'In the old days,' he went on, 'one Dobson was parson here. He was Vicar when I was wed in this church. A jovial fellow, even if he was a papist . . .'.

'A papist, sir? In the King's Church?'

'A papist he was. He put water in the wine and then drank it himself. After him was one Osbaldeston, who was at least a man of decent family. A reading parson too—a thing much to be commended.'

'Reading?' Margery was puzzled. Was it matter for note in Whalley that the parson could read?

'Aye, reading.' Roger gave his explanation in the same sardonic tone. 'He read what's set in the Prayer Book, and that being done, he made an end and suffered us to be gone. But this rogue Ormerod, who's plagued us these six years, is not content with that. He's got him a Preaching Licence, and now we don't know when we'll dine.'

Margery gurgled with amusement. She was finding that her cousin's humours sat lightly on her.

'I've known the like before,' she said. 'How does this Master Ormerod preach?'

'Like a quinsied duck. And when I told him so, the rogue babbled of our great-uncle.'

'Who?'

'The sainted Alexander.' Roger grinned, and then

changed his topic abruptly. 'There's one thing of merit about a parish church—you have to ride to it.'

'So I note. But . . .'

'Which means there are horses to put up. And where there are stables there's commonly an inn—hard by the church. We'll comfort our throats before we heave insults at the Devil.'

Margery was shaking with laughter as she followed Roger to the inn. Her cousin, it seemed, took a lighter view of Sunday's duties than her brothers had ever done.

Once in the church, she found the well-remembered order. The Bidding Prayer was made, the Psalms chanted, the Lessons read, just as had been done every Sunday since she could remember. Master Ormerod, black gowned and grave of mien, and wearing a surplice deliberately torn to show his contempt of it, gave her no trouble. She recognised him at sight as a puritan divine of the breed she knew so well; and when he came to his pulpit and gave out his text from the twenty-sixth chapter of Leviticus, she sighed wearily. Idols and graven images meant the old familiar sermon against Popery.

So it proved, and Margery was not interested. She had heard it too often, and now she allowed her thoughts to wander. And not her thoughts only; for a quick glance at Roger showed him to be blatantly asleep, and Margery, perceiving that there was no vigilant guardian at her side this day, turned her head a little and let her eyes go roaming too.

She was in a huge family pew, and this in itself was odd. She had marked the inscription on it as they came in. *Factum Est Per Rogerum Nowell,* the deep-cut letters had said; and the date, *MCCCCCCX,* was of only a year ago. And what, she was asking herself, did a solitary widower want with this great horse box?

The church was packed, as well it might be when there were churchwardens quick to present the laggards, and magistrates as quick to exact the shilling fine. Margery wriggled in her pleated safeguard as sun and crowd combined to heat the church. She twisted to the side, and a chapel took her eye. Or should she call it a chantry? She was not versed in such niceties. But she was at least curious about this one, for it held four women sitting alone, and not a man among them. She looked again, and saw that its windows had stained glass; and in the glass were the arms of Nowell.

Margery grew attentive. There were the three cups sable in their field of argent, and below them were two figures; apparently they were of man and wife, and seven sons knelt by him and seven daughters by her. Beyond doubt this was some family memorial. But what, then, was this chapel?

Master Ormerod turned his glass and went booming on about idolatrous images of saints. Margery left him to it. She was stickily hot by now, and in no mood to give ear to a sermon she knew as well as he did. She began to pick out the lettering below the figures and she groped in her memory for what rudiments of scholarship she had. *Orate pro animabus Rogeri Nowell armigeri*—that was easy enough—*et Gratiae uxoris ejus*—and Grace his wife—*et pro bono statu Johannis*—that, she thought, must mean the well-being of John—*primogeniti Rogeri*—firstborn of Roger—*cum fratribus et sororibus suis*—these must be the kneeling figures . . .

Margery halted and frowned at it. The next was not quite so easy—*qui istam fenestram fieri fecerunt*. It was something about the window, but—Margery dropped her eyes from the glass as she pondered it; and she saw the women who sat in the chapel. Abruptly her thoughts changed. One of these women was looking at her.

Margery swung her head hastily, and stared dutifully at the preacher. But she caught no word that he was saying. Her mind was in turmoil, and she had feelings of guilt, horribly mixed with a sudden fear; and all at once she was aware that her heart was beating faster than it should. She had to brace her shoulders and steady her breathing before she could ask herself why this was.

Certainly it was odd. She began to disbelieve it, and cautiously she let her head turn to the chapel again. Warily, she took another glance; and she had a flood of relief when she saw that the woman was now apparently intent on the sermon. Margery took the chance and began to study her attentively.

Disbelief began to mount. How could she have been frightened by this decorous lady? For decorous she surely was. Every fold of her sleek black taffeta, every pleat in her white lace collar, spoke decorum; and there was a fine elegance, and a precise good taste too, in the snowy satin of her stomacher and in the silver lace that gleamed and sparkled on the taffeta. It all blended perfectly with her raven hair. The white plumes in her tall black beaver swayed gently as she nodded quiet approval of the sermon. There was nothing rustic here, and surely nothing frightening either. The lady made an admirable picture, and Margery found herself envying the skill and good taste that had gone to compose it.

The heat in the church was getting overpowering; and Margery, dabbing cautiously at her face with her hand kerchief of cambric, wondered if taffeta was cooler than she had supposed. Certainly there was no sign of distress in the sharply-chiselled face under the fine black beaver. Margery's attention left the clothes and fastened on the face. It was almost too sharply chiselled. A pale oval face this, with small delicate ears, a straight sharp nose, and a chin that receded a little. Margery was not sure that she liked that pointed chin; and the small thin-lipped mouth had a droop at the corners that set her wondering what this woman was like to live with. And while she wondered, the woman turned quickly; and her dark deep-set eyes looked full into Margery's.

Margery jerked upright. She could not look away. The dark glittering eyes held hers; they were deep dark pools, radiating force, wave after wave of it, and of a sudden Margery was cold. In the heat of the church, while her clothes clung damply to her, a shiver crept up her back, to find her heart and set it pounding; and then in an instant, as if a cloud had been swept from the sun, the cold was gone. The heat was with her again, and the dark-eyed woman was giving her a smile as sweet and gracious as might be dared in any church.

Margery gasped with relief, and turned hurriedly to Master Ormerod again. But Master Ormerod was ending at last, and some deep instinct was rousing Roger from his slumbers. Margery shook herself into a becoming propriety as the Blessing was given.

There was a surge of departing; and no sooner was Margery on her feet than she was aware of eyes turned curiously upon her, as gentlemen wondered who this was, and ladies made sharp appraisement of the orange-tawny. Margery stiffened, and made sure that her shoulders were truly braced. Roger, saturnine in cloak and doublet of black velvet, with gold lace and gilded cords, crinkled with amusement as he took it all in. Thereafter he was in no hurry. He gave Margery his arm and went sauntering down the aisle, gazing blandly at the roof; while Margery, half proud and half nervous, was at pains to saunter as carelessly as he. This was a change from black grogram and a sister's watchful eye.

They came blinking into the sunlight, and Margery was hoping now for some meetings, and perhaps some talk, with one or other of these gentlemen whom Roger surely knew. But in that she was disappointed. For even while Roger stood looking about him and drawing on his gloves, the lady from the chapel, the lady of the black taffeta and the silver lace, bore down upon them purposefully. Margery grew suddenly tense, and for a moment the cold tingle touched her spine. But it faded as soon as it had come. There was surely nothing here to disturb her peace; the lady was all graciousness, and her smile was charming as she glanced inquiringly at Roger. He bowed politely and did what was plainly needed.

'Give me leave, ma'am, to present my cousin Mistress Whitaker. She's my guest just now. Cousin, here's Mistress Nutter, wife of Richard—of the Rough Lee.'

The dark eyes were on Margery again, but now they had a light that matched the quivering smile. Margery hastily recalled her manners and made the curtsey that was due. It was punctiliously acknowledged.

'You are most welcome to Pendle, mistress.' The diction was perfect, and the voice a tone deeper than Margery had expected. 'But the gossip runs that you've come alone, no woman with you?'

'Why yes, ma'am, I have. But I'm my cousin's guest.'

Mistress Nutter rippled into laughter.

'We'll acquit you of the improprieties, mistress, and surely Master Nowell too.'

'Madam, my thanks!'

If Margery's keen ears found a hint of irony in Roger's bland tone, there was nothing in his bearing to support it.

He was standing very straight and sober in his black and gold, one gloved hand holding his prayer book while the other rested lightly on the gilded hilt of his ceremonial sword—the very picture of a courteous gentleman who waits at his ease while the ladies talk.

Mistress Nutter chose to be arch.

'I had meant to convey, sir, that your cousin should have some courtesies from her own sex as well as from yours. You'd not confine her to a monastery?'

'Indeed no, ma'am.' Roger was as bland as before. 'Nor to a nunnery either. She was not born under such a star if I judge aright.'

The laugh rippled again.

'It's very well, sir.' She turned directly to Margery. 'You've been already to my poor house, as I'm told, and I'm sorry you'd so sad an errand. Please to come again, and soon. We'll try then to give you friendlier welcome.'

Margery stood stiffly, her thoughts whirling as she sought for escape. There was something here that she mistrusted, and the memory of that chilling glance in the church came vividly to her as she stood. She knew she had no wish to go again to the Rough Lee, to be the guest of this woman whose dark eyes stabbed like icicles. Then, while she still groped for words of refusal, she was sinking into a quick curtsey and saying how pleased she would be to go.

She was almost relieved when she had said it. There was, after all, no other answer within the courtesies, and she could not stand in silence for ever. She would at least have time to brace herself before the ordeal came.

Mistress Nutter dipped acknowledgment of the curtsey. She smiled acknowledgment of the acceptance. For a moment the dark eyes gleamed, and Margery stiffened again as a ghost of a shiver came and went. But before she had found a word to say, Mistress Nutter had turned to Roger and was speaking with a most becoming gravity.

'I'm in your debt, sir, for the pains you took when poor Mitton died last week.'

'Not so, ma'am. A simple duty.' Roger's smooth tone expressed nothing.

'Aye sir, duty no doubt. But duty most zealously performed. I say again that we're in your debt. And we much regret that so much was laid upon you.'

'Let's keep regrets, ma'am, for Mitton's death.'

'Aye indeed.' She nodded decorous agreement. 'Poor Mitton! A faithful servant, sir, and I do not know how I shall find his like....'

It almost sounded as though that might be the cause of her regret.

'What of these women, sir?' Her question came sharply while Margery was musing.

'Women, ma'am?'

'These Demdikes. I've heard such tales ...'

'From whom, may I ask?'

The first edge of sharpness had come into Roger's voice as he slipped his question quickly. But Mistress Nutter was not disturbed. She answered him easily.

'From my servants, sir. They're in such flutterings . . .'

'You'll hardly heed such gossip, ma'am.'

The dark eyes lost their light. They were very steady when she spoke again.

'May we be serious, Master Nowell? Mitton dies something oddly. Some women of an ill sort are seen. Then a magistrate puts them to the question. May I not suppose ... ?'

'You may suppose, ma'am, that if there'd been anything found against them they'd have been committed.'

Mistress Nutter stood in silence. Then she nodded thoughtfully.

'I understand, sir. Then I'll take my leave.' She turned quickly to Margery. 'You bear it in mind, mistress? No long delay!'

Margery's curtsey was formal. Roger's bow was solemn. Mistress Nutter outdid them both. Her curtsey was perfect, and her smile was charming as she turned about and went tripping lightly through the churchyard gate.

'What the Devil!'

Roger was staring at her retreating back, and for a moment Margery was startled. But the old sardonic tone was back in his voice, and she felt her forehead crinkle with relief. Here was something she could deal with at her ease.

'Sir?'

The lift of her eyebrows said the rest, and Roger asked no more. He explained himself pithily.

'She's mighty civil,' he said. 'And when Alice Nutter's

mighty civil, it commonly means that she wants something. At this moment I don't perceive what it is. Did you mark that chantry?'

'Aye, sir. And the glass in it.'

Black-and-silver went trotting past the gate on a fine black horse with silver lace on a black saddle-cloth. Roger swept his beaver punctiliously. Then he stood in silence.

'Touching this chantry, sir?'

Margery prompted him as the silence lengthened, and at once he was in his light humour again. He moved down the deserted path.

'We'll go to the inn,' he said. 'My throat needs cosseting again. But touching this chantry, little cousin, it's ours, as you'll have marked from the glass. For these hundred years it's been ours, for which we're at charges each year of six shillings and eightpence. But while I was away from here there were some who took it to themselves, and even when I was back they declared that they should continue in the use of it.'

He stood aside to let her pass through the gate, and again she had to prompt him.

'And you answered?'

'Mildly as a coted dove. Only saying that I'd run a foot of steel through the next that did. Since which time, these gentlemen have not used my chantry.'

'No, sir? And yet . . .'

'Aye, little cousin—and yet?' His forehead was crinkling now. 'For though they kept themselves from my chantry, they bade their ladies sit therein—whom I could not well call to account.'

'I perceive the difficulty, sir.' Her solemn tone matched his. 'And then?'

'The Devil whispered in my ear—and I, in my turn, whispered in the ear of Alice Nutter . . .'

'To her content, I trust?'

'To her infinite content. For the Nutters, being, when all is said, no more than yeomen, are not graced with a pew in church. They must sit with the common sort—which irked our Alice sorely. So I gave her leave to sit within my chantry—*my* chantry, do you see, little cousin?'

'Aye, sir. Which she does?'

'Which you saw her do. And one by one the high-born

ladies find them seating elsewhere. And I—I found me a little pew within a barn . . .'

'A barn!' Margery was shaking with laughter.

'Aye, a barn—where it had been these seventy years, some puling monk having stayed it from the church when first our people made it. So I hauled it within and set it where you see, for such comfort as it has.'

The lift of his eyebrows sent Margery into helpless laughter at his oddities; but under the laughter a more serious thought was stirring in her. She was coming to see, more and more clearly, why there might be some who did not love Roger Nowell.

They came to the inn, and suddenly his mood had another shift. He stopped by the door and regarded her gravely.

'I had the thought,' he said, 'that you were not at ease with Alice Nutter?'

Margery's eyes were as steady as his.

'I'll not deny it, sir. I was most ill at ease.'

He nodded, and at once the banter was back in his voice.

'Little cousin,' he said solemnly, 'you've a most excellent good nose.'

9

The King's Justice

Master Nicholas Banister, Squire of Altham and a Justice of the Peace and Quorum, rode to Read the next morning. He came on the wings of a gusty wind that set grey clouds chasing in a patterned sky, and he swung from his horse in bright sunshine with his cloak black from the rain of the spattering showers.

His coming was expected, and he had the welcome that belongs to an old friend. Roger was out in the wind to greet him. There was a groom to take his horse, and Tom Peyton to see to his servant's needs. There was hot spiced ale to warm his heart, a chair set ready by a tended fire, and cheesecakes warming before it. Sandals and gown of his own were waiting as change from his boots and cloak, and a long white pipe and leaves of tobacco were ready at his call.

Margery, too, was ready. She had, indeed, been ready this past hour, for the bustle of preparation had warned her and roused her curiosity. After her experience with Richard Baldwin she was taking no more risks, least of all with this man who was Roger's nearest friend; and today she was trim and demure in the black saye kirtle and the flowered sarcenet gown. She had, indeed, given it the white lace collar, but that no more than lightened it; it did not mar its propriety.

She saw through the window Master Banister's coming, and as he and Roger walked together to the great door, she moved discreetly into the window, thankful that this was between showers and that there was sunlight for her hair; and when Master Banister, cloak swaying and spurs jingling, swept into the room in haste to be at the fire, she was admirably poised for him to see.

He stopped as though he were frozen.

'Lord of Grace, Roger! What's this?' he burst out. 'Is she your own?'

Roger's crinkling smile showed his pleasure, and Margery, catching sight of it as she made her curtsey, let her face melt into its twin. It was not wasted on Master Banister.

'Roger! Roger!' he said. 'Tell me more. Whose is she?'

Roger was laughing now.

'I've told you, Nick, she's my cousin only, and distant at that. I could wish she were nearer. But she's Margery Whitaker, not Nowell.'

'Whitaker is it?' Master Banister untied his cloak and stood considering her. 'You bring her here from nowhere and say she's not yours? I'll believe you, Roger, but there'll be those in Pendle who won't.'

'I nothing doubt it. But we neglect your comfort.' Roger jerked at the bell cord, and at once there was bustle for Master Banister's needs. Margery took his cloak, Roger saw to his ale, and his own servant came hurrying to tug off his boots and help him into gown and sandals. It gave Margery a chance to consider him. He was a tall spare man, perhaps a few years older than Roger, and not so broad nor so robust; but his lithe figure and browned face told of good health, and there was a hint of hidden reserves in the ease of his movements. His hair and beard were grey now, and it was plain that he had felt the chill of this blustering morning. But his spirits had not been chilled, and his hazel eyes were bright and clear. Just now they were a-twinkle with pleasure; and Margery, sensing the honesty and kindliness that lay in them, knew already that she liked Nick Banister.

'Margery Whitaker,' he repeated. 'I would it had been Nowell, as with such a look it should have been. But it's the less matter since I'll call her by no more than the Margery. That's if she'll give me leave. What say you, lass?'

'Why, gladly, sir.' Margery was pleased. This augured friendliness, and she hoped it might be a hint to Roger, who was still calling her little cousin.

'That's well answered,' he said, and busied himself with a

cheesecake in the comfort of an elbow-chair. Roger leaned across to replenish his ale.

'I'll not have you neglected, Nick. The less so since we've work to do.'

'Lord of Grace!' said Master Banister cheerfully. 'It's ever so with you Pendle folk, Roger. What's for today?'

It was as a Justice of the Peace, the nearest among Roger's neighbours, that Master Banister had made his visit. It was established between these two that unless some more urgent matter should intervene, Nick Banister should ride to Read each Monday and Roger to Altham each Wednesday. At each house the host conducted the business, and his guest became active only when some matter rose that required the sitting of two Justices together.

Roger propped himself against the chimney-shelf.

'It's what we've had before,' he answered. 'There's matter of a girl to be bound apprentice. There's a fellow taken begging and presented as a rogue. And there's the usual calendar from the Newchurch.'

Nick Banister laughed.

'Meaning your Richard Baldwin, I take it—still hot against sinners?'

'Hot as the Devil's nose. But it's to be remembered he's churchwarden there, and has duties.'

'Which afflict him sorely.' Nick Banister heaved to his feet. 'The sooner started, the sooner ended. Let's be to it.'

The two men moved to the door together, but before they reached it Nick Banister paused.

'What of your Margery?' he said. 'Is she banished from this? By her face she's agog with interest.'

'Is it so?' Roger turned, smiling. 'Come in if you've a mind to, and choose your own moment.'

Ten minutes later Margery moved quietly through the side door of what Roger, half mockingly, called his Justice Room—by which he meant that he had taken advantage of the present emptiness of his house to set aside a convenient room for this use. A long table of shining oak ran across one end of it, and set against the table, with their backs to the wall behind, were elbow-chairs for the two Justices. Each end of the table had an empty chair, and another half-dozen chairs were set against the walls; in one of these sat an elderly white-haired man whom Margery did not know; in another sat Richard Baldwin.

Nick Banister was at his ease in his chair, his long legs stretched beneath the table and his furred gown pulled comfortably. A smiling lift of his eyebrows welcomed Margery and directed her to a chair by the wall. She tip-toed to it and then gave her attention to Roger.

He had pushed his chair back to the wall and was on his feet, standing with his head a little down and his fingers on the table before him. To his left, and beyond the table, stood Jim Wilsey, cheerful and untidy as ever. In front of the table a burly rough-bearded fellow in rags and tatters stood guarded by four sturdy men who formed the Watch that day.

Apparently Roger had heard as much of this matter as he wanted, for he brought it to a quick end even as Margery found her seat.

'Enough,' he said. 'You're a known noted rogue and you'd best have stayed elsewhere. Here you shall have your deserts.'

He took a quick glance to his left, where Nick Banister sat in silence. A slight nod signified assent, and Roger turned to his front again.

'William Walker,' he said formally, 'being presented and convicted as a known and noted rogue, and for begging and trespass. To be soundly whipped according to law. And to sit in the stocks the space of six hours.'

He waved a hand at Tom Peyton, who seemed to have a status here, and the unfortunate trespasser was hustled out without a chance even to struggle. Roger seated himself, took pen and ink, and wrote laboriously on a paper that lay on the table before him.

Margery turned to look about her, and found Richard Baldwin, in the next chair, viewing her gravely. She suffered it without embarrassment, well knowing that he could not condemn her appearance this day. The black saye was impeccably puritan, as Margery knew; Prudence had seen to that. Evidently it had its effect, for Baldwin looked almost benign as he considered her.

'Next,' said Roger suddenly, and the white-haired man sitting beyond Baldwin came quickly to his feet. From the back of the room a sturdy middle-aged yeoman stood out.

'Thomas Shaw, yeoman, of Higham,' called Tom Peyton loudly. 'Presented by Christopher Swyer of Barley, Overseer of the Poor, for that he did refuse to have bound unto him an apprentice, and to live within his house, one Ellen Hay, being a poor child of eleven years or thereabouts and without known parents.'

Evidently this was not a criminal case, and it soon became a not unfriendly argument. It quickly emerged that Thomas Shaw was not seriously refusing to take the girl. He was merely standing out for better terms; and the white-haired Swyer, acting on behalf of the Overseers who would have to pay for it, was trying to get the indenture accepted cheaply.

The argument, speeded by some comments and suggestions from Roger, was soon at an end, and the details began to be agreed. As each point was settled, Roger had to set it down on paper, and seemingly he found this no light labour. The watchful Margery saw his trouble. Roger had plainly no facile hand with a pen, and Margery remembered with a new understanding the brevity of his letters to her brothers. Now, with these details to set down, and the argument to heed, guide and judge, he was obviously labouring. A sudden impulse of sympathy brought Margery to her feet, and she tip-toed to the end of the table. She took the empty chair at his right hand, and spoke quietly as he stared in surprise.

'I'll be your clerk, sir,' she said.

Roger's surprise became evident, and Nick Banister stirred in his chair. Richard Baldwin sat up sharply, and the argument stopped abruptly. Here, it seemed, was a new and astonishing notion, and for a moment Roger held silence. Then he nodded.

'I'll be in your debt if you can,' he said. And without more ado he pushed to her the papers, the sandshaker, the jar of quills and the ink-horn. Then he left her to it while he gave his attention to Thomas Shaw again.

'You agree, then, to furnish the girl with good and sufficient clothing, of sort proper to her station?'

It was not very difficult. Margery had been well-schooled in writing and she kept pace without undue labour. In half the time that had once seemed likely, Ellen Hay was bound apprentice for the term of seven years, and her indenture, signed by her master, and by Christopher Swyer for the Overseers, had been duly witnessed by the Justices as the law required.

'Next,' said Roger cheerfully, and Tom Peyton sang it out as before.

'James Hunt, labourer, of Wheathead. Presented by Richard Baldwin of the mill, churchwarden, for that he did fail to present a female child of him and his wife to the Minister of the Newchurch for lawful Baptism within one month of the birth of the said child according to law.'

This gave no trouble, and within two minutes Margery had it in writing that James Hunt was fined twelvepence for his neglect, and a frown from Richard Baldwin was hinting that he thought this insufficient.

'John Dodgson, labourer, of Fence,' called Peyton. 'Presented by Richard Baldwin of the mill, churchwarden, for that he did tipple in an alehouse during the time of Divine Service on the Sunday last agone. . . .'

Again it was easy, and soon Margery had recorded fines of twelvepence against John Dodgson and twenty shillings against the keeper of the alehouse. Then Tom Peyton was calling out again.

'Anne Redfern, widow of Thomas Redfern of the Rough Lee. Presented by Richard Baldwin of the mill, churchwarden, for that she came not to the Newchurch for Divine Service the Sunday last agone, namely the eighth day of September.'

Margery looked up quickly at this mention of the Rough Lee, wondering what manner of woman this might be, and whether she was perhaps a servant in the Nutter household. One glance disposed of that notion. The woman now before the table was clearly no indoor servant. She was too browned, too slovenly, and altogether too dirty for that. She was a woman of between thirty and forty, in the poorest of clothes; and there was that about her which roused Margery's keenest scrutiny—something which set her suddenly in mind of the Demdike women of the Malkin Tower. It was not physical likeness. This Anne Redfern with her fair hair and blue eyes must at one time have had pretensions to being a beauty. She was broadening now, and she had evidently taken no care of herself, but there were still signs of what she had been. But for all the physical disparity, there was enough in her slouching stance and drooping head, in the sullen twist of her mouth and the hard glitter of her eyes, to recall to Margery the shifty dark-haired Alizon. And when Roger spoke it seemed that he was of the same mind, for the impersonal tone in which he had dealt with others had changed now to something colder and harder.

'If you were not in the church, where were you?' he demanded.

'At home.' The answer came sullenly.

'Doing what?'

'A-seeing to my mother.'

Roger's frosty stare indicated his disbelief.

'What ailed her?'

Anne Redfern fidgeted and kept her eyes on the floor.

'You'd best tell what's asked.' Roger's voice came sharply now. 'What ailed her?'

The woman looked mutinous, and for a moment Margery thought she might spit as Elizabeth Device had done. But she controlled her temper and made shift to answer.

'Her age, like enough,' she said. 'She'd a rheum of the eyes, and great warch in her bones.'

Roger nodded slightly as though he accepted this. But his next question seemed to surprise the woman.

'What age has your daughter?'

'My . . .' She stopped, confused and suspicious.

'Your daughter, I said. What's her age?'

'Fourteen last St. Peter's day.'

'Where was she, the time of Divine Service?'

Anne Redfern flung her head back and scowled viciously. Evidently she had seen the trap. Roger's voice came with an edge.

'I wait an answer. Where was she? She was not in the church, I'm told.'

The woman's lips twisted in malice, but no answer came. Roger ignored her and turned to Margery.

'I find it plain,' he said. 'Either she or the girl could have done what was needed. It did not need both. Set it down at the full fine of twelvepence, to be paid by next Wednesday's noon.'

Anne Redfern found her voice as Margery's pen began to scratch.

'Twelvepence!' she spluttered. 'And me without one!'

But Roger was not impressed.

'Tell that to another,' was his curt answer. 'You're a known lingerer and a liar too, for which I'll call your churchwarden to witness. What says he?'

Richard Baldwin spoke decisively.

'She's the one and she's the other, and much that's worse besides.'

'Even so. Twelvepence let it stay. And if it be not paid as required you're for the Preston Sessions, and I doubt not gaol thereafter.'

He ended on that. Nick Banister came to his feet and the two men went out together. Margery stayed to collect her writings, and as she moved slowly to the door Richard Baldwin intercepted her.

'You're schooled in more than the Scriptures, mistress,' he told her. 'I would as much might be said of my own daughter. Grace can write her name and a few words more, but she'll not make a clerk. You'll be a pride to them that reared you.'

Margery, with a quick thought of Prudence and Alexander, was by no means sure of that sentiment; but she offered no contradiction.

'You're very gracious, Master Baldwin,' she said. 'I do my poor best.'

'None so poor, mistress, none so poor. You'll remember that there's a welcome if you'll ride so far as Wheathead?'

'That I'll surely do.'

She smiled very graciously and went demurely out. But the smile had broadened into a grin before she reached the parlour. Richard Baldwin, after all, had not been so very difficult.

But in the parlour some more compliments awaited her. Roger said he had not known what a talented cousin he had, and Nick Banister went further.

'If I'd a son not wed,' he told her, 'I'd be in talk with Roger about you.'

She coloured at that; and groping for an answer she could find no proper one. Perhaps Roger saw her difficulty, for he changed the topic abruptly.

'This Redfern woman,' he said. 'Did I deal too hardly with her?'

Nick Banister pursed his lips.

'No,' he said at length. 'It's not the first time she's been presented.'

'Nor the last, if I know her. But you remember her, do you?'

'Tolerably. She's of the infernal sisterhood you keep in Pendle, is she not?'

'The infernal . . .' Roger laughed. 'Our witch brood, hey? I think she is—she and her chattering dam.'

'Roger, you talk in riddles. Who chatters?'

'This Redfern's mother. The crone mutters to herself without ending, though there's scarce a word to be made out. For which cause she's called the Chattox, though I've heard her true name's Whittle.'

'Whittle? That's a name could have come from the same cause.'

Roger nodded.

'It may have done. But Nick, there's trouble again with the other brood—the Demdikes. Have you heard that Mitton's dead?'

'I have not. Who is Mitton?'

Roger told the tale briefly and added some details of the doings at the Malkin Tower. Nick Banister listened attentively, quietly sipping his ale while his eyes seldom left Roger's face.

'So?' he said slowly when Roger had at last ended. 'It's you and Baldwin at odds again, is it?'

'That's not to be shirked. He'd have had me tear confession from them—which is not my way.'

'Nor mine. Yet have a care of that man, Roger. He could be dangerous. What of the witches?'

'You call them so?'

'At the least, it's what they'd call themselves. But of this Mitton, Roger. What killed him?'

'I'd say his heart burst. He was over-fat for running in the heat. I've seen the like before.'

'As have I. But this whelp, as you called her. What did she think?'

'Alizon?' Roger spoke carefully. 'I think Alizon supposed the Demdike's arts had struck the man.'

'Why say you that?'

'Nick, you press me like an attorney. It's no wonder

you're of the Quorum. I say it because she was very sorely scared.'

'Of more than seeing the man fall?'

'Aye. From what I'm told, she hared it up the hill as though the Devil were nosing her back parts. But what of it?'

Nick Banister answered him very gravely, and Margery suddenly saw how very bright and shrewd his eyes had grown.

'These women, Roger, are what I've called them—a sisterhood. If they have not the powers that Baldwin supposes, at least they think they have. In that they're at one with Baldwin. I don't doubt that this Alizon truly supposes that the Demdike struck Mitton down—and I don't doubt that the Demdike supposes it, aye and willed it too. They're an evil sisterhood, Roger, and dangerous. They think they can kill, and, believing that, they sometimes do kill. Killing's none so hard when your victim's crazed with fear. They're evil, they're murderous, and they're dangerous. Look to it, Roger, and be not at too great odds with Baldwin. He could be a stout friend and a willing, when there's such villainy abroad.'

Roger's slow smile betrayed nothing.

'You have the right of it, Nick,' he answered quietly. 'I don't doubt that. And yet . . .'

'Yet what?'

But Roger did not answer that directly. He drained his ale-mug thoughtfully, and then he seemed to answer a question that had not been asked.

'I ask myself,' he said, 'who'll pay the Redfern's fine.'

10

Undercurrents

Roger's question was answered within two days. On the Wednesday morning he made ready to ride to Altham, as his custom was, and he was just about to mount when a horseman rode up to the house. Roger had brief speech with him and then presented him to Margery as Miles, son of Richard Nutter of the Rough Lee.

'He has moneys to pay on behalf of one Anne Redfern,' said Roger. 'Be pleased, therefore, to give him quittance for that. Give him also some proper entertainment. Fare you well.'

And on that, without any more words, Roger was away. Tom Peyton went clattering behind him, and Margery was left standing on the gravel wondering whether she should infer displeasure from his abrupt departure, or amusement from a suspicious crinkling she had seen in his forehead. But that, she reminded herself, she might ponder later. At the moment she had a social duty to perform, and she was by no means sure how to perform it.

She turned to Miles Nutter, and for a moment they stood considering each other. He was a young man of perhaps eighteen or twenty years, and Margery's first note was that he was uncommonly good-looking. He was slim, slight, and of a medium stature, trim and almost dapper, and holding himself briskly erect. His face, neat and delicate in its lines, was pleasant and vivacious, and it was bronzed enough to blend pleasantly with black hair that had a natural curl. His doublet, breeches, and cloak were of murrey serge, his hat of black beaver, his boots of soft yellow leather; and Margery, observing these things, was thankful that she had been minded to go riding, and was therefore already in her orange-tawny. Master Nutter held himself well. He stood with an easy smile, hat in hand, at the side of his horse; and Margery was pleased with him. As far as looks went she approved of Master Nutter, and she gave him a very friendly smile.

He bowed with less clumsiness than most men showed. Then he passed his horse to the waiting groom.

'I'll regret it,' he said politely, 'if my coming intrudes upon your affairs, madam.'

'It does not,' she told him promptly. She liked his airy voice, and nobody had ever called her madam before. She was disposed to favour Master Nutter. 'I've no affairs of note this morning, sir. Pray come within, and I'll give you the quittance my cousin ordered.'

He stood gracefully aside to let her pass, and as she led him in he chatted easily in his light tones.

'I'm ashamed that you should be plagued with quittances for pence, madam. But I'm told you'll know the occasion for it. This Anne Redfern dwells on my father's land, and my mother has some softness . . .'

'No doubt, sir.' She thought it prudent to interrupt. It would be safer than an argument about his mother, and softness was not the first of the qualities Margery would have attributed to the lady.

She solemnly took his proffered pence and then busied herself with the writing of what she hoped would pass as a quittance. She had no idea what form it should take, but she need not have been troubled. He took it without a reading and quickly stowed it in his pouch. Apparently he was more interested in Margery than in the quittance; yet a shyness seemed upon him now, as though he were reluctant to speak what was in his mind. Margery thought she had better help him.

'You'll drink a cup of ale, sir?' she said, and pulled at the bell cord. 'You'll need it after riding through so fresh a morning.'

He accepted it pleasantly, and Margery moved to the window as he drank. There was sunlight there that could pick a glint of red.

Master Nutter seemed encouraged.

'It is indeed a very fresh morning, madam.' He was looking thoughtfully at the orange-tawny. 'I—er—I have to ride yet a little further this day—up into Goldshaw. Has any yet conducted you to Goldshaw, madam?'

'No, sir.' An eye flickered and a forehead crinkled. 'I've heard talk of it, but not yet seen it.'

Ten minutes later they trotted out together into a fine September morning with a soft west wind and a sky of cobalt blue. They went in an amiable silence, and Margery told herself that there was much to be said for these easy Lancashire customs. She would certainly not have been given this freedom at home, but Roger had specifically told her that in the Forest she might ride where and with whom she chose; the Forest folk had easy ways and were not given to raising eyebrows at nothing. So Margery rode at ease, and found happiness enough in the cool air and the greens and blues of the morning.

He led her by the road she had ridden when she had gone with Roger to the Rough Lee. But before they had come to the Hoarstones, Master Nutter, still chattering amiably of everything and nothing, turned abruptly into a side-road, and they dropped steeply into the valley where the Sabden brook glittered in the morning sun.

'I've messages for my Uncle Anthony,' he explained. 'He lives up in Goldshaw here, with his sister who's my aunt.'

'Your mother's sister, is it?'

Margery was in some disappointment. She had expected a morning spent roving on this hillside, and a visit to a second Alice Nutter was a much less tempting prospect. But he was in haste to reassure her.

'Not so,' he said quickly. 'It's from my father's side. My uncle in Goldshaw is younger brother to my father. He's a widower now, and his sister, being my Aunt Margaret, dwells with him and keeps his house. In full style she's Mistress Crook, but she's widowed too, and it serves her turn to dwell with him. This road leads to the Newchurch, but here's where we leave it.'

They were at the bottom of the hill and had just splashed across the brook. Master Nutter turned to ride down it, but soon he had left it and was leading up a gulley in the hillside. Margery followed without protest. She was at least partly reassured. The proposed visit certainly suited her worse than the ride she had expected; but she had liked

Dick Nutter, and if his brother and sister were after his pattern they might be tolerable folk to visit. And when all was said, they were Roger's neighbours, and there might be nothing lost by knowing what they were like.

Two minutes on the climbing track brought them to a modest house, squat, comfortable and unpretentious, sure of itself in the strength that the grey stone gave. It was set in a fringe of pines, linked by a blackthorn hedge; in the Winter it might have had an air of gloom, but on this brilliant morning the grey stones were gleaming in the sun, and the fringeing pines gave a cool and pleasant shade.

Master Nutter was assiduous. He helped Margery to dismount; he opened the gate; he led the horses, and when the fine oak door swung open he was in haste to present her to the man who stood quietly beneath the low stone lintel.

He might have spared his breath in that, for one look told Margery that here was Dick Nutter's brother. He had the same spare and wiry figure, the same sandy hair, the same look of decent honesty; and this Anthony had also a kindliness of eye that won him Margery's liking at once. In a soft quiet voice he gave her friendly welcome, and he led her into a small square hall, stoutly panelled in oak. To her right, an oaken stair led to chambers above; before her, an oaken door stood open to show a cool stone-flagged kitchen; to her left, another door led to a sunlit parlour, likewise panelled in oak. Anthony Nutter took Margery's cloak while his nephew hurried into the parlour; and at once his voice was lifted in greeting to his Aunt Margaret. Anthony Nutter smiled at the sound of it, and then stood aside as an ancient servitor came waddling out of the kitchen and went to the horses. Anthony was smiling again as he viewed the old fellow's back; then he turned to Margery and took her into the parlour.

Aunt Margaret turned out to be a pleasant middle-aged woman, soft of speech and kindly of face. She offered the friendliest of welcomes, and produced ale, and cakes, and an apple tart of surpassing excellence. The welcome, and the unassuming friendliness of the house, soon melted Margery's carefully-assumed dignity and set her chattering freely. Miles, too, had plenty to say for himself. He turned to Margery with a very boyish grin and offered her more of the apple tart.

Margery hesitated. She was in her usual state of suppressed hunger, and it was an excellent tart. But she was a guest on a first visit—and the tart, when all was said, did not belong to Miles.

Margaret Crook gave an understanding smile.

'Now no holding back for the looks of things, please. It was made for the boy's visit, and it shall end with that.'

Her affectionate glance at Miles, and his smiling response, were not lost on Margery. It looked like the spoiled nephew of the favourite aunt. Margery ceased to hesitate, and sank her teeth into apple tart instead.

'I'm glad it's liked,' said Mistress Crook. 'Though I must not take all the credit for it. It's of a special making, and I had it from Miles's mother. Have you met Mistress Nutter yet?'

Margery, having her mouth full, nodded.

'She's the best of cooks,' Mistress Crook went on. 'She's skilled in all things, and not least in that.'

'Spoken like yourself, my dear. If you spoke of the Devil, you'd find his good parts.'

This was Anthony Nutter, breaking suddenly into the talk from the hearth, where he was leaning his shoulders against the littered shelf that ran above it. He had said no more till now than some polite greetings, and his sudden intervention surprised them all. His sister shook her head in vigorous disapproval.

'Tony! Tony!' she said. 'You must stop saying things like that. What will Mistress Whitaker think?'

'Think? Of me, or of Alice? Which?'

'Of both of you, Tony. And you might remember that Miles is here. Alice is his mother, even though you forget it.'

But Anthony Nutter was unabashed. He broke into a shy, affectionate smile.

'So she is, my dear. So she is. Though he takes more after you. And you, my dear, are the sweetest thing made, and it's beyond your powers to think hardly of any.'

His smile was disarming, and his sister laughed openly.

'Take no more notice of him, Miles,' she said. 'It's the humour he's in. Tell me now, what news have you for me?'

This led to family gossip, and Margery left Miles to it. Anthony, she noticed, had left the hearth and was standing in the sunlight of the open window, with his hair rippling faintly in the soft wind that blew through the casement. On impulse she went across to him, and he waved her to the low seat, done in blue linen, that ran under the window. Himself, he remained standing as he looked her over gravely. Apparently he was satisfied, for he nodded as though pleased.

'You're kin to Roger Nowell, are you not?' he asked without prelude.

'Yes.'

She answered him simply, for she felt already that this was a man to be dealt with plainly.

He nodded again, and his answer had a plainness that surprised her.

'Inheritance made him an Esquire. God made him a gentleman. Have that in mind, for you'll meet some who'll blacken him.'

The slow, puckering smile came on him again.

'Enough of that!' he said. 'I'll be having you in flight from me. Such earnestness on a September morning! Are you come for long?'

She laughed.

'Truly sir, I know not. But I think I'm here till my cousin tires of me.'

'That should be long. I doubt not that your presence gladdens him.'

She was surprised at the warmth that his answer stirred in her. There was a patent sincerity about Anthony Nutter which gave power to his words.

'You are too good, sir,' was all she could find to say.

'Polite belittlement! But I know of what I speak. Roger Nowell had daughters, and now they're gone, and his house is the emptier for that—as mine has been since my Anne is gone.'

'Your daughter, sir?'

'Aye.' He hesitated. 'She was of your age,' he went on. 'She died. Just two years agone.'

'Oh!' Margery came to a stop, not knowing what she could say.

'Be at ease. It was not your fault.' His smile was a little twisted now. 'These things are of God, and I doubt not He has care for His own. But perhaps we talk too long. Miles seems astir.'

Miles was. He had risen and was looking inquiringly at Margery. She nodded, aware that for a first visit she had stayed long enough.

But as Miles sought her cloak, her host had yet a word to say; and he said it with the direct simplicity that seemed to be his way.

'You've met Alice—my brother's wife?'

'Only once.'

'It's enough. She might be called—powerful.'

Margery's faint nod gave cautious assent. She knew exactly what he meant.

'You and I,' he continued, 'have not to live with her. Miles has. Moreover, he's her son . . .'

'Yes?'

'He's a good lad at heart. If you come to think him more under his mother than a lad should be—why then, have charity of thought.'

If she wondered why he thought it needful to say that, she had no chance to ask him; for Miles came up with her cloak and she had to turn to thank him. Then there were friendly partings, with Mistress Crook wordily insistent that she should come again, and Anthony quietly confirming that. Then they took leave, Miles calling gay farewells as he held her stirrup.

He led her down the track by which they had come. He seemed to have grown silent now, but Margery had a clear question to ask. She asked it as they crossed the Sabden brook.

'Your uncle spoke to me,' she said, 'of a daughter who had died. What was it that took her off?'

'Anne?' he answered. 'Poor Anne! Aye, she was my cousin.'

He fell silent again, and Margery began to be irritated.

'Aye, sir. Your cousin, to be sure. I had guessed as much. But, pray, what did she die of?'

'Why, as to that . . .' He seemed out of humour. 'I cannot well say. It was very sudden. Some said . . .'

Again he stopped, and she knew she ought to press this no further. But press it she did, curiosity getting the better of manners.

'What did some say?' she asked bluntly.

'Why, they said so many things that—that I know not what they said.'

And at that she had to leave it. She could not in decency press it further, and they toiled up the hill in an awkward silence, he disconcerted and she irritated. In the same silence they came to the main road again, and he turned to the right as was needful if they were to return to Read. But Margery stopped at the turning.

'I'll not need escort from here, sir,' she told him. 'You've distance enough in your road to the Rough Lee. My thanks, sir, for your kindnesses.'

He demurred at that, insisting that it was his plain duty to escort her home, and thus irritating Margery even more. To insist on the duty of it, and speak not at all of the pleasure of it, was by no means what she thought proper; and she was wondering how she might best tell him so. She had had quite enough of Miles Nutter for one morning. She thought his aunt pleasant and his uncle charming; but Miles himself, for all his good looks, had fallen in her estimation. She found him a silent and tactless fellow, and she faced him now with a steadiness of eye that should have warned him.

'I've no wish to have you a slave to duty, sir. I pray you, take your leave.'

She thought he was about to expostulate when she saw, to her further anger, that he was not even looking at her. He was looking over her shoulder at something beyond, and she turned sharply to see what it was. Then she had to contrive a hasty smile as Richard Baldwin rode up; and Richard Baldwin, she thought, did not look pleased.

'Good day to you, mistress! And to you, Miles!'

It was civilly said, but his face was impassive and his voice had a chill.

There was exchange of greetings and Margery sought for some softening approach. But Miles Nutter cut her short.

'I'm for the Rough Lee,' he said to Baldwin. 'May we ride together?'

'Surely. Then I'll take leave, mistress. Good day to you!'

He rode off, and Miles, with a flourish of his hat and not another word spoken, rode after him.

Margery sat her horse in silence, furious that he had presumed to do what she had bidden him do. It was a humiliating end to a morning which had once held hope and promise, and her teeth were holding her lip stiffly as she thought of it.

'What the Devil ails the fellow?' she asked herself. And then her lip eased into a smile, and she all but laughed as she perceived how her thoughts had somehow dressed themselves in Roger Nowell's clothing. It made her feel better, and she was almost good humoured as she turned her horse. But she was thoughtful as she rode home. Questions were pressing upon her. What had happened to Anne Nutter? Why had Miles behaved so oddly? And what irked Richard Baldwin?

It seemed that life in Pendle had its undercurrents; and some of them ran muddily.

11

The Chapel-of-Ease

Her questions were still unanswered when Sunday came; and she was therefore by no means displeased when Roger announced, after breakfast, that he would not ride to Whalley church that day, but would attend Service at the Newchurch instead. As a Justice, he thought it wise that he should occasionally see and be seen at the Forest church; and what day more proper than this, when a new Churchwarden was to be sworn as successor to the departed Mitton? He put the question as he blew tobacco smoke, and Margery was in haste to agree with him. She had learned that Alice Nutter went to Whalley church alone, and that her husband and son went to the Newchurch.

They rode out together along the Forest road, Roger chatting genially and seeming less out of humour than he had been a week before on the way to Whalley. Margery, remembering the dislike he had expressed for Master Ormerod, asked who the Vicar of the Newchurch might be.

'He's not a Vicar,' was the answer, 'but a Curate only. The Newchurch is in Whalley Parish, being a Chapel-of-Ease—for the ease, that is, of those who dwell too far from Whalley. One called Town has it, and has some grains of sense, if we count by the reckoning proper to Curates. It's true the rogue preaches, but not so vilely as Ormerod. Wherefore is our Baldwin at thrust of dagger with him.'

His cheerful tone belied his words, and Margery laughed once more at the oddities of her cousin. Then her laughter faded as the thought came that not the least of Roger's virtues was his knack of knowing when not to ask questions. She had said nothing to him of her ride with Miles Nutter except the bare statement that they had ridden to Anthony Nutter's house together; and Roger, though his eyebrows had lifted at her sharp tone, had asked no questions. This, she now thought, was a forbearance new to her, and very different from what she would have had from her brothers. They would certainly have questioned her rigorously, asking whom she had met, what had been said, and what had been answered. It had never occurred to her brothers that Margery was of an age to have some thoughts and hopes as private to herself. She smiled now at the thought of the scene that would have followed; for she knew only too well how her family's tactless prying would have provoked her to a resentment which she could not have voiced openly, and how she would in consequence have turned sullen and evasive, with resulting accusations of stupidity and insolence.

'You smile broadly. May I share it?'

Roger's bland question, cutting into her reverie, roused her to the present, and at once she became aware that they were passing the spot where she had parted so angrily from Miles Nutter on that mid-week morning. She looked happily across at Roger, appreciating his forbearance, and as they dropped steeply down to the brook she told him the whole tale.

He heard her attentively, and when she had come to an end she watched him nervously, eager for his comments and yet apprehensive lest he think her an idle babbler.

His comment, when it came, had his usual terseness.

'As to young Miles,' he said, 'Anthony's right. The lad's of good heart but in some fear of his mother. As to Anne Nutter, she died in bed and of I know not what. In which ignorance I stand alone, the rest of Pendle being very sure.'

His sombre tone gave the clue to that, but she had to ask it.

'Saying what?' she asked, already knowing the answer.

'You've already guessed it. That she died by craft of witches.'

'Oh!' Her mind saw Anthony Nutter's sad and kindly smile, and she thought this Pendle gossip hideous. Then another question reared before her.

'The Demdikes?' she asked.

'A few say it. But the most say Chattox, mother of that Redfern of the other day.'

She pondered that as they crossed the brook. Then she came to her other problem.

'And what of Master Baldwin?' she asked. 'Something had vexed him. But what?'

'That's less sure. One thing could be that he guessed you'd been at Anthony's. It was the most likely house for Miles to have come from on that road.'

'But what of that? It's no improper house to visit, surely?'

'Baldwin might say differently. He's mighty hot against all papists.'

'Papists?' Margery had raised her voice in surprise.

'Aye—all but.'

'But surely the Nutters—Miles himself, and his parents . . .'

'Aye, aye—of the puritan sort. At least Dick is, and Alice says she is. But that's nothing to it. In this county there's many a family that's so split, the half being puritan and the rest being papists. And so it is with the Nutters. We've had two of that name taken as Massing Priests, and duly hanged and gutted. So it's no matter for surprise that Tony and his sister are Church-papists.'

'Church-papists? Meaning what?'

'Is it new to you? A Church-papist is a papist in all things but one—which is that he saves the recusancy fines by some church attendance, rare and grudging. Thus do Anthony and his Margaret, and because of that our Baldwin loves them not. Nor will he smile on their guests. Are you answered?'

'In some sort.' Margery patted her horse's neck thoughtfully. 'How long might it take to gain understanding of this life in Pendle?'

He laughed.

'That I know not. My stay here's been too short.'

'I believe you, sir.'

Margery answered him feelingly, and she said no more till they had climbed at last to the Newchurch. These Pendle undercurrents were bewildering. She had thought herself well established with Richard Baldwin as an earnest puritan, and now it seemed that that was in jeopardy. And what was she to do? She had no wish to avoid Anthony Nutter to please Richard Baldwin. She liked Anthony, and she wanted to know more of him. Yet she had a liking for stout old Richard too. And Miles? Did his puritan mother object to his visiting his papist uncle? Was that the cause of his awkwardness? And what of Anne Nutter, and this foul tale of witchcraft and the Chattox woman? What lay behind all that? Above all, how was she, Margery, to steer her way through these whirling muddy currents?

The horse-minders hurried to them as they dismounted, and one glance into the Newchurch told Margery that here she was far from Whalley. Here were none of the dignities of a wealthy parish church. Here were no stained glasses and family pews, no memorials and coats-of-arms. Of pews there were only two in this grey little chapel on the hill; there was a simple one near the Altar, free to any of the better sort who might attend; and there was a low box-pew by the West door, where the four churchwardens might sit in watchful dignity. There were benches against the walls for the sick and aged; and that was all. The rest might stand, for there was no ease for the many in this Chapel-of-Ease.

Richard Baldwin, gowned and dignified, and with his black Staff-of-Office in his hand, met them at the door and greeted them as if he were truly pleased that they were there. He led them to the pew by the Altar, and Margery, smiling thanks at him, got a response that came as near to a smile as could be expected of a puritan in church. Evidently she was forgiven.

'I'll need to leave you,' he said. 'With a warden short, there's a deal to watch.'

He marched off, his feet swishing in the rushes, and at once disappointment came. Dick Nutter arrived, smiling shyly, and sat himself next to Roger. But where was Miles? For Dick Nutter had come alone.

Apparently Roger noted this, for without ado he asked the question.

'Miles?' was the answer. 'He's ridden to Whalley this day with his mother. I know not why.'

This was irritating; and the more Margery considered it, the worse it got. For if Miles had deliberately gone to the unusual church to make a meeting, he would be only too likely to suppose that Margery had done the same. Which was maddening. Not to see him, yet to have him suppose that she had tried to see him, made vexation enough to heighten her colour and set her foot tapping angrily in the rushes.

Then uproar broke out to disturb her thoughts, and she turned sharply; but it was only the Beadle whipping the dogs out of church to let Service begin. Then the Wardens took their seats, watchful by the door lest any should try to leave, and a moment later Master Town, black-gowned and of puritan demeanour, was reading the Sentences; the Service had begun its familiar course. Margery took it easily until Master Town came to his tiny pulpit and gave as his text the ninth verse of the sixth chapter of Galatians. Then she was alert at once. For this verse is an exhortation to good works, as indeed the whole chapter is, and Margery knew well enough that it was from the third chapter, which exalts the power of Faith, that the puritan preachers were wont to draw their texts. It was an odd choice, and she wondered what Richard Baldwin would think of it. She leaned back and prepared to listen with attention.

That she had cause for attention was soon plain. Master Town was no Calvinist. He began conventionally enough, with an onslaught on the corruptions of the Flesh and the pretensions of the Bishop of Rome. This was quite safe; all the Elect could nod approvingly. But before long Master Town was exhorting his flock to be zealous in good works and never weary in well-doing. He grew eloquent on this, and soon he was not only commending the doing of good works, but was plainly hinting that here was a road to Grace, even for the graceless. Margery sat bright-eyed and intent, missing nothing of its significance. For this was no Calvinism; it was rank Arminianism, belittling the power of Faith and offering to the many a hope of escape from their predestined doom. It was enough to rouse high anger in any Calvinist, and again Margery wondered how Richard was taking it. She was sorry that he was out of her sight; one glance at his face might have told her what manner of puritan he was.

Roger seemed in no hurry to get away when the Service was done, and Richard Baldwin certainly treated them handsomely. He escorted them out into the churchyard, and he sent a fellow to fetch their horses; then he apologised for leaving them as he went to see the lesser folk out of the church. Roger fell into talk with Dick Nutter, and Margery stood aside, warming in the sunlight and watching the people stream out. Wilsey, the tall, untidy Constable, gave her a wide grin, and then her eyes fastened on a group who were just emerging. Unmistakably, it was old Demdike, of the Malkin Tower, who made the centre of the group, her deep little eyes blinking as they met the light. To her left, supporting her as she walked, was the sullen Alizon; to her right, Squinting Lizzie rolled her unpleasant eyes; the half-witted Jemmy lurched and slobbered behind. A pace after him came Anne Redfern of the fair hair and the blue eyes, but still with the vicious set to her shapely face. Margery looked them over with distaste, sure that they were at the church only from fear of the law and Roger Nowell. Then her interest re-kindled at the sight of a bent and aged woman at Anne Redfern's side, a woman who went sturdily for her age, peering left and right, and muttering to herself in an unceasing flow of sound. This, surely, must be the Chattox, Anne Redfern's mother.

Richard Baldwin came out again and threaded through the press to Margery's side. He eyed her steadily.

'And what,' he asked grimly, 'did Mistress Whitaker think of *that*?'

She knew that he meant the sermon, and she had her answer ready. But before she could voice it there was noisy interruption. There was a stir and bustle in the crowd, and a yell of fury came from Alizon Device as Anne Redfern's hand slapped viciously across her cheek.

'You goddam bitch!' screamed Alizon, rubbing at her tingling face.

'That's for a whoring drab! Here's another!'

And Anne Redfern's hand slapped as viciously into the girl's other cheek.

Roger Nowell, standing cloaked and hatted by the gate as he waited for his horse, moved swiftly. Three quick strides down the path took him within striking distance. His long muscular arm swung back, shaking out his whip. Then the thong whistled across the Redfern's shoulders, exploding there like a thunderclap. The woman screamed like an injured horse and leapt madly away. Alizon, stunned with surprise, wasted a precious second gaping, and when she turned to run she was too late. Roger timed it perfectly, and the lash caught her thighs as she turned; her shrill scream testified to the sting of it.

Margery turned to Richard Baldwin and saw him grimly pleased. Then inspiration came to her.

'There's a verse in the seventy-eighth Psalm, is there not?' she said. 'Nearing the end of the Psalm, I think . . .'

He stood rigid, clearly searching his memory. Then a slow smile spread over his face as he gave her the quotation:

'He smote his enemies in the hinder parts and put them to a perpetual shame.' Something like a chuckle came from Richard Baldwin. 'Well said, mistress, and well remembered too.'

They walked together up towards the gate, and his face sobered as he spoke again.

'But I was asking you,' he said, 'what you thought of the sermon?'

Margery was prompt with her calculated answer.

'Fervid, sir. And eloquent. Yet I thought it smacked somewhat of the Arminian Sectaries.'

She spoke slowly, as though she were thinking it out, and she knew from his face that she had judged well.

Those who came up the sloping path a moment later saw what set them blinking. On the road by the gate above, a smiling girl, gay in orange-tawny and a laced and feathered hat, was mounting a fine grey mare. And at her side, his brown face beaming with goodwill, one hand at her horse's head and the other holding her stirrup, was that stout old puritan, Richard Baldwin of the mill.

12

The Mill at Wheathead

Miles Nutter appeared again the next morning.

He appeared, but he could not be spoken to. For this was Monday, and Roger, supported by Nick Banister, was dispensing justice according to custom; and he had clearly taken it for granted that Margery would again be his Clerk. It thus came about that when she looked up after recording a fine of five shillings imposed on John Bulcock, who had been drunk enough to swear at the Constable, she saw through the window the trim and elegant figure of Master Nutter as he rode up to the house. Which was most provoking. For the Justices' Clerk was busy, and had to set down the complicated story of Elizabeth Carr who maintained that the fourpence a week allowed to her by the Overseers was insufficient; and while Margery was recording the Justices' decision that Elizabeth Carr should in future have sixpence, she heard again the clop of hooves on the gravel, and, again, through the window, she had a glimpse of Master Nutter's back as he rode away.

She inquired into that as soon as the session was ended. Young Master Nutter, she was told, had indeed sought speech with her, but when he had learned that she was occupied he had at once called for his horse, declaring that he would not wait that day; and with some vague talk of the morrow he had at once departed.

Margery listened without comment, and went away thoughtful. Young Master Nutter, it seemed, had still something to learn. She thought he had a great deal to learn if he supposed she was to be dealt with so. And if it should suit his convenience to wait upon her the next morning, he should have disappointment for his pains; she would ride to Wheathead and make her promised visit to Richard Baldwin.

She was away early the next morning, and she got off the Forest road as soon as she could—lest she meet Master Nutter riding to Read. She went down to the Sabden brook, as though she were bound for Goldshaw; if she continued on this road she would come to the Newchurch, and Tom Peyton had explained to her that beyond the Newchurch this road would lead her to Barley and thus to Wheathead. This morning she rode in homespuns in place of the orange-tawny. Roger, who seemed to have a trick of remembering things, had been as good as his word, and the clothes he had promised her had been laid out for her inspection the night before. There was a cloak of russet serge, of the quality called puke—which meant that it was of a fine weave and dyed in the wool. There was a riding-skirt of the same, simpler and less pleated than the orange-tawny safeguard. There was a sleeved jerkin of soft brown leather, and boots and gloves to match it. And as a final proof that Roger remembered, there was a pair of breeches in the russet serge. She had fingered them dubiously, asking herself if she dare be seen in them. She had seen their advantages, but she had left them at home this morning; safe and practical though they were, they were not her choice for a first visit to Richard Baldwin.

She rode easily and without haste, for her mind was pleasantly occupied with another problem of clothes. Roger's generosity had gone farther than the homespuns. From some old family chest he had suddenly produced a full ten yards of flame-tint satin, sleek, soft and shining, and had flung it to Margery with the jest that if it was too gay for a puritan she had his leave to turn papist; and Margery, who cared nothing at all for his jests if only she might have the satin, had coo'd with delight and made away with it on the instant. She was now considering what to do with it. She was well enough versed in the fashions to know exactly what she wanted. She was a competent needlewoman when she chose to be, and Anne Sowerbutts was at least useful. The making of a kirtle was therefore possible. But she would need buttons and thread, laces and silken points, all of a fit quality; and she could not plan the kirtle in detail until she knew just what was to be had. That, she thought, was the immediate problem. How and from whom did one buy such things in Pendle? This she must now discover, and it was no use asking a man.

She came to the Sabden brook and began the steep climb to the Newchurch. Tom Peyton had given her clear directions. She must go past the church and down a steep and curving hill which would bring her to the Pendle Water, flowing down a great rent in the hillside. Once past this rent, which Tom had called a clough, she must cross the Water, and at once she would be in Barley; and in the street of Barley she would find a lesser stream flowing to the Pendle Water. This lesser stream, if she rode up it, would lead her to the mill at Wheathead.

Her thoughts reverted to the kirtle and its trimmings. She was wondering if she could properly ask Mistress Baldwin, if she should chance to meet her, about the laces and the buttons. Perhaps not about laces, she thought, remembering her puritan status. But surely she could ask about buttons? The strictest puritan could scarcely condemn a girl for wanting buttons.

Round a bend of the stony track a horseman came, riding swiftly towards her. Abruptly, Margery stopped thinking about buttons. Something in his slim build and graceful carriage was familiar, and in another minute he was close enough for all doubt to be ended. Here was Miles Nutter.

'God's Grace!' said Roger Nowell's cousin, and reined in to await events.

Either he was sunk in thought or he was misled by her homespuns. He gave no sign of knowing her until he had come abreast; he had, indeed, almost passed her when he realised who it was. He was prompt enough then. He wheeled skilfully, and came up to her, his horse pawing and his hat a-flourish.

'What fortune's this?' he said. 'I'm enchanted, madam! But may I know your purpose this day?'

It was civilly spoken. Margery gave him credit for that—and for good looks too, as he waited in front of her, dapper and smiling, his beaver in his hand and his black curls a-flutter in the wind. Her answer was more encouraging than she had intended it to be.

'I ride out, sir. I take the air and I view these moorlands.'

No need to mention Wheathead until he had declared himself further. He did so very promptly.

'May I have the honour, madam? I was on my way to Read to learn if I could be more fortunate than yesterday. May I view the moorlands at your side?'

Again it was civilly spoken. It did not, indeed, explain his blunders of yesterday, nor what he was doing on this unlikely track; but it was not an answer that could well be resented. Margery accepted it gracefully.

'I shall be happy of your escort, sir.'

He was at her side at once, and together they began the climb to the Newchurch. But somehow speech seemed to have failed Master Nutter, and they rode in a silence which each seemed to expect the other to break. It lengthened and became acute, and Margery found herself forced to speak first.

'I saw you yesterday,' she told him as they passed the little church. 'But I saw you only through glass. I had no chance to speak with you.'

He evidently saw the implied question, for his embarrassment was plain. 'It was my regret,' he said at length. 'I was so pressed for time. I had indeed scarcely a minute.'

'Then I wonder, sir, that you thought fit to appear at all. That must have cost you many minutes.'

Miles Nutter positively reddened. He had clearly no answer, and his distress was so apparent that Margery began to feel sorry for him. For all his odd behaviour, there was something likeable in him and she decided to draw it out.

'I think we'd best forget it,' she said. 'This is another day, and a better one. We view the moorland. Let that be all.'

His relief was palpable. He roused himself at once and began to talk amiably, pointing out the clough and the stream that sparkled in it. Margery said little, thinking that it would be better to let him talk than to make him listen, and she confined herself to a few prompting questions.

But when they came to the Pendle Water he turned sharply from the road, making along the stream towards the clough. Then he halted, seeing that Margery did not follow.

'We may climb a part of this clough,' he explained, 'and if we then bear to the left we may come down into Goldshaw. It's a most pleasant ride.'

'No doubt, sir. But I've ridden through Goldshaw already. Is not Barley yonder across the water? I planned to ride that way.'

'There's naught of interest in Barley. Believe me, madam, I do know this ground. The clough's our proper way.'

Margery began to be irritated again. He had freely offered to escort her, and she had supposed that to mean that he would escort her where she chose to go. Apparently he took a higher view of the privilege of an escort. But she kept her temper and spoke him fairly.

'Since I'm new to Pendle, sir, may I not be humoured? I've a mind to ride to Barley and thence to Wheathead. Will you not suffer me, sir?'

'Wheathead! Madam, I do assure you there's nothing at Wheathead, nor yet at Barley. Believe me, if you please, we'd waste our time.'

He seemed heated about it, and Margery began to lose patience.

'By your leave, sir, there's at Wheathead a mill where I'm invited to visit. That's my purpose, sir, and surely a very proper one?'

'Proper enough.' He spoke without conviction. 'Yet I'll be most grateful, madam, if you'd ride this way with me. It would . . . it would give me much pleasure.'

He ended lamely, and still his earnestness seemed out of proportion. Certainly, she thought, he was none too obliging. It seemed that she was to fit his whims in all matters; and that, indeed, had been his attitude yesterday. She was not disposed to comply.

'I ride to Wheathead,' she answered firmly. 'Do I have the honour of your escort, sir?'

To a gentleman of manners there was only one answer to make, and she could see in his face that he knew it. But he did not make it.

'Madam, I do beg you . . .' Every line of his body showed his unhappiness, but he clung to what he had determined. 'I'm not for such a ride this day. It grows late, and . . . and I'd best be returning.'

And without another word he turned his horse, splashed through the stream, and went cantering off down its farther bank. His hat waved in farewell, but he did not turn his head.

Margery sat her horse in silence, her cheeks red and her eyes glittering. This was rudeness almost to the point of insult, and inexplicable rudeness at that. She was still flushed and angry as she found the lesser stream and followed it through the village of Barley and out to the moorland beyond. The fellow, she thought, was clearly impossible. He ended every meeting with a display of contempt for her, and she must see to it that he had no further opportunity. And again a hot anger went sweeping through her as she thought of it.

Above her a curlew called, and at that she looked up into a clear blue sky, richer from the white of the billowing clouds. She looked down at the clear stream, splashing and gurgling at her feet. She saw the mossy stones and the tufted grass that swayed and shivered in the moorland wind. She felt the wind in her hair. And the curlew called again.

Margery felt better. She began to think more clearly, and soon she was asking herself what lay between Miles Nutter and Richard Baldwin. For Miles Nutter had left her abruptly this day when a visit to Richard Baldwin was proposed. Surely there was something here? Margery frowned with perplexity. These Pendle undercurrents ran deeper than she liked, and the mud in them was thick.

She had not much further to go. In another mile she found that the stream had cut itself a channel and was running between banks. She rounded a bend and came suddenly upon a rippling pool, deepened by a low stone dam, grey and mossy; and beside the dam was a sturdy grey mill, its timbered wheel churning steadily in the seething torrent from the sluice. Fifty yards back, on the rising ground above, was a low stone house, squat and sturdy as the mill, and flanked by granary and stables. A horsed wagon stood on a road beyond the granary, and men were loading sacks into it under the watchful eye of Richard Baldwin, who stood by the open door with a tally-stick in his hand.

He turned as he heard the oncoming horse, and it was evident that he had quickly recognised the rider. He lifted his tally-stick in friendly greeting, and as he came to meet her he laid it on the low stone wall that ran beside the pool.

'You're well come,' he told her. 'I'm glad indeed to see you here.'

And Margery believed him. He stood by her stirrup, his

face aglow in the sun as he looked up at her, and there was no mistaking the sincerity of the man. The strong brown face, the firm mouth, the steady deep-set eyes, gave proof enough of that. His eyes, too, were without the hardness that could so quickly cloud them; nothing shone from them now but pleasure.

He held her stirrup as she slipped from her horse, and then he stood in silence, looking down at her from his greater height and nodding approval of her russet homespuns. She stood his scrutiny without apprehensions, knowing that he must approve. Her clothes fairly matched his own, she thought, as she noted his russet breeches and leather jerkin, and the tucked-up sleeves of his white shirt. He was open-necked, bare-headed and dusty, as befitted one of his creed. Margery gave them credit for that. These puritans were not idlers, and master though this man was in the mill, his own hands would take their share of the burden.

He called a lad to take her horse, and then he led her past the mill and up the bank of the pool to the house beyond. The heavy oak door, set under a low stone lintel, was ajar, and gave passage to a clatter of voices from within; and as he led her to it, the door swung fully open and a girl appeared, standing quietly under the stone.

Richard Baldwin was smiling affectionately as he spoke.

'Here's Mistress Whitaker, Grace. Come from Read as she promised.' He turned to Margery. 'I grow proud of my daughter these days,' he added.

Grace Baldwin smiled prettily, and her father stepped back, his gaze moving from the one girl to the other as she and Margery eyed each other.

He had some reason to be proud of his daughter, as Margery quickly perceived. She judged Grace Baldwin to be almost of her own age and of much the same height and figure. Her steady eyes and chestnut hair were plainly from her father, but her brown face had a pleasing softness that was certainly not his. Yet there was no undue weakness here, for her mouth was moulded after her father's fashion, and there was staunchness to be read in the firm little chin below her white teeth. She held herself well, and stood trim and self-possessed in a brown kirtle of twilled woollen saye, with laced collar and a white cambric cap.

She addressed herself directly to Margery.

'From what I've heard, mistress, he's proud of his guest too. But come within, and I'll help you from your cloak.'

Margery found herself smiling; something in this fresh and friendly voice attracted her and made her wish to be friendly in return.

'You're kind,' she said. 'And I'll be glad to be rid of it.'

She followed the girl through the open door into a big low stone-flagged kitchen. The open door and the windows to left and right of it let the light flood over the scrubbed top of the great table that filled the centre and bore an array of plates, spoons and knives, all set ready for impending dinner. Beyond the table, facing the door and taking the eye at once, was a huge fireplace—a round stone arch, full fifteen feet across, and having deep within it the stone hearth and the low benches that ran on either side of it. Over the red and powdery heart of the fire was a great iron pot, three chains running from its rings to a blackened hook in the arch above; and from the pot, clear through its heavy lid, came the sharp crackle of boiling fat. Lesser pots hung from lesser hooks, and sent wisps of cheerful steam to join the blue smoke that curled from the outer logs.

A great oak dresser took one whole side of the room, and by it, slicing cubes from a great loaf of the barley bread, was a woman whom Margery knew at once to be Grace's mother; here was the same pleasant face and the same friendly air, and here also was the plumpness that might come to Grace in later years. Without any fuss she made Margery welcome, and clearly took it for granted that she would dine with them. Nor did Margery need persuading to that; for one thing she liked these Baldwins and wanted to know more of them, particularly of Grace; and for another thing she was hungry, and the scent from that crackling pot was a temptation in itself.

Grace carried her off to her own neat bedchamber to dispose of cloak and hat, and she stayed to chat while it was done. Again Margery needed no persuading; apart from the liking she already felt for Grace, she was attracted by the plain friendliness of these Lancashire folk, and after the restrictions that had hedged her at home she was feeling appreciative of the freedom their easy customs gave. To be free to roam at large without an escort, to find a yeoman's home that gave this easy hospitality to the kin of an Esquire, to be given this frank welcome by a yeoman's daughter; all this appealed to Margery and made it imperative that she should conduct herself as their ways required.

'I've been hearing of you from my father,' said Grace pleasantly. 'A tale of virtues that might surprise you.'

'It would. A tale of faults is what I'm more used to.'

'From whom?'

'My brothers, mostly.'

Grace laughed. 'That's the way of brothers. Take no heed of them. I don't.'

'Nor I, I fear. But you give me news.'

'Of what?'

'Of having brothers. I had not heard of them.'

'No? But that's my father's way. Trust him to say less than he might. But I've two brothers. Richard's in the Low Countries, learning of their ways of milling, and there's John who studies in Geneva. Are you ready?'

'Almost. That's the way, as I've noted.'

'How?'

'Brothers go forth to learn and do. Sisters stay at home.'

'And work. You say it truly. Yet is it so with you, mistress?'

Margery grimaced at that, and felt a little ashamed of her present ease.

'Just now I'm visiting,' she explained. 'But it's so with me at home. And enough to do, I assure you.'

'You need not assure me. I've noticed there's enough to do, and especially since I've been alone to do it.'

'I think I'm ready now. Does that mean a sister married?'

With her hand already on the door, Grace stopped short.

'No,' she said, and looked steadily at Margery. 'Has my father not said it? Margaret's dead this twelvemonth and more. It—it was talk of Pendle.'

Margery stared, and a thought that chilled came creeping through her. The sunlit room struck cold and menacing.

'What—what did she die of?'

Grace Baldwin looked away uneasily.

'That's in darkness. Who's to tell?'

'Please?'

'You've guessed already. She died of witches' harm. On her twelfth birthday.'

13

The Miller's Daughter

'O Lord Who hast made all things that are put to our use, we do humbly move Thee for Grace that we may see Thy bounty in that which is set before us now, and that we may eat thereof in thankful heart and lowly mind. Amen.'

Richard Baldwin, his brown face gleaming in the flood of sunlight, spoke his prayer in a high, clear voice. Then he glanced the length of his table and nodded; and with scrape of feet and creak of chairs, his company seated themselves. He sat himself at the head of his table, his wife to his right and Margery to his left. Grace was next to Margery, and beyond her was the pewter salt-bowl. Below that were the three journeymen, the two apprentices and the two serving-maids; for Richard Baldwin saw himself accountable to God for the well-being of all whom God had committed to his charge and authority. He would exert the authority as became a Master Miller; but he would also see to his charge as became a man with the Spirit in him. His wife and children were his family in the eyes of men, but all who worked with him were his family in the eyes of God. He saw it so, and he performed it so.

Now, while the others sat, he stood to carve for his family; and while his wife politely regretted that it was but a poor meal to set before a guest, he grew busy with the four legs of a sheep that lay hot and smoking on the huge pewter dish before him. One of the wenches pattered to his side to spoon out the boiled carrots, while the other came to carry the plates; the apprentices poured and carried ale, and soon the whole sharp-set company had their faces down, with knives and bread-cubes plying busily.

Mistress Baldwin made small-talk, and for once Margery was glad of it. It helped her to keep her mind from the ugly questions that were seething in it. She forced herself to leave thoughts of the Pendle witches, these dark tales of youthful death, and to give heed only to the sunlit room, the clatter of knives and plates, and the easy talk around her.

'I heard you're of Lambeth, mistress?' her hostess was saying, and suddenly Margery realised that the question was meant for her.

'True,' she answered. 'I was bred there.'

'And you have yourself known the Lord Archbishop? You're to be envied, mistress.'

'I—I was no doubt fortunate.'

'Fortunate indeed. And the Dean? I mean your venerable cousin—is it cousin?'

'Great-uncle, I think. I fear I was too young to hear him.'

'That's a pity. Truly venerable, as I've heard.' Mistress Baldwin nodded sagely.

Her husband approved of that.

'Much to be respected,' he said. 'And of sound doctrine, from what I'm told.'

A quick thought came to Margery.

'Have you read any of his works, Master Baldwin?'

'Alas, no! Such books are rare to come by in Pendle, where there's none visits but a petty-chapman.'

'That's hard indeed.' Margery's voice was grave. 'But touching my great-uncle's works, I have by me his *Homily On The Justice Of God*. I had it for reading on my journey here, and it's most freely at your service if you'd wish to use it.'

'I'd wish indeed!' There was eagerness in his voice. 'That's if it's not depriving you . . .'

'By no means, and I'll see you have it. Oh!'

'But what, mistress?'

'I—I'd forgot. There are some few pages spoiled. I—I had to take them out. But . . .'

'No matter, if there be more that remain. I'll be right glad of it. But . . .' He cocked an ear to the door. 'What's that? Grace, do you hear aught?'

He struck his knife sharply on the table and the chatter died away. In the silence, a man's voice came through the half-closed door, a rich and jovial voice that sang lustily.

'The sailor led the serving-maid
Right lovingly by hand-oh!
And she as daintily arrayed
As any in the land-oh!'

'It's Fat Jack!' Mistress Baldwin spoke excitedly.

'Aye, the bawling rogue!' said her husband, and in spite of his words his tone held pleasure rather than censure.

The song went on, swelling nearer and louder,

'Her kirtle was of damask rare,
Her gown of satin fine-oh!
The ribbons in her golden hair
With tinsel were ashine-oh!'

There was a tramp of sturdy feet now, to hammer the rhythm of it. One of the apprentices got a sign from his master's eye, and moved to the door as the song continued.

'The sailor's eye did drop a wink,
And thereat she did flush-oh!
Which turned her cheek to softest pink,
The pink of Maiden's Blush-oh!'

The apprentice swung the door fully open and disclosed the singer, poised to knock with a staff of well-worn ash. He sloped it down instead, and stood peering into the room.

'Good day to ye, master! Good day to ye all!' His rich voice came booming under the rafters. 'Who wants pins today?'

He was a huge man. With his broad shoulders and six feet of height, he must always have been big, but now he was huge. He had bulging arms and legs, a great corpulent middle, and a plump and shining face as round and red as the rising moon. It looked oddly like the moon, thought Margery as she saw the great grin that slashed across it, and the eyes that twinkled so merrily in it.

'Come you in, Jack. Come you in, and be rid of that pack. You'll be easier so.'

Richard Baldwin spoke cheerfully and with welcome in

his voice. 'Fill a mug for Jack, one of you,' he added, and an apprentice bustled to it.

The stranger wanted no more invitation. He stepped inside, and his shoulders went through the curious wriggle that rids a man of his pack—a heavy pack, this, and of value, if the care that he gave it was not misplaced.

Margery turned to Grace at her side and raised an eyebrow in question. Grace answered easily enough under cover of the chatter that had sprung up again.

'It's Jack Law,' she explained. 'He's the chapman. He comes every quarter. He's pins and laces and thread, and little books, and broadsheets, and I know not what besides.'

Margery nodded.

'Fat Jack?' she asked.

'What else? Look at him. Though my father won't call him that. He says it mocks infirmity. But everyone else does, even my mother.'

'And you?'

'And I. You heard his song?'

'Having ears, I did.'

Grace laughed softly.

'He always sings that. It announces his coming. It has some scores of verses, and I don't think my father approves of it at all. He says it's light and lewd, bless him!'

'I know. But tell me . . .'

Margery looked round warily and was reassured. The chapman had his shining face uplifted beneath a quart pot. Richard Baldwin was carving meat for him. The serving girls were seeing to his other needs, and Mistress Baldwin was overseeing that. None was attending to her and Grace.

'Tell me,' she said. 'What kind of laces does he carry?'

Grace laughed understandingly and went into details. Fat Jack, she explained, would have in his pack only the simple, and the cheap and gaudy, but he would soon procure better for those who wanted it. Margery nodded dubiously. She had no objection to telling the chapman what she wanted, but hardly in the hearing of the Baldwins. Then she caught Grace's eye and saw that the girl had guessed.

'They'll be about him like swarming bees,' said Grace, 'as soon as he opens his pack, and he'll be here the afternoon. It's a great day for us when the chapman comes. So if you've need of more than pins, you'd best have him visit you at Read.'

'And will he?'

'I'll warrant he will. Leave it to me, mistress. Give me a hint of your needs, and I'll drop a word in his ear before he goes.'

'I'll be grateful to you.'

Margery began to talk about the kirtle, about what she planned and what she would need. She kept it up till Richard's knife hit the table again to bring them to their feet while he gave thanks to God for their meal. Then the chapman's pack was opened and Grace's prophecy was fulfilled. Swarming bees was an apt simile.

'I'll have to leave you,' said Margery. 'I'm over-spending my time.'

It was not precisely true, but it would serve. Her welcome had been of the kindest and she would not outstay it. Better to free them now to dote on the chapman's pack; especially Grace, for it would be Grace who would stand aside from the tempting pack to talk with her. Margery's liking for Grace was rapidly growing.

'I'll get my cloak and then take leave,' she said.

Grace made no attempt to dissuade her. Perhaps she was too honest for such insincerities. She led back to her bedchamber and helped Margery into her cloak.

'You've been something more than kind,' said Margery, peering at herself in the little steel mirror. 'May I come again?'

'Of course. I was hoping you would.'

'Truly?'

'Truly indeed, mistress.' Grace paused and then explained herself more fully. 'It's lonely here at Wheathead, where we've few visitors, and one who's welcome is the more welcome for that. Come again when you can, mistress, and whenever you can.'

Margery spun on her heel to face her.

'I'll come,' she said. 'Have no doubt of that. But there's one thing. Be pleased to stop calling me mistress. It's formal and it's cold, and there's not the need for it. My name's Margery, and I'd have no other. Is that clear?'

Grace coloured a little.

'Clear enough, if you wish it so. I'd no wish to be cold,

believe me. But I've some schooling in manners, and my father's not an Esquire.'

'Nor mine. Did you think it?'

'At least you're Master Nowell's kin.'

'Distant kin, and poor at that. My father was a divine, and as lean as a pulpit mouse. So let's have an end to forms. Is it clear now—Grace?'

Grace looked at her steadily and nodded.

'Aye, quite clear. And sweetly said. But I see you're ready. Come to my father.'

They went through together, and Mistress Baldwin disentangled herself from the press to make a friendly farewell. Her husband sent an apprentice to get Margery's horse, and then himself walked slowly out into the sunlight with the two girls.

'Hark to them!' he said smilingly. 'Chattering like sparrows, and all for such fripperies! They'd have the afternoon to it if they had their way.' He was almost benign about it. 'They shall have their hour, and then there's work to do. And for you within doors, Grace, as well as for us without.'

'I know it, Father. Yet have charity. He comes but seldom.'

'It's perhaps enough. All being said, his wares are vanities.'

'True, sir.' This was Margery, coming to Grace's help. 'Yet not vanities of vanities, surely?'

'Well said! They're harmless as such things go. And I've a liking for Jack Law.'

'That's common, it seems. He must be of stout heart. His pack's not light.'

'Nor is he. But you say it well. His heart's of the stoutest, and it carries him many a mile.'

The horse was being led up, and they stopped by the millhouse to wait for it.

'He's from Colne, across the river yonder,' Richard explained. 'He left there yesterday, and he was at the Rough Lee last night, where he stayed till morning.'

'The Rough Lee?' Grace's voice was suddenly sharp.

'So he's just said. Why should he not?'

'There's no reason. But I wonder that Miles did not speak of him this morning.'

Margery caught her breath sharply. Miles of the Rough Lee could only be Miles Nutter. Which meant . . .

'No doubt he thought nothing of it.' Richard's answer broke into her thought, and she made herself pay heed to him.

'You'll remember the book you spoke of?' he reminded her.

'Surely I will.'

He helped her to mount.

'Good day to you, mistress. We've been glad of your visit. Let it not be your last!'

'It shall not. I promise that. Good day, and my thanks! You'll give my message to the chapman, Grace?'

'I will. And you'll come soon, Margery?'

'I will indeed.'

She trotted off down the bank of the stream, leaving Richard Baldwin to stare in surprise at his daughter's sudden familiarity. But of this, Margery saw nothing. She was too deeply sunk in thought. She knew now why Miles Nutter had been on that unlikely road. He had been visiting the mill, and Margery could think of no reason why he should not. But why in the world could he not have said so?

She passed through Barley, found the Pendle Water, and decided to follow it down. She knew she could get home that way, and this grassy track was set about with arching trees whose cool shade looked attractive. Margery wanted to think.

There could be no doubt that Miles Nutter had been at the mill. Grace had distinctly said that Miles had not spoken of the chapman . . .

Margery whistled softly and called herself a fool. It was suddenly so obvious. For Grace had not spoken of Master Nutter, nor even of Miles Nutter. She had simply spoken of Miles. And Grace, as Margery had just learned, was not one to use a plain Christian name without some encouragement.

Margery dismounted and sat herself on the grassy bank. She wanted to think this out, and she was asking herself where her wits had been this day. If she supposed that something existed between Miles and Grace, that could certainly account for his being unwilling to ride to the mill at Margery's side. It might account, too, for old Richard's seeming displeasure when he had met Miles escorting Margery from Goldshaw the other day.

The shade was cool, for the bank was thick with pine and larch and rowan. Margery stretched herself comfortably as she considered this. It was easy enough to suppose that Miles Nutter had two faces, that he was paying court to her and Grace at the same time; there need be nothing unbelievable in that. But could she think that Miles was paying court to her? Certainly he was showing very little ardour. And if he had little ardour, why should he wantonly lay up trouble for himself?

Margery sighed with perplexity, and her thoughts turned to that chilling tale of Margaret Baldwin. If this girl had been at all like the cool and friendly Grace, it was no matter for wonder that Richard Baldwin was savage against the witches. He was not a man to doubt a witch's power to give effect to her malice. Again Margery sighed. She had not this easy certainty. After what she had seen at the Malkin Tower the other day, she did not doubt the malice; but she did doubt the power.

There was a sudden rustle in the sloping bank above. Leaves swayed and parted, and Jennet Device came slithering down the steep grass, ending on her back at Margery's feet.

' 'Lo!' said Jennet cheerfully. 'I've been looking.'

'Looking at what, Jennet?' Margery was smiling at the child, almost thankful for her interruption.

'You.' Jennet's answer was characteristically blunt. 'You—sitting like that.'

Her eyes strayed to the grazing horse, and it suddenly dawned on Margery that the saddle-bags were the point of interest. She laughed.

'I'm sorry, Jennet. I don't think there's any cheese today. Let's look, shall we?'

They explored the bags together and found a pair of apples, which Jennet seemed to think an acceptable substitute. She sank her white teeth into one without delay, while Margery stretched on the grass again.

'I saw you Sunday,' said Jennet suddenly.

'Did you? Where?'

'Church.'

The scene in the churchyard came suddenly to life in

Margery's mind, and she had a quick vision of Alizon Device and Anne Redfern, and of Roger's drastic quelling of their quarrel.

'Where were you, Jennet?' she asked.

'Hid,' said Jennet briefly.

'Why?'

'Chattox and that Anne.'

'Oh, I see.' Margery stopped to consider this queer self-possessed child. Had she cause to fear Anne Redfern?

Jennet gurgled suddenly, and spat out bits of apple. Margery realised that she was laughing.

'Did you see?' asked Jennet.

'See what?'

'Alizon and that Anne. And Master Nowell. I did laugh!'

'Jennet!'

Margery was a little shocked, but Jennet was laughing merrily.

'Alizon can't sit down,' she gurgled.

'Jennet! You shouldn't laugh at that.'

'Why not?'

This was disconcerting. Margery had no answer ready.

'I hope Anne's sore,' said Jennet brightly.

'Why?'

'She's bad. They're all bad, the Chattox. Even Granny's feared of them. And they broke our fire-house.'

'They what?'

But Jennet was not listening. She was crouching on all fours and giving ear to something else. Then she sank back again as though reassured.

'I thought it was Alizon,' she explained. 'She's with Granny, begging in Barley.'

'You don't seem to like Alizon?'

'She's a bitch. I saw you this morning.'

Margery gasped. She had thought herself quick-witted, but this child's shifts were bewildering.

'Going to Baldwin's,' explained Jennet. 'And *he* doesn't like Alizon.'

'Perhaps he doesn't. But why doesn't he?'

'He chased her. And Granny too. Off his land. Granny said she'd pray for him.'

'She'd what?'

'Pray still and loud, was what she said. She did, too.'

The chill that lurked in Pendle swept over Margery again. She was getting to know it now, and to hate it. What tale was this that the child was telling? Granny must be old Demdike, the woman of the Malkin Tower. Prayer by Demdike? What sort of prayer, and to Whom? And 'still', in Jennet's usage, would mean 'unceasingly'. Margery twitched with discomfort, and Jennet munched steadily at the second apple.

'And what happened?'

Margery spoke at last, and her own voice sounded strange to her.

'A girl died,' said Jennet briefly. 'At Baldwin's.'

She twisted suddenly round, and pushed her fair hair back from her forehead to show a dry white scar.

'Alizon!' she said. 'When she was buried.'

'When who was buried, Jennet?'

'Margaret. Alizon was drunk. She threw a pot at me. That's why . . .'

Jennet stopped abruptly and crouched tensely. Then she was away up the grassy bank, wobbling like an excited rabbit. There was a flutter of leaves, and she was gone.

Margery jumped to her feet. Faintly, up the track, she heard voices, and she knew at once that this must be Demdike and her Alizon. And at that she realised that she, like Jennet, had no wish to be seen by them, by this Alizon who threw pots, and this Demdike who prayed so still and loud. Before they had rounded the bend, Margery was at horse again, riding through the woodland to the road, to home, and sanity.

14

The Fates are Three

With Michaelmas upon them, Roger grew concerned over the matter of a Constable.

Churchwardens and Overseers, he explained, were elected at Easter, but the Constable at Michaelmas. The election lay with the Vestry, and the Vestry, said Roger, were as laggard as so many slugs; for here was Michaelmas upon them, and no man yet named to succeed Jim Wilsey in his distasteful office. Roger grew perturbed. It was not proper, he said, for the Forest hamlets to be without a Constable; and moreover the Quarter Sessions were at hand, and the Bench would have a sharp word to say if they heard of such neglect. As usual, it was Roger who had to see to it, and he took such a tone with the Twelve who made the Vestry that they hastily met and as hastily elected one Hargreaves of Goldshaw to be Constable for the forthcoming year. Once the election had been done, the office could not be refused, and the Twelve spared no time on Hargreaves' anguished protests; they went to their homes and left him to it.

Roger was not pleased. The Twelve, he said, had not between them wit enough to furnish out a maggot. Did not all men know that this Hargreaves was a rank papist, only just this side recusancy? And was that a judicious choice? But there was nothing to be done now that the election had been lawfully made. Roger had to accept it, and Margery attended him as Clerk when Henry Hargreaves, Yeoman, of Goldshaw Booth, was sworn before the Justice in the ancient forms.

She eyed this Hargreaves with interest as he took the oath.

He was all brown. He had jerkin and breeches of brown. He had a brown and sunburned face, big and smiling. He had twinkling brown eyes and a crop of brown hair; a big fellow, plump, well fed, and sure of himself. He had a big jovial voice, and he said cheerily that he knew nothing of Constable's work but would see what he could make of it. He would need, he said, some instruction; and Roger tersely told him that he would get it.

Then Hargreaves turned to Margery and told her, to her surprise, that he had a message for her.

'It's from Tony Nutter,' he explained. 'He and I are neighbours up in Goldshaw, and he'd have you know that you'll be welcome at his house when next you please to ride that way.'

She found that heartening. She was pleased that Tony had remembered her, and she was pleased to have a reason for calling on him again; she wanted to learn more about his daughter who had died, so she thanked this Hargreaves politely, and considered him anew. Apparently he was on good terms with Tony Nutter, and because of that, and because they were both papists, she supposed they might have the same outlook on affairs and people. Margery had not forgotten Tony's warm words about Roger, and if this Hargreaves shared that sentiment he might make a more helpful Constable than Roger seemed disposed to expect.

On that she left him, perceiving that he and Roger had much to discuss. But two days later she acted on the invitation Hargreaves had brought, and she rode unheralded into Goldshaw. Tony Nutter came out himself to help her unhorse, while the old servitor hovered behind him to lead the beast away.

Anthony led her in at once and took her to his sister, who received her smilingly and cut short her polite apologies.

'We're glad to see you,' she said. 'We wished you to come. That's why Tony sent the message.'

She went to see to the cake and ale, leaving Tony to help Margery from her cloak.

'We expected you,' he said. 'Harry brought your answer.'

'Harry?'

'Neighbour Hargreaves, should I say? Our new Constable. And what does Roger Nowell say to that?'

Margery hesitated. It might not be tactful to repeat Roger's comments to a fellow-papist. Fortunately Margaret Crook's return provided a diversion.

'What's this about neighbour Hargreaves?' she asked.

Tony took his ale to the hearth and leaned comfortably against the chimney-shelf.

'I was asking what Roger Nowell thinks of him as Constable,' he replied.

'He should be pleased.' Mistress Crook nodded vigorously. 'Harry's a good fellow, and he's an honest man too, which is more than can be said of some we've had as Constables. He'll be a very proper Constable. Everybody knows that. They wouldn't have made him Constable if they hadn't. This cake's not what it should be, is it? It's sad as Lent. It's those elm logs, Tony. I've told you before, you can't keep a proper heat with elm.'

'Then we'll have more of the ash.' Tony was smiling at his sister's chatter. 'But of Harry as Constable, proper's not the word that all would use.' He looked whimsically at Margery. 'I hear you've been at Wheathead?'

'Why yes. But some days ago.'

She was asking herself how he knew. There was a warning in that, she thought. Everybody seemed to know everything in Pendle, and that might be worth remembering.

'Richard Baldwin might say improper,' he went on quietly. 'A stout heretic, our Richard—which Harry is not. You knew that?'

His question was to Margery, and it embarrassed her. She had no tactful answer ready. Fortunately he did not wait for one.

'Harry Hargreaves holds to the Faith of his fathers,' he went on, looking very straightly at her. 'So does his wife, and so do I, and Margaret here. And that's the core of the matter. He's an odd choice for Constable.'

His sister's chatter filled the silence as he ended.

'I think he'll be a very proper Constable,' she insisted. 'And I'm sure everybody else will think so too, except a few sourfaces.'

'What about our Alice? She's heretic enough, and a sourface too.'

'Oh—Alice?' Mistress Crook seemed disconcerted. 'I'm

sure Alice will give credit where credit's due. Alice speaks fair of everyone.'

'Aye, so she—speaks. And talk of the Devil! Who's this?'

They all looked to the window as a horseman rode up. Margaret Crook came to her feet delightedly.

'It's Miles,' she said. 'I'm so pleased. He could not have come better, bless him!'

She hurried out, and Tony, with an amused glance at Margery, strolled after her. Margery sat stiffly, her lips tight with annoyance. In her opinion, Miles could not have come worse. She had thought herself in a fair way to learning what she wanted to know, and now there would be no more of it. And here, in this house, she could not deal with Miles Nutter as she wished to. She thought his coming most inopportune.

What he thought of it himself, she could not decide. He came in with his aunt, and greeted Margery civilly and without apparent embarrassment. She followed his lead and the proper civilities were exchanged. But thereafter it was Mistress Crook who led the idle talk, and Miles and Margery did no more than follow politely. Tony stayed by the hearth in a silence prolonged enough to set Margery wondering what thoughts were stirring in his shrewd, observant head.

She rose and took her leave as soon as she decently could, and at once Miles was on his feet to do the same. It was plain that he meant to ride with her, and it would look odd if she were to raise objections; so she let him have his way, and they rode off together down the steep track to the Sabden brook.

She put it to his credit that he lost no time then in coming to the point.

'I owe you apology, madam. I'm very conscious of it, and most regretful.'

Margery made no comment, and when he glanced almost appealingly at her he found her wrapped in a frosty dignity that chilled him as much as it surprised him. He did not know that it also surprised Margery, who had not known she had it until she suddenly assumed it. Then she spoke crisply.

'If you had good reason not to ride to Wheathead, sir,

you might have said so with more frankness—and certainly with a deal more courtesy.'

His head reared at that, and she knew it had stung. He had no good answer, but he did his best.

'I certainly erred,' he said. 'The circumstances were very . . .' He stopped, plainly distressed. 'Oh, I'm sorry. I'd no wish to . . .'

He did not finish that, but took to staring at his horse's neck. Margery kept her frosty air, but under it she was feeling warmer towards him. His sudden descent from formal speech to that simplicity had pleased her, and had revived her belief that he had decent notions behind his foolishness. But she would not let him know that yet. A spell of banishment would do him no harm. Besides, Margery was pleased with this new-found dignity; it promised to be useful, and she wanted to practise it. So she drew rein and then faced him squarely when he stopped beside her.

'Master Nutter,' she said. 'It's ill talking when there are resentments to cloud it. And that's our present case, as you well know.' She waved him into silence when he tried to speak. 'The moon was young last night, as I chanced to see. When it's come to full you may seek me again if you're so minded. And by that time I'll no doubt know my answer.'

And before he had found a word she was trotting away in unbroken dignity. That, she thought, had been excellently done. She had shown him as much kindness as he had deserved, and perhaps more; and she had left herself free to decide as she chose. Best of all, she had discovered this new dignity, which she must certainly cherish and preserve against a day of greater need. It was very well.

But she had been so concerned for that dignity that she had ridden from him without any thought of where she was going; and when she came to earth again, and began to give heed to her whereabouts, she discovered to her annoyance that she had been making towards the Rough Lee and was, indeed, close upon it. Certainly that would not do this day, and she made her escape, as she had done before, by turning up the steep lane that led to the wooded ridge. But this time she continued up the lane beyond the ridge, and soon she was on the shoulder of a hill from which, a mile away across the valley, she could see what looked like the Barley road. That tempted her, and she turned from the lane to the grassy slope. But by this time she was feeling more than hungry. She thought of the bread and cheese in her bags, and cast about for a halting place. She had not far to seek. Below her in the valley, not ten minutes' ride away, a coppice of fresh young trees broke the smooth green of the grass and promised a welcome shade. Margery left the track and made directly for the coppice.

She stretched herself lazily on the tufted grass, flinging off her hat to let the wind through her hair. She ate at leisure, lying on her back and watching the white clouds chasing in the blue above. A mood of content was on her, and she was disposed to be grateful to God and Roger Nowell, who had between them given her all this in place of the sweating kitchen in the house at Holborn. She wondered idly what Prudence was doing this day; whatever she was doing, she would not have this sun and wind and grass to grace it. Margery looked round happily to savour them to the full, and her eyes took in the trees behind her. Something struck her as odd and in another moment she was sitting erect and looking keenly.

Unquestionably it was odd. These were the outer trees of the coppice she had seen from the track; all were young and much of a size; but between them, filling the spaces between their trunks, were cut boughs and sprays of brushwood.

Margery considered it thoughtfully, asking herself who had done it and why. Then, with her curiosity rising, she got to her feet and walked across to see more closely. That satisfied her that this was no accident of wind or weather. The boughs and brushwood had certainly been put there by human hands, and put there to make a barrier; it was not a stout barrier, but it would suffice to persuade a wandering sheep to go elsewhere. And again Margery asked herself why.

She walked slowly round the coppice, and soon she found what looked like an entrance, for here there was only a single bough joining a pair of trees. She dipped under it and made her way cautiously along a trodden track. Thirty paces brought her to a clearing in the trees, and here she stopped and stood staring.

It was an odd sight. The clearing was of some size, and large enough for its centre to be full in sunlight, clear of all shadow from the trees; and here, in this sunlit centre, tall plants grew thickly. Margery moved slowly among them, peering at them and asking herself what they were. Certainly she had not seen such plants before. And as she looked, she noted also that the soil between them was looser and less choked with grass than it was elsewhere; almost, it had an air of cultivation.

She gave her attention to the plants again. Most of them rose above her waist. They had large dull-green leaves, paired with surprisingly small ones, and carried on stout and branching stems. The plants had borne flowers earlier in the summer, and most of the flowers had fruited; but here and there a late flower remained, and very odd flowers they were—big, bell-shaped, and of a curious pale purple. A few late fruits remained too, and these were as odd as the flowers; they looked like small black plums, smooth and shining, and still wrapped in the green leaflets that had once cupped the purple flowers.

Margery's mind was alert by now. Only a few late fruits remained; then where had the others gone? Birds? There seemed to be no birds about these plants. Children? Children would hardly roam to this lonely coppice, and they might not be tempted if they did; there was something repellent about these purple flowers. Then she remembered the boughs and the brushwood and the air of cultivation. Had the missing fruits been picked? Margery stood puzzled and thoughtful.

She bent down and picked one of the shining fruits. The over-ripe pulp squashed easily, and the juice spurted over her fingers. She threw it away in disgust, and stood contemplating the scene. Her fingers felt sticky from the juice, and she put them thoughtlessly into her mouth to lick them clean. Then she spat viciously as an acrid bitterness assailed her tongue. She spat again, and her tongue was dry and numbed.

At that she left it. She had had enough of this place, and as soon as she could come up with her horse she was away, riding down the hillside, grateful for the sunlight and watchful for the Barley road. Yet she did not ride at ease. Her mouth had dried as though she had thirsted for hours, and the fingers that had held the fruit felt dry and taut and strangely numbed.

She was in thoughtful mood when she got home, and the mood lasted while she drank ale to allay that strange thirst, while she washed, and changed her clothes, and made ready for supper. It persisted after supper, even though she was at last able to assure herself that her mouth and fingers had returned to normal.

It grew quiet then, in the parlour, as they sipped their wine and felt the warmth of the fire. Roger was tired after his day at Altham, and he turned sleepy in the comfort of his elbow-chair. Margery sat silent and thoughtful. Then she remembered the book called a Herbal which he had shown her on a night so long ago, and as he dozed she got quietly from her chair and took it from the ingle-shelf. And while the fire crackled, and the chill of night crept down from the Hill, through the Forest and over the house, she sat with a candle beside her and the book on her lap, steadily turning the thick, soft pages.

It was sleepy work. She was tired from the saddle, and soothed by sun and wind; and her eyes grew heavy in the glow from the fire. But she persisted, turning page after page while the logs burned white and Roger dozed by his forgotten wine. Twice she tip-toed to the hearth and mended the fire, and it was burning low for the third time when she found what she sought. Then sleepiness left her abruptly.

This plant with the purple flowers, she read, was known to some as Atropos; and that startled her, as well it might. For she had learning enough to know that the Fates are Three. The first is Clotho, who spins the thread of life; the second is Lachesis, who measures the length that each shall have; and the third is Atropos—who cuts the thread of life.

She gave attention to the Herbal again. This plant, it seemed, was known best to the Italians, a people famed for their subtle skill with poisons. It was as a poison that they held it in most regard, and a man who drank this juice would surely die, crazed and raving. But the Italians had another use for this plant, and a strange one. Their ladies would squeeze these shining fruits, and run drops of the juice into their eyes; which would then open wide, and become big, dark and staring; and the Italians, who seemed to think that this enhanced the beauty of their ladies, had therefore named this plant, in their own tongue, La Bella Donna.

The dying fire fell together and spluttered into sudden flame. It roused Roger and he sat up, blinking in the rush of light.

'What's this?' he said, and stared at her. 'Do you see ghosts?'

'I—I think I do,' she answered slowly.

'God's Grace! You've an edge to your voice tonight.' He was fully awake now. 'What's the tale?'

She told him, fully and completely; and he listened without comment, sitting quietly in his chair and never taking his eyes off her face. When she had ended he rose, still without speaking, and drained his wine. He threw more logs on the fire, and propped his shoulders against the chimney-shelf. In the same silence she lifted her face, and her eyes met his. She shut the Herbal and let it lie on her lap unheeded.

'To die raving?' Roger spoke first. 'Meaning to twist and writhe and rant, and see what isn't there?'

'I—I take it so.'

'It *is* so. I've seen it so.'

He turned from her and leaned on his elbow, staring at the sizzling logs.

'And eyes agape, you say? Big and wide?'

'So the Herbal says.'

'It says truth. That, too, I've seen in Pendle.' He turned to face her again. 'What foulness have you unearthed?' he asked her quietly.

Margery came to her feet and stood by him. He lifted his eyes from the logs to meet hers, his lean aquiline face set and grave.

'This raving, sir, and these wide eyes. You've seen them here—in a dying man?'

'It was a dying girl I had in mind.'

'Oh!' The chill that came from nowhere was surging up her back. 'You—you mean Margaret Baldwin?'

He shook his head slowly.

'Not for aught that I've heard. It was Anne Nutter . . .'

'Oh!'

For a moment the sunlit room in Goldshaw reared before Margery's eyes—with Miles Nutter eating his aunt's apple-tart, and the kindly, soft-voiced Anthony standing by the open window telling of his girl who had died. Then, as quickly as that had come, it had gone; and Margery was back with the fire and the candles and the grim-faced Roger.

'She raved of the Chattox,' he was saying. 'And her eyes were even so.'

He slapped the chimney-shelf as though irritated. Then he went abruptly to the table and poured himself wine.

'We needn't thirst,' he said.

He held out the crystal jug that held the wine, and after a moment's hesitation Margery took her glass to be filled. Wine, she thought, might help this moment.

Roger raised his glass, and there was a faint smile on his face as he viewed her across the wine.

'You've done well,' he told her, 'uncommonly well. Nevertheless . . .'

She looked up at him, and she had a hint of a smile to match his.

'Nevertheless,' he continued, 'it would be a decent prudence if we spoke of it to none just now. Such matters . . .'

He broke off and sipped thoughtfully at his wine.

'That a witch has malice I've known these many years. That she has more than malice I've held in doubt. That, perhaps, might bear a second thought.'

Margery nodded assent. And later, when she took her candle and went slowly up the stair to bed, she was still in thought; a witch's curse, it seemed, might truly cut the thread of life—in Pendle.

15

The Eve of All Hallows

Now came October, and a vast brewing of ale. Ale of a sort might be, and often was, brewed at any time, but no ale of the year was held to equal the October brew. Other ales were smaller stuff, good enough for a salty thirst or a kitchen revel; but to the honoured guest, to the man of quality, there was nothing to be offered but the four-year-old October.

Margery soon discovered that everybody was expected to help. To read and write and cast accounts were skills rare in Pendle, and she who had them was made to use them. Soon she was busy from morning till night, checking quantities of grain and firing delivered, riding here and there to inquire for grain and firing not delivered; and when that was done, and the brew in progress, she must record the quantities placed in barrel, and check and pay the wages of the helpers. She was kept so occupied that the full of the moon had come and gone before she remembered that Miles Nutter had not sought her out. She told Roger of this, and he laughed at her. Miles, he said, would be like the rest of Pendle—busy brewing. Nobody ever visited anybody till the October brew was done; they were all too busy brewing.

Then the weather broke. It had lasted beyond its season, and the brew had been done in days that could have been September. Margery, in particular, had been grateful as she rode her busy miles in sunshine. But a morning came at last when she woke to the splash and patter of rain on the windows, and she knew that St. Luke's summer was gone at last. Grey mists of rain were sweeping up the valley on the wings of the south-west wind, and when she looked for the hills they were not there; all high Pendle was lost in the swirling rain, and when, after breakfast, she peered sulkily through the streaming glass and wondered if she would be able to ride that day, Roger laughed at her. If she were not out of her mind, he said, she would ride nowhere that day, nor the next day; and to her great discontent Roger was right. For three days and nights the streaming flood poured down; and then, in the night, the wind came out of the north-west, and it blew. It blew like no wind she had ever known, and when she ventured out on foot she was aghast at its force. She came home hatless, wet and muddy, to spend the rest of the day by a fire that kept flaring back at her in maddening waves of smoke; and she learned that night that the rose-red curtains of her bed were not for decoration only; they were all that stood between her head and the vicious draught from the ill-fitting casements.

In this wind Nick Banister rode across from Altham.

He came, as usual, to support Roger in the giving of Justice, and Margery plied a busy pen as she recorded the complicated case of William Lee, who complained that he had been harshly refused relief by Christopher Swyer, Overseer of the Poor. To which it was answered that an Overseer could not be expected to leave his brew to bandy words with an idle vagabond whom all men knew to be more in need of a whipping than of pence; and when William Lee grew heated at this, Richard Baldwin intervened to charge the said William Lee with drunkenness, profane swearing, and wilful absence from church. It made a difficult morning, and Margery was heartily glad when William Lee was at last handed over to the Constable to be set forthwith into the stocks; the wind would no doubt cool him when he got there.

She had a word with Richard Baldwin afterwards, and she gave him her great-uncle's *Homily,* which she had been at some pains to make as decent as she could. His thanks were earnest, and Margery was still smiling when she walked into Roger's parlour to find him deep in talk with Nick Banister. He broke off as she came in.

'I've been telling Nick of your coppice,' he said, 'and of the plants within it. You may tell him yourself what the Herbal says.'

She did her best at that, and Nick Banister, easy in his furred gown, stretched his legs lazily as he looked at her.

'We've all heard of subtle poisons,' he said, 'but I did not know we grew them here at home. The land was tilled, you say?'

'It had some look of tillage, sir.'

'Very like. By whom, Roger?'

'Who's to say?' Roger blew smoke of tobacco and spoke lazily. 'It's a lonely spot. Of our witch brood, the nearest might be the Chattox crew. They live up behind the Rough Lee, on Dick Nutter's land.'

'The Chattox, hey? The chattering one, and that Redfern chit of the other day? Poor husbandmen, I'd think. No . . .' He laid his pipe aside thoughtfully. 'There's more to it than that, Roger. Who delved and planted matters little. Any groundling might be put to that. But who has learning enough to know of this and order it?'

'Again, who's to say? Whoever's ordered it is of no common breed.'

'Common enough for the common hangman. But this Anne Nutter—did she speak any name in her ravings?'

'Chattox,' said Roger tersely.

'Did she so?' was the dry answer, and at that Nick Banister left it. Ten minutes later he rode away, his hat pulled low, and his cloak jerking and twitching in a wind that was blowing as hard as ever. Margery looked at it gloomily, and wondered if it would blow for ever; and Roger laughed as he told her it could.

But it went out with the month, and the last day of October was grey and quiet. Margery spent it within doors, for she had word that the chapman was come and had asked speech with her; and there was Fat Jack, mountainous and rubicund, to lay before her the tinsel, the silver lace, the covered buttons and the silken points. She looked at them with delight, and she was deep in consideration of costs when Roger wandered in. He checked in his walk as he saw the display, and he stood there, thumbs in girdle, crinkling with amusement while Margery reddened with annoyance. But he chose to say, as he went out, that when she had at length made up her mind what she wanted she might send Fat Jack to him for payment; and Margery promptly forgave him his amusement. He might laugh as much as he pleased on those terms, and she took all the chapman had, which was a good deal; except for some cloth-of-gold to make a girdle there was all she wanted for her new kirtle; and even that, the chapman said, should be brought to her within the month. Grace had evidently given a very proper message to Jack Law.

It gave Margery a pleasant morning, and through the afternoon she was busy with Anne Sowerbutts and the flame-tint satin. She came from that with no more than time enough to prepare herself for supper, and when she tripped down the stair, trim in saye and sarcenet, she found Roger already in his parlour, leaning against the chimney-shelf and thoughtfully sipping his wine.

Something struck her as odd, and for the moment it eluded her.

She stopped short when she saw what it was. Roger had not donned his red velvet; he was still in jerkin and breeches, and if she thought this was an oversight, a quick glance round corrected her. By the door his boots stood ready, and on the ingle-shelf were his hat and cloak; and by his cloak was his sword. It was this that gave her warning, for she had not seen it since Preston; except for the gilded toy he wore on Sundays, Roger never troubled with a sword in Pendle.

From the cloak and the sword she turned her gaze to Roger.

'Is aught wrong, sir?' she asked.

'No—not yet,' was his curt answer.

It was not reassuring. Nor was his tone, but she thought she might risk one more question.

'Is the matter secret?' she asked.

'In the sense you mean it, no.'

'Then may I know it?'

But his answer to that was a question.

'What day's tomorrow?' he asked.

'Why, the—the first of November.'

He took the scent of his wine thoughtfully.

'True,' he said. 'But that's puritan wording. How would Tony Nutter call it?'

Her forehead puckered at that till she saw his meaning. Tony Nutter would remember the Saints.

'He'd say All Saints' Day, surely?'

Roger nodded.

'Or in Lancashire, All Hallows. And this, therefore, is the eve of All Hallows. There are certain nights in the year when the Devil stirs our witches and foulness walks abroad. This is such a night, and it's well to be prepared.'

Then Margery understood. Roger was expecting trouble in the Forest and was ready to ride at short warning. She looked again at the boots and the sword, and then back to Roger.

'You'll take me with you, sir—when you ride?'

'Is it work for you?'

'I was at the Malkin Tower—and at the poison coppice. Will you keep me from it now?'

He looked her over gravely, and his face relaxed.

'So be it, then. You've the blood that fits you for it. And if it gets tangled I may be glad of your wits. But in the dark we put safety first. It's breeches for you.'

She made no demur at that, nor wished to. She saw the good sense of it, and she went off in haste to make the change. But she was a little nervous as she struggled hastily into her riding-clothes. She had heard as a child so many tales of the night and its dangers, tales of sprites and goblins, of noxious mists and the vapours of the midnight air, that she was soon confused between belief and unbelief, and clinging to an illogical notion that she would be safe from all these as long as Roger was there.

Roger, it seemed, was in no hurry. Apparently he meant to wait till he had word of some alarm, and no word came. He explained that every night a Watch of four men, chosen in rotation, patrolled the Forest as a precaution against wandering rogues. This Watch was under the general orders of the Constable, and tonight, at Roger's insistence, Hargreaves had doubled the Watch and had undertaken to lead it himself. All of them were to be mounted, and at the first serious trouble one of them was to ride to Read. It was for this call that Roger was waiting.

Supper passed without incident, and then they were back in the parlour with the wine and the comfits and the mended fire. Their talk lingered and died, and still no call came. Only the heavy ticking of the clock broke the ordered silence of the room. Margery grew drowsy as excitement left her and tedium took its place. She thought of the witches and the Malkin Tower and the death of Anne Nutter; but it was all too complicated, and her thoughts turned to her new kirtle and the exact placing of the lace upon it. Then even that was too much effort, and her thoughts strayed to Grace Baldwin, surely locked within doors tonight by a father who was likely to be grave about goblins. And Richard himself? What would he be doing this night?

Margery sat up suddenly and became alert. Roger was on his feet, prowling round the room and fidgeting with things. Clearly he was growing uneasy. Margery kept her eyes on him, and he turned suddenly and saw her watching.

'There's some vileness stewing now,' he said. 'I have the scent of it. But what help's that without a guide?'

He began to pace the room again, and something of his restless humour passed to Margery; she, too, was on her feet, her ear cocked for hoof-beats on the gravel outside. But all stayed quiet; and if evil stalked, it stalked in silence.

A tap at the door brought Tom Peyton into the room, and Roger was agog for news. But Tom had only come to ask if more logs should be brought.

Roger shook his head impatiently.

'We've logs enough,' he said. 'What's o-clock?'

'Close on eight, sir.'

'When decent folk would be abed. There's no mistake about the double Watch, Tom?'

'Hargreaves made promise, sir.'

'Aye.' Roger stared gloomily at the fire and stirred the logs with his foot. 'What a Watch to stay for!' he burst out. 'A half-dozen ploughboys and a pair of yeomen, with a papist captain! And all melted to their boots from fear of sprites! God's Grace, what a Watch!'

He paused for a moment and then turned with decision in his face.

'We ride,' he said. 'Never stay for my boots, man! See to your own—and the horses.'

'Aye, aye, sir.'

Tom Peyton vanished, and Roger laughed happily. With decision taken, he was himself again. He flung Margery's boots across the floor to her and began tugging on his own; and when she prudently threw more logs on the fire, he called to her to hurry.

The horses had not been exercised that day, and someone had been generous with the corn. They went off at a cracking pace, Margery alongside Roger, and Tom a few paces behind with a great burly fellow named Joe Rimmer at his side. The night was fine and dry, with a light breeze out of the south-west and pale stars over their heads. But the rising moon hung over Burnley, red and bloodshot, and away to windward the stars were blotted out. And as Margery pulled her cloak tight, the wind puffed suddenly in her face. She knew these signs. A red moon, and cloud to the south-west on a rising wind, meant rain, and rain in plenty.

Some two hours later they drew rein near Fence and took thought what to do. They had been to the Newchurch and to Barley, thence down the Pendle Water, and then by the lower road to Fence. They had seen nothing that should not have been seen. They had covered a dozen miles and more, and seen not so much as the Watch. Nothing had met them but silence. All Pendle was snug with bolted doors and shuttered windows.

Margery shivered as she sat her horse, for the softness had gone from the night and the cold had got through her cloak. He feet were cold in her boots, and her fingers stiff in her gloves. She looked up at a cheerless sky. The cloud had crept steadily on till the ragged fringes of it were touching the moon; and the first scattered raindrops came pattering down as Roger spoke.

'The Devil's folk hide well,' he said. 'Tell me not that they're abed. That's for honest folk.'

He flung his head back as though he were listening, and Margery strained her ears in sympathy. But there was nothing but the sigh of the wind and the patter of the rain. Then the cloud-fringe covered the moon, and the sudden darkness made the rain seem louder.

Tom Peyton came edging up to Roger.

'Beg pardon, sir . . .'

'You needn't, Tom. What is it?'

'There's a country tale, sir, the Devil sits astride those stones this night.'

'Stones?' Roger whistled softly. 'The Hoarstones, you mean? God's Grace, Tom! I think you have it.'

He peered through the gloom at Margery, and she heard his short laugh.

'The Devil must have lulled my wits,' he said. 'I could not have forgot Hoarstones else.'

The clatter of the horses broke the silence as he led them quickly along the short track to the stones. It gave Margery time to remember the cluster of great old stones that leaned and toppled in what might once have been a circle. If the Devil and his witches chose to be abroad this night, these stones were as likely a spot as any.

But at the Hoarstones silence met them. They halted on the track, not two score paces from the stones, and they looked and listened. All stayed dark and still. They had outdistanced the rain, and nothing but soft wind broke the silence.

Roger looked left and right, then at the stones again.

'All quiet,' he said, 'and plaguey cold. But I've a feeling about this. We'll go closer.'

He moved off the track, letting his horse step carefully on the stony ground. The others followed, the iron-shod hooves ringing noisily.

'Enough to rouse any Devil,' said Tom Peyton cheerfully. 'Hell's Light! What's that?'

The blowing cloud had streamed from the moon, and the stones shone silver in a flood of light. Sharp and black against the biggest, a man was crouching, bareheaded and bent. He turned to them, and they saw his face, white above his black cloak. Then, as they stared, he set something carefully to the ground. In another instant he had leapt between the stones and they heard his running feet.

The three men were after him on the instant, and Margery let them go. That was man's work, and with horses and the moon to help them they could scarcely miss him. Meanwhile, she would see what it was that this man had set so carefully to the ground. She swung stiffly out of her saddle and walked unsteadily, her feet numb in her long boots. Then she stopped and caught her breath sharply.

'God's Grace!'

It came from her quickly, and it was not irreverent. She peered again and dropped to her knees to see better.

'God's Grace!' she said again.

She leaned forward and picked from the cold stone the small white body of a naked child.

She opened her cloak to give some sort of covering; then she turned to let the moon pour its light on her burden. Roger Nowell, riding back into the circle, was off his horse in one swift movement.

'Margery! What have you?'

In silence she parted her cloak to show him. She was still on her knees and she stayed so, looking mutely up at him, the moon full on her white face.

'Dead?' he asked.

Margery bent her head and forced her mind to move calmly. It was an infant boy she held, and seemingly not a week old. He lay inert in her arms, still and quiet, and when she tore her gloves off, her chilled fingers could feel no warmth in the tiny body.

'I—I think so,' she answered slowly.

She felt again and as her fingers moved over the child's forehead she drew them back in surprise. She felt again. It was as she had thought. The child's face was wet.

'Exposed to die,' said Roger softly, and his voice was colder than the night.

Margery looked round her, wondering. There was water in a tiny rill nearby, but the stones at her feet were dry. Evidently the rain-shower had not yet reached so far. Then the cloud-fringe was on the moon again, and nothing but the loom of things remained. Margery shivered and pulled her cloak tight as the rain came down in a hissing wave.

A clatter of hooves broke into her thoughts as the two servants walked their horses into the circle. The man who had fled came trudging with them, his wrists made fast to Tom Peyton's saddle. He was still hatless and he had lost his cloak. That, and no more, could be seen of him in the gloom.

'Make him secure and walk him along,' cracked Roger. 'He has matter to explain.'

Margery came suddenly to her feet, thinking that she had been bemused for too long.

'I'm taking him home,' she said shrilly, and she was speaking of the child, not the man. 'Maybe life's still a spark.'

She found her stirrup somehow, and without asking any leave she was away, riding swiftly and dangerously, her right arm under her cloak pressing the small cold body to her own.

'God's Grace!' called Roger, as she went swaying into the rainswept dark. A minute later he came up with her at a full gallop, and he bore her close company through the miles that lay ahead.

The rain made the night its own.

16

The English Mission

The child was dead.

When Margery was at last convinced of that, and had laid him down in decency, she trailed wearily to the parlour and told Roger.

He was rid of his boots and cloak and stood brooding by the dying fire, his wineglass in his hand.

'What else?' he asked curtly, and stretched out to pour wine for her.

'Drink it,' he told her sharply. 'By your face, you've need of it.'

She did as he bade her, and then dropped heavily into her chair. For the first time in her young life she was feeling at the end of her strength, and she sprawled limply, her face white and strained.

Roger bent down, stirred the fire, and mended it.

'I think Nick Banister was right,' he said. 'Evil is the just word. And now there's justice to do.'

He straightened himself and looked keenly at Margery.

'You've come to no harm,' he said. 'Sleep's your only need, and you may take it to your heart that you've borne yourself well this night. There's more in you than I looked for when I summoned you to Pendle.'

That went to heart; and it roused her, as perhaps he had meant it to do. The fire, too, was springing up as the dry wood flared and crackled, and the warmth of it was reaching her. Between that and the wine she began to feel a glow, and a touch of colour crept back into her cheeks. She got to her feet and slipped out of her cloak, and with Roger's help she rid herself of her boots. Then she contrived a smile.

'There's more in Pendle than I looked for when I had your summons,' she answered.

'That I'll believe,' he said grimly, and he poured the wine again.

Footsteps rang on the boards outside, and a sharp rap on the door heralded Tom Peyton and his fellow. Wet, cold and muddy, they came in briskly, their prisoner between them, and Roger received the man with a cold and hostile stare. For a moment he said nothing, standing in silence and looking the man over with keen attention.

Margery twisted in her chair and mustered her attention to do the same. She saw a stocky, well-built man of middle height and perhaps in his early thirties; thick-set, black of hair, and blue of chin. He held himself erect and returned Roger's stare with something like composure. He was in a pitiable state; he was still without hat or cloak, soaked with rain and shivering with cold; his sallow cheeks were white, his eyes heavy, and he looked tired to desperation. But he stood quietly and without protest, and he took a quick glance at Margery with eyes that showed intelligence in spite of their fatigue.

'That's enough, Tom.' Roger was speaking quietly. 'You two go for warmth and a drink. You've earned both, and I can do what remains. Off you go—but stay near the bell.'

Tom looked relieved. It seemed more than he had hoped for, and the two of them disappeared quickly enough. Roger looked steadily at the man before him.

'Your name?' he asked.

'Thompson.'

The sound of his voice made Margery look up sharply. It had the accent of the country—yet it was not wholly of the country. She listened keenly.

'No doubt.' Roger spoke calmly. 'But your true name?'

The man stayed silent, calmly meeting Roger's eyes, but saying nothing.

'What's that about your neck?'

Roger snapped the question suddenly, and the man stirred uneasily. But still he said nothing, and Margery, looking intently, saw round his neck what appeared to be a thin silk cord. Roger snapped again.

'I mean what's about it now—not what's likely to be about it when the Assizes are done.'

The man drew breath sharply. Then he drooped his head as if in acquiescence. He took the cord between his fingers and drew from within his shirt a small silver Cross, delicately wrought in filigree. He let it hang by the cord, and he stood again composed and silent.

'It's as I supposed,' said Roger slowly. 'I'll guess your name. Southworth, is it not? And noted as a seditious Jesuit?'

The man inclined his head again.

'I am Christopher Southworth,' he answered quietly, and his country accent was gone; this was the voice of education.

'And a Jesuit?' asked Roger.

'No.' The answer was firm.

'At the least then, a Seminary Priest?'

'I am of Douai.'

'Which we call a Seminary. And her to preach sedition?'

'I preach no sedition.'

'We'll say, then, a Massing Priest, sent to do that Rite?'

The man bowed again.

'I am of the English Mission,' he said simply.

Roger's voice hardened.

'Is it a part of that Mission to bring cold death to children?'

A faint flush crept into the man's pale cheeks.

'I brought to that child, not death, but life,' he answered deliberately.

'Life?' There was anger in Roger's voice.

'That was my word. Life, I brought.'

There was silence as the men stared at each other. Then Margery jumped from her chair in agitation. She had seen his meaning.

'Oh!' she burst out. 'Oh! He's a priest—and the child's face—it was wet . . .'

She stopped, her breath coming quickly, and looked wildly from the one man to the other.

'Grace of God!' said Roger softly.

'Exactly that,' came the quiet rejoinder.

Roger retreated to the hearth, and his fingers fidgeted uneasily.

'Let us have this plain,' he said. 'You are telling us, Master Seminary, that you gave Baptism to that child?'

'No less.'

'The child being then alive?'

'There were movements.'

'You heard us coming?'

'On those stones—I did.'

'And you stayed for us?'

'I stayed to do my Office.'

'God's Grace, man! I'll own your courage.'

Roger's eyes dropped as if this embarrassed him. Margery could hold silence no longer.

'By your leave, sir,' she said, 'this man is no doubt a papist, but I do not think he is a rogue.'

'Nor I. But what of that?'

'By his looks, sir, he is in very poor and unhappy case. May he not have some comforts?'

Roger stood impassive, his face betraying nothing; but he gave it longer thought than Margery had expected. Then he nodded slightly.

'Contrive them,' he said shortly.

She took him at his word, and moved her chair forward to the fire. Her eyes gave the invitation, but Christopher Southworth hesitated till he saw Roger's wave of assent; then he moved forward and sank heavily into the chair.

'My thanks,' he said quietly.

Margery looked round. She had barely sipped her second glass of wine, and now she took it up, set it brimming, and gave it to the priest. Then, seeing him still shiver, she picked her cloak from the press where she had thrown it, and set it about his wet shoulders. He looked up as she did so.

He drank the wine in silence, and when the glass was empty and he would have set it down, it was Roger himself who leaned across and filled it again.

'A gracious charity,' said Christopher Southworth. 'At least you do not join malice to heresy.'

'I've faults enough without that,' said Roger tersely. 'But of this child that's dead—why thought you that he stood in need of Baptism?'

The priest considered that before he spoke.

'I came to those stones,' he said at length, 'on my way to —to where I had to go. And by the stones I saw the child. I saw him plain, the moon being then very bright. And seeing him so, all naked, and in that spot and upon this night, I made bold to guess who had set him there and why.'

He hesitated, and Roger had to prompt him.

'Your guess being?'

'I make no doubt, Master Nowell, that you well know what all men know—that this Forest of Pendle gives harbourage and nurture to a very vile brood of witches?'

'I do know. You suppose, then, that the witches set out this child?'

'What else? Is it not their way?'

'That I know not—except that this child is not the first. Why should witches do such murder?'

A touch of surprise came over the priest.

'You ask me that?'

'I do. How shall it profit them?'

'It might profit their hellish Master.' The priest's voice had become very grave. 'They are a very vile and wanton crew, damned of God and damned of man, wholly given to the work of evil.'

He paused, and his face wrinkled with disgust.

'A baby's fat may make an ointment,' he went on slowly, 'and such an ointment may be used to kill. They know of herbs to season it . . .'

'Herbs!' Roger was sharp on that, and his eyes met Margery's. 'What herbs, if you please?'

'I do not know. I am not initiate in evil.'

Roger smiled grimly.

'In spite of which, Master Southworth, it seems that you have more than an idle knowledge of these things.'

'Is my duty less?'

'Duty? In the English Mission?'

'In the Church of God. For how shall His servants combat what they do not know?'

Roger glanced at Margery.

'What of Ormerod?' he wondered. 'What do he and his like know of this, save texts to be cited? I doubt, sir papist, that so much is known in the Church of this realm.'

'I spoke of the Church of God,' was the dry answer.

'God's Grace!' Roger was smiling faintly. 'For a man so circumstanced, you've an impudence that warms me. But you have not yet answered my question. Granting that the hellish sisters did expose that child, why suppose him to be not yet baptised? And why such a death?'

'It is the ritual of Hell. Laid upon the stones as a sacrifice to their Master. But a child baptised is a child of God, not acceptable to Hell.'

'You reason shrewdly. And I say again, you have more than idle knowledge.'

A hint of a smile greeted this.

'It's no matter for marvel. Such knowledge is not hard to come by. There are books in plenty, and of authority.'

'Books?' Roger smiled at the thought. 'There's Foxe's *Martyrs,* to be sure, and some wild tales in Holinshed. And the King's own *Demonology,* which I was lately at charges for.' He laughed. 'I sweated the half way through it and find it an endless talk between one Philomathes who knows too little and one Epistemon who knows too much. But what says Margery to this? You have some show of learning.'

Margery scoured her memory for fragments of brotherly talk.

'I remember a Dialogue by one Daneau of Geneva,' she said. 'And another by a Master Gifford. And there's a Discourse by one Perkins. But these, from what I've heard, have no great show of authority.'

'Authority,' said Master Southworth crisply, 'should not be sought in heretics. If you would have authority, read Bodin or Delrio or Remi. Or Grilland or Boguet or Sinistrari. Or best of all, the *Malleus Maleficarum*. These, truly, teach with authority.'

Roger disposed swiftly of this catalogue.

'They are not here to be read,' he said.

'That's to be deplored.' The priest spoke earnestly. 'If I had known your need before I was taken, I would have contrived something. As it is . . .'

He broke off and shrugged helplessly.

'Aye, as it is.' Roger spoke slowly and soberly. 'As it is, sir, you're taken. And I, sir, am a Justice.'

His tone was warning enough, and the priest rose quietly to his feet.

'You know the Statute, Master Southworth? You are beyond doubt what it calls a priest made in the parts beyond the seas according to the Order and Rites of the Romish Church. And for such a one to enter into this realm is Treason. For which it is very certain that any Judge of Assize will send you to be hanged and drawn.'

The priest said nothing, but his pale face was whiter and more haggard than before. Margery felt herself shudder. She knew as well as he did the horror that was boded. For in that sentence, drawing meant exactly what it meant when one spoke of drawing a chicken—except that the chicken had the privilege of being killed first, which the priest had not. He was hanged merely as a formality, for seconds only, before being lowered to the bench where the long knives waited, and a fire crackled to burn what the knives took out.

Margery shivered. She looked appealingly from the one man to the other; from the priest standing rigid to Roger standing with his head sunk in thought. The silence grew oppressive, and the fire crackled suddenly. It put her in mind of that other fire, and for a moment she felt sick.

Roger lifted his head. He had the ghost of a smile as he addressed her.

'Will you tell me,' he asked, 'how I'm to work that on a man who warms by my fire and drinks my wine?'

'Oh! You mean that he . . .'

'Peace!' He waved her into silence and stood in thought again.

The priest spoke quietly to Margery.

'Whatever may befall,' he said, 'let me give you thanks for kindness shown to—to one who had need of it.'

But Margery did not heed him. She was looking at Roger, and Roger was acting oddly.

He walked slowly to the window and flung back the damask curtains. The window-glass was black against the night, and the driving rain drummed noisily on it. Roger swung the wrought-iron latch and pushed the casement open. The candles flickered and the curtains billowed as the raindrops came spattering blackly on the damask. For a few moments Roger stayed, looking out into the night. Then he pulled the casement shut, and latched it lightly. He turned to the room again, leaving the curtains parted, and he spoke, as it seemed, to Margery.

'One of these nights we'll have some rogue climb in by that window,' he said. 'It's but six feet from the ground and there's ivy there to help.' He paused to brush raindrops from his hair. 'A vile night,' he added. 'Once out there, you'd not be seen by friend or foe at five paces.'

He came slowly to her as she stood by the hearth.

'If I'm to commit this fellow, we'll need paper for the drawing of a Mittimus. We'd best go seek it.'

It was, in fact, in the press behind him, as Margery well knew. But his meaning was clear by now.

'Aye, sir,' she said. 'We'd best go seek it.' And she went out with him.

When they returned the room was empty. The candles were flickering and the curtains swaying in the wind from the open window. The cloak she had lent the priest lay folded on the table; and on it, gleaming against the russet, was the silver filigree Cross.

17

The Lady Bountiful

Anne Sowerbutts drew back the bed-curtains to let a flood of light come in; and Margery woke reluctantly. The strong light set her blinking, and she turned away from it to bury her head again. But Anne was insistent. She had a word from Master Nowell, she said; and that made Margery turn again, to stretch and yawn, and then to listen. It had been a short night after the exertion and excitement, and she had heavy eyes in an aching head. But she made herself listen, and she learned that Roger would ride out as soon as he had breakfasted and would welcome her company if she chose to give it. If not, she might lie abed; but he wished to have her answer.

She made the effort and found him heartily at table, seemingly no whit the worse for his late hours. The rain had passed now; there were wisps of white driving across a blue sky, and a pale sunlight was flooding over the breakfast table.

'I've spoiled your sleep,' he told her smilingly as she sank into her sunlit chair. 'Spare your denials. You're still blinking like a noontide owl. But a ride to Goldshaw will blow that away. I think we'll rouse Hargreaves.'

A lifted eyebrow was all the answer he got to that. Margery had her mouth full.

'Hargreaves,' he went on affably, 'was little use enough last night, so we'll let him be busied this fine morning. He shall stir his great hulk and seek for parents who mourn a child.'

Margery checked in her eating and called herself callous. In this pleasant sunlight she had forgotten that little helpless body. But Roger was speaking again, and now more gravely.

'That we found a dead child last night,' he was saying, 'will soon be known to all. That's for the common ear. That a man was taken and contrived an escape could be given out also if it had to be. It's a thing that could be explained, though if we don't brag of it there'll be few to ask of it. But that the man who escaped was more than a nameless rogue—that is for you and me alone. Is that understood?'

'Aye, sir. And secure.'

'It had best be. That same Statute has severities for those who comfort a Massing Priest. And one thing more . . .'

He paused, and his gaze was steady on the brown leather jerkin she was wearing with her russets. Then she understood, and her face coloured. Bright against the brown leather, she had the silver Cross.

He smiled as he saw that she had understood.

'Our papist had a discretion,' he told her. 'He wore it, but within. Do you the same. A Cross, to be sure, is not in itself a papist thing. It's not like a Crucifix or an Agnus Dei. A loyal subject may wear one. But you'd best not let that one be seen. It's not of common work—and it may be known in Pendle.'

That was not to be disputed. Margery had already noted that folk in Pendle had a trick of knowing the affairs of others, and when she rode out with Roger into the sunlight the silver Cross was safely masked within her jerkin. They had fresh horses this morning, restless and eager beasts who made little of the road to Goldshaw; it was the road that led to Tony Nutter's, but a little short of that, a lane branched off and brought them to a squat and firm-built farmstead. Harry Hargreaves pushed his cheerful face out of a byre as they rode up.

If Roger supposed that his visit would disconcert a none too zealous Constable, he was wrong. Hargreaves' face lit with pleasure when he saw them. He welcomed them warmly and insisted on taking them to his parlour, where his wife, a tiny and bird-like woman, almost laughably small against her great husband, joined in his welcome and gave them hospitality that was ahead of the hour. For a moment Margery suspected that here was effusiveness meant to allay wrath, but she was soon sure that it was not; these Hargreaves were not of that breed.

Roger related briefly what could safely be told of the night's doings, and Hargreaves listened stolidly. He ran his fingers through his brown curls, and his brown face slipped into a twinkling smile that went oddly with his grave words.

'It's bad, sir,' he said. 'It's worse than bad. I think the Devil stalks in old Pendle these days, and there's none of us that's safe—not us, nor our children either. Whose child was it, sir?'

'That's for the Constable to discover. I'm here to bid you begin.'

'I'll look to that, sir. I'll not spare trouble if we can lay these limbs of Hell in gaol. They're beyond fitness to live. They should be burned from the body of us, sir, burned out root and branch.'

The man's earnestness was plain, and Margery observed it with interest; it gave her the thought that if the Constable and the Churchwarden were at odds on all else, they were seemingly at one in this; it might have been Richard Baldwin speaking.

But Roger remained cool.

'Burned, do you say?' he answered. 'It's hanging, not burning, that's provided, and not that till there's proof. And proof's what we lack. Why do you say it's these limbs of Hell?'

'Does a soul doubt it, sir?'

'Maybe not—in Pendle. But a Judge at Lancaster might. Some proof is needed. If you can furnish it, or even the shade of it, I'll commit.'

'Aye, sir. The whole damned coven. But more of the ale, sir? And you, mistress?'

But Roger was not to be tempted. He had overmuch to do, he said, and at that he took a cordial leave and went trotting down the lane, Margery beside him.

'It's plaguey odd,' he said suddenly, as they came out of the lane. 'That fellow was positively joyed to see us. I'll swear he was. I'd thought he'd be shy of us this morning after what he didn't do last night. But not a whit! He was joyed to see us, and I'm asking why.'

He halted to consider it, and Margery countered his question with another.

'Did you mark, sir, that when you spoke of that poor child he showed no surprise?'

Roger's head jerked up.

'Where do you steer?' he asked sharply. Then his eyes narrowed and he spoke slowly. 'You've wits like a whetted razor. And you see truly. It was even so. No surprise at all. But you'll have some thought behind this?'

'I asked myself if it was indeed news to him.'

'God's Grace, girl! You go deeper than makes for comfort. But it could be so. Then who's been talking?'

Margery studied her horse's head intently.

'Not you, sir. Nor I. And I think your servants may be trusted. There remains Master Southworth.'

'Ha! Our Seminary, is it?' Roger looked round him shrewdly. 'That's well said. And I see we're well placed for a visit to papist Nutter. A word with Tony might be of interest. He's thick with Hargreaves.'

A short three minutes brought them to the house in the pines, and once again they had gracious and friendly welcome.

'It warms me to see you here—both of you,' said Anthony as he led them in. 'I hope to see you many times again.'

'Handsomely spoken, Tony.' But Roger's tone was dry. 'To what do I owe this warmth?'

'To yourself.' Tony Nutter was not flinching from it. 'Yourself, you kindle it.'

'My neighbours, I fear, seem agreed to take another view. What's this of a dead child?'

Margery, just settling herself on the window-seat, held her breath. She had hardly expected such speed, but she saw at once the trap it concealed. Tony Nutter did not.

'Child?' he said. 'Have you not heard . . .'

'Have you?'

The question came with a snap, and Tony stopped short as he saw what was implied. But he did not lose his poise. He stayed collected, and the dignity that was inherent in him broadened and grew plain to see.

'Master Nowell,' he said calmly. 'You know as well as any man that we who are of the old Faith must needs keep an ear to the ground. Hearing's keenest so.'

Roger nodded.

'Thus distant hooves are heard, I'm told—especially flying hooves. But let be! I'm not here to search your garrets. But of this child, Tony. Who can tell me its parents?'

'I cannot. I've heard it suggested . . .'

'I'll not ask by whom. But what?'

'That . . . that this poor child was some witch woman's bastard.'

'It could be.' Roger sounded doubtful. 'But why?'

'It would give two reasons for . . . for what was done.'

'The other being to be rid of it?'

'Just that.'

Roger sipped his ale in silent thought. Tony Nutter stood watchful; and his sister, coming in to place cake on the table, caught his eye and for once held silence too.

'Death has some queer shapes in Pendle,' said Roger at last.

'Need you tell me that?' was the quiet answer.

'I'm sorry. You meant your daughter. I had not meant to remind you.'

Tony Nutter would have answered that, but his sister would have none of it. She had sat silent for long enough, and now she swept into the talk like a whirl of autumn leaves.

'You're not to talk of it to him, Master Nowell. It's bad for him. Any talk of Anne, and he can talk of naught else for the day, and he goes to his bed at night in a humour black as a pall. It's more than bad for him, and we'll have more cheerful talk by your leave.'

'My most willing leave.' Roger looked her over whimsically and put her to her favourite topic. 'How is Master Miles these days?'

That was enough for Mistress Crook, and she was away on it at once. Miles did excellently. He visited her each week, and never once had he let the weather stay him. But that was his way. And then Mistress Crook, among whose talents discernment seemed to have no place, fixed a beaming eye on Margery and hoped to see her and Miles visiting together again. That, she thought, had been very proper. . . .

There was some more of this, and Margery sat in discomfort. It was not a topic she wished to discuss, least of all with this garrulous lady. But to her relief, Roger was also showing signs of impatience, and they were not lost on the thoughtful Tony. He seized a moment as his sister paused for needed breath.

'You're the soul of charity, my dear,' he said. 'You give Miles all the virtues. And truly, he has at least some of them.'

'Some!' Mistress Crook sounded indignant. 'Now don't pretend not to agree with me, Tony, because you know you do. You know quite well you think the world of him. He's as good as son and heir to you now.'

'Heir indeed, but not quite son,' said her brother quietly. 'But I think we detain our guests.'

Roger had obviously had enough, and he was already on his feet and tying his cloak. They stayed to take courteous leave, and Anthony walked out with them to the horses which the old servitor had in readiness. He stayed by the gate as they rode away, and once again Margery found herself feeling warmly for this kindly, courteous man whose life was bleak and empty. She said so to Roger, and he nodded.

'I told you once,' he said, 'that in this County we do not harry papists for the sport of it. It's such men as Tony Nutter who put us in that humour.'

They came to the Sabden brook and Roger led up the hill away from Read.

'We're for the Newchurch next,' he said. 'Best see Curate Town about that burial. But you're thoughtful this bright morning. What is it?'

'That Master Nutter plainly knew of the child—which must surely mean Master Southworth.'

'Not a doubt of it. Nor need we doubt that when that Seminary left us he knew which house would shelter him. Like enough he's there now. There's another trifle too . . .'

'Yes?'

'If he found that house in last night's storm, he's no newcomer to Pendle. Though that's to be expected. He'll have been bred nearby. Some sprig of the Salmesbury Southworths, no doubt.'

They came to the Newchurch and found that they had had their pains for nothing; they learned at the curate's house that there was a Theological Exercise in Burnley church that day, and Master Town was away to bear his part in it; he would not be back till the next night.

'No matter,' said Roger cheerfully. 'The sun's still high and the horses fresh. We'll ride to Wheathead and bid the churchwarden take order for that. It's fairly in his scope. And as he and Town are at odds like dog and bear, there may be sport in it. Turn your horse.'

Margery was not displeased. She would be glad to see Richard Baldwin, and very glad to see Grace. Moreover she was getting hungry, and the thought occurred to her that if Richard Baldwin pressed them to his table he would have no hard task with her.

'It's in my mind,' said Roger thoughtfully, as they went cautiously down the long curving hill, 'that these papists may know more of witches than we do. That Seminary, now. Set him against such a one as Ormerod, or for that matter against our Baldwin. The Seminary spoke to the point, and his point was salted. But what's in Ormerod or Baldwin but rant, and a deal of wind? Moreover . . . Hell and the Devil!'

Margery saw it at once. Fifty yards in front of them a squalid tumble-down cottage stood by the roadside in an unkempt garden, and walking out of that garden to a fine horse tethered by the road was a woman Margery knew at once. Beyond all doubt it was Alice Nutter.

There was no avoiding the encounter, and Margery, glancing sideways, saw Roger brace himself for it. He swept off his hat with a courteous flourish.

'Good day to you, ma'am!'

'Good day, sir! And to you, mistress.'

Mistress Nutter had already mounted, and her way seemed to lie with theirs. The three horses went down the hill together.

'You find me busy, Master Nowell.' Mistress Nutter's voice was bright and cheerful. 'You'll guess the cause of it.'

'Not so, ma'am. Pray enlighten me?'

She drew attention to a basket made fast to her saddle, and Margery saw from a quick glance that it was empty save for a white cloth.

'We have duties of charity, all of us,' said Mistress Nutter vigorously. She was very assured this morning. 'We must look to the needy, sir, as our duty is. A cake or two and a little cheese. These things may help in days of grief.'

But Roger was not impressed.

'Whose grief?' he asked dryly.

'Master Nowell!' She was almost arch about it. 'You surely know that Eliza Howgate was lately brought to bed? A sin, no doubt, and to be deplored. It's a backsliding too common in these days. But women are sometimes weak.'

'Meaning that she's a mother and should not be?'

'In a sense, yes.'

'In what sense, if you please?'

Roger's dry tone seemed to rankle, and the dark head reared as she answered:

'The gift of life, sir, was not vouchsafed to that poor child.'

'Was it not?' Roger's change of tone was barely perceptible, but Margery's keen senses had it. 'Do you say, ma'am, that there's a child dead?'

'Alas, sir! Yes.'

The horses ambled on, the iron shoes scraping in the grit, while Roger stared silently at Alice Nutter.

'Was it born dead, or has it—become dead?'

'Sir!' The voice quivered, but her eyes were as steady as his. 'Is it needful, sir, to put that on a woman in her time of trouble?'

'Put what, if you please, ma'am?' His voice was bland now, and Margery caught a hint of mockery in it. 'Of two misfortunes, I do but ask which.'

'Your pardon, sir. I had mistaken you.' It came quickly, but there was a pause before Mistress Nutter explained herself. 'The child, if you please, was born dead and was of need buried directly. That was three days agone, and Eliza Howgate is still abed.'

'Poor soul!' The sardonic note in Roger's voice belied his words. 'But I'm obliged to you, ma'am. You give me news.'

'Because you pressed me to it, sir.' She paused again, and then seemed to hurry on. 'A stillborn child is not matter to be blazed abroad. Nor is its burial. But we women hear such tales where men do not. You'll be secret, sir, I trust?'

'As the grave, ma'am.'

The dark eyes flickered suddenly, and for a moment a cold shiver struck through Margery. But it was gone in an instant, and then Alice Nutter was turning to her with the most friendly of smiles.

'We've been waiting for you at the Rough Lee, mistress,

and you surely know you'll be welcome. Are we not to be thus honoured?'

The smile was lighting her face now, and her eyes were almost merry. Margaret sat stiffly and sought desperately for a way of escape.

'I've been so busied, ma'am. I've found so much to see and learn in Pendle . . .'

'Aye, to be sure. Yet do not be too agog to learn of Pendle, mistress . . .'

The dark eyes had lost their merriment. They were inscrutable as she changed her tone again.

'We'll hope to see you then at our poor house—Miles and I?'

'I'm honoured, ma'am.' There seemed nothing else to say.

'Then Miles shall wait upon you and fix a day.' Mistress Nutter nodded as though all that was settled. Then she turned again to Roger as they came at last to the bottom of the hill and the Pendle Water flowing from its clough.

'Do our roads part, sir?'

'We're for Wheathead, ma'am.'

'And I for the Rough Lee. Then you'll give me leave, sir. I've much to do this day.'

'Your servant, ma'am.'

Roger's beaver swept again, and she left him with a gracious smile as she crossed the Water and went trotting down its tree-fringed road. But Roger made no move towards Wheathead. The hoof-beats died away in the trees, and still he did not move. He sat his horse stiffly by the rippling stream, and the sunlight came from the water to throw a quivering pattern on his grave impassive face. The silence lengthened, and Margery heard the splashing of the stream and the sigh of the wind in the leafless trees behind her. Above her there were white clouds sailing in a pale blue sky, and the sun had warmth enough to tempt her to untie her cloak.

'Can your wits cut through that?' asked Roger suddenly, and she came out of her reverie and gave him full attention; his tone demanded it.

'Of the child, sir—at that house yonder?'

He nodded.

'Aye. Of this child she called stillborn.'

Margery collected her thoughts and spoke carefully.

'It would be an odd chance if it were not the same child.'

'Odd indeed, at that house. Know you of these Howgates?'

'Not a whit.'

'The woman's a reputed witch. And the man's Kit Howgate, a bastard of our Demdike, and left-hand brother to that swivel-eyed Elizabeth.'

Margery whistled softly. She had not suspected this.

'And Alice Nutter—she visits *there*?'

'So we saw—as the Lady Bountiful! That's her favoured pastime, and it disposes some to speak well of her. I'm asking now if it covers some other things.'

Roger paused, and his sombre eyes gazed steadily at Margery.

'She railed at me that I put something on Eliza Howgate. What was it that she supposed me to have put upon the woman?'

Margery met his gaze squarely. She had expected this, and her eyes were as steady as his.

'Your words should have meant what you pretended, sir—which, of two misfortunes? They could also have meant the truth.'

'Meaning the child on the stones?'

'Aye, sir. Just that.'

'As you say—just that. And Alice was so hot on it, and in such haste to deny . . .'

The rippling stream filled the silence as he ended. It was Margery who found words first.

'If it's *that* she was in haste to deny . . .'

'She must know something of it.' Roger's eyes had never left Margery's. 'And will you tell me how she knew—if she did know?'

'This Howgate, perhaps?'

'Not so.' He shook his head decisively. 'For if she was in haste to deny, she must have supposed me to know something of the matter too. She would not have denied what she supposed I did not know. And how could the Howgates have told of our last night's doings?'

Again there was silence as Margery followed his thought.

'There's Tony Nutter,' she said slowly. 'He surely knows, and she's his sister-in-law . . .'

'Whom he loves like the sweating sickness. He'd spill no

papist secrets there, even if she'd had time to seek him out.'

Margery nodded.

'I thought of that also.'

'Yet she knew. Call it guessing if you wish, but I say she knew. I've a whim about it, as Nick Banister might say. And again I ask, who told her?'

'There's one thing possible . . .' Margery spoke doubtfully.

'But continue. In charity, continue.'

'It's been in my mind that whoever laid that child upon the stones might have stayed hid—to watch what befell.'

'God's Grace, lass!' He tapped his saddle thoughtfully. 'You see it always. Which should mean that whoever laid the child has contact with our Alice. One asks why.'

'Aye, sir. It's a thing . . . a thing not to be expected.'

'There's much in Pendle not to be expected. Now there's one thing more, and this the most ill scented.' He gazed, hard-eyed, at Margery, and his nostrils were quivering with disgust. 'Your poison herb, and baby's fat, and raving death—Anne Nutter may have died so?'

'It . . . it has that look.'

'Mark it then.' His words came slowly. 'This Alice is ambitious for her son. She'd have him an Esquire . . .'

'So it's said.'

'Tony Nutter dropped it this morning that the boy's his heir. Now why did that come about?'

Margery felt her eyes widen; and a chill she had known before came gnawing at her spine as she took his meaning. She stared at him speechless.

His voice came again, quietly and remorselessly.

'Why did that come about?'

'Because Anne died,' she answered, and hardly heard her voice.

18

Ambition's Track

'And that's not all,' said Roger slowly.

He broke an unhappy silence. Margery stayed quiet and waited.

'It comes back to me now,' he went on, 'that there was another Nutter who died oddly and to the profit of the Rough Lee.'

'And . . . and in that manner?'

'That I know not. It was twenty years agone, and memories grow dim. Yet Tony and his Margaret should know something of it if their minds be but jogged a little.' He nodded thoughtfully. 'That shall be my work. I'll go visiting again. And you—get you to Wheathead and deal with Baldwin for me in the matter of this burial.'

'Telling him what?'

'That's with you. You know my mind and you've wit enough to judge what's safe. Now get you gone. We'll talk at supper.'

He wheeled his horse and cantered off. Margery watched him go. Then she rode quietly across the stream and through Barley village, her eyes unseeing and her thoughts in turmoil. For what was suggested was as plain as it was foul: that these witch women, ignorant and evil, danced to another's tune and for another's profit; and as she thought of it, there came back to her the memory of Nick Banister, sitting at ease by Roger's fire and asking who had learning enough to order that lonely coppice.

She passed through the village and came to the higher upland, where the stream splashed on the stones and the wind had a keener edge. She rounded the bend and came to the pool and the mill and the wheel in the seething froth. And then her head reared. For there was Grace, sitting in the sunlight by a spinning-wheel that clicked and chattered; And at her side, lounging on the low stone wall and very much at his ease, was Miles Nutter.

They came to their feet as they saw who it was, and Miles was plainly out of countenance. Grace stood quiet and composed, and Margery scanned her keenly, suspecting that a shade of embarrassment hid behind that friendly smile. If it was so, it had Margery's sympathy. This was a meeting she could well have done without; she thought she had enough in her mind this day without having to deal with Miles Nutter too.

'This is pleasure,' said Grace. 'And not one we had expected.'

'I'd not expected it myself, but I've messages for your father, and of some urgency.'

'I'll take you to him. It's a month and more since we saw you.'

'Blame weather and witches, if you please.'

'And brewing. I know how it is. Miles here has missed you too.'

'I didn't know he'd sought me.'

Margery turned to Miles for the first time, thinking she could not continue to ignore him. He reddened under her gaze and twisted awkwardly. But before he had found words the door of the millhouse opened and Richard Baldwin came out, his brown face aglow. Margery turned to him with relief.

'This is a kindness,' he said heartily. 'It will please us all.'

Margery took a quick glance at Miles and doubted that sentiment; then she came quickly to the point.

'Truly, sir,' she said, 'it's not kindness. It's need. I have messages from my cousin.'

'Is it so?' His face grew graver. 'I doubt that bodes no good at this season. But come within. I'll have a lad care for your horse.'

But Miles Nutter interposed. He came forward and took her bridle.

'At least let me serve you in this,' he said, and Margery hastened to give him a gracious answer.

'I'll be grateful,' she told him smilingly. Anything, she

thought, that might ease this moment, if only for Grace's sake.

She followed Richard into the big kitchen and from there into a small parlour which she judged must be private to himself. It had only a table, a pair of chairs and a bookshelf; and she swept an expert glance over this as she took the proffered chair. There were manuscript books which she thought must be the mill accounts; there was the heavy quarto Geneva Bible, Calvin's *Institutio*, and a dozen or so of lesser works of the sort that had graced her brothers' shelves. And open on the table, clearly in present use, was her own copy of the *Homily On The Justice Of God*.

'Now, mistress. What of these messages?'

She turned to the tiny hearth and warmed her hands thoughtfully while she considered what words she should use. Then suppressing what she thought dangerous, she told him all she thought safe of the doings of the night. He listened quietly, but she saw plainly from his hardening face that he was stirred by her relation.

'They hold all together and keep themselves close,' he quoted as she ended. 'Shall they escape for their wickedness? Thou, O God, in Thy displeasure shalt cast them down.'

He sat in silence after that, and only his smouldering eyes showed how deeply he was moved. Margery ran over her memory of the Psalms.

'The pestilence that walketh in darkness,' she said. 'The sickness that destroyeth in the noonday.'

He was nodding approval of that before she had realised that her thought had been with Anne Nutter, rather than with a dead child.

'It's even so,' he said. 'But I feared there would be some vileness yesternight. I'll be right glad to be done with all these Saints' Days, and not with some only. They're occasions ever for lewdness by the vulgar and worse by the wicked.'

Then he became practical.

'This child must have decent burial, to be sure. But can it be at the Newchurch, or indeed at any church? Can we suppose there has been Baptism?'

That took Margery by surprise, and she all but blurted out too much. She checked just in time, and hastily sought for an answer. But she had not been bred among divines without learning something of equivocation.

'I think,' she told him carefully, 'that our Church permits Baptism by those who are not its Ministers when there is *extremis*.'

'Ha!' His eyes lit at that. 'So much was done then? This child was alive when found?'

'Yes. Alive, and was then baptised.'

'Thanks be to God! I ask now, who thought of that?'

'Does it signify?'

'I'll take that as my answer. I make you my compliments.'

She accepted them placidly, telling herself that she had earned them in one way, if not in another. She thought she had managed that adroitly, and without an untruth.

'That being so,' he said, 'there's no reason why the child should not lie in the ground of the Newchurch, and I'll urge that on Master Town. A well-intentioned man, mistress—well-intentioned I'll grant, but he errs. He errs grievously. You've noted he's corroded with the Arminian pestilence, but he has errors added to that. Now this day he goes to Burnley where he's to uphold . . .'

He was still expounding what he called the Infralapsarian heresies of the curate when Grace came in to call them to dinner. He continued his discourse throughout the meal, and Margery had to keep her mind alert lest she make some foolish answer. One thing eased her; she noted that Miles Nutter was no longer to be seen. But when dinner was done and Thanks had been given, she looked appealingly to Grace, who at once carried her off to her own small room on pretext of tidying hair.

'Thanks!' said Margery briefly.

Grace laughed.

'I thought you were very brave. Listening to such talk can be trying work.'

'I've served a sound apprenticeship to it.' Margery smiled ruefully. 'It runs in my family at home.'

'You were very tactful.' Grace seated herself on her bed and left the only chair to Margery. 'And you were very tactful with Miles before dinner.'

Grace was obviously making an opening and Margery was anxious to help her; the sooner this was cleared, the better.

'As to that,' she answered, 'to be perfectly plain, I begin to find Master Nutter an embarrassment.'

'I'm sure you do. You've been treated with too little courtesy, and it's time you knew the truth of this.'

'There's no reason why I should. It's his affair and perhaps yours, but it's not mine. I'm not a maker of trouble.'

'Listen, Margery . . .' Grace was insistent. 'It's best for us all that you should know the truth of this. So listen.'

It was not an easy tale for Grace to tell, and she looked at her bed more than at Margery. But in the end she had it plain. Margery had supposed correctly that something lay between Grace and Miles Nutter. It was indeed more than that, and it would have ripened into a betrothal but for one thing—the uncompromising opposition of Alice Nutter. On that, Grace was forthright. Alice Nutter, she said, had no mind that her Miles should, as she phrased it, throw himself at a yeoman's girl. Dick Nutter, himself a yeoman, would have made no trouble; Richard Baldwin might have been persuaded; but Alice would have none of it. Her son was to rise in the world; he was to end as an Esquire, and he must find a wife in the family of an Esquire. Nothing less would do, and Miles was straitly forbidden to have dealings of any kind with Grace. Forbidden meetings naturally followed.

'You make it very plain,' said Margery. 'It explains what seemed odd discourtesies. I perceive his embarrassments. But it does not explain why he sought me at all. Why could he not leave me in peace?'

Grace hesitated.

'Judge him not too harshly for that,' she said at length. 'It would truly bring blame on most. But not only Miles. With such a mother, and with her so insistent, what could he do but comply? You've met Alice Nutter, Margery? You know the force that's in her.'

'I do. But are you saying that it was Alice Nutter who set him on to go a-riding with me?'

'No less.'

'But why? In the name of what makes sense—why?'

'Are you not kin to an Esquire?'

'God's Grace!' Roger's exclamation came from her before she could check it. 'It was for *that* that he rode with me?'

'At her insistence. Only at that. Though it's sour hearing for you.'

'Pay no need to that. I don't want your Miles, and I've taken no hurt. But how of your father? Had he no word to say?'

'That Miles visits me, he knows. It could not be otherwise. And he has said no word against it—or against Miles. Why should he? Miles is a yeoman's son, and . . .' Grace had coloured as she sought for words. 'And it might be thought a proper match.'

'Proper indeed. But if it be forbidden by . . .'

'Don't you see it? My father knows all things of it but that. Miles has not spoken of his mother's commands.'

'But she herself? Surely she . . .'

'Then you don't know Alice Nutter. Trust her for that! A most kindly gracious lady, our Alice! She's friend to all the world—and lays her commands in secret.'

Margery sat silent. Unbelievable though it was, she believed it. It fitted, she thought, with what else she knew—and fitted, too, with what had been darkly hinted. Was nothing done with decency in Pendle? Was there nothing here but misery? The child dead in the night; the hunted priest; Anne Nutter, darkly dead; Margaret Baldwin; and now this! And what would come next?

'My poor Grace!' she said quietly. 'I think I see it all—and believe it too. Now what would you have me do? I'm yours to serve in all things.'

Grace lifted moist eyes to Margery's.

'Just this,' she answered steadily. 'Forgive Miles. Be understanding. And if he's driven to call on you again, resent it not but show him some courtesies.'

Margery agreed at once.

'All that most willingly, and it's little enough. But would it not be better if I were to refuse to see him? Even his mother could scarcely insist on his visits after that.'

But Grace would not agree. She showed instead some signs of alarm.

'God forbid!' she burst out. 'Margery, you don't know Alice Nutter as Miles and I do. She's wicked, Margery. Truly she is, and she's dangerous. God forgive me for saying it, but she is. I know not what would follow if you drove it so. For pity's sake, let it be.'

Margery clung to a coolness that was slipping from her. This, from the gentle Grace, was perturbing; and again she had Roger's dark thoughts surging in her mind. Then she forced herself to be steady, and she phrased her question carefully.

'This wickedness of Alice Nutter, Grace. I think I could believe in that. But tell me, what form does it take?'

'I'd feel safer if I knew. Even Miles does not know. I think he guesses something, but he has not told me. All being said, how could he?'

'He couldn't. I perceive that.' Margery came to her feet. 'But Grace, you're looking strained. You'll be better beyond doors at your spinning wheel. And I'll be better on my road. But be sure I'll do as you've asked.'

They parted amiably, and Margery took due and cordial leave of Richard Baldwin. But once she was round the bend and out of their sight she rode fast. She was in haste to talk with Roger, and there was a chaos in her mind that was not pleasant. Until yesterday Pendle had been a rustic place, unhappily plagued by some vicious women. Now the picture had changed, and a much more formidable person had come into view; vaguely indeed, but not less alarmingly for that.

In the end she hurried too much, and she was home before Roger; and not until supper was done were they free from attendance and able to talk at ease. But once they were back in the parlour, with the fire and the candles and the wine, Roger lost no time in coming to what was in his mind. 'You took order with Baldwin for that burial?' he asked without prelude.

'Yes.' She did not trouble to explain how. 'But there's some more. It was a secret, to speak truly. Nevertheless . . .'

'You take no risk with me,' he assured her. 'Country gossip's not among my faults.'

'I know.' She told him briefly of Grace's tale and of the doings of Miles Nutter.

It stung his pride and angered him.

'Here's a tale!' he snapped. 'She'd make you a creature for her advancement, would she? She'd link her lad with you, and through you with me, and through me with half the quality of Lancashire? Was she drunk when she thought of it?'

But he cooled and listened calmly to the rest of it. Then he grew heated again when he learned that Miles Nutter might yet be calling on Margery.

'Do you lend yourself to this?' he asked angrily. But he cooled again when she explained the matter.

'You may lay this to your credit,' he told her. 'If I thought less well of your wits, I'd forbid it shortly. As it is . . .' He regarded her smilingly. 'As it is, you've a face that will call men from afar, but you've some cool sense within it—or I'd not talk with you as I do. Have it your way then. Be civil to the lad if you wish. But let him not call too often, lest neighbours gossip.'

That was well said, and Margery knew it. She promised that at once, and then waited for his next. He came to it without pause.

'First,' he said, 'a detail about Anne Nutter. A little before she died they had Alizon Device come a-begging to the house. She got into the kitchen, where Anne, a charitable soul, seems to have given her some small thing. And apparently there was some talk. After all the two girls were of an age, and Alizon can be a lively chit when she tries. There was a jest, it seems, and a laugh or two. Into which comes the Chattox, also a-begging, and at once she starts cursing—holding that Anne was laughing at *her*.'

'And then?'

Roger shrugged.

'Who knows? But Anne took sick the next day and died within the month.'

'So soon?' Margery frowned over it. 'On the face of it there's no link with Mistress Nutter there.'

'No.' Roger hesitated. 'Except the profit that may fall to Miles. And this: these Chattox dwell on the Nutter land, and none believes they pay a rent. Do they perhaps pay by service done?'

Margery nodded, seeing the point in that.

'One other matter.' There was a grimmer note now in Roger's voice. 'I've been looking into that affair of the earlier Nutter, and I've learned at least something from Tony.'

He paused, and Margery was erect in her chair. Roger's tone was ominous.

'Dick Nutter was *not* the eldest son. He was the second

son, Tony being the third. The eldest, and hence the heir, was Robert.'

'Yes?'

'This Robert, some twenty years back, was in the service of Sir Richard Shuttleworth of Gawthorpe, and while in that service he died. That's known to all.'

'So that Dick inherited in his place?'

'And Alice with him.'

Margery's voice came softly.

'How did this Robert die?'

'That's what I've been learning. He went to Wales with Sir Richard. On the way home he took sick, and he was left at Chester with his body-servant. He died there at Candlemas.'

Margery made her thoughts stay cool.

'If there was none with him but his servant, it can hardly have been the work of our Pendle witches—or of Alice Nutter.'

Roger eyed her steadily, and an odd smile lurked in the corners of his mouth.

'That servant,' he said, 'was Thomas Redfern, now dead. Thomas Redfern, husband of Anne Redfern and son-in-law to the Chattox—who dwells on the Nutter land.'

19

Martinmas

To Anthony Nutter it was Martinmas; to Richard Baldwin, who had abrogated the Saints, it was the eleventh of November; to Margery and some others it was Roger Nowell's birthday, a day marked off from other days.

At breakfast he had Margery's congratulations, to which he brusquely answered that it was his fiftieth birthday and he could wish that it were not; but he accepted with obvious pleasure the leather riding-gloves she had decorated for him in silver lace—first fruits of her dealings with Fat Jack the chapman. And after breakfast, the day being Monday, came Nick Banister from Altham with flint and tinder neat in a silver box, with Roger's initials worked on the spring-loaded lid. That pleased Roger too, and the three of them were in high good humour when they went to the weekly administration of justice. And when this work was done and they were back in the parlour, they found another visitor. Thomas Heber, Roger's son-in-law, had ridden over from Marton, his home in Craven, with gifts and good wishes, and a special letter from Anne Heber to her father.

Margery was presented, and he looked her over with such unconcealed thoroughness that she suspected he had a special wifely commission to observe and report. She hoped her own inspection of him was better concealed, but it was certainly as thorough. He was a short and thick-set man of perhaps a year or two beyond thirty, heavier of body and redder of face than he need have been, and having some air of dullness about him; well intentioned, perhaps, but none too intelligent, and surely too fond of the table and the bottle. But he was hearty and friendly, and he bore a pressing invitation that Roger and Margery should be guests at Marton over Christmas.

They went happily in to dinner, sociable from the wine that Roger had for once brought out at noon. Margery enjoyed it, for she found that she was expected to play hostess to the guests; and this, after some preliminary nervousness, she found to be a matter much to her liking. Nor was it difficult, for Tom Heber wanted no entertaining. He was a jovial fellow, loud-voiced and self-assured, and it soon emerged that he had some esteem of himself as a teller of tales. But little by little, as the wine sank lower, his tales became more and more of the stable, until it dawned on Margery that here was a social problem.

It was Nick Banister who showed her how to solve it. He began to talk of the troubles that beset a Justice of the Peace, and as Tom Heber was lately in the Commission for Yorkshire, and vastly proud of it, he must needs cap anything that was said; and when Roger had a word to say about the way Lieutenants of a County had of issuing peremptory orders to Justices, Tom Heber could not hold back an instant. He had a tale to tell, he said, that bore on exactly that. He had caught a Jesuit and . . .

'A what?'

Roger's voice cut in sharply. Then he relaxed, and spoke quietly.

'That's of interest, Tom. By what name?'

Tom Heber's fist thumped the table.

'One of your folk, sir. One of yours. The rogue's a Southworth of your Salmesbury brood.'

'Christopher Southworth?' This was from Nick Banister.

'Aye, that same. D'ye know of him, then?'

'We had some warning that he was at large.'

'As had we.' Tom Heber drained his glass and set it down with a clatter. 'Wherefore, when some of us were after the wildfowl at Tom Lister's place, and we started this black-cloaked rogue from a coppice, we made a guess at it and stayed him with our fowling-pieces.'

'And then?' Roger spoke steadily.

'Why, we had his name out of him, and a confession of what he was . . .'

'A Jesuit?'

'Called himself a priest only. Which is the same damned thing, hey?'

Roger let that pass.

'And where is he now?'

'That's what's odd. That's what I'm telling.' Tom drank thirstily and then explained himself. 'We lodged him safely, and I wrote of it to our Lieutenant, never doubting I'd have orders to send the Romish rat to York. And do I get them, hey? Do I get them?'

He drank again and eyed them truculently.

'I wait a week without a word. Then when I'm thinking there's a messenger dead, up comes a letter long as a parson's nose. The fellow's treasons, it says, are all done in Lancashire, and your Earl of Derby is to have him first for a question or two. So he's to go on loan, as 'twere, to Lathom, for which service I'm to part with him. And did ye ever hear the like of it?'

'It's not common,' said Roger, and Margery noted that he had quietly placed the wine by his own elbow. 'And is this therefore done?'

'Half.' Tom Heber seemed to be searching for a wine-jug he could not clearly see.

'Half? Meaning what, if you please?'

'Meaning that your Earl sent one of his own gentlemen to escort the rogue.' He hiccoughed suddenly. 'Gentleman is it? A gay young spark, all lace and fripperies. And he's to take my rogue from me, blast him! Where's the cursed wine? I'm dry as lenten pease.'

He heaved forward in his chair and stretched across the table for what he could not reach. Then, of a sudden, he sagged across the table and lay gasping like a stranded fish. Roger rose quickly and threw him back into his chair, where he slumped in a snoring sleep.

'Get you back into the parlour, Margery,' said Roger, quickly. 'He's no sight for you.'

She obeyed without a word, and until they came to her she sat alone, staring into the fire. That Tom Heber was drunk disturbed her not at all. It was, as she knew very well, the common failing of country gentlemen and the daily habit of many of them. It was the thought of Christopher Southworth and what awaited him beyond Lathom that pounded through her head and set her staring at the fire, till she saw in fancy the glow of the scaffold fire and the gleam of the waiting knives. She knew something of such work. In her weeks at Holborn she had walked more than once over London Bridge and seen the heads on the flanking pikes; and once, by the Charing Cross, there had been a pair of legs to stink and blacken in the sun. All London knew what treason meant, and Margery shuddered sickly. She had liked Christopher Southworth.

It spoilt the day. Roger did his best when he and Nick came in. They had roused Tom Heber and soused his hair with water, and he was almost himself again. The talk grew friendly once more, and partings were cordial as the guests rode away; and when they were gone Roger talked of many things that were far away from treason. Margery did her best to follow him, but the brooding melancholy stayed. It stayed with her throughout the night, and she was positively pleased the next morning when Miles Nutter suddenly appeared after breakfast and desired speech with her. She was already dressed for riding, and was hoping that the wind on the hill would blow the vapours from her. So she did not keep Miles in suspense; within a few minutes she was riding out with him.

She dealt easily with him. As soon as they were out of earshot of others she saw him look diffidently at her as if he were feeling for words; she cut him short in it.

'You need not give me explanations,' she told him. 'I've had them and I've accepted them and there's no more needs be said.'

His face cleared at once and relief spread over it. Once again Margery found herself thinking that there was something attractive in Miles Nutter. If these clouds could be dispersed there might yet be good cause to give congratulations to Grace.

'You're the soul of kindness, madam,' he said quickly.

'Not so. It's merely that I've some sense, and much liking for Grace.' She paused and caught his eye. 'And perhaps a little for you also if you now deal honestly with me.'

'Be sure of that,' he insisted warmly. 'I'll not fail you henceforth in that. Be very sure of it, madam.'

'That's well. On those terms we can be friends. In token of which you may stop calling me madam. Let's deal simply. Whither do we ride this day?'

It soon appeared, as she expected it would, that he was eager to be at Wheathead, and as Margery was willing enough for a word with Grace, they were soon making for the Newchurch, chatting amiably of everything and nothing as they went. With his mind now at ease, Miles Nutter was an excellent companion.

They were at the mill before noon, and if Margery had any doubts of the propriety of accepting his escort, they melted in the radiance of the smile she had from Grace. Miles, too, was at his best, and both he and Grace seemed to suppose that all was now well; only Margery was clear-sighted enough to see that it was not. Only a passing embarrassment had been dispersed; the hostility of Alice Nutter remained; and Margery, thinking of that, and of the deeper and darker shadows that hung about the Rough Lee, found her thoughts flow gloomily. She was not in humour this day with the chattering pair at her side, and of a sudden she was on her feet and declaring that she would ride on alone; and she persisted in spite of their protests. At their insistence she stayed for dinner in the great stone-flagged kitchen, and then she was away, riding into the clear, pale sun of a November afternoon, desperate to be clear of this air of doubts and thwarted hopes, and eager to be alone.

This time she did not ride past the pool and down the stream to Barley, as she had always done before. Instead, she went up past the granary and then turned to her right into the road that flanked it. This road, she knew, must lead her to the point where the Forest road curled away to Gisburn, and from that point her way home would be as easy as from any other. Yet as things befell, she never reached that point; for in a mile, the road she was riding brought her to an upland valley where a bridle track led off, and here in the rough grass she found a thin and trickling stream which must surely find its way into the Pendle Water far below. It tempted her, and after a little thought she left the road and followed the rough and winding bank. A half-hour's riding confirmed her guess when she found herself on the slope of the long, wooded ridge that ran behind the Rough Lee; she had ridden this before.

She followed the stream down almost to the road, and then she halted on a wooded knoll to survey the ground. The Forest road ran past the knoll, a bare ten yards away;

to her left was the hill by the Malkin Tower, with the road coming steeply down from it; to her right, the road dipped between grassy banks as the stream splashed across it to join the Pendle Water. Margery sat thoughtful, asking herself what she should do.

Up to her left a hoof clattered on a stone, and Margery's thoughts changed abruptly. She turned alertly as four horsemen came into view, riding slowly down from the Gisburn road. She moved warily into the fringe of pines on the knoll, thinking that it might be prudent not to be seen by four strange men in this lonely dell; then, from the pines, she scanned them more keenly; and what she saw set her heart pounding. The men were in two pairs, and the pair behind had the look of servants; of the pair in front, one was a gay gentleman, bright in a cloak of green and a gold-laced hat with orange plumes; but it was the man at his side, the man in the black cloak and the sombre hat, who stirred the recognition that set Margery into turmoil. Here, beyond doubt, was Christopher Southworth.

She understood at once. The priest was on his way to Lathom House for questioning; and the gentleman in green must be the gay young spark of Tom Heber's tale, sent by the Earl as escort for the prisoner; this, after all, was their natural road out of Yorkshire into Lancashire, and no doubt they were now in search of quarters for the night.

Margery's mind was racing. All her sympathy was with the prisoner, going so quietly to Lathom and the awful death that lay beyond, and the thought hammered in her that sympathy was not enough. She must *do* something, do something that would help, do something somehow, and not sit gaping like a fool at a peepshow; somehow and by some means she must raise a diversion and hope that the priest would have wit enough to profit by it.

She swung her horse as the riders came to the knoll, and as they entered the dip in the road she rode wildly at the bank of it, as though in haste to cross the narrow road. Then chance gave her what she could not have contrived; for the bank to the road was steep, and her horse stumbled and reared. Margery left her saddle altogether; she went clear over the horse's head and thudded into the bank beyond the road.

Fortune was with her, or her young life might have ended

there. The October wind had piled the dead leaves thick against the bank, and their soft cushion eased her fall. It broke no bones but it knocked the wind out of her, so that she writhed and twisted, fighting wildly for breath in a long-drawn noisy whooping.

There were sudden voices and a clatter of hooves; and as she blinked and gasped, her shoulders were seized from nowhere and pressed to the ground. Hands took her wrists, and her arms were pulled up and out and down, and then her wrists were driven hard into her stomach. It was drastic, it was primitive, and it was painful. But it was effective; it forced the rest of the wind out of her and let her breathing begin afresh; she sweated and panted, but she knew it was passing.

Through moist and blinking eyes she became aware of a blue sky and a cloud that floated in it; and beside the cloud, and seeming to float with it, was a collar of gold-laced green; and above the collar was a brown and sun-tanned face that had laughing eyes and a cheerful grin. Margery saw the picture slowly, as memory and understanding returned.

Then she remembered her purpose, and at once she was contriving further. She took to blinking again, and she added a few gasps for better effect while the thought crossed her mind that this gentleman in green looked a very proper gentleman. Then she took to rolling, as though in pain, and as she rolled to the side she took a quick glimpse of the road; a few paces away, one of the servants, his eyes fast on her, sat a horse and held two others; beyond him was his fellow-servant, calming Margery's horse which he had evidently chased and caught.

'You're not hurt. Stop grunting and get up.'

Margery gasped again, and this time it was genuine. She had not expected that. Sympathy, she thought, would have been more proper. But that must wait; there were other things more urgent, and the first of them was to see along the road to the other side. So she ignored his words and began to heave about again.

'Pray tell me: are you afflicted of St. Vitus?'

The voice came again, and Margery was suddenly still. This gentleman seemed to know too much. And did she detect amusement in his airy voice? She felt herself colour, and to conceal that she rolled right over; and very calmly and deliberately, the gentleman prodded her with the handle of his whip.

She was on her feet, spluttering with indignation, before she had thought at all. And as this gentleman stood in front of her, placidly shaking out his cloak, his brown face was alive with laughter.

Then Margery remembered. Careless now, she looked openly around her, and relief flooded over her. Far from the road, a good quarter-mile down the little stream, Christopher Southworth was at full gallop towards a belt of trees and tangled scrub.

'Lord of Hell!'

The gentleman took his horse at a leap, and with one darted glance at Margery he was away, his two servants scampering wildly after him. Margery shook herself and began to smooth her cloak. Then her eyes strayed again to the belt of scrub, and suddenly she laughed with relief; if Christopher Southworth let himself be caught in that tangle and with that start, it would be his own fault. But she was thoughtful as she picked her hat from the wet leaves and walked stiffly towards her grazing horse; it had occurred to her that the sooner Roger knew of all this, the better.

Yet her mind was not wholly on that as she rode home; from somewhere the thought intruded that she would like to know more of this gentleman in green.

20

The Gentleman from Lathom

Roger was flattering, for his first thought was for Margery. Not till he was assured that she had taken no hurt would he let her finish her tale, and even then he came back to it, seeking to know how she had fallen and how her breathing had so forcibly been put to rights. He heard her in detail, and then he nodded.

'The fellow has some understanding of things,' was his sage comment.

Margery suppressed the retort that the fellow seemed to have too much understanding of some things. Instead, she went on to say that Christopher Southworth must surely have got clear.

'Not a doubt of it,' said Roger. 'He'll know the ground, which these Lathom men will not. And as for you—if you had your deserts you'd be sent to Lathom in his stead.'

'Why?'

'You're the slyest fox in Pendle, as I've for some time been supposing. It was chance, was it, that brought you blundering on the Seminary and his guard?'

Margery reddened. She had said nothing about motives, but Roger was another who sometimes knew too much. And then she saw his forehead crinkle.

'It's well that we can see eye to eye,' he was saying. 'All being said, it was craftily done, and I've liking enough for the Seminary to have no wish to see him gutted.' He looked her over with his eyebrows lifting in the familiar style. 'Impudence in petticoats is what I'd call you, little cousin.'

Margery began to feel at ease. This was something she knew how to deal with, and her face took on solemnity.

'You call me sly, sir? And impudent? Pray, sir, whence should I have gleaned such qualities?'

'Our sainted great-uncle might have told you. He told me often enough. Now of this man from Lathom—a gentleman, you say?'

'By looks and speech, certainly.'

'Some description of him?'

Margery gave her mind to that, and then spoke slowly.

'He's of a good stature, and something broad of shoulder. He holds erect, and his face is lean and brown. His hair of the same, and his eyes hazel. His nose a little out of shape, and when he smiles his teeth shine very white.'

'His age?'

'Young. Twenty perhaps, or a little more.'

'And his dress?'

'Murrey serge, with a cloak of green—likewise trimmed orange, as his beaver is too.'

Roger nodded.

'He seems to have had your best attention.'

She caught his dry tone, and she pouted at him as she saw his meaning; and all she got for that was an impish grin from a cousin who could be as sly as herself.

'I don't recall the fellow,' he said. 'Let us hope his memory does not match yours.'

He strolled to the window and stood with thumbs in girdle looking idly out at the darkening sky.

'Did the fellow ride a chestnut?' he asked suddenly. 'With a white blaze on the head?'

'Just that.' Margery was surprised. 'But do you know the beast, sir?'

She got no answer, but his steady gaze through the glass served instead, and Margery went running to his side to gape at what she saw. Coming quietly over the gravel were three horsemen, two servants and a gentleman in green.

'God's Grace!' said Margery, and Roger hooted with laughter at her.

'He comes most happily,' he said, 'and now we'll hear his tale. *We*, I said,' he added as Margery made for the door. 'You may stay by me and hear it too.'

'Not like this?'

'What vexes you?'

'Look at me!'

Her anguished tone set him laughing again. She had gone to him as soon as she had entered the house, and she was still as she had been—muddy and wet, her clothes spattered and her hair awry. She took a quick glance in the hanging mirror and was horrified. But before she could protest again, Tom Peyton was in to announce that Master Francis Hilliard desired speech with Master Nowell.

'In here,' said Roger briefly, and Tom disappeared. Margery shot a despairing glance at Roger and got another grin for her pains.

'The price of impudence,' he whispered cheerfully.

Then, before she could answer that, the latch had clicked again, and the Earl of Derby's gentleman was bowing in the doorway.

'Master Nowell, sir?'

'The same, sir.'

'And a Justice of the Peace, sir?'

'I have that honour.'

'It's my cause for intruding, sir. I serve the Earl of Derby and have need of help.'

'Which you shall surely have. However'—Roger's formal tone eased—'you've some dust from the road, and a glass of wine may help you state your need. Come from the door, sir, and feel the fire. Master Hilliard, is it?'

'Francis Hilliard, at your service, sir.'

He slipped easily into a smile as he came forward, and Margery, who had pressed into the shadows in the corner, watched approvingly. It was her first leisured view of him, and she noted now his easy carriage and firm step, the hint of humour and vitality in his face. Her first impression, she thought, had been correct. Master Hilliard had much to commend him. And when Roger spoke again her keen ears detected a shade of warmth in his tone, as if he too approved.

'Give me leave, sir,' he said, 'to present you to my most cherished cousin, Mistress Margery Whitaker.'

That was handsomely said, and Margery had a quick glow of pleasure at it. She stepped from the shadows, and her first glance was for Roger.

'That's gracious, sir,' she told him. 'I trust I'm worth the cherishing?'

'You trust it: I believe it,' said Roger gallantly.

Margery turned happily to Master Hilliard. She had forgotten for the moment her dusty disarray, and there was colour in her cheeks and a sparkle in her eye as she faced him in the firelight.

'Your servant, sir,' she said formally; but she winged the words with a smile born of pleasure and excitement.

'Madam!'

Master Hilliard got no further than that. She saw his eyes widen and his jaw stiffen, and she guessed that he had not recognised her, had perhaps not even seen her, till she came from the shadows. Now she came quickly to his help.

'I'm in your debt, sir, for service rendered this day. I thank you.'

'And I also.' This was Roger in quick support of her. 'My cousin, sir, has told me of her fall, and I suppose it to be you who brought her to her feet. My thanks go with hers.'

'Aye, sir. I brought her to her feet.'

Master Hilliard's quick glance at Margery told her that he remembered also how he had brought her to her feet. 'I trust, madam, that you came to no hurt?'

She saw the mischief in his eyes, and she chose to take it as a challenge.

'None that distresses me, sir. Yet I've something to repay when a time shall serve.'

He nodded as though he accepted that. Then his tone became more serious.

'I fear I used you but roughly, madam. And certainly I deserted you in haste and with exceeding ill manners. I must plead a pressing urgency.'

'I guessed it, sir. Pray make no apology for that.'

'You're gracious.' He turned briskly to Roger. 'It's this, sir, that sets me in need of your help.'

'I'll not hear of it till you've sunk your wine.' There was a firm friendliness in Roger's voice now. 'Pray be seated, sir.'

Master Hilliard obeyed with his eyes on Margery, and it was she who poured his wine and carried it to him. She kept her hand on the glass as he took it, and for a moment she stood gravely at his side.

'You'll perceive from this,' she told him, 'that I do not hold resentments.'

Their eyes met and she saw relief in his. Then she stepped

back and was in haste to carry Roger's wine. He took it courteously, and she had in return a smile that pleased her, and a glance of sardonic amusement which did not disconcert her. She was coming to know her Roger.

She lit the candles herself, for she was not minded to summon servants. Then she gave ear to Master Hilliard's tale, and she and Roger listened gravely while he related what they could not well admit to knowing already. Margery's distressing accident, he said, had so engrossed his own and his servants' attention that the sly papist had seized his moment and made off; only on that account, said Master Hilliard, had he departed so abruptly and discourteously.

He turned aside from his tale to ask forgiveness for that. Apparently he was reassured, for he was soon at his tale again. He had ridden hard, he said, in pursuit of the rogue but had not so much as set eyes on him; and soon it had been plain that in such a country he would need local help if search were to succeed; he had therefore stopped at the first house he had come to, and had there inquired for the next Justice.

'Which, sir,' he ended, 'is how I come to be here. And you'll no doubt perceive what help it is I ask. This Southworth is a State prisoner, and of some importance.'

Roger did not answer directly. He walked thoughtfully to the window, where the light had almost gone and the glass was showing more of the room's reflection than of the darkening sky beyond. For a moment he stood in thought, peering through the glass; then he swept the curtains across and turned to the room again.

'If you could find nothing of him by day,' he said, 'we'd surely find as little by night. It must stay till morning. Meanwhile, sir, you are our guest. I'll have your horses put up and your servants seen to. For your own comfort, my cousin here shall take order.'

Margery was on her feet at once in high approval of this. Nor did Master Hilliard say it nay, and in a very few minutes he had been conducted to a bedchamber while his own servants ran busily to open his bags and see to his comforts. Margery assured herself that all was in hand, and then began to think of her own needs. In the talk she had contrived to forget her untidiness, and the returning thought of it appalled her. She almost ran to the stair, and she was three steps up when Roger detained her. She turned, and stood looking down on him as he came to the foot of the stair.

'A pretty case we're in,' he remarked pleasantly, and she knew the sardonic mood had him. 'It has its dangers. Two things I count fortunate.'

'You relieve me, sir.' Her expression was matching his. 'These things being?'

'The one, that you seem in some manner to have acquired this young man's goodwill. The other . . .'

'I'm all attention, sir . . .'

'Is a certain talent for deception that seems natural in you.'

She nodded, and her retort came crisply.

'It derives, no doubt, from our sainted great-uncle.'

She stayed for no more, but ran lightly up the stair. His delighted chuckle followed her.

She came to her bedchamber, looked at her reflection in the mirror, and shuddered; and thereafter she was at more than usual pains with her tiring. It was deplorable that this should have come upon her when the kirtle of flame-tint satin was but half made, but there was no help for that; she must do what she could with the black saye, and she did it with zest and care. It was, she told herself, not too bad; and if she herself had seen it too often, at least Master Hilliard had not. And there was some silver lace that graced it now, and some more on the sarcenet gown. Master Hilliard, perhaps, might have seen worse.

Apparently he had. Margery was down the stair the last of the three, and there was Roger brave in his wine-red velvet, languid in the glow from the fire; and there at his side was Master Hilliard, elegant now in scarlet velvet, laced with gold and slashed with yellow satin which matched the vivid starch in his slim collar. No country fellow, this Master Hilliard, and not a man to travel with half-filled bags; that was as Margery had foreseen.

She was not, it seemed, as he had foreseen. He turned politely as she entered; and then he checked and stood rigid, his eyes fast on her as she stood silent in the doorway.

'You keep your eyes upon me, sir?'

Her tone made it a question, and she thought to have

him in confusion with it. But he had more composure than she had guessed, and he turned it deftly.

'Madam—if this were the Great Hall at Lathom, and there were three score of us within, I do assure you they'd all have eyes upon you. Madam, my compliments!'

It was bravely said, and Margery was excited as she sought a quick answer.

'I find a courtier, sir . . .' It was the best she could devise. 'I had not expected it, in Pendle. Sir, I return your compliments.'

He was quick to bow, and at once she took the chance of that and showed him the elegance of her curtsey. She stayed in it, knowing it to become her, and her sparkling eyes met his. From the fireside, Roger raised his glass.

'You make pretty play,' he said. 'I'd add my own compliments if I thought they were wanted.'

They turned to him at once, both on the edge of speech. Each checked to give way to the other, and it was Roger himself who had the first word.

'Enough,' he said. 'Just now there's a greater need. Let's to supper!'

It was a happy meal, even though the talk languished. They were hungry enough for that, and it did nothing to spoil their harmony; and afterwards, when they were settled at ease in the parlour, the bright fire brought content and the wine lured them into talk. Master Hilliard showed an engaging interest. He wanted to know more of Margery, who she was, what things pleased her, and how she spent her days. She let him have the answers, for she was at least as curious about him, and she supposed that what she gave she might expect to have returned. So, while Roger sat in watchful silence, there was question and answer, thrust and parry, probe and evasion; and from the sum of it, Margery gleaned what she sought.

This Master Hilliard, she learned, was from Warwickshire, where his father was a gentleman of some substance. There was, however, an elder brother who would inherit the estate, so that this Francis had his way to make in the world. On his mother's side he was kin to the Listers of Westby, and when he had had an invitation to visit them he had at once accepted it. He had spent last Christmas at Westby, and had found liking enough for the North Parts to tempt him to leave Warwickshire; he had found also the opportunity to do so, and he had seized it with the promptness that becomes a younger son. For while he was at Westby, hospitality for a night was sought by a gentleman returning to Lancaster, a Master Covell . . .

'Covell?' Roger cut sharply into the talk at that. 'Tom Covell, would it be? Or Edmund?'

'Why sir, I did hear him called Tom. I know nothing of an Edmund.'

Roger laughed.

'You will, when you've cause to lodge at Lancaster. Know you Tom Covell's work?'

'I understood him to be Governor of the Castle there.'

'God's Grace, man!' Roger laughed uproariously. 'That's Tom Covell to the last inch. He'd laugh himself to jelly if he heard it.'

Master Hilliard began to look grave.

'Do I learn, sir, that I have been cozened?'

'Not so much as that, and there's no cause for heat. Tom Covell's the County's jester. Besides, there's colour in that tale. Lancaster Castle has the gaol in it, and Tom governs that. Not precisely the Castle, you understand, but the Castle gaol. The old rogue!'

'Rogue, sir?'

Again Roger laughed.

'Take not that to heart either, for I've salted what I've said. Tom Covell's of the best, and he orders that gaol as none has ever done before him. He's rogue only when it comes to costs. He must be waxing fat, he and his precious brother Edmund. Edmund is host of the *George* and Tom sends him his custom. And when Master Sheriff has to feed the judges and their crew at the Assizes, Tom will see to it —with Edmund's help and at a price! Rogue, did I say? I was Sheriff of this County last year, and Tom Covell had some eighty pounds from me for it.'

'Eighty pounds?' Margery sounded appalled. 'Eighty pounds, sir? And for what, if you please?'

'Meat for lawyers and hay for horses. Or would it be the other way? But we're losing this tale. Tom Covell was at Westby, you say?'

'Aye, sir. At Christmas.' Master Hilliard took up his tale again. He had liked Master Covell. They had all liked

Master Covell, and he had been pressed to lengthen his stay. One consequence of that had been a letter in his own hand, commending Master Francis Hilliard to the Earl of Derby as a gentleman worthy of employment. Master Hilliard, scenting advancement in this, had forthwith hastened to Lathom and presented the letter; and His Lordship had read it with respect.

'He would,' said Roger. 'Covell's no fool. And he's of some weight in the County. Besides the gaol, he's a Coroner and a Justice of both Peace and Quorum. A letter from him would be heeded by any man. And what followed?'

What followed had been the appointment of Master Hilliard as a Gentleman of His Lordship's Household, and it had been in that capacity that he had been sent to Marton to escort the papist Southworth.

'Whom you seem to have lost,' said Roger dryly. 'I doubt if it will please milord.'

But Master Hilliard was not perturbed.

'That's as may be,' he answered easily. 'There was naught else I could have done.'

But Roger remained dry.

'Which is to say,' he commented, 'that you found more interest in Margery here than in your Seminary.'

'Am I then in fault for that?'

'I did not say you were. But then I know Margery and milord does not. He might see it differently.'

'His Lordship must surely . . .'

'Must does not apply to His Lordship. I'm not unfriendly in this, but I advise you to show some zeal. Precisely what help did you suppose I could give?'

'I had thought, sir, that you were best placed to order search and inquiry. I do not know this Pendle.'

'Who does? But as to search, that's to waste time if you mean by it no more than to ride at large and hope to sight the fellow. Inquiry I'll put in train. It's best done in shadow. As for knowing Pendle . . .'

Roger paused, a half smile on his lips.

'That shall be Margery's work. She has, in some fashion, brought this upon you and she shall help to mend it. She may conduct you in Pendle.'

That had Master Hilliard's prompt approval. He thanked Roger heartily and then came promptly to what seemed to interest him most. Would Mistress Whitaker be pleased to ride with him on the morrow and show him something of this Pendle?

But Margery did not answer precisely as he might have wished. She had, indeed, no intention of not riding with him on the morrow, and whether Roger had ordered it as retribution or out of tact, she neither knew nor cared. Either way, it suited her excellently. But this Master Hilliard, she thought, seemed a shade sure of himself; and something might be risked here. Her voice expressed nothing as she answered.

'Certainly I shall ride with you,' she told him calmly. 'My cousin has ordered it, and I shall show him obedience.'

That left Master Hilliard guessing. She read as much in his eyes and was well content. And the morrow, she thought, might look to itself. She turned the talk to other things.

Yet it was Roger who had the last word, as she might have foreseen. He took her, as he often did at bedtime, to the foot of the stair, and lit her candle.

'When you marry,' he told her cheerfully, 'I'll approve no husband who has not a stout arm. He'll need it if he's to keep you in a decent order. Meantime, you're well placed in Pendle.'

She was all innocence as she looked down on him.

'Why in Pendle, sir?'

'You weave enchantments. God keep you!'

21

The Scent of Evil

Nothing in Pendle, Margery told herself, ever went as it should. There seemed indeed to be a curse on the place.

She pouted through the window, and her whip slapped angrily against her boot. For here was a cool November morning, grey and windless, with a pale sun and the mist still hanging by the trees—a morning made in Heaven for those who would go a-riding. And here at her side was Master Hilliard, booted and spurred, and cloaked in green and gold. And there were the horses, pawing impatiently at the gravel. And there, beyond the horses, riding towards the house over that same gravel, was Miles Nutter. He could hardly have timed it worse.

She was bound to receive him, and he came briskly into the house. Then he saw Master Hilliard and checked abruptly.

'I'm sorry,' he said politely. 'Perhaps I intrude?'

Margery had to echo his politeness.

'You do not intrude, Miles. We have a guest in the house. That's all.'

She presented Master Hilliard, and formal bows were exchanged. Then Miles turned to her again.

'I hate to seem discourteous, Margery, but I've messages for you, if you please.'

Margery nodded. She and Miles were on easy terms by now.

'From Grace, I hope.' She turned to Master Hilliard. 'You'll give me leave?'

'Most certainly. I'll look the horses over. They're scraping the gravel.'

He went out with an easy nod to Miles, and Margery stared thoughtfully at his retreating back. She was considering that she might need her wits in dealing with a man who could so quickly give so deft an answer. It was wholly courteous, but it had a nice reminder that she was engaged to ride with him and had best not delay too long.

Miles said his say quickly enough once he had her alone. It was an urgent and unwelcome request that she should at last make her promised visit to the Rough Lee. His mother, he explained, had been daily expecting it, and was now asking difficult questions about his daily doings. And Grace, he added, was becoming anxious and unhappy about it. Margery hesitated. She did not like Alice Nutter and she did not want to visit the Rough Lee. On the other hand she did want to help Grace, and to appear at the Rough Lee on easy terms with Miles might make affairs flow smoother for him and Grace. Which, as far as it went, was well enough. But to appear on easy terms with Miles, whether at the Rough Lee or anywhere else, would not help her with Master Hilliard. Or—would it? She pursed her lips as she considered that. Master Hilliard did seem a shade sure of himself—and of her. Barely perceptibly, Margery nodded. Then she turned to Miles.

'You shall have your way, Miles,' she told him. 'But we shall have to ask this Master Hilliard to ride with us. He's my cousin's guest, and it's laid on me to show him something of the Forest.'

'Willingly,' said Miles, who would obviously have assented to much more than that to get Margery to the Rough Lee. 'It's good of you, and it will please Grace as much as me.'

They went out to the gravel, and while Miles sought his horse Master Hilliard helped Margery to mount. She had a quick word with him then.

'It's very fortunate,' she said. 'This Master Nutter comes nicely to the moment, and he may be useful. His home is far up the Forest, near to where your priest escaped, and the folk there are more likely than others to have heard whatever's whispered. So I've grasped at opportunity and said we'll ride so far with him. That's to your taste, I hope?'

'I'm guided by you,' he answered, and she thought his tone lacked warmth. 'Where is this house?'

She let Miles answer that, and he did so cheerfully. Master Hilliard, who evidently did not mean to be outshone, roused himself to talk; and Margery, riding between the two men, had the best of both of them. They went up the Forest in a merry chatter of tongues, and if Miles Nutter was pleased when they got to the Rough Lee, he was probably alone in that.

Alice Nutter received them graciously. She had, as Margery well perceived, a trick of being dressed to the last detail in whatever would colour the picture that she offered. This morning she was the housewife, the mistress of the Rough Lee; busy to be sure, but not too busy to give time and gracious welcome to her guests; and her kirtle of corded black taffeta with the white lace cap and collar supported this perfectly. She received them at the door. She had an affectionate smile for her son, a friendly one for Margery, a gracious one for Master Hilliard. She led them to her parlour, erect and dignified; and as a last telling detail, keys jingled from her girdle of silver chain. It was perfectly done, and nothing of it was lost on Margery. She saw every point, and her eyes opened a little in admiration; no bungler, this assured and observant lady.

'I give you welcome of the warmest,' was her greeting to Margery. 'I've heard a deal about you from Miles, and I've been asking when we should have this honour.'

'Miles has been my good friend, madam. I'm much in his debt. I'm still learning this Pendle Forest, and Miles has been the best of guides.'

'I'm glad you say it. Truly, he does know it well—as indeed he should.' She turned lightly to Master Hilliard. 'Pray, sir, do you stay in Pendle long? If so, we shall hope for your better acquaintance.'

It seemed no more than a proper courtesy, but Margery, sitting wary and alert, thought she detected more than that. Was this perhaps what Mistress Nutter was most concerned to know? If she had indeed designs on Margery for Miles, she might well be concerned about the length of Master Hilliard's stay.

And Master Hilliard, knowing nothing of these Pendle undercurrents, made the worst of answers.

'In truth, madam, I know not. And I must give apology for our intrusion.' Clearly, he was concerned to be polite.

'May I plead urgency, madam? For indeed we should not have intruded upon you had there not been pressing cause.'

Very faintly, like a snake in the dry grass, the taffeta rustled. Mistress Nutter sat a shade more erect.

'Indeed, sir? Pray acquaint me then with the purpose of this visit.'

Master Hilliard wanted no more invitation. He plunged forthwith into the tale of his papist, and Mistress Nutter gave him attentive ear while Margery sat aghast, angry with herself as a fool for not foreseeing this. This visit had been intended to placate Mistress Nutter, who was now being told that it had been made only because it appeared that she might be useful. Margery pressed her lips and waited stiffly.

But Mistress Nutter did not lose her poise. She heard him to the end, and then sat as if in thought.

'I've not heard of a priest at large,' she said at length, 'but I'll make inquiry into that, and have my husband do the like. Between us, we may hear some whisper, and if we do you may be assured you shall hear of it at once. We are loyal folk in this house, sir, and we'll gladly give proof of it.'

Then the door opened and a serving maid was in with the ale and cheese-cakes that were usual, and with an apple tart that was not so usual. Mistress Nutter bestirred herself and saw to her guests' comforts. She did it graciously; she had a proper smile and she chatted lightly; she was quick to bring them all into the talk, and her guests responded accordingly. Margery bit into her apple tart and found it to be all that Margaret Crook had said it would be. Then she roused herself and took her part in the talk, and she did it with a vivacity that brought admiring glances from both the men. Master Hilliard said some proper things; Miles chattered easily, and his mother was benign and dignified in the centre; all the requirements were satisfied. But Margery was not at ease. Alice Nutter had been angered, not placated; all that was uncertain was whether her anger was directed more against Margery or more against this Master Hilliard who had her company. For all this woman's seeming benevolence, there was one thing she could not conceal from senses as keen as Margery's; the power that lay in her was pouring from her now, wave after hostile wave of it. She sat by her table, placid, composed and smiling, with the power flooding from her. Miles had a watchful eye on her; Master Hilliard glanced more and more at her, till he was almost staring; and Margery felt a known and hideous chill begin to touch her back. Her talk faltered and failed, and her fingers pressed sharply into her palms as she strove to stay calm.

It was Master Hilliard who broke the party. He came suddenly to his feet and announced abruptly that he must be on his way. He had much to see before dusk, he said, and Mistress Whitaker had promised to conduct him; and he said it with a glance at her so direct that its meaning could not be lost. It was not tactful; it was scarcely even courteous; but nobody showed resentment. Miles looked positively relieved; his mother kept her poise unshaken and let nothing of her thoughts be seen; and Margery, who at another time might have disputed this assumption that she was his to command, now swallowed it meekly. She would have swallowed much more than that, she told herself, to get out of this house.

There were polite leavetakings, and again the proper things were said. Nothing escaped that could make a ripple on the placid surface. But Margery, saying her polite farewell, met Mistress Nutter's eyes, and found in their black deeps a gleam that froze her. She was trembling as she got to her horse, and once they were clear of the house Master Hilliard had to bestir himself to keep pace with her.

Miles had made no offer to come with them, and they were riding alone. Margery had led up the steep lane, away from the road and towards the high ridge that ran behind the pasture; something in her was clamouring for its cool heights, and she kept the pace with hardly a thought for her companion till he ranged alongside her.

'Is it your wish to kill the horses?' he asked bluntly.

That brought her eyes to his, and suddenly the tension broke. His brown face was easing into a smile that was sane and cool and friendly, and Margery relaxed. She pulled her horse to a halt and smiled back at him. It was a smile of relief; but the relief was overwhelming, and she felt a dimple in her cheek and a crinkle in her forehead as the smile spread. Master Hilliard was a bare yard away, and he had the full effect of it.

'I'm sorry for that,' he said quickly. 'The truth of it is . . .'

He hesitated. 'I'm sorry if Mistress Nutter is your friend, but the truth is . . .'

Again he stopped and it was Margery who ended his sentence for him.

'The truth is,' she said, 'that you were mighty ill at ease with her.'

'I was indeed! I've not felt the like before with any woman—or man. And you, madam, were you at ease?'

'No,' she answered simply, 'I was not.'

They ambled on in silence till Margery suddenly drew rein again. It had occurred to her that this climbing lane must soon bring her to the sight of that coppice where tall plants grew; and this day she did not wish to see that coppice and have thought of what it hid. She turned abruptly from the lane and made off along the wooded ridge; without protest, he followed.

'I was most ill at ease,' she told him suddenly. 'And not for the first time. It's ever so with Alice Nutter.'

'I'll believe you,' he said fervently. And again there was silence as the horses picked an unhurried way. Master Hilliard was looking at her thoughtfully.

'Yet Master Miles,' he said suddenly, 'seemed a very tolerable fellow. Do you find him so?'

Margery's mind became alert. She had the thought that this was less casual than it seemed; he was, perhaps, probing, and she was quick to assure him.

'I find him likeable,' she said. Then she pointed up the hill towards Wheathead. 'There's a girl yonder who's my good friend and finds him more than likeable.'

'Ah!' He seemed relieved. 'And he returns that good sentiment?'

'Yes. Though that's a confidence.'

'A safe one, I assure you, madam. He's perhaps to be envied.'

'In that, yes. But to live with such a mother? I've no envy for that.'

'Nor I.' He hesitated again. 'Yet one thing more I could envy him.'

'Which is?'

'His easy speech with you, where I must be formal—as you perceive, madam.'

Margery laughed openly. She was in friendly humour with him now.

'You may have the like privilege if you wish it,' she told him. 'I hereby absolve you from all formality.'

His face took on a broad grin.

'Margery, the day improves. Now, whither do we ride?'

She laughed at him again, and then she paused to consider. They had ridden most of the length of the ridge, and before them a stream crossed their track. She saw it first with surprise and then with amusement, and her face was crinkling as she turned from the path and led down the stream.

'What's to do?' he asked as he saw her amusement.

'This stream,' she answered. 'It's the one I was riding down yesterday when I first set eyes on you.'

'When you spilled from your horse—by that knoll yonder?'

'Just that.'

'My thanks for being told. Permit me, if you please.'

He passed in front of her and then pulled his horse back to a safe walk as they came to the knoll. Margery, behind him, had to match her speed to his.

'You'll be safer if I lead you,' he assured her heartily.

That was plain enough, but Margery preferred to be slow of understanding.

'Meaning what, if you please?'

'Meaning that you all but broke your silly neck yesterday, and I'm not minded to have you succeed this day.'

Margery's eyes opened a little. He was certainly dropping the formalities, and she was disposed to test this further.

'So you impose caution by constraining me?'

His answer came quickly. 'If you journey with me there'll be moments when you'll conform.'

Her eyes opened wider as she went slowly past the knoll, staring thoughtfully at the orange-plumed hat that jogged in front of her; and when they were come safely into the road she stopped, and sat considering him.

'How did you say you were named?' she asked.

'Francis.' His tone told her he was at a guess.

'Francis, is it? Is that what your mother calls you?'

'My mother? No—she shortens it and calls me Frank.'

'She does well.'

He stared blankly at her till understanding broke upon him. Then his smile came, and it broadened happily.

'A hit!' he said easily. 'A very true and proper hit! I won't tell you what I think of you for it.'

'Why not?'

'It might make you vain.'

It was her turn to smile when understanding came.

'Make me vain, do you say? My brothers, I fear, would account that superfluous labour. But if you've sisters, I'd like to hear them talk.'

His smile returned and she waited happily for his answer. But it never came; behind them a twig snapped loudly, and his answer was lost as they both turned. Standing on the grass verge, a bare five paces away, and certainly within hearing distance, was Anne Redfern of the shapely face and the shifty eyes.

Margery stiffened as she looked. She had not set eyes on Anne Redfern since that Sunday at the Newchurch when Roger had so quickly quelled the quarrel. She remembered that incident now, and she had the feeling that Anne Redfern was remembering it, too. The woman's eyes were vicious as she looked from Margery to the man who sat his horse so near to her. The thin mouth twisted to an open leer as she moved backwards to the ditch and hedge behind her; there she paused, and of a sudden she loosed a laugh that was an insult—a laugh blatant with obscene suggestion.

Then she was through the hedge and away, and Margery caught Frank Hilliard's arm as he was dismounting to pursue.

'Let be!' she said urgently. 'For pity's sake, let be!'

'After that?'

'Aye, after that. She's not worth your arm. And we've hatreds enough already, here in Pendle.'

He assented—unwillingly and with a grumble, but he assented. They went deviously home. But Margery had no warmth from the pale sun and no pleasure from their talk. The woman's malice had been too plain, and Margery remembered unhappily that this Redfern had been wife to a servant whose master had died at Chester one fateful Candlemas. Now the woman dwelt on the Nutter land, for which she surely gave obedience to the Rough Lee. Margery remembered again the dark eyes that had gleamed so coldly in that house not an hour ago; and remembering them, she felt a sudden dread. Soon and somehow she might expect the mud to stir in these Pendle undercurrents, and when it stirred it would surely disturb what seemed a present happiness. Happiness, she now thought, was a quality that did not flourish in the lee of Pendle Hill.

She had not long to wait. There were two cool November days in which all was peace, days in which Margery rode with Frank Hilliard and made pretence of searching for a papist priest. She saw to it, indeed, that he did not ride to a grey house in Goldshaw, nor to any other place where a priest might be thought to lurk; but apart from that she was content to ride at large with him, chattering about everything and coming to grips about nothing. On the second day she rode with him to Wheathead and presented him to Grace; and when they were home again, and before even they were out of their riding-clothes, a horseman rode in, haggard and dusty. He bore the Derby colours, and he carried a written order from the Earl that Master Francis Hilliard was to return forthwith to Lathom—no delay permitted. It gave no reason and it showed no courtesy.

He broke the seal and read; then, without speaking, he showed it to Margery, and as soon as she had read she was apprehensive. The thing, she thought, was redolent of trouble, and her conscience was uneasy as she thought of a priest escaped, and the part she had played in that.

Roger was lazing in his parlour when they burst in on him and thrust the paper beneath his nose. He read it in silence, and then he handed it back.

'You ride at dawn,' he said.

'Dawn?' Margery was aghast.

'Dawn, I said. That's meant to be obeyed.'

'Aye, sir.' This was Frank Hilliard, and there was a note of resentment in his voice. 'But do you mark the tone of it? Why that? It's not His Lordship's way.'

'It's his way when he's angered. You'd best obey orders.'

'Aye, sir. But—what's so angered him?'

'That's to be learned at Lathom. But the order's plain that you're to ride forthwith—which does not mean at your leisure.' The half smile was on Roger as he scanned the rueful faces before him. 'Other things apart,' he added quietly, 'to obey orders is commonly the path of wisdom.'

22

The Dark House of Nutter

Frank Hilliard obeyed orders. He breakfasted by candles and rode at first light. Margery hauled herself out of bed and came sleepily down the stair to see him off; she detested dressing in the dark, but this time she felt she could do no less; there was something on her conscience here.

Mist hung over the gravel as he mounted, and Margery stood shivering in the cold grey light, her gown pulled tightly round her.

'I want to know what befalls,' she told him.

'You shall,' he assured her. 'Whatever it is, you shall know. Meantime, have some care for yourself. I've no wish to hear of you with a broken neck.'

At another time there would have been a retort to that, but now, in this sleepy hour, her mind felt numbed; and she was still standing by his stirrup, looking up at him, when Roger walked quietly out of the door. He surprised them both, for neither had guessed that he was astir.

'Just one word,' he said. 'When you've leisure and can leave Lathom, you make yourself our guest again, if it so please you.'

'It pleases me mightily.' Frank Hilliard was prompt in his answer. But then he seemed to have a second thought, and he looked almost doubtingly at Margery. 'That is,' he went on, 'if Margery's of that mind too?'

'I've no mind but my cousin's,' said Margery, trying to blend manners with equivocation, and he laughed.

'That suffices,' he said. 'I'm your promised guest then.'

'It's something past dawn,' said Roger quietly.

'Aye, sir. Then I'll be off. God keep you—both!'

He went boisterously away, his two servants clattering

behind him. Margery watched them go, and then she walked slowly to the door, and for all her bickerings with him she felt cold and lonely now that he had gone. Roger stood in silence on the gravel, and she turned to him impulsively. She had just realised that he had roused and dressed in the dawn to give that invitation and that he had done it for her sake. Whether she wanted it given or not she had a very warm feeling for this thoughtful cousin.

'In with you,' he said suddenly. 'It's cold out here.' He slipped his arm round her and urged her through the doorway. Then he paused to look her over.

'You're early from bed,' he told her.

Margery spun round, wide awake and alert for anything. She knew that tone of old, and she wondered what sly thrust was coming. But he had no more to say. He merely passed his fingers lightly over her hair—and something rustled. Margery gasped with annoyance as she clapped her hand on a stray curling-paper she had overlooked and left in.

'Lord of Hell!' she said, echoing the words of the man her thoughts had flown to. Then she looked ruefully at Roger, caught his grin, and gave herself to reluctant laughter.

'Now go furbish yourself,' he told her. 'It's cold for empty stomachs, and we'll be better for breakfast.'

She took her time at it, and when she at last came down Roger was ending his breakfast. By the time she had ended hers a red sun was lifting over the leafless trees, and Roger walked to the window to watch the thinning mist.

'It improves,' he said. 'I think we'll go a-riding.'

'As you will.' Margery thought she might as well ride as mope. 'And whither?'

'Goldshaw.' Roger spoke decisively. 'We'll call on Harry Hargreaves.'

'The Constable?'

'Why not? It's time he was asked for news of a Massing priest. He was told to inquire.'

'Oh!' Margery was nervous of this. 'Do you think he'll have news?'

'Since he's a papist I'm quite sure he won't. So a zealous magistrate may safely ask him.'

Margery was amused. She had a continuing interest in Roger's subtleties.

'Then why be at such trouble?'

'It proves my zeal. And a visit to Hargreaves will make it natural for us to pay respects to his neighbour.'

Margery stared blankly. She was beginning to understand why some were not at ease with Roger Nowell.

'Tony Nutter?' she asked at length.

'*You* may chat with him. My own trust is in his sister.'

That made it no clearer, but she had to be content with it. Getting information from Roger when he did not mean to give it was not a hopeful undertaking, as she well knew. Margery gave it up and went off to make ready.

The interview with Hargreaves went as Roger had foretold. The Constable was apologetic. He had made all possible inquiry and had learned nothing; he was very sorry, but it was not to be mended. All of which drew no more than a nonchalant nod from Roger. He thanked the zealous Constable, drained his mug of October, and took a friendly leave.

The next short journey was quickly made, and soon the old servitor was leading away their horses while Tony Nutter greeted them heartily.

'You're guests we've wanted,' he said. 'Come within.'

'You're cordial this day, Tony. You're sure we're no burden?'

'Very sure. You're never a burden, either of you.'

'Never?' Margery saw Roger's forehead crinkle as he spoke. 'That should mean you've never guests I shouldn't meet. However . . .'

They went into the little parlour, cosy with a fire on this grey morning, and then Tony had a word for Margery.

'You of all,' he told her, 'will never be a burden here. Be sure of that. We've been hearing lately of your doings.'

'You're gracious, sir.'

Margery was being cautious. She had the thought that something of this warmth had to do with an escaping priest, and if that were so she might do well to pick her words with care. Apparently Roger thought the same, and he went at it boldly. 'Here's fine talk, Tony! First you accuse her of a treason, and then you all but thank her for it. Let be, man!'

'As you will.' Tony Nutter was unabashed. 'I did but strive to be plain.'

Then Mistress Crook came bustling in, and she left them

in no doubt of her feelings. She was profuse in her hospitality; there were the cheese-cakes and the famous apple-tart; there were plums, dried and set in sugar; there were nuts, all the way from the Spice Islands; and there were little strips of salted fish to raise a thirst for the prime October which her brother was spicing by the fire. And with it all was her babbling chatter, profuse, eager and indiscreet.

'We're in your debt for ever,' she told Margery. 'I do hope you were not hurt. Horses are such dreadful things to fall from.'

'Madam, I . . .' Margery felt baffled. This was too blatant. However much these people knew or guessed, there was surely a limit to what should be said aloud. But Roger came skilfully to her help.

'How is Master Miles?' he asked, as he had once done before; and, as before, it was bait enough for Mistress Crook. Miles was charming. She did so hope affairs would turn out well for Miles. He surely deserved it. And then indiscretion had his aunt by the ear again.

'I hope you'll think so too,' she told Margery. 'I hear he has been much in your company of late, and I was so glad you went with him to the Rough Lee. You'll be there again soon, let us hope?'

Once again it was Roger who answered for her.

'I doubt that,' he said dryly. 'Margery is no doubt shy to speak of it, but she's avoiding those parts for a while.'

Mistress Crook reared, and Margery became tense and alert. This was not an answer she would have expected. It had an air of indiscretion, and that was not Roger's way. But his tone had not been idle, and again Margery asked herself what the purpose was that had brought him to this house this day. And had he not said that he would put his trust in Mistress Crook? But now he was speaking again.

'The truth is,' he was saying, 'that Margery is presently shy of the Rough Lee. She had some encounter there with the Redfern woman.'

'That creature!' Mistress Crook began to bristle. 'What has she done now? Pray tell me of it.'

Roger sat at ease and answered lightly.

'Done? She can scarce be said to have done anything. She presumed to a resentment that Margery should be on that land. That's all.'

'Brother Dick's land?'

'So I'd have said. But from what Margery says, the Redfern fancies it as her own land.'

Margery sat in silence and left him to it. This, of course, was not at all what she had said, but Roger evidently knew what he was about. Mistress Crook was becoming angry.

'Her own!' she snapped. 'Her own indeed! I never could understand why Dick allows that family on the land at all.'

'He doesn't,' said Tony quietly. 'It's Alice who does that, as we all know.'

'Alice, then. It's the same thing.'

'Not quite—thank Heaven!'

'Don't say that, Tony. But to allow these Chattox there after what Robert said . . .'

Tony looked at her indulgently.

'That was a long time agone,' he said slowly.

'And what of that? He said it, just the same. And then he died—all alone there, and away from us all.'

'Not quite alone.'

Tony's quiet answer struck coldly, and Margery sat very still, her thoughts flying back to what Roger had told her of the Robert Nutter who had died at Chester. Tony's meaning had been plain, for Robert had not been alone; there had been a servant with him.

'No. Not alone.' There was a smouldering anger in her voice now. 'And I still tell you, Tony, you know what Robert said.'

Roger came quietly into the talk.

'You speak in mysteries,' he complained. 'What did your brother say?'

Tony gave him the short answer.

'Robert? He said he was bewitched—by the Chattox.'

Roger turned slowly to Margaret Crook.

'You think, then, that your brother was indeed bewitched?'

'Of course he was.' Margaret was indignant. 'What else could it be—with such women and after such a quarrel?'

'I can't judge that,' said Roger. 'I know something of the women, but nothing of a quarrel.'

'Then never mind about that. But there was a quarrel, a dreadful quarrel, and Robert wanted the women put off the land and our father wouldn't. He said he didn't believe it, but of course it was our grandfather that wouldn't when you come down to the truth of it.'

She was growing incoherent, and Roger lifted a protesting hand.

'Please,' he said. 'I get lost. Tell me, when was this?'

'Just before Robert died—the summer before.'

'And Robert died when?'

'Twenty years come Candlemas.'

Roger nodded.

'So there was a quarrel, and your brother asked your father to turn these people off the land? Is that it?'

'Yes.'

'But they were not turned off?'

'No. And that's what I've been telling you. It would have been our grandfather.'

'How?'

Margaret looked pitying at Roger, as though surprised at his stupidity. The understanding Tony intervened to make it plain.

'Margaret means,' he said, 'that our mother had died, and our father had therefore taken us to live for a time with his own parents—our grandparents. So the fact was our father did not at that time own the land. He'd not yet inherited, and he could not have turned these people off it. It would have needed our grandfather to do that.'

'That's plainer.' Roger spoke thoughtfully. 'And your grandfather, being asked, would not? Is that it?'

'That was his wife.'

'His wife? You mean that your grandfather might have turned these people off, but that his wife, being your grandmother, hindered him in that?'

'I take it so. But it's an old tale and best let die.'

Tony Nutter spoke as though he would gladly change the topic, but Roger would have none of it.

'Why,' he asked gently, 'should your grandmother protect a witch-brood against her own grandson?'

'Because she was a witch herself.'

Margaret had snapped the answer before her brother could speak. When he did speak, he was almost chiding.

'Margaret, my dear!' was all he said.

'But it's true,' she insisted. 'You know very well it's true. Why else did she stop him? And why else did she make

Robert have that dreadful Tom Redfern as his servant? And if it come to that, why else did she bring Alice here and marry her to Dick?'

She ended in a silence that chilled. Roger sat impassive, and Margery, catching his eye, read in it a warning which she did not need; she had no intention of intruding herself while the Nutter secrets were tumbling out.

Tony Nutter turned to face Roger squarely. There was a flush in his cheeks and he was plainly embarrassed, but he spoke calmly.

'Since it's gone so far, you'd best have the rest of it,' he said slowly.

'I'd be grateful.'

Tony smiled wistfully.

'Near twenty years agone, remember. Anne Redfern was sweet seventeen then, and sweet she was to look on. She was newly wed to this Thomas Redfern, and brother Robert—here's nothing of credit, but it's the truth—brother Robert tried to have his pleasure of her. Which she would have none of . . .'

'That being the quarrel?'

'Just that. Even then, she'd a tongue like a sewer, and Robert had the reek of it. That angered him and he threatened.'

'Threatened what?'

'Anything and everything, though I never learned the rights of it. He was taken of a fever, you see, and for a week he retched and vomited—till Margaret here took him in charge, and he thrived on a broth she made. But in all his ravings he cursed the Chattox, vowing it was their foul arts had struck him.'

Margery stole a glance at Roger and saw him staring at the floor. And Tony went on quietly.

'That was when our grandmother came nosing into the thing—she and Alice.'

'Alice?' Roger looked up at that.

'No other.' Tony was speaking deliberately now. 'Alice had come out of Trawden a month before. Grandmother said she was kin, and called her cousin. And already she'd been pressing Robert to marry her.'

'Robert, was it? Not Dick?'

'Robert it was—at first. But he liked her as little as the

rest of us did, and he was man enough to say so. Maybe it was that. Or maybe Alice turned cool of him when he was taken with the Redfern. Or maybe it was because he fell sick just then. We'll never know. But at least there was no more heard of his marrying Alice. But they pressed him to another thing.'

'Yes?'

'Grandmother, with virtuous Alice at her side, must needs have it that he owed amends to these Redferns for wrongs done—though in truth it hadn't gone so far. But that's how it was, and by what acts they pressed him, none of us ever knew. All that's certain is that when he went into Wales with Shuttleworth, he took Tom Redfern with him as body-servant—and I mind the fellow's leer as they rode off.'

'Don't speak of it, Tony. It was dreadful.'

Margaret's voice was shaking, and her brother went over to her, standing by her side and stroking her shoulder softly as she turned away from them. Margery, glancing again at Roger, saw him with a face of stone, and she knew he was probing because he felt he must.

'I take it then,' he said quietly, 'that your brother took this fellow only because he had to. He had not come to love the Chattox brood?'

Tony smiled wanly.

'I mind his saying, before he took horse, that whenever he should be home again he'd clap the whole brood where they'd be glad to chew their own lice.'

And Tony Nutter turned to the fire, his face white and wretched. His sister's face was buried in her cupped hands.

'And Alice?' said Roger softly.

'She turned on Dick and married him out of hand.' Tony was speaking with his back to them, his face still to the fire. 'Dick's softer than Robert ever was, and he could not stand against them. He was wed at Christmas that year. And the next we knew was Tom Redfern back among us, to tell of Robert dead at Chester.'

Tony's foot stirred the fire viciously. Then he turned quickly to face them.

'The one satisfaction I had,' he said grimly, 'was the end of Tom Redfern.'

'Don't, Tony. Don't,' whispered Margaret miserably.

'Of Tom Redfern?' Roger was quietly insistent.

'Aye. He swaggered it for a week, as one knowing more than his betters. Then the sickness had him, and he retched his way to Hell.'

He ended, and the strained silence wrapped the room. Margery stirred uneasily, and Roger drew deep breath.

'An odd sickness, that,' he remarked dryly.

'Yes.' Tony looked him squarely in the eye. 'In the summer it took my father, and he was dead by Michaelmas. And before the year was out, my grandfather was gone. And brother Dick ruled at the Rough Lee.'

'Ruled, do you say?'

Tony smiled sourly.

'Owned might be the better word,' he agreed.

Roger nodded and seemed to consider. Then he spoke deliberately.

'These sicknesses, Tony—did no thought ever come to you about them?'

But Tony Nutter would not answer that. He looked at the fire, and evaded.

'Some things are with God,' he said quietly. 'And best left with Him.'

But Roger thought, and then slowly shook his head.

'All things are with God, Tony, and the more so when they're left undone by men. But have we therefore a duty to leave all things undone?'

He came quietly to his feet.

'I had meant to make pretence,' he said, 'that we'd come on you by chance. I'll not tell that tale now. You see which way I drift.'

Tony nodded.

'I'll pray that God be with you,' he answered. 'May He keep us all!'

'Amen to that! And now we'll take our leave. I'm grateful for your tale.'

Margery was on her feet at once. This room was oppressive to her now, and she was glad of the cool fresh air as they rode down to the brook.

Roger had only one comment to make.

'If I take to retching,' he said tersely, 'cook my broth yourself.'

23

Clouds over Wheathead

Tony Nutter's tale did what few things could do; it spoiled Margery's sleep.

Neither she nor Roger had much to say of it that evening; they seemed to agree that it was best left in a decent quiet. But their minds were on it, as they both knew, and Margery brooded unhappily. She had had a glimpse into a home that must have been horrible; for the Rough Lee, twenty years before, could have been nothing less than that. Margery's thoughts were on the motherless children in that fear-drenched house: the doomed Robert, linked by hate to a gloating servant; the soft and friendly Dick, forced to a marriage he must have loathed; the sensitive keen-eyed Tony, seeing all and hating all; the kindly talkative Margaret, clinging perhaps to Tony as the shadows deepened around her; and all of them young, eager and helpless. They must have been near Margery's present age when a prim, dark Alice had come into their home from Trawden, come to stay, and wed, and rule. And that dreadful grandmother who had called this Alice kin: what of her? Margery shivered as the picture came alive in her mind.

She was not eager to blow her candles that night, and when at last she did blow them, she slept badly; and as she passed fitfully from sleep to waking, and from waking to sleep, and most of all when she was in the twilight that is neither, scenes and figures began to float before her in a strange mad medley. There was Alice Nutter, sitting like a frozen rock in a cold that spread and numbed; there was a slim young Nutter, riding into Wales with a monstrous black-cloaked servant leering at his back; there was a grandmother, vague and misty, who chuckled spitefully and lifted a finger to bring dark Alice running; there was Tony, always with his face twisted in misery; and Margaret, sometimes as a young girl slim and cowering, and sometimes as she had been yesterday, hunched by a fire with her head buried in her hands. And between them all, with them and yet not of them, was Frank Hilliard, flitting strangely from one picture to another, and always in danger from the chuckle or the cold.

The darkness of exhaustion dimmed the pictures in the end, and Margery slept heavily. When she came down to breakfast, heavy-eyed and late, Roger took one look at her and then jerked her thoughts to other matters.

'Tom Peyton had a word for me while you were still abed,' he told her. 'There's some trouble, it seems, at Wheathead, though I don't yet know the rights of it. The Device woman's been here with some complaint. Apparently Baldwin's whip caressed her shoulders—though why she thinks that's matter for complaint the Devil knows best.'

Margery nodded.

'Which Device would that be, sir?'

'Elizabeth—the one that squints. So I'd have you ride to Wheathead and get the truth of it for me.'

'I'll try.'

'If you can't, who can?' Roger's eyebrows lifted in the familiar style. 'Baldwin has a softness for his sister-puritan.'

Margery laughed, not at all displeased, and went off for her riding-clothes. A ride to Wheathead might cool her head this day.

She found the millpool smooth and black under a cold grey sky. There was no sign of Grace, but Richard Baldwin received her amiably and took her through the stone-flagged kitchen to his own austere room, where the account-books nestled against the Bible. Margery came to the point at once, and two steely eyes under a lowering brow met hers as she ended.

'She complains, does she?' he said coldly. 'I dealt lightly, and if Master Nowell wants my counsel it is that he has the Constable bestow what I spared.'

Elizabeth Device, he explained, had come a-begging yesterday, and when she had been refused she had not gone; instead, she had hung about through the morning, pestering the apprentices and frightening the serving maids with the roll of her hideous eyes. At last, in an unguarded moment, she had been allowed to slip into an empty kitchen; and Richard himself, coming at that moment from his small room, had seen her trying the larder door.

'By God's providing,' he said, 'I'd a whip handy, and I drove her off. But lightly, let it be known. She had less than a poor dozen, and she ran howling. That's all of it.'

He evidently considered that the matter was at an end, for his expression changed. He was positively benevolent as he told Margery that he had now ended the admirable *Homily* she had so kindly lent him. She must credit him with gratitude for the loan—and she must certainly stay for dinner.

A hungry Margery accepted promptly. She had a high opinion of the Baldwin dinners. But where, she asked, was Grace?

A cold shadow came across his face.

'She's in her chamber,' he said shortly. 'However, you may visit her there and talk with her. I give leave for that.'

Margery bit her lip in time to restrain comment. She knew at once what this meant. Grace was confined to her room for some offence, and could have no talk without special leave. Margery knew all about the discipline of puritan homes.

She thanked him quietly, glad that leave had been given, and with no more said she went back through the kitchen and made her way to Grace's room. The click of the spinning-wheel greeted her as she raised the latch and entered.

The little room was cold and bleak. Grace sat on a stool in the wan grey light from the low window, her foot pressing the treadle while her fingers guided the skeins. She looked cold. Her face looked pinched and her fingers blue, and there was a shawl draped about her shoulders; but warmth shot into her eyes as Margery entered.

'Margery!' She jumped up from the wheel. 'I heard your coming, but I tried not to hope you'd be let in here.'

Margery sat herself in the single chair.

'Hope or no hope, I'm in—and with leave duly given. What's your offence?'

'Offence!' Grace pouted at it. 'Did my father not tell you?'

'Not a word, except that I might enter. Which was enough to tell me there's been offence.'

'You seem to know of these things.'

'I've some cause to. But what was it?'

Grace pulled a wry mouth at that.

'It came from the kirtle you're making. I'd a word with Fat Jack, and he told me you'd had your laces. That set me thinking of it, and I . . . I wanted its like. And in short, I got a sermon on pomps and vanities . . .'

'In short, do you say? Not if I know that sermon.'

Grace smiled ruefully.

'No, not in short. But I was foolish. I disputed against it . . .'

'Oh dear!'

'So I said—later. And here I've been, these three days.'

'Three?' Margery considered that, and then went to what she thought was the root of the matter.

'What have you had to eat?'

Grace looked disgusted.

'Some bread—and all the water I want. I'm getting dreadfully hungry.'

Margery nodded sympathetically.

'I know. One does. Though why any should suppose that makes you want a kirtle less, I can't think.'

'It seems they do suppose it.' Grace went back to her spinning-wheel. 'I'd best be at work again. I've a task set.'

'Then you'll be wise to achieve it.'

The wheel went clicking, and Margery watched with understanding. She had had all this herself too often not to understand.

'One thing these weeks in Pendle have taught me,' she said slowly.

'Yes?'

'Such discipline afflicts us all. They're the common lot. But there's one thing that can end them.'

'And what's that?'

'Leaving the house you're reared in. Journey to Pendle did that for me. And for you, Grace, there'll be an end when you're wed.'

The skeins dropped from Grace's fingers.

'What counsel's that?' she asked brusquely. 'What chance have I? You know how it is.'

Margery tried to speak hopefully.

'Could it not be contrived? Miles is certainly willing, and your father could be persuaded.'

'Oh, my father? Oh yes, my father—he'd consent. But what of Alice Nutter? She never will.'

'It's as bad as that? Never?'

'Never.' The wheel clicked viciously as Grace stamped on the treadle. 'You're teasing me, Margery!'

'Grace! I never . . .'

'Never's the word, and never it will be. And that's my choice. I can wed where I don't wish; or I can sit till I'm grey, waiting for consent that won't be given. I'm plainly a miller's girl, and below her high notice. There'll be nothing of consent while Alice Nutter lives.'

Margery made no answer. She had not seen this anger in the friendly Grace before, and she was telling herself that she should have foreseen it. Grace, after all, was her father's daughter, and at this moment she looked it. And then, as Margery sat silent, a new and ugly thought crept into her mind. How many people were there in Pendle whose lives would be sweeter if Alice Nutter ceased to live? It startled her, and she tried hastily to put it behind her; it would not do, she thought, to let such broodings slip out to be heard by the kindly Grace.

The clicking slowed and stopped. Grace dropped the skeins to her lap and looked deliberately at Margery.

'If Alice Nutter were to die,' she said slowly, while Margery sat aghast, 'I ask myself who'd mourn for her. I should not. I could not. And—this is horrible, Margery—I don't think Miles could either, even though she's his mother.'

Margery sat breathless with a chilling shiver in her back. These, from Grace, were words from a pit of misery.

And then, to her unspeakable relief, Richard Baldwin looked in, smiling.

'Come to dinner,' he said pleasantly. 'Both of you.'

Grace jumped happily to her feet at words that meant she was forgiven, but the door had shut before she could speak. But the tension had broken, and they looked at each other easily.

'That,' said Margery, 'was a most timely coming.'

'In more ways than one. How's my hair?'

They went to dinner as though they had chatted of no

more than trifles, and to Margery's surprise it was a happy hour. Richard Baldwin could be hard and he could be narrow, but he could not be petty; and having called Grace from her room he quickly made it plain that she was restored in full. He greeted her pleasantly and carved generously for her; soon he was at pains to bring her into the talk, and under this treatment Grace revived rapidly. The food and friendship dissipated her ill humours, and Margery was exerting herself in light talk that might help; by the time the meal was done and Thanks had been given, Grace was again her own placid and contented self.

But afterwards, when they had left the table, they had an echo of their earlier talk. Richard was back in the mill, the serving-maids were busy, and Grace, who had had quite enough of her own room, drew Margery into a corner of the warm kitchen.

'What was said before would be best forgotten,' she said. 'It was foolish talk, and wicked—some of it.'

Margery looked her in the eye.

'Forgetting what's been said is easier willed than done,' she answered. 'We shall not forget it, either of us, as you well know.'

Grace looked uneasy.

'You see too clearly for your talk to be always comfortable,' she said. 'But at least it need not be spoken of. That's a thing we can . . .'

Grace stopped short, an ear lifted to the door. A babble of shouting had broken out by the pool, a woman's voice, high pitched and shrill, vying with angry tones from Richard Baldwin. Grace took one startled look at Margery and then darted to the door. Margery followed in the same alarm, harbouring a vague thought that this must be Elizabeth Device again.

She was nearly right in her guess. It was not Elizabeth but it was the young Alizon; and with her, wheezing and snarling, was the aged Demdike. They were standing together by the smooth, black pool, and in front of them, his voice raised high in anger, was Richard Baldwin.

'Payment?' he was saying savagely. 'Payment, and to Satan's brood? What madness has you?'

Demdike, bent and wizened, faced him coolly, her little eyes blinking in the grey light.

'You'd my daughter's help, and you'd best pay what's due for it,' she croaked; and a panting Alizon dared a laugh.

Richard Baldwin turned slightly as he became aware of Grace and Margery; without turning fully, he addressed his daughter.

'Grace, be into the house and fetch my whip. Hasten!'

Grace went off at a run. She knew better than to disobey that. Her father turned deliberately to Alizon Device.

'You shall be paid your due,' he said grimly. 'And in the coin that paid your mother.'

Alizon turned white. The threat was not idle, as she well knew. She took one glance at his granite face and another at the open door. Then Grace came running, whip in hand, and a quaking Alizon turned and ran.

Richard took the whip from Grace and faced the aged Demdike. The woman made no move to go, and the watchful Margery thought her foolish; if she supposed her age would be a sure protection, she did not know the puritans; compassion for witches, young or old, had no place in the puritan creed.

'Get from off my ground,' said Richard slowly; and his tone had a cold fury that made Margery hold her breath. 'Get from off my ground,' he repeated. 'From my ground and from my sight.'

He paused, and his steely eyes passed from the Demdike to Alizon, standing defiant a safe fifty yards away. He spoke again to the woman in front of him.

'Assure the whelp,' he said softly, 'that she shall have her payment.' Then his voice swelled in anger. 'Payment? Payment to a witch and a whore? Aye—and if God shows me His favour I'll get you your payment. And that's to hang the one and brand the other. And now be off—clear from my ground.'

Demdike turned slowly, feeling blindly with her stick for the low grey wall by the pool.

'Hang yourself,' she muttered as she went.

She shuffled along, tapping at the wall with her stick. Then she stopped and looked back malignantly.

'I'll pray for you,' she said over her shoulder. 'For you and yours.'

A hateful chill struck Margery. How was it that this woman prayed? Still and loud, young Jennet had said.

The tapping stick moved along the wall, and a venomous chuckle came faintly on the wind. Richard Baldwin stood rigid, and there was sweat on his face as he fought for control. Then, with a gentleness that was strange in him, his arm was round Grace.

'Margaret!' he whispered.

He whispered it almost to himself, and Grace looked up in agitation as she heard her sister's name. Margery stood frozen. Margaret Baldwin's death had followed a Demdike prayer.

Richard looked steadily at Grace.

'If you'd not been here to see,' he said, 'I'd have killed her then.'

His arm dropped, and without another word he turned and went quietly into the house. The door-latch clicked, and the girls were alone in the fading afternoon. From a heavy sky, cold raindrops pattered suddenly.

Margery rode home blindly, and let her horse find the way. Yet her crowding thoughts were not so much with Richard as with Grace. Richard's quarrel with the Demdike was his own affair, but Grace's troubles came nearer to Margery. Here was something she could feel more vividly; and here, too, was something that turned on Alice Nutter, and Alice Nutter was growing very large in Margery's thoughts. Her imagination was still lit by Tony's tale, and the half-dreams it had brought in the night. She was beginning to see Alice Nutter as the spider who spun these Pendle webs, and suddenly she shivered at the image of that; webs made her think of the thread of life, which is spun, and measured—and cut.

She went straight to Roger in his parlour and told him the whole tale. He nodded calmly.

'Begging with a threat,' was his comment. 'They send Elizabeth here to complain, and the other two go there. If she's paid for help she didn't give, they'll withdraw complaint. That would be the pattern of it. Which shows they don't know our Baldwin.'

'Or didn't. I think they've learnt. I've told you what he called them. And witch is no doubt true of Demdike. But what of the other?'

'Also true.' Roger laughed shortly. 'A June night and a dry ditch—that's our Alizon.'

Then he turned sympathetic eyes on Margery and looked her over keenly.

'You're looking almost haggard,' he told her. 'And that's not to be permitted. Your looks are too good to spoil. You've had two bad days, and like as not a bad night between. Quiet evening and early bed for you, little cousin.'

She gave him half a smile at that address, but she had no protest to make. Roger was right, and Margery knew it. She was very tired now, and she was dragging wearily as she went to dress decently for supper. Yet she did not, in the end, have her quiet evening, nor was she early to bed. She was just into her kirtle before supper when there was the sudden noise of a horse on the gravel outside, a knocking at the great door, and Tom Peyton's steady tread going to it. Margery slipped out of her bedchamber, her ears agog, and at once she heard Frank Hilliard's brisk tones as he inquired for Master Nowell.

It was enough for Margery. It served as a tonic, and made her forget her tiredness. After the stresses of the last two days there was something exciting and sustaining in the thought that she might again, for a few days, have his cheerful confident face at her side. The thought set her in a glow, and she went impulsively down the stair as Roger came quietly out of his parlour.

'So soon?' she called.

'Aye,' he said quietly. 'So soon.'

'You're well come,' she told him. 'Well indeed.'

She turned to Roger, as though inviting him to add his word to that. But Roger did not share her raptures; he kept his experienced eyes on the younger man's face, and when he spoke his tone was grave.

'What trouble are you in?' he asked quietly.

Margery's smile faded quickly as she looked from the one man to the other. Then she listened anxiously as Frank Hilliard told his tale. He told it where he stood, barely inside the door, with his gloves still in his hands and cloak still dusty about his shoulders. Yesterday's early start, he said, had brought him to Lathom by the afternoon, and he had at once gone to the Earl's closet. He had sent in his name—and had been denied audience. Through the evening he had stayed in the ante-room, cooling his heels and asking himself what this portended. Not till midnight had he been admitted, and when he was at last in the closet his reception had been cold and hostile. A frigid Earl had as good as accused him, not merely of negligence, but almost of connivance in the escape of Christopher Southworth, priest. The audience had ended with His Lordship's curt command that Master Hilliard should at once depart from Lathom, and should not presume to return until that meddlesome priest had been re-taken—how or by whom did not signify. Master Hilliard had been given no chance to make a protest. A chamberlain had at once swung the door for him, and he had fancied as he left that even the clerk at the side-table was permitting himself the insolence of a smile.

He ended his tale and looked diffidently at Roger.

'The only comfort I had, sir, was the scope of the invitation you sent me off with. And—and in short, sir, here I am.'

'You did well.' Roger spoke gravely. 'As Margery has said, you're well come. So be at ease on that score.'

He lapsed into silence, and Margery's agitation grew. She had feared that there might be some recriminations over the priest's escape, but it had never occurred to her that anything more than carelessness could be in question. An accusation of connivance, even if there was little to support it, was another thing, and Margery had no wish to see so grave a charge laid at Frank's door. Her liking for him apart, she knew well enough that she was herself the true culprit here, and that he was merely paying for what she had contrived. She glanced round her unhappily. Frank was still standing quietly with his eyes on Roger, whose face seemed carved from stone. Tom Peyton lurked in the shadows, missing nothing; and the door creaked suddenly as the wind swayed it.

'I never could hold that fellow's name,' said Roger slowly. 'What is it, Tom?'

'Which fellow, sir?'

'The fellow at Lathom. Alice Nutter's nephew, or whatever he calls himself . . .'

'Potter, sir.'

'Potter it is.' Roger spoke it grimly. 'Matthew Potter, a Clerk of the Closet—hard by His Lordship's ear.'

24

The Breaking Storm

Master Ormerod's sermon the next morning was no more to Roger's taste than might have been expected. He slept through most of it, and then came out of the church in a fine sardonic humour.

'There's a windy rogue,' he grumbled as they came into the churchyard. 'Wind enough for a May-Day bladder, and sense by the same reckoning. I'll get me a cloak with a higher collar.'

'Collar is it?' Frank Hilliard was answering him from Margery's other side. 'I've never known why the Scold's Collar can't be fitted to a windy parson. There's many a woman bitten it for less.'

Margery's forehead began to crinkle. She could never resist this kind of thing.

'It's the woman who commonly suffers,' she said provocatively. 'As this morning.'

Roger's eyebrows took their familiar lift.

'How?'

'I stayed awake.'

His laughter gave scandal to some worthy worshippers, and Margery waited warily for the retort which it would not be in his nature to forgo. But this time he did forgo it. The gleam perished from his eyes and the laugh from his lips; his shoulders stiffened, and his face froze to formality. Margery suddenly understood, and she turned quickly as Alice Nutter came upon them.

Roger's beaver swept impeccably. Frank's followed. The two curtseys came a second later, the one exact and the other elegant.

'Your servant, ma'am. We are all your servants.'

He was half smiling and wholly assured; and Margery, stealing a quick glance, marvelled at his easy air; only the steadiness of his eyes gave hint of his wariness.

'I had not expected the pleasure of seeing Master Hilliard here this morning.'

It was very properly said, and her tone could not be called discourteous; it had something that compelled attention; that was all. But Frank Hilliard began to look diffident.

'In truth, ma'am, I'd hardly expected it myself,' he answered, and Alice Nutter nodded pleasantly.

'Life brings surprises, Master Hilliard. Perhaps we should be glad of that. To know what is in store for us might not always breed happiness. Do you not think so, mistress?'

Without warning the dark eyes were on Margery, and for a moment her mind was a frightened chaos. Power and menace were shooting from those depths, and a wild urge was on her to turn and run. Then, as if from a far, cold distance, she heard her own voice.

'It's very true, ma'am. And it's most true for those who do least heed it.'

Where she had that answer from, she never knew. The voice was hers, but the words were not; they seemed to come to her from outside herself. And while she wondered at them, a new thought came flooding through her, sweeping away fear and bringing assurance. To be frightened of Alice Nutter, to wait passively while she wove her schemes, was to wait for sure disaster; as well might a rabbit wait upon a stoat. But to meet Alice Nutter with force and daring would be to meet her with what she had never known; and that might find her unprepared. Margery's eyes grew bright and hard as understanding grew within her.

But Alice Nutter was speaking again.

'As you say, mistress.' Her voice was rasping now, almost as though she found presumption here. 'That's more true than you know. How true you'll learn—if you live to be a proper age.'

Margery's retort came promptly.

'I'm already learning, ma'am. I'm in wonder at what I've learned—since I came to Pendle.'

The last of the worshippers, threading past this group

who blocked the path, looked askance at the tense and silent figures. Mistress Nutter's forehead was twitching, and her eyes had seething fury now. Then Roger's voice came steadily.

'Life, ma'am, can be most uncertain—for all of us. As a Justice, I've had cause to notice that.'

Alice Nutter spun to face him, and he met her with a cold assurance that seemed to disconcert her. For a moment she stood at gaze, rising almost on her toes. Then she relaxed. Her face eased; her forehead smoothed; the fury faded; the smile was back on her lips.

'We grow earnest, sir, for so fair a day. But I must take my leave. Your servant, sir . . .'

Her curtsey was punctiliously acknowledged, and at once she was away, walking quickly in search of her horse. And with her the tension went also. Margery turned to Roger in relief, and his eyes met hers. But it was Frank Hilliard who chose to speak first.

'It's very odd,' he complained. 'There's more here than I understand.'

'I nothing doubt it,' said Roger tersely.

He offered no further enlightenment, and he rode home in a brooding silence, leaving Margery to deal with Frank as she saw fit; and as she had no mind now for what must be difficult, she turned their talk to lightnesses. They chattered airily, and both with apparent enjoyment. But under her chatter Margery was brooding. The encounter with Alice Nutter had been more than trivial, and Margery was feeling in much need of a quiet talk with Roger.

She had it that afternoon, and it did not bring the comfort she had expected. When dinner was done, Frank went off reluctantly to write some account of affairs for his father in Warwickshire. He was, he said, a very poor hand with a pen, and he would welcome Margery's experienced help. But on that Roger interposed firmly. He kept Margery in his parlour, and he spoke his mind with more precision than she relished; and he did not even mention Alice Nutter.

'Why,' he asked, 'did young Hilliard return here in such haste from Lathom?'

Margery was perplexed. She had thought this obvious, and she said as much.

'He was invited. And he had promised to come.'

Roger nodded.

'I'd not forgotten that. And more likely than not it's as you say. Yet there are some other possibilities, and where so much is tangled it's well to have clear what can be clear.'

Margery began to be interested. Evidently Roger was not talking at random.

'There are some other possibilities,' he repeated calmly. 'You've not seen Lathom yet?'

'No. But . . .'

'It's almost a palace. From which it follows that life at Lathom is almost life in a court.'

He paused; and Margery sat attentive, wondering what was coming.

'Life in a court,' said Roger slowly, 'teaches a man to look to his advancement—to set it before all things. And many a courtier has set it before his honour.'

He paused again, and Margery sat tensely. There was an ominous ring in this, and his grave tone supported it.

'Bear in mind,' he was saying, 'that this Frank is a younger son. And it's the way of things that a younger son must look to himself if he's to avoid poverty.'

'He shows no sign of poverty. There's nothing mean in his apparel.'

Margery's sharp tone suggested that Roger's words had stung. But he answered her quietly.

'That's to be expected. There's no advancement in a court for the man who's shabby, so he must look to that before all things. He must dine off salted fish, and be at charges for a velvet cloak. That's the courtier's hell. And if he loses his lord's favour . . .'

Again Roger paused, and Margery waited unhappily. She was too shrewd to doubt the truth of this—in general. But was it true of Frank Hilliard in particular?

'Aye,' she said at last. 'And if he loses his lord's favour? What then?'

Roger looked her in the eye.

'Then he must retrench, and sharply. He might begin by parting with his servants.'

That went home, and Margery jumped to her feet in agitation. She had wondered where the two servants were who had attended Frank when he first appeared in Pendle.

This was no pleasant picture that Roger was painting for her.

'Where do you lead me?' she asked suddenly. 'Whither does this tend?'

He answered that without haste.

'If Frank Hilliard returned here, as it's very possible he did, in simple consequence of invitation given . . .'

'Yes?'

'Then that should mean, little cousin, that *you* are the attraction. You, your form and feature, your taste and talent, talk and disposition—all, in short, which in sum is you.'

Margery felt her cheeks tingling.

'I know nothing of that,' she said. 'But if it is so, what then?'

'That would be for you to answer—if it is so.'

His tone had a dryness that brought her to earth again. She looked at him steadily.

'Will you be more plain, sir? Whither does this tend?'

'It would appear,' he said deliberately, 'that his return to milord's favour depends on the taking of Master Southworth, the Seminary. And to that, he might have hoped to find some pointer here.'

'Here?'

'Shall I say, then, in your company?'

Margery's temper fired at that.

'What?' she blazed. 'He'd have me serve such ends? He'd use me slyly?'

'He may have thought you'd used him—slyly.'

Her fire died suddenly, quenched in that cold logic. That, after all, was precisely what she had done.

She looked helplessly at Roger, and to her unspeakable relief there was the hint of a smile in the corners of his mouth. She seized on that as an omen, and a faint warmth began to creep through her chilled thoughts as he spoke again.

'Now mark,' he said. 'I spoke of possibilities, and I rate this no higher. It is a possibility, and no more. I'm not one of those who would drop poison between you and him. And the truth is, I do not judge young Hilliard to be a knave.' He paused, and his steady eyes held hers while that sank in. 'I have, down the years, known knaves in plenty and honest men not a few. And between them I'd judge Frank Hilliard to be the honest man. You may take that to your comfort.'

He stopped, and for a moment the smile took life. Then it died again, and his quiet tones went on.

'But the possibility remains. It's to be reckoned with, even if it's thought unlikely. Which comes to this—that you must guard your tongue. That is all. There must be no giving of full confidence, especially in what touches Master Southworth. On that topic, silence can lose you nothing, and chatter might lose you all. Is that plain?'

Margery let her head droop. It was more plain than pleasant.

'Aye, sir,' she answered. 'It's plain enough.'

He seemed to have no more to say, and Margery had no wish for more. She had not even the wish to ask him what he had thought of Alice Nutter that morning. But later, as she sat aside and brooded, those threatening exchanges held her thoughts. If Roger had been right in supposing that Alice Nutter had used her kinsman at Lathom to drop to the Earl a poisoned tale about the escape of a priest, her motive must surely have been to secure the removal from Pendle of a man whose presence spoiled her plans; she might reasonably have expected that Frank Hilliard would be instantly called from Pendle to render account at Lathom; and surprise at seeing him in Whalley church this day might well have provoked her to indiscretion. And what next? Malice seemed certain now, and it would not be for Margery alone; there would be enough of it to embrace Frank too.

Margery grew uneasy. She had brought Frank into enough trouble already without exposing him to more. Her uneasiness grew as she considered it, and soon she was anxious to lay it before Roger and have his shrewd counsel. Yet that, at this present moment, she could not do; for now Frank was back in the room, chatting with Roger about Lathom and the affairs of the County, and in his hearing she could hardly broach such a matter as this—especially after Roger's warning. So she had to wait. She had to wait through the evening for an opportunity that did not come, and in the end she had to resign herself to leaving the matter till the morrow.

But the morrow brought cares enough of its own. It was

a Monday; which meant that Nick Banister was joined with Roger in the giving of justice, and Margery, as their now indispensable Clerk, had to sit the length of the session with them. And the session was neither short nor easy, for Richard Baldwin soon showed himself to be in truculent mood. He began with five presentations for absence from the Newchurch, and then he presented Elizabeth Demdike and her granddaughter, Alizon Device, for begging and trespass on his land the preceding Saturday; and Elizabeth Device, daughter to the said Demdike, promptly rolled her diverging eyes over the Justices and their Clerk as she asked leave to bring charges of assault and profane swearing against Richard Baldwin of the mill, churchwarden.

Roger was not pleased. He was not pleased with any of them, and his expression showed it. Margery took one look at his face and then bent thoughtfully over her paper as she set down the details of the charges; then she chose a new goose-quill from the jar in front of her and began to trim it with her small knife; a new pen, she thought, was likely to be needed before all this had been ended. And Nick Banister cleared his throat and drew his chair forward to Roger's side.

Roger spoke with crisp precision. Elizabeth Demdike, he said, had a licence to beg, and since she was all but blind it was reasonable that her granddaughter, Alizon Device, should lead her; the presentation for begging must therefore fail. Licence to beg necessarily implied licence to enter upon land in order to beg, and the presentation for trespass must therefore depend on whether the women had or had not departed peacefully from the land when lawfully ordered so to do.

Nick Banister nodded approval. Both Justices turned patiently to Richard Baldwin, and Margery, catching sight of his face, put down her penknife and let the goose-quill wait; she had seen that look on a puritan face before.

He came slowly to his feet, grasping the table with a grip that blanched his knuckles, and he spoke in a ringing voice that was tremulous with anger. He had, he said, been merciful before the Lord, and had presented for slight matters only—for begging and trespass; but since his mercy was rejected, the one charge dismissed and the other held in doubt, he would now ask leave to withdraw both; instead, he would present for conjuring evil spirits with intent to harm him in his soul and body.

He ended on a note of fine fervour, and at once he plunged into an exultant recitation of the thirty-fifth Psalm. He had got as far as the seventh verse before Roger's icy voice cut in and stopped him.

'Enough!' he snapped. 'This is not a Meeting House. Set that down.'

And Margery was so far gone in consternation that he had to slap the table angrily before she realised that his last command was for her. She was in haste then to obey, and her pen scratched noisily as she set the new charge down. She was in no doubt about its gravity. Begging and trespass, as Baldwin had truly said, were trivial matters, punishable at worst by a whipping from the Constable and a few hours in the stocks; but this new charge was capital. King James had never forgotten the North Berwick witches of twenty years ago; they had confessed to raising the storm that had all but drowned him as he brought his Queen from Denmark; and a dozen years later, when he came to reign in England, he had quickly been urgent with his Parliament to enact that the conjuring of spirits, for any intent whatever, should be punished with death. Margery knew all about this Statute; she had learned enough of law for that in her weeks as Clerk, and Roger's frigid displeasure gave her no surprise; this was a charge that no Justice could take lightly.

Then Richard Baldwin was on his feet again to give his sworn evidence, and this, as Margery knew it must be, was slender. It came to no more than a recital of last Saturday's quarrel with heavy stress laid on Demdike's threat to pray for him and his. That, he declared, could mean nothing less than the conjuring of spirits to do him harm.

'That's to be considered,' said Roger calmly. 'But you've not only charged the woman. You've charged the granddaughter too. What threat did the girl make?'

She had of course made none, and Baldwin had to admit it. Roger promptly dismissed the charge against Alizon, and Margery, glancing at Baldwin as she duly recorded this, saw his face stiff and white with fury. Nervously, she wondered what was coming next.

'Now the Demdike,' said Roger. 'What has she to say?'

The stick tapped aggressively as the old woman made her

slow way to the table. And what she had to say was simple; she coolly swore that she had never said anything of the sort; and then, at her request, Alizon was heard, and fervently swore the same.

Again Margery glanced nervously at Richard Baldwin. But he had mastered himself now, and his hard face had no more expression than Roger's. He received Roger's inquiring look with a calm nod.

'I've sworn to it,' he said, 'and there's two, of a certain sort, sworn against me. Now let my daughter be heard. The Lord forewarned me of the need, and I've been at pains to bring her here.'

Margery had not suspected this, and she sat still, restraining surprise, as Grace rose from an unobtrusive seat at the back and came to the table. There she spoke quietly, and Margery thought she was embarrassed and reluctant; but her words were clear as she told of the quarrel and of hearing Demdike's threat. She ended, and would have gone back to her seat, but Margery intervened and pulled her into a chair at the table, next to her own.

'You'll stay by me now I've found you,' she whispered. Then she gave heed again as Baldwin spoke once more.

'That's two sworn against two,' he announced. 'There's yet a third to swear to it.'

Roger nodded patiently.

'Who?' he asked.

'Mistress Whitaker.'

Margery jerked up in surprise. She had not thought of this; it was obvious enough, but it had somehow not occurred to her. But she saw Roger's nod of assent, and she knew she could make no objection. So she went to the front of the table, and in the simplest words she could muster she corroborated what Grace had said.

'That's three to two,' said Richard Baldwin quietly.

Roger nodded, and then, as he stood in thoughtful silence, Nick Banister intervened. He leaned forward in his elbow-chair.

'Master Baldwin, has harm of any sort come to you or yours since these threats were made?'

That was unexpected, and for a moment it had Richard Baldwin at a loss. Then he spoke of great unease of spirit that had lain upon him since the Saturday. Nick Banister nodded. Then Roger pushed his chair back and seated himself; a moment later the two Justices were together in whispered talk.

Margery looked across to Richard Baldwin and ventured the ghost of a smile, which he acknowledged with a barely perceptible nod. Then she turned to Grace at her side.

'I wish this had not come,' she whispered.

Grace smiled ruefully.

'I know,' she whispered back. 'It was that word of praying for him that did it. You heard what he said at the time. It set him in mind of how Margaret died, and he's been speaking of the Lord's Just Vengeance ever since. Mother and I worked on him that he should make it no more than trespass, and we thought we'd prevailed. But you see how it is?'

Margery nodded. She did see, and she saw also what Grace perhaps did not see: that if Richadd Baldwin did not get his Just Vengeance he might well develop a festering resentment against Roger; and Roger, she thought, had trouble enough on his hands without that.

Grace was whispering again.

'If the Demdikes can indeed do us harm, they'll surely do it—after this.'

Margery looked up quickly, and one glance at Demdike was enough. The old crone was still standing there beyond the table, and her dark little eyes, seemingly none so blind now, were flickering from Grace to Margery and back again, as though there were two others she would now pray for still and loud. Margery looked, and shivered as she caught that evil glance; here was that Pendle cold again.

A chair scraped behind her, and the Justices had ended their colloquy. Roger came to his feet again. He considered the Demdike sombrely, and then he spoke decisively.

'We accept it that Elizabeth Demdike and Alizon Device did enter upon the land of Richard Baldwin at Wheathead, and did not depart peacefully when ordered so to do. This we find to be trespass. We accept it also that Elizabeth Demdike did use words meaning that she did intend to invoke spirits to the harm of Richard Baldwin.'

Roger paused, and when he resumed he spoke more to Baldwin than to Demdike.

'There is testimony that this Demdike intended to invoke

spirits, but none that she did in fact do so. And certainly there's no tale of such harm done as might flow from spirit's work.' He paused again, and he was looking very steadily at the man before him. 'What needs to be proved under the Statute is that she did actually invoke; and that has not been proved. There has not even been an attempt to prove it. And proof that she merely intended to do so, which is what we've had, is not enough. We do not, therefore, think proper to commit to Assize on this.'

He stopped; and suddenly the goose-quills shivered in their jar as Richard Baldwin smote the table with clenched fist. But before he could speak Nick Banister had leaned forward and was interposing in Roger's support.

'In short, Master Baldwin, there's proof of intent to invoke, but none of invoking with intent—which is what any Judge at Lancaster would require. And to be plain with you, if we let this go to Lancaster it will not get past the Grand Jury.'

Richard Baldwin, white-faced and silent, turned from the silent Justices to his own daughter; and Margery, intercepting that look, had a rush of sympathy for him. It was the look he had had two days ago when Demdike's evil word had wrung from him his Margaret's name; and as he now stood rigid, looking at his girl who lived, he was as surely thinking of the other who had died—died, as he was sure, from a Demdike charm. And suddenly, from Margery's side, Grace rose and ran to him.

He put a protecting arm round her. Then, standing so, he turned to the magistrates beyond the table and spoke in a voice that was not quite steady.

'I am answered,' he said. 'And in the days to come, I'll put my trust in the Lord of Hosts, and in Him only.'

Demdike's stick began to tap the floor, almost as though she were applauding; and at that he turned on her and Alizon with a white-faced fury that set them shrinking quickly back.

'And as for them,' he quoted, 'Thou, O God, shalt bring them into the pit of destruction.'

He turned his back on the standing Justices, who had yet some words to speak; and with no leave asked, and no farewell said, he left them. His arm was still round Grace as he went quickly out.

25

Aftermath

Margery turned in alarm as Roger's chair went clattering back. He was on his feet, strained and erect, his nostrils dilating and his brows drawn down in anger. But before he could speak, Nick Banister stretched out a long arm and plucked his sleeve. Roger spun round, and for a moment the two old friends were eye to eye. Then the older man prevailed, and slowly and a shade sullenly Roger sank back into his chair. He shrugged, as though to say that another might now manage this affair, and as if in acceptance of that, Nick Banister came to his feet, speaking crisply.

'Master Nowell has announced,' he said, 'that we find Elizabeth Demdike guilty of a trespass. For that she shall sit in the stocks the space of six hours.' He looked sternly across at her. 'Take note that only your age spares you a whipping before the stocks. Quiet!'

He waved her into awed silence when she would have spoken, and Margery sat wondering; she had not suspected this steely dignity in friendly Nick.

'Alizon Device . . .' The ring in his voice brought Alizon to her properest manners. 'You too have trespassed, and you too shall sit the six hours out. You too shall note that you should have been whipped but for the need to spare your grandmother.' He turned quickly to Hargreaves. 'Constable, you shall set above the stocks a paper having in great letters "Evil Tongues Makes Evil Lives". Enough!'

He beckoned to Roger, and the two men went quietly out. Margery clutched at her papers, and without waiting to gather her quills and ink-horn, she ran after them. Sitting through such a scene as an impassive clerk had been a heavy trial, and now she felt desperate to talk of it. Yet at once she was thwarted, for Anne Sowerbutts pounced upon her with a tale of a poor pedlar who had been waiting these two hours to lay his cloth-of-gold before her; and soon it would be too late for the poor man to reach another house this day. Margery bit her lip with annoyance, but as she had undoubtedly been urgent with him to bring the cloth-of-gold she could hardly refuse to receive it now. So Fat Jack was produced, slightly the worse for the ale that had beguiled the tedium of his wait, and the cloth-of-gold was duly bought. But it took a full ten minutes, and Margery had barely escaped from him, and was running to the parlour, when Frank Hilliard intercepted her. Again she bit her lip as she remembered that she had promised to ride with him in the hour before dinner; and for once she failed in a promise. She swept him and his importunities aside, telling him shortly that she must be with Roger; and then she brushed past him and ran. The quarrel that had flared so openly between Richard Baldwin and her Roger was nagging at her mind; and she did not pause to reflect that this might not be a prudent way of dealing with Frank Hilliard.

She burst into the parlour and came upon them much as she had expected, Roger with his shoulders to the shelf above the hearth, and Nick Banister at ease in the elbow-chair. Roger, ale-mug in one hand and tobacco-pipe in the other, was speaking his mind about Richard Baldwin, and to Margery's huge relief he was speaking it calmly.

'He has a head stuffed with witches,' he was saying, 'and the moon crammed in on top to addle all. God's Grace, Nick! Here's no uncommon tale. She that squints went first, and I don't doubt she went with a plan of thieving. That's her trade. So Baldwin whipped her, and he showed some sense in that, I grant. Then the old beldame creaked along to see what could be got . . .'

'More fool her! He's not the man for that.'

'Nor for any crooked thing. So they quarrel, and what's odd in that? At which the Demdike curses—and is there anything at all odd in that?'

'Baldwin did not say it was odd. He said it was a threat to bewitch him. And in that, Roger, I'm at one with Baldwin.'

Roger's eyebrows lifted; but Nick nodded calmly, as though to confirm what he had said.

'I've told you before, Roger, that these women are evil and dangerous, a sisterhood of Hell. And I've told you that I do not put it beyond them to kill in deed, as well as in wish. And hard on that came Margery here, with her foul tale of plants fruiting in a coppice. That showed how it might be done. Yet for all of it, Roger, I fear you still do not give weight to these women and their threats. Baldwin does—more indeed than I do. But I tell you, Roger: if he errs in that, his error's not wider than yours.'

'Yet you agreed with me not to commit to Assize?'

'Under the Statute we could do no other. She threatened to work evil, and I don't doubt she's tried. So far she's not succeeded, and till she does we can't commit. That's how I see it. But Roger . . .'

His tone was warning of earnestness, and both his listeners felt it.

'Yes?' said Roger quietly.

'Baldwin will no doubt look to his daughter. Look you to Margery.'

'Margery?'

'Aye, Margery. She and the Baldwin girl swore Demdike to the stocks, and that's a thing the beldame may remember.'

'God's Grace, Nick!' There was a note in Roger's voice that Margery had not heard before. 'If she tries that—if harm comes to Margery . . .'

'Just so! You begin to understand.'

'Understand? Understand what?'

'How Baldwin feels. And *he* has a daughter dead, remember.'

Roger stood staring, and his ale-mug came slowly down as his arm dropped. Margery stood tense, half frightened and half bewildered. And then Roger spoke slowly.

'Nick,' he said. 'You've the subtlety of the first serpent, and I make you my thanks. I . . . I'll find it in me to forgive our Baldwin. I'll even forgive him the way of his departing this day. Nevertheless, I fear the harm's done.'

'Meaning?'

'That I may forgive Baldwin, but it's less likely that Baldwin will forgive me—or you. It's not in his nature.'

'I fear you talk sense there, Roger. More of it than I've liking for. These puritans are as you say.'

He sipped his ale thoughtfully, and Margery, alert and watchful, saw how grave his face had become; and suddenly, as she watched him, he turned directly to her.

'You've puritan connections, have you not?'

It was unexpected, and she was a little flustered. Her answer came nervously.

'I . . . I used to have, sir.'

'You could no doubt have them still—for Baldwin—if you so desired?'

'For him? Why, yes sir, I think I could.'

He nodded, as if well pleased.

'It's said that the peacemakers are blessed. It's your chance to lay treasure in Heaven. Make what peace you can—for the sake of many.'

He took horse soon after that, and was away. But his words lingered, for his earnestness had been impressive; and Margery was soon sure that here was charge laid upon her which she might neglect only at peril of soul. Nor would she delay, and the next morning, under a grey December sky, she rode to Wheathead, Frank Hilliard at her side.

She was not glad of his company, and that, she reflected grimly, showed the degree to which her thoughts were occupied. On another morning she would have found him the best of company for such a ride, but this day her thoughts were elsewhere, and she found it hard to show him a proper interest. The task Nick Banister had imposed on her needed all her thoughts, for Richard Baldwin would be in no forgiving humour. Margery was sure of that. She knew these puritans only too well, and she was perfectly aware that their God was a Lord of Hosts, much more given to smiting the adversary than to forgiving him. Her task would not be easy, and she was finding Frank a distraction from her attempts to plan an approach.

Nor was Frank himself in the best of humours, and when Margery finally gave up her attempts to think, she became uneasily aware that his usual good spirits were not with him; once or twice she caught a glance that seemed to carry a positive displeasure, and she found herself wondering if this flowed from her brusque handling of him yesterday. That, she thought, might be better than to have him suspicious of her dealings in the Southworth affair, but it was certainly unpleasant; and between that and Roger's hints of his possible motive in riding with her at all, she found herself all but out of patience, and hard put to it to keep courtesy in their talk.

They came to Wheathead at last, and certainly they could not complain of their reception. Grace was clearly delighted, and in no time she had them in the arch of the great hearth, where the glowing warmth brought a pleasing tingle to ears and fingers numb from the ride. Frank seemed to thaw in mind as well as body, and he returned cheerful answers to Grace's talk.

'You're well come, both of you,' she said. 'We're so lonely here we'd say that to most, but when it's a friend of Margery's we say it and mean it. I'm told you're new to this Hill of ours?'

He grinned cheerfully and said he was learning.

'Learning what?' This was Margery, alert for possible double meanings, but he only laughed.

'At least I learn that it's a plaguey cold hill for a winter ride.'

'Yes, it has a chill at times.'

Grace had answered him gravely, and again Margery looked up sharply. She knew two kinds of cold on Pendle Hill.

'How is it—since yesterday?' she asked suddenly, and for a moment Grace sat silent.

'It's been dreadful,' she said at last. 'I spoke the truth when I said I'd have welcomed almost any visitor this morning.'

'Dreadful—from your father?'

'Yes. He's taken it hard.'

'Meaning that he's resentful.'

'Yes. You see . . .'

'Towards me also?'

'No.' Grace managed a smile. 'No, not to you, Margery. He says you spoke the truth, and had no part in what else was done.'

'Will someone enlighten me?'

Frank asked it quietly, and Margery understood at once. She had told him briefly of yesterday's proceedings, but these undercurrents ran deeper than that. A moment of further thought showed her that he might safely be told, for nothing in this touched Christopher Southworth. But before she could speak, the door swung open and Richard Baldwin came stamping in.

'Ha!' he said. 'I thought I heard voices. Master Hilliard, you are welcome here. And what of you, mistress? Are you still among our friends?'

'I hope so. Is there reason why I should not be?'

He considered that thoughtfully before he answered, and Margery waited anxiously, realising that in his usual blunt fashion he had come to essentials at once.

'No,' he answered slowly. 'We've no quarrel with you, neither I nor mine. You bore true witness and took no other part.'

She made no pretence of misunderstanding him. She must come to the matter some time and it might as well be now. But she had the scent of his humour and she spoke a little nervously.

'I'm charged with some messages,' she said. 'Messages from my cousin and also from Master Banister—particularly Master Banister.'

She watched him keenly. She saw the shade of doubt in his eye, and she was pleased with herself for having had the wit to use Nick Banister's name. Evidently he still had some respect for it.

'Is it so?' There was suspicion in his voice. 'You'd best come to my parlour then.'

He led to the door, and Margery had a word for Grace.

'Enlighten Frank for me,' she said, and then she followed to the parlour.

'These messages?' he said curtly.

He made no prelude, and Margery caught nothing of promise in his tone. She looked round quickly, and at once she observed the open Bible on the table in front of him. She craned her neck as she seated herself, and saw that it was open at the hundred-and-ninth Psalm—significant reading. Then she realised that he was waiting.

'My cousin and Master Banister,' she began. She hesitated, and then plunged on with a fine disregard of detail. 'It seems that they are but little removed from you in the way they view this Demdike. It's a difference only as to how her works may best be brought home to her.'

His hand slapped the Bible angrily, but she went on

quickly, giving him no chance of courteous interruption. She surprised herself with the tale she made of it. She reminded him of his treatment of Elizabeth Device, and she mentioned Roger's approval of it. Then, mixing Roger and Nick Banister into one, she told him of their belief that Demdike had indeed set out to cast a charm; she glossed over their doubts of the potency of the charm, and hurried on to credit Roger with a dictum about giving a witch rope enough to hang herself. She represented the whole affair as a mere difference of policy, and then she drew once more on her imagination for a wholly fictitious quotation from Roger: 'Better send her to the Summer Assize and have her hang, than send her at Lent to be acquitted.' She was pleased with that, as having the true ring of Roger in it, and on the whole she thought she had kept surprisingly near the truth. She looked at Richard with some satisfaction, and as a final shot she invented a warning message from Roger, bidding him have a special care of Grace.

He looked her over coldly.

'Why?' he asked.

'He thinks the Demdike may have disliked being sworn to the stocks.'

'She did.' There was satisfaction in his tone at last. 'And the whelp even more. I was at trouble to visit them as they sat. I'd some hopes the people would have stoned them and thus made an end, but I should have known better.' He smiled bitterly. 'There were some three-score folk a-watch, and all but one were too frightened of the Demdike power to lift a finger.'

'And the one?'

'Some honest soul—I could not learn his name—had hung a dead cat from the whelp's neck. It's guts were laid open and spilled upon her. She spat her curses at the stink.' He smiled again. 'Did I say I could not learn the fellow's name?'

'You said so.'

'Yet I made a guess. There was a smile on our Constable that set me thinking. I'll say it for Harry Hargreaves, papist though he is, that he knows what's proper for a witch.'

Then the smile faded and his eyes were hard again.

'So I don't doubt their malice, and I'll have a care for Grace. There was not the need to warn me. Yet it was well intended, and you may take my thanks to Master Nowell for that thought. And bid him in his turn look to you, mistress. You, also, bore testimony against the abhorred of God.'

At least he had spoken of thanks to Roger. Margery seized on that and pressed it further, speaking urgently of Roger's helpful goodwill. He pondered that darkly before he gave answer.

'That he has goodwill, I'll believe,' he said at length. 'That it's helpful, I see no reason to believe. He's a deal too tender to the ungodly. They could have been sent to the Lent Assize, and if anything of proof was lacking it might have been had.'

'But how, if you please?'

'There's juice in the driest apple if it be but pressed enough. So with these women. They were not so much as swum.'

'Swum?'

'Aye, in the nearest water. It's a cleansing way with witches. If they float, there's proof of guilt. If they sink, there's hope of drowning. And either way the world's the cleaner.'

And there he left it. He rose and said he must be back in the mill, and there was nothing for Margery to do but accept that. But she was not wholly dissatisfied; at least there was some hope, and all might yet be well if there was no more alarm of witches. And at that her satisfaction faded, for of course there would be more alarm of witches; if a cow died, or a rick took blaze, if even the ale were sour, the Demdike hand could be seen by a man who meant to see it. And then? He had given warning that he would trust in the Lord of Hosts—which meant, as Margery supposed, that he would follow his impulse and believe it to be the will of God. That was the way of puritans, as she well knew. It was at the centre of their creed that each should read his Bible and decide for himself what the will of God might be; and not every man could be trusted to decide with sense in such dark and tangled causes. Margery's heart sank at the thought of a Demdike killed, and Roger committing Richard Baldwin for the trial of his life at Lancaster. If Richard were hanged at Lancaster, it could even be on

Margery's testimony. She stood in the doorway, looked across at Grace, and felt sick.

Grace, however, looked happier. She had apparently got quickly to good terms with Frank, and they were sitting on opposite sides of the hearth, chattering easily. And at once Margery disturbed their harmony. She felt that in her present mood, and with her present thoughts, she must get out of this house. She could not, this day, sit at dinner with Richard Baldwin and think of what he might soon provoke; so she told Frank they must be going, and he was not pleased. Grace looked disappointed, and that made Margery feel selfish; but she stuck to it, feeling that to stay would be more than she could bear, and a rather sulky Frank went in search of the horses. Margery took the chance of a word with Grace.

'I'm sorry,' she said, 'but it's not the day to linger. Everyone's at odds with someone, but who's to say what may come next?'

'I know.' Grace spoke soberly. 'It may be better soon.'

'I hope so. I fear Frank's not pleased.'

'No. But Margery . . .'

'Yes?'

'Have a care for him. There's such a web of hatred here.'

'Here?'

'In Pendle, I mean. Miles had a word to say . . .'

'Miles?' Margery was almost startled. Yesterday's affair had so filled her mind that she had all but forgotten the Rough Lee, but this reminder brought her to the alert at once; it was not safe to forget the Rough Lee.

'What did Miles say?' she asked anxiously.

'Not very much, and even that not plain. But I did glean that Alice Nutter had not thought to see your Frank on Sunday. She supposed him gone from Pendle.'

'So I'll believe. But what more?'

'Nothing that's sure. But . . .'

'Go on.'

'Miles thought his mother was displeased—and something more than displeased. She said little, it seems, but Miles knows her ways.'

'I'm getting to know them myself. So you think there's mischief brewing?'

'Yes. And if that woman brews it . . .'

Grace broke off quickly as Frank was heard walking the horses to the door. But enough had been said to send a second cloud over Margery's thoughts and to deepen her gloom to something like despair. Everyone she knew in Pendle seemed to be in trouble or in danger, and most of them must look to themselves; but Frank Hilliard must be her special care, since all that touched him lay at her own door. She was asking herself now if she had not a duty to get him out of Pendle, and brooding darkly on that, she stayed in her thoughts and let him do without her talk.

They passed through Barley, and as they left it behind and made down the Pendle Water, Margery's thoughts came swiftly to earth. Coming along the wooded road, moving wearily, with bent head and tapping stick, was old Demdike, the dark-haired Alizon slouching with her. Both looked to the ground as the horses went past, and Margery kept her eyes to the front. But then she yielded to temptation and turned her head for a quick look; and at once she regretted it, for it gave her a glimpse, which she did not quickly forget, of two faces turned to her, the one lined and old and the other young and vicious, but both alike twisted in a living hurting hate.

'And who the Devil may those be?'

Frank's voice came from her side to disturb the thought, and she remembered with surprise that he had not seen these two before; he had heard of them but he had not seen them, and he showed a quick interest when he learned who they were.

'I wish I'd known sooner,' he said. 'I'd have viewed them the more keenly as we passed.'

He looked across at Margery, and this time she could not avoid his eye.

'What's the truth of it?' he demanded suddenly.

'Truth of what?'

'Of all these tales. Of what you told me yesterday, and of what Grace yonder had to say to me this morning. What's behind it all?'

Margery hesitated. She wanted to talk. She wanted to talk to someone of all this, and she wanted to talk to him in particular; and she knew, too, that talk of such sort might do much to ease the stiffness that was growing between them. But caution was alive in her, and Roger's warning words were clear in her mind. True, he had been speaking mostly of the Southworth affair, but Margery well knew that confidences, once started, have a way of running on; and her very liking for Frank, the very temptation she felt to talk deeply with him now, gave warning that here was a path that might prove both steep and slippery. And she was too tired and strained to think as quickly and clearly as she would need to in such a talk.

She thought she could not risk it, and she put him off with vague words. At once she saw the resentment in his eyes, and she guessed that his wish to draw her into talk had sprung as much from friendship as from curiosity; and in rejecting that, she had in a sense rejected him. Her unhappiness grew, and his matched hers. Silence came upon them, and they rode home with hardly a spoken word.

It was a relief when Roger told her that he had written to his son-in-law, Tom Heber, accepting the invitation for Christmas that Tom had brought them at Martinmas. They would spend the Twelve Days out of Pendle, said Roger. The break would be good for both of them; and as for Frank, he might come with them if he chose; he would be sure of welcome at Marton.

But Frank would have none of it. He said stiffly that there was not the need for it; he lacked neither friends nor kin, and he would betake himself to his own folk. He was very proper and dignified when he added that there should be no delay in his departure from Read.

Roger made no comment, but all expression had faded from his face as he remarked that Frank must decide that for himself. And Margery, who had no illusions about Frank's attitude, was now in such a humour that she was almost glad of it.

26

Taffeta and Velvet

Frank kept to his resolution. He left the next morning, riding unattended in a cold grey mist. Once again Margery stood outside the door to see him go, but this time her feelings were different. His farewell when he rode to Lathom had been warm and hopeful, today his civilities had a chill that matched the mist. He expressed no regret, and said nothing of seeing her again; he did not even say where he was going. He thanked Roger courteously for kindness done, spoke a formal word of thanks to Margery, and then rode away. Margery stood in the mist, silent and lonely, nursing the helpless feeling that something had gone from her, as it need not have gone if the fates had dealt a little kinder; that, she thought, was the way of things under Pendle Hill.

'What was it that set you at such odds?'

Roger's voice startled her. She had not guessed that he was still behind her on the gravel, and her memory flashed to that other morning when he had done the like.

'Odds?' she repeated vaguely.

'Aye—like dogs and a baited bear.'

He took her arm and led her into the parlour where the fire glowed red and hot ale steamed before it; and at once she thought of Frank, with his face cold in the mist, and she shivered in the radiant warmth.

'What ails you, lass?'

The kindness in his voice broke her guard, and she found herself clinging to him while she groped for the hand kerchief which was meant for airs and graces. Roger was too wise to interfere; he left her to it and became lost in the proper spicing of his heated ale. Soon she had recovered herself, and she watched him affectionately as he sipped critically at the spiced October. And suddenly she was pouring out the story.

'A thought too much cinnamon,' was his comment as she ended. 'So you think this to be the last of him?'

She stared at him as he delicately sifted powdered ginger into the ale to correct the cinnamon.

'I . . . I hardly know.'

It had occurred to her that Roger was taking this very calmly; and since Roger was assuredly not callous, it followed that Roger must see some hopes.

'Tell me,' she said fiercely, 'tell me what I may think.'

'A dangerous venture, that.' He sipped the ale again and seemed satisfied. 'But you've done well. Here's an uncertain world, and there's more wisdom in silence than in talk. Apart from which, he'll not prize you the less for it when pique's died down.'

His calmness was the right medicine. It infected Margery, and she began to think clearly again.

'That might be. But I've to see him against first. And I do not know so much as the way he rides.'

'North,' said Roger promptly. 'I heeded his going.'

'North, was it? But whither?'

'Where you will.' He sipped his ale placidly. 'There's but one true road here. You may ride into the Forest or you may ride out of it. He rode in.'

'So?' Margery's voice was eager.

'Again, what you will. Myself, I remember that the Forest road leads to Gisburn—and the Listers are his kin.'

'The Listers?'

'Of Westby, hard by Gisburn. A pleasant spot.' Roger reached for his boots. 'And finely placed—ten miles short of Marton, on the road that we must ride.'

And suddenly Margery took to laughing. Roger said nothing, but he watched her warily as he tugged his boots on.

'You think he'll visit Marton?' she asked him suddenly.

'Who knows? But it's no long ride. Nor need he lack a reason if he should seek one.'

'How?' She was cool again now.

'Family greetings.' He pulled his cloak about his shoulders. 'Jane Lister is a Heber. She's Tom's sister. That might be convenient. And now I'm for Altham. Curse these Wednesdays!'

He was away at that, and for an hour Margery was buoyant. But the mood did not last when she was alone, with no one to talk with and nothing to do. Soon she began to despond; by afternoon she was moping, and by nightfall she was a misery. She had hardly a greeting for Roger when he returned, and she sat through supper in a black silence, trying to tell herself that it was all for the best since she had certainly had a duty to get Frank out of Pendle.

Roger seemed to notice nothing, though twice, when she looked up suddenly, she found his eyes upon her. But later, as he sat lazily with his wine, he startled her by asking suddenly whether azure would suit him. For a moment she doubted if she had heard him fully.

'Azure,' he repeated calmly as she shook her wits together and sat up. 'It's a colour, is it not? I think of a new doublet.'

Margery began to get interested. She was always interested in clothes. But why a new doublet? And she was quite sure that azure would *not* suit Roger.

'May I . . . may I know what it's for?' she asked doubtfully.

'For Marton. What else? We'll be there the Twelve Days, and with junketings each night. Am I to be the same throughout, like a seed-time scarecrow?'

But Roger got no answer to that. It had occurred to Margery that here was a problem that did not touch Roger only, and her mind was running hastily through the contents of her wardrobe. She stared at him in consternation, and gave herself to estimating his mood. Then she stood with her hair under the candles, gave him her most crinkling smile, and told him in urgent accents that she must herself have some new clothes for the occasion, if she were not to bring disgrace on him, his house and his family. She watched him anxiously as his sardonic eyebrows rose, and then, seeing no displeasure there, she hastened to state her needs. The flame-satin kirtle was all but finished, and that would be well enough as far as it went; but she would need at least one more kirtle and a new gown too. She had only the flowered sarcenet, and that was getting known. Besides, it would not go with flame satin. Scarlet would be the best, she thought. Scarlet was the most useful of all colours . . .

'Also the most expensive, is it not?' said Roger blandly. 'But go on.'

Margery blinked. It was; but she had not expected Roger to know that. But he had told her to go on, so she went on. The second kirtle, she explained, could be of white. White, she said, was always attractive . . .

'It denotes innocence, does it not?' said Roger, with a wooden face. And Margery nearly choked. Roger knew too much.

'Yes,' she had to answer. 'I . . . I've been told it does.'

'Very proper. For a young girl. But pray continue.'

She continued hurriedly, thinking it better not to linger on this. The point was, she said, that a scarlet gown could be worn with either kirtle—the flame or the white.

'To speak again of this white,' said Roger, halting her in full flood. 'What's it to be made of?'

Margery steadied herself. Then she took a deep breath and told him she had always thought white looked best in damask. She watched him anxiously when she had said that, hoping he would not know that damask cost even more than satin. He had no right to know that, of course, but it was well not to be too sure—with Roger.

'Certainly the best,' he agreed dryly. 'That's why it's worn at the Court. What of the gown?'

Margery bit her lip. It sounded very much as if Roger did know about damask. So she spoke cautiously about the gown. Of course it would look best in velvet—scarlet velvet. That would be specially good with white—and warm too, if the nights should be chilly.

'What if there's a fire in the house?' said Roger.

She pulled a face at that and admitted that a good taffeta might do. A silk taffeta was always sweet and cool. Then, thinking she had better make some concession, she admitted that peach was a good colour, and a cheaper dye than scarlet.

'Will peach go with flame?' demanded Roger suddenly. And a startled Margery hastily collected her wits and agreed that it would not. Scarlet, she said, it would have to be.

'Scarlet,' said Roger like an echo. 'Taffeta or velvet?'

'Velvet,' said Margery promptly, and Roger laughed, and asked, as blandly as ever, if that was all.

Margery, who was beginning to feel nervous, had to admit that it was not. Of course the other things were trifles, but gown and kirtle did need accessories. There would have to be some collars, a girdle or two, a few petticoats and . . .

But Roger cut her short. He was not, he said, a tire-woman, and he would not have her reduce him to that rank. She might sort these matters with herself, or with Anne Sowerbutts, or with the Devil if she pleased. But tomorrow he would ride with her to Preston, where she might harry the mercers like a plague from Egypt. Meantime, she would do well to get pen and ink, and list her needs—if, indeed, there was paper enough to carry the tale of them. Then he laughed as he saw he was wasting his breath. Margery was already hunting for the ink-horn.

Her pen was still scratching when the fire had burned hollow and the first of the candles began to gutter, and her head was still a whirl of details when Roger made an end and hounded her off to bed. She turned on the stair, as her custom now was, her carrying-candle in one hand and her sheaf of notes in the other, and she bade him good night as he stood looking up at her. She smiled happily upon him, for the troubles of the day had flown; nor did her excited mind pause to ask what meaning might lie in the inscrutable smile that flickered on his face.

She was too busy to mope in the days that followed. The work at Preston took longer than she had expected, and there was a night spent at the *Angel* before all was done, all things bought, and sempstresses found who would undertake so long a task in so short a time. They would be hard put to it, she thought, as she made little drawings to illustrate her notes; for Roger had seemed in a melting mood, and he had remembered without its being hinted to him that the next week would see her birthday. On pretext of that, she had got not only the white damask and the scarlet velvet, but the taffeta too, in a rich, warm shade of orange. So there were two gowns to be made, as well as the damask kirtle, and as she must certainly have them different the sheaf of notes had to be expanded.

It was nightfall of the morrow when they were home again, and at once Margery entered on some busy days. She could not, for very shame, have everything done for her by sempstresses, and there was work in plenty for herself and Anne Sowerbutts. There was sarcenet and saye to be made into petticoats, gloves to embroider, white lace to be worked into collars, and a new hat of real beaver fur to be trimmed and plumed. Then she had to leave the work half done while she rode with Roger to Preston again, to try the gowns and kirtle and buy more threads and laces. She was far too busy to pine for anybody, and she had scarcely a thought of Alice Nutter.

Only once did Pendle intrude itself upon her. In the week in which they were to leave, she had an unexpected encounter. She had walked with Roger through the stables, and she chose to return alone through the back of the house. This brought her past the kitchen, and as she passed its open door her keen ears picked from the chatter a voice she thought she knew. She stopped, turned, and marched into the kitchen; and at once there was an excited yelp as Jennet Device came scampering up to her.

Margery was as pleased as she was surprised. She had a persistent liking for the grey-eyed Jennet, and it was weeks since she had seen the child.

''Lo,' said Jennet in her matter-of-fact tones. 'You well again?'

'Well?' Margery permitted herself a blink of surprise. 'I've not been sick, Jennet.'

'No?' Jennet seemed unconvinced, but she was quite unperturbed; and suddenly she bit fiercely into a huge piece of apple tart someone had given her. 'You fell off a horse,' she added cheerfully.

'Did I? How did you know that?'

'Saw you.'

Margery became interested, and her interest sharpened as she asked herself how much this child knew. Jennet's attack on the tart had smeared her to the ears with apple syrup, and she was now unconcernedly licking her fingers as she wiped it off.

'When was this, Jennet?' asked Margery quietly.

'Martin's Day.'

The strong white teeth sank into the tart again, and it was plain that there would be an interval before Jennet could possibly speak again. Margery thought quickly, and suddenly realised that there were three kitchen-maids in front of her, all with bulging eyes and gaping ears; and there was no telling what this queer child would say next. Margery decided to take no risks.

'Come with me, Jennet,' she said, to the obvious dismay of the maids. She left the kitchen and made for Roger's parlour. Jennet, busy removing a second layer of syrup from her ears, trotted behind like an obedient dog.

It was the half-hour before dinner, and Roger was sitting quietly with his ale when the two of them walked in.

'This,' said Margery briefly, 'is Jennet Device, Alizon's sister.'

'The Devil she is!' Roger turned in his chair and looked keenly at the child, who returned his stare unabashed and went on wiping her ears. Then Roger's face relaxed and his smile appeared.

'I remember you, little maid,' he told her solemnly, and Jennet, as if she liked his tone, broke into a grin.

'What's that on your fingers?'

'Apple.'

Jennet spoke the word between licks, and Margery expanded it for her.

'Jennet's been eating apple tart,' she exclaimed. 'She's quick at it, but not neat.'

'So it seems.' Roger contemplated Jennet with open amusement. 'You like apple tart, little maid?'

A gurgle from Jennet seemed to mean that she did.

'Is there apple tart at the Malkin Tower?'

Jennet shook her head, and Roger's smile broadened.

'Are there no apples there?'

'No oven.'

The terse answer was so prompt that Margery burst out laughing as she saw its meaning; if no more than apples had been lacking, Jennet would have come by them somehow.

'And to what,' asked Roger, 'do I owe this pleasure?'

Margery realised that this question was for her, and she answered it quickly.

'I found Jennet in the kitchen—with a half-dozen wenches cocking ears. And Jennet says she saw my fall at Martinmas.'

Roger seldom needed long explanations, and Margery read in his eyes that he had seen the point at once. But his immediate response was indirect. He spoke again to Jennet.

'In the kitchen? Do you want to eat dinner there?'

Jennet's face lit with eagerness, and the watchful Margery knew that a bait had been offered and taken.

'You shall if you wish,' said Roger carelessly. 'Did you see anyone else at Martinmas?'

Jennet began to count on her fingers.

'Five,' she said at length. Then she stood waiting quietly, as if her shrewd mind had understood that she must answer obediently if she wanted her dinner.

'Five?' Roger gave the word a slight stress. 'And who were they?'

Jennet ticked them off on her sticky fingers.

'The gentleman,' she began, 'the one in green. And two serving men. And a papist . . .'

'That's four.' Roger's voice betrayed nothing. 'And who else?'

'There was Anne. She was hid.'

Roger's face stayed impassive, but for a moment his eyes sought Margery's. Then he turned to Jennet again.

'Which Anne was that?'

'Redfern.'

'Was it? And was she hid with you?'

The little head shook vigorously.

'Not me with Anne. Pig-dung's sweeter.'

'Well said, little maid! But whither did these people go?'

Jennet wrinkled her forehead, and her sticky fingers began to count again.

'The papist rode off. The gentleman after him—but he didn't catch him.'

'Why not?'

'Too late.' Jennet grinned broadly at Margery in explanation of that, and Roger went tactfully to his next question.

'Where did the papist go when he wasn't caught?'

'Don't know,' said Jennet slowly.

'Guess?'

'Goldshaw.'

Roger made no comment, but his swift glance at Margery showed that he was impressed by Jennet's knowledge.

'And Anne Redfern.' he said. 'Where did she go?'

'Rough Lee.'

There was no hesitation this time; the answer came pat,

and Margery saw Roger's knuckles whiten as he gripped his chair.

'Why did she go to the Rough Lee?'

'Tell our Alice.'

'Impudent child!' But there was no reproof in Roger's tone. 'Why should Anne Redfern tell our—tell Mistress Nutter?'

'She's frighted of her.'

'Is she? And are you?'

The little head nodded.

'And do you go there to tell her things?'

'Not me!'

'Why not—if you're frighted?'

'She can't catch *me*.'

'Well said, little maid!' Roger laughed, and then seemed to decide that Jennet had had enough. 'You shall have your dinner now. Do you come here often?'

Jennet pursed her lips and considered that cautiously.

'Now and then,' she admitted at length.

'I've not seen you here before.' Roger laughed again as Jennet began to look mutinous. 'Which means that when you come here you don't let me see you. Is that it?'

With a little hesitation, Jennet nodded again.

'It's very well, Jennet.' Roger was smiling openly at her. 'You need not hide next time. I give you leave to come again.' He turned to Margery. 'See she has dinner in the kitchen.'

'I will. Come along, Jennet.'

She made for the door, and she had pushed Jennet through it when Roger spoke again.

'If there's another apple tart, give it her. She's earned it.'

When Margery came back to the parlour, Roger had left his chair and was leaning against the chimney-shelf. He looked up as she came in.

'I think we know now,' he said slowly, 'how Alice Nutter was able to send some hurtful words to Lathom. But that's the lesser matter. What of this child?'

'Jennet? She's shrewd for her age. And well informed.'

'Uncommonly well informed. And what she does not know she guesses—shrewdly, as you say. But consider . . .' Roger was speaking soberly now. 'She's shrewd and knowledgeable. She has two sharp eyes and a trick of hiding herself. And even when she's not hid, who'd take heed of such a child? She may see all and be seen by none. She's had some favours from you and she has hopes of more. And as far as we may judge, we have her goodwill. Now, add that up.'

'You mean . . .' Margery hesitated. 'You mean that she could be, in some sort, a spy?'

'She was born to that trade. Nor, I think, should we scruple to use her. We're in no case for niceties. We've fair warrant for a spy. So look to it, and keep her fee'd.'

'Fee'd?' Margery laughed. 'I'll do better than that. I'll keep her fed.'

27

The Traveller by Night

Three days later they rode to Marton.

Tom Heber, red, plump and jovial, greeted them noisily. From behind him a swarm of children were released to fling themselves at Roger with whoops of delight; and into this uproar came Anne Heber, laughing and protesting, to give welcome to her father. Margery hung back, and watched with eyes that missed nothing. Anne Heber, she noted, did not take after Roger. She was a pleasant, fair-haired woman, with a soft, clear skin and calm, friendly eyes; at seventeen she had probably been fragile and alluring; at twenty-nine she looked broad, placid and capable. Margery considered the six children, and thought them sufficient explanation of that.

Margery was presented, and Anne showed herself friendly. She had one eye for Margery and one for the orange-tawny, and she seemed to approve of both. Then she led within doors, and Margery, following her up the stair, had a backward glance at a Roger who was new to her—a Roger sitting in the arch of the great door and bestowing sugared plums, in strict rotation, on the clamouring children. Evidently he was an old friend to them, and Margery was first surprised at that and then surprised at herself for not foreseeing it.

Dusk was on the house when she came down the stair, and the candles lit her flame satin to a glow that matched the scarlet gown. Below her was an excited buzz, for this was Christmas Eve and it was open house to all who came. Expectancy was in the air, and the boughs of evergreen that hung from wall and ceiling gave mystery as well as colour.

Margery went down excitedly, very willing to take her part in these Christmas revellings, whatever they might be. On that she knew herself to be ignorant, for Christmas had always been a mild and decorous season in her mother's puritan home. She knew also that Christmas in the North Parts had the repute of being never mild and not always decorous; but what the North Country customs actually were, she did not know. She had asked Roger, and he had firmly refused to enlighten her; he had retired instead behind an impish grin and had told her that she would learn.

She did. There were plenty to teach her, and they found her a willing pupil. It was a mixed company: an Esquire or two, half a dozen gentlemen and a score of yeomen, all with their wives and the elders of their sons and daughters. Already they had forgotten distinctions, and it was hard to tell in the throng which was the gentleman and which the yeoman. But at least none was in doubt about Margery, for though she had not contrived it her late appearance turned to her profit; it meant that they were all there to see her when she halted, half way down the stair, to survey the scene. And see her they did; the warmth of her flame and scarlet, the red glint the candles had found in her hair, her widening eyes and her cheeks flushed with excitement, all joined to make a picture rare in Craven; and a burly yeoman, taking the freedom that Christmas gave, raised his ale-mug in a cheerful swing and set the company turning to see what this apparition was. Roger was prompt on that; he slipped through the throng, gay in his wine-red velvet, and came to the foot of the stair to take her hand and announce her formally to the company.

It set her breath fluttering. Quiet days at Lambeth had not prepared her for this before so many. But she faced them boldly, even if the hand that clutched Roger's did feel moist and sticky; and then, firmly telling herself that her flame satin, with its yellow lace and French farthingale, was second to nothing in this company, she made her curtsey twice—first to Roger alone, and then to them all; and while she held herself, poised and still, in that most gracious gesture, a wild and incongruous thought came shooting through her mind—a thought of sister Prudence come by some miracle into this room; Prudence, with her hair lifting and her jaw dropping at the sight of her young sister now. It was too much for Margery; her mind leapt at it, and with a crinkling forehead she went off into gurgling laughter.

That conquered them all, and at once she found herself one of them, and therefore at her ease; and with that came confidence, and she plunged joyously into the whirl of it. There was dancing, and of this she was nervous, for she knew little enough about it; dancing had not been one of the things her family had taught her. But to her infinite relief, it was Roger who first took her hand and led her out; and if her performance in the Galliard was not skilful, it matched in that the performances of many others in the company. They did not, she thought, have much love for the Galliard; they danced it once, apparently as a concession to the forms of things, and thereafter they abandoned it and kept themselves to what Margery would have called the Branle. The French had called it that when they devised it, and in southern England, where men looked respectfully to France for guidance in polite affairs, it was still so called; but here in the North Parts, where it was not the way of men to look respectfully to anybody, they called it the Brawl; and after that manner they danced it. It gave Margery little trouble; for placing of feet, as she soon perceived, counted for very little in the Brawl; all that mattered was that at every opportunity everybody kissed somebody. The staid and dignified sat cautiously aside, but the younger yeomanry went at it with zest, and they plainly thought it a vast improvement on the Galliard.

Roger evidently considered that he had done his duty when he led Margery in the Galliard. After that he left her to fend for herself; and she fended very well in a gay press of yeomen's sons and daughters. She learnt the Brawl; she learnt their quick blunt repartee; she learnt the purpose of the sprigs of mistletoe that hid so coyly in the hanging evergreens. In no long time Margery was enjoying herself; this sort of Christmas seemed to her to have much to commend it, and when she said as much to a red-haired young yeoman who was just then at her side, he laughed excitedly and told her that if she wanted to learn more she should hold tight to Old Ball's tail; nor, as he swept her again into the Brawl, would he tell her what he meant by that odd remark.

Then came supper, crowded, generous, and informal.

Margery, in the middle of an excited group, found herself trying to keep up the talk while she dealt hungrily with a great basin of what looked like yellow cream and was, she learned, the traditional frumenty—wheat, boiled in milk and flavoured with cinnamon and sugar. With it was a queer oatmeal bread which she had not seen before; they told her it was called jannock, and that the proper thing to do was to dip it in the frumenty and then eat it while it dripped. Then came what they called mincepies, shaped like a manger to tell them of a Birth, and stuffed with every kind of spice to tell them of Gifts that had come from the East. There was cold goose with wheaten bread; and nuts and sugar and plums; and mug after mug of the prime October to help it down. Then, when all was done and the hungriest stuffed to repletion, the clatter died and the talk sank to whispers; and without any order given, the company moved from the centre of the room and pressed themselves against the dark panels of the walls. Then a trumpet blared and drums banged noisily; the doors were flung wide, and into the room, tumbling in joyous somersaults, his motley a wild flurry of blue and yellow, came the man who meant Christmas—the crazy Lord of Misrule.

He had a thunderous welcome, and pretended to be angered by it. He belaboured the nearest with his sceptre—an inflated bladder, swinging by a cord from a two-foot stick—and he roared lustily for silence. Since they were so insolent, he told them, they should do penance in proper form. He stalked fiercely round the room, pulling his painted face into grotesque frowns, and Margery, sitting cross-legged on the floor in the front of the throng, suddenly hiccoughed with excitement and amusement. She was promptly punished with the bladder, a great thundering slap that knocked her off her balance and sent her sprawling against her red-haired yeoman, while the room rocked in a gale of laughter. Again the Lord of Misrule waved his bladder for silence, and slowly the laughter died until he could be heard again. They should, he said, do penance by paying homage to his horse—a marvellous proper horse, he said, who was named Old Ball; and whatever more the Lord of Misrule may have meant to say was lost for ever in the stamping and cheering that greeted this.

Again the doors were set wide; again the Lord of Misrule

plied his bladder for silence; again the hush throbbed with expectancy. Then, cavorting through the doorway, neighing, kicking, and jumping clear from the floor, came the monstrous image of a horse. The stamping and cheering rose to madness, with shrieks and whistles and bangings of mugs. Margery took one look at Old Ball and then swayed helplessly against her neighbour, hurting her ribs with laughter. Old Ball was a huge horse's head, crazily done in wood and canvas; the round bottoms of wine-bottles formed his eyes, and his teeth were painted wooden pegs; below, two stout sticks took the weight and pretended to be his front legs; a great sheet of canvas made his body, and concealed the man who was his hind legs and who worked his tail and jaws; for both moved. There was a great tail of red-bound rope, which flapped wildly; and there was a lower jaw which moved creakingly up and down; and from out of this fantastic mouth there stuck a great iron ladle, gaily hung with ribbons.

The Lord of Misrule swung his bladder, and Old Ball came prancing obediently; and at a shouted command he went romping round the circle, rearing on his hind legs and whinnying noisily, while the applause came in deafening waves. Then, as the laughter began to die, Old Ball went snorting at a stout and bearded yeoman; the jaw moved with a creak, and the yeoman's arm was seized by the painted teeth. He led the laughter himself, while he felt in his pouch; from it he produced two pennies, which he flung into the beribboned ladle. Old Ball promptly released him, and the ladle was suddenly withdrawn between the painted jaws; from somewhere within the beast there was a metallic clang as the pennies dropped, and then the ladle shot out again as Old Ball went snorting after his next victim. This was a portly gentleman in murrey velvet, who jovially produced a silver shilling; another yeoman paid his twopence; Roger was the next, and flung a whole crown into the ladle; a yeoman's wife and somebody's fair-haired daughter gave a penny each; the wife of an Esquire produced a florin; and Old Ball continued inexorably round the circle. But the crowd was growing restless, and began to stir. Someone flung a coin; another followed, and another; and soon coins were being flung at the ladle from all sides, and the Lord of Misrule was jumping wildly after those that fell. Then the climax came. The musicians who had played for the dancing suddenly struck up again, and Old Ball went stamping round the room to the thump of a marching tune. The staid and portly moved hurriedly aside, and the rest rushed wildly at the tail of red-wrapped rope; as many as could get a grip hung fiercely to it and the rest hung as fiercely to them; and soon three-quarters of the company were solemnly tramping a circle in tow of that crazy horse. Then the music came faster—and faster—and faster still. The solemn tramp became a jogging trot; the trot became an unsteady run; and soon there was a wild and whirling romp, till the man in the canvas horse stumbled and fell headlong. His followers sprawled on top of him, and their followers fell across them in a wild hooting chaos while the music ended abruptly in a screech of discord.

Margery was gasping for breath. Her head was in someone's back, and a laughing nut-brown girl was sprawling across her legs. At her side, the red-haired yeoman, one arm still round Margery, was disentangling himself from a plump girl in green. Across the room, Anne Heber, who had gone into it with the best of them, was being hauled to her feet by Roger. Everywhere fathers were grinning and blowing, while mothers looked anxiously at sons and reprovingly at daughters. And girls who had not yet extricated themselves were being given swift reminders that the mistletoe still hung in the greenery above.

Then Tom Heber was on his feet, hot and happy, with a face like a Harvest Moon. He banged noisily with a mug, and the clamour fell away as the company ranged themselves against the walls once more. Tom saw it done, and then he walked, with what steadiness he could summon, to the hearth. In silence he laid on the stones a silver crown and a quart of ale, and Margery noticed that this space had been left clear; there was a press round every wall, but the space by the hearth was clear.

The chatter died to expectancy again, and they stood and sat and shuffled, while breath was regained, kirtles smoothed, and doublets pulled into shape. Then, loud and brazen, the clock struck twelve, and the First Day of Christmas was come. There was the inevitable cheer, and then silence again. Evidently they were expecting something, and a quiet buzz of talk broke out as they waited.

Margery, squatting on the floor next to the brown-faced girl, asked what was to come next. The girl abandoned a hopeless attempt to smooth her collar, and explained; they were waiting, she said, for the man who should first come in by the outer door and carry Christmas with him. The quality of this first-comer, she went on, was a matter of importance, for if he was a mean fellow it would be but a mean Christmas; everybody was therefore hoping that he would be a man of at least some quality. Margery nodded, and began to feel the excitement that was mounting again in the room, while the nut-brown girl went chattering on. There would not be long to wait, she said, for there were always some who went a-roving with this intent; but the thing was never contrived, and none could tell who it might be. But whoever it was he would have the crown and the quart of ale as his fee, and thereafter he would be the guest of honour in what . . .

The nut-brown girl stopped short in her sentence and cocked an ear. Others did the like, and the buzz of talk died like a quenched candle. Unmistakably, through bolted door and shuttered window, the clop of horses could be heard. Surprise came into faces, and here and there a man came tensely to his feet, First-comers were wont to come on foot, and this might not be a reveller.

The horses came on and then stopped. Boots crunched on the gravel, and then a thunderous knocking split the silence. Men looked at one another, and a great voice came booming through the oak.

'Open,' it cried, 'by the sainted Christopher! Here's Christmas on a horse! Who'll draw bolt for him?'

That was better. Faces relaxed and smiles appeared. This was a jovial voice, a rich and hearty voice, clearly proclaiming that if its owner was not a reveller he soon would be. There was a buzz and stir from the company, and in it Roger's voice came clearly across the room.

'God's Grace!' he was saying. 'Of all the bawling rogues! It's Tom Covell.'

Then Tom Heber went rolling to the door, his Anne beside him, while the company stood, craning necks and stretching toes to see the better. Jointly, the Hebers drew the bolt and turned the latch, and the door swung open.

'God 'a'mercy!' said the jovial voice. 'I was fearing you were drunk, or else abed.'

He stepped through the arch, and he seemed to fill it as he came. He stopped on the threshold to pull his beaver off, and he stood there plain to view: a great mountain of a man, broad and corpulent; a man of perhaps fifty years, with a round, red face, a grizzled, brown beard, and deep brown eyes that rolled and twinkled merrily.

Tom Heber did his best at a bow.

'Master Covell?' he asked.

'Now who else should it be, hey?' The man's laugh came rolling out, as rich and hearty as his voice. 'One look at me and I'm known for life. And I mind you from last year. You're Tom Heber. And this your wife?'

'Aye, but let that bide.' Anne Heber was answering him herself. 'What signifies, Master Covell, is that you're first-comer here. Your ale and crown lie ready.'

'First-comer, hey?' His laugh came rolling as he led boisterously to the hearth. 'Did I not say I was Christmas on a horse?'

Again his great laugh rolled out, and the company found it infectious. Margery felt it too, but her curiosity had roused now, and it quenched her laughter. She was asking herself what had brought this man to Marton at this strange hour—this man, she remembered, who ruled the gaol at Lancaster, and had stood sponsor to Frank Hilliard. Whatever his purpose, he bore proof of a wet road and a wetter night; his cloak was black and soft with rain, and the wet mud was dripping from his boots as he took his stance on the hearth, his back to the fire and his red face beaming.

He drained his quart at a single draught, and thereby established himself with this company; the yeoman had respect for a man who could do that. Then he blinked, and peered at the empty mug.

'That's a poor pot,' he growled, and beamed at them again.

'How?' Anne Heber was smiling at his antics.

'Thick-bottomed as a milk wench. Leaves no room for ale.'

In the roar that followed this, Anne gestured to the hovering servants; and at that, Tom Covell set the silver crown spinning on his great hand.

'If there's to be more ale, I'll part with the crown,' he said. 'Some wench shall have it.'

'Aye, to be sure.' Anne was laughing at him as she spoke. 'But which wench?'

'Why, the prettiest.'

Her husband guffawed.

'Aye, the prettiest. But which is that, hey?'

'The one with the best legs.'

The answer came with a grin, and suddenly Tom Covell sent the crown spinning across the floor, to be scampered for by all who cared to chase it. His laugh rolled out again as he saw the crush, and he watched it genially, swaying gently on the hearth, his hands behind his back and his legs planted apart. Margery stayed out of the rush and let the crown go by. She was considering this man, appraising him critically; a man who was friend to Roger and benefactor to Frank Hilliard might prove important in her affairs; and a man who held such places in the County must surely be more than the roisterer he seemed.

A servant came hurrying with more ale, and that put Master Covell in mind of something else.

'I've two horses on your gravel,' he told Tom Heber. 'They were sweating, and soon they'll be chilled. I've a servant too—of a sort. He's chilled all the time.'

'Pest take me! I'd forgot.' Tom Heber turned to the man who had brought the ale. 'Wake those idle grooms and let them see to the horses. And yourself, take Master Covell's servant and make the rogue drunk.'

'That's no labour,' said Master Covell helpfully. 'He's quicklime in his guts, and steams at the first quart.'

He pulled at his second ale, and then beamed on the company again.

'What a plague do we stay for?' he asked. 'Is there no music here?'

The drums went thumping at his word, and in no time he had them all dancing again, and dancing now with an added zest, as if they had drawn new spirits from the exuberant fellow. The red-haired lad swooped on Margery and pulled her gaily into the dance. She went with a laugh, but under the laugh her thoughts were stirring; the feeling was growing in her that more than chance had brought this traveller by night; and as soon as the dance was ended she made apologies and slipped away. It was time, she thought, to have a word with Roger.

But Roger had disappeared; and so had Tom Covell.

28

'To Drive Away Sorrow'

Christmas Day was now a half-hour old, and the crowd was thinning as one after another made ready for journey home. Tom Heber was wandering about offering last mugs of ale, and Anne was busy with the stirrup-cups of soup. Outside, there was noise and bustle as horses were led from the crowded stables; inside, there was talk and flurry as waiting husbands stamped impatiently and wives ran scolding after lagging daughters. Margery discovered her velvet gown, long since discarded in the heat, and slipped it on; she drew it tightly round her, and went strolling through the great door to see what might be seen.

The rain had cleared, but the night was dark and raw. Lanterns had been set by the door, and the gravel seemed filled with horses. Everywhere men were mounting, some with ease and some with trouble; for the ale had been strong and the air was cold, and not every yeoman found his stirrup at the first attempt. But soon all were up, and wives and daughters were being helped up too, to sit pillion behind husbands and brothers. Servants were running with the lighted horse-lanterns, one to each rider, and soon the lanterns were in clusters as neighbours joined to ride in groups for their greater safety. There was shouting and laughter, calls of thanks and farewell, and then the Hebers were waving from the warmly lighted doorway. Margery went to join them there as the hoofbeats receded. Then the noise grew less, and soon the lanterns had dwindled to pin-points that jogged and danced. Anne Heber yawned and led the way in.

Margery followed, undecided what to do. She was still

wondering how Roger was occupied; he was surely with Tom Covell, and something was surely portended by this midnight arrival. Tom Covell, she remembered, was a Coroner and a Justice of the Peace and Quorum, as well as being Governor of the gaol at Lancaster; such a man would hardly ride through this, of all nights in the year, without a purpose.

A snore disturbed her thoughts. Heat and ale had overcome Tom Heber at last; he sprawled, open-mouthed, in a chair, his legs stuck stiffly out and his red face twitching. Margery considered him thoughtfully, asking herself how she would have fared if Fate had sent her to a cousin cast in such a mould, instead of to her own Roger. She knew how easily it could have been so; for Tom Heber, not Roger Nowell, was the pattern of a country gentleman.

She looked further. Anne Heber had disappeared, and Margery guessed that she was seeing to it herself that the children were safely in their beds; that would no doubt take a little time, and Margery's eyes moved to the firmly shut door of a little parlour which had been given to Roger as his own; it was private to him while he was in this house, and Margery had little doubt that he and Tom Covell were in it now. For a moment she considered. Then she tossed her head wilfully and marched boldly at the door; at need, she told herself, she could show a proper surprise at seeing Master Covell within.

She tapped politely and then walked straight in. By the little hearth, Roger was leaning in his favoured pose, and Tom Covell was filling the elbow-chair; he was something more than filling it, as was apparent when he began to heave himself out of it.

'Don't curtsey,' he told her cheerfully, as he saw her point her toe in preparation. 'If you do, I'll have to bow, and I'm a deal too fat for scrapings.'

He was on his feet, rocking a little and breathing heavily, and his grin sent Margery into a smile.

'We'll give you absolution,' said Roger from the hearth. 'But here's the lass herself. And here's Tom Covell, and you'll have heard talk of him.'

'Aye, sir.' Margery's amusement was growing as she turned again to Master Covell.

'Your servant, sir.' She said it formally, and she only just checked the curtsey that would have followed so naturally.

'Servant!' he growled. 'You should have let me say that. I say it to all the girls, and when they're as pretty as you, I mean it.'

He eased himself into the chair again, leaving her without an answer. Tom Covell was something new in Margery's experience. Her mother's circle had not included men like this, and the thought of him suddenly dropped among them came quickly to her, and sent her into gurgling laughter; then she recovered her manners and eyed Tom Covell anxiously. But he seemed delighted; his grin had broadened and he was sitting back, wheezing and chuckling.

Roger leaned forward, and his foot hooked a small leather-covered stool from the wall.

'You'd best be seated,' he told her. 'Covell's here from Westby, and with a word to say that touches you.'

Margery's smile faded. Word from Westby must be word of Frank Hilliard, and Roger's tone had been sober. She took the stool, and without a word she seated herself and sat still and erect, her hands clasped and her kirtle smoothly spread. In silence she looked anxiously at them, and waited for one of them to speak.

It was Roger who spoke. The Council of the North, he said, had met at York, and Tom Covell, returning from that to Lancaster, had chosen to break his journey at Westby, as he had done the year before. There, also as he had done a year before, he had met Frank Hilliard; and there had been some talk between them.

'How is he?' Margery put in impulsively.

'Sad.' Master Covell gave her the answer himself. 'Sad as a dripping tree. But that's no matter. That's as he should be. I've grieved as hard myself in the days when I went a-wenching and was crossed in love. He'll get past that, and it's no matter. What's of weight is that the lad's sour . . .'

'Sour?'

'As the green crab juice. And there's an oddity about that.' Tom Covell paused, and nothing of the jester was left in him now. 'This sourness is some three days old, no more —though he's been there these three weeks, as I'm told. I'd some talk with Jane Lister . . .'

He went on to explain it at some length. Mistress Lister had been perplexed. She had found Frank something out of humour when he had arrived from Read, but that had not distressed her; it was no more, she said, than was proper after the events he had related; and under it he had been buoyant, making no secret of his intention to visit Marton at Christmas and there put all to rights. And then, all in an hour, he had changed. A bitterness had come into his talk, and there had been no more said of a ride to Marton. He had declared instead that he should go to his home and stay there. He had had enough, he said, of these North Parts and their folk. He would stay out of courtesy till Christmas was in, and then he would be away to his home in Warwickshire, there to stay until some proper employment should offer; he would not return to Lancashire, nor to the service of a nobleman whose words and conduct he resented.

'And that's the drift and set of it.' Tom Covell came to an end and looked steadily at Margery with eyes that were now grown very bright and keen. 'I tried to learn what scent he was nosing, but he only grumbled that it was not his tale to tell. Then I tried Tom Lister, and he as good as bade me to the Devil.'

'And Jane?' Roger spoke quietly.

'As foxed as I.'

'And you've come here to tell us this?'

The big man shrugged, and for a moment he seemed almost shy.

'I like the lad,' he explained slowly. 'And knowing you and yours, Roger, I made the guess that the lass might be worth the liking too—as she surely is.' He turned to her with a smile that set her blushing. 'What do you say to it all, lass?'

'I . . . I know not what to say. It's exceeding kind of you, sir, to . . .'

'Tom . . .' Roger cut in sharply as if he had seen her confusion. 'Exceeding kind of you it surely is, but there'll be more to it than that. You did not ride here at this hour, on this night, to do no more than tell a tale. Now what's in your mind?'

Tom Covell sat mute, as though he collected his thoughts. Then he spoke gravely.

'The lad means it,' he said slowly. 'He's the sort that does. He'll stay through tomorrow—or today, as it is now, and at tomorrow's dawn he'll be away. And being away, he'll remain away. That's bad. But what's worse, he'll take his sourness with him, and it will stay with him while he lives.' His thick shoulders shrugged again. 'That's all I've a right to say. It's for you and your lass here to say if it's to be permitted.'

'How's it to be stopped?'

'It's but ten miles to Westby. A letter sent at dawn could have him here by nightfall. There's time enough.'

'Only just.' Roger was smiling at him from the hearth. 'Time enough, but none to spare. Which is why you rode in rain on Christmas Eve.'

Another twitch of the shoulders was the only answer to that, and Roger turned to Margery.

'It's for you to speak,' he said. 'Do we send such a letter?'

'Not "we", Roger.' Tom Covell was grinning again. 'There's but one voice he'll heed.'

'Very like. So it stays with Margery.'

She wriggled on her stool in acute discomfort, but it was plain that she must say something. She had been taking it for granted that Frank would somehow appear at Marton during Christmas. She had made the white damask kirtle with that foremost in her mind, and now . . .

Roger, as usual, came quickly to her help.

'There's a need for courtesy in this,' he said. 'All being said, you owe him something—more, perhaps, than he owes you. It would be proper to give him thanks of a decent warmth before he departs these shires. Or at least, you could represent it so . . .'

The hint was enough, and Margery came quickly to her feet. Roger produced writing needs, and soon her pen was busy. She wrote shortly and quickly:

I hear from the wind that you purpose to depart from the North Parts. I owe you much thanks for kindness done, and it's ill work setting thanks on cold paper. But if you will ride this way your welcome shall not lack warmth. Pray bring with you no thought that might cast a chill on

Margery.

She passed it invitingly to Roger.

'Subtle as the serpent,' was his comment. 'He may find in it what he pleases, yet nothing that you can't deny.'

She wondered if that was censure; but as she folded it and applied the wax, he took his signet from his finger and passed it to her; and that, she thought, was surely the seal of his approval.

'I'll take order for sending this,' he told her. 'For yourself, get you to bed. It's well past one, and you'll have heavy eyes at noon.'

She had. She slept heavily, tired by the long and arduous evening, and she knew nothing of the lad who rode into the Christmas dawn with the paper that bore the arms of Nowell. But she was astir when Tom Covell called for his horses some two hours short of noon, and she was at his stirrup when he mounted. He grinned ruefully at her and hoped she would enjoy her dinner.

'I'll miss mine,' he grumbled. 'But there's no help for that. I've wife and family at Lancaster, and a man should sup with his own on this night. Fare you well—and deal softly with the lad.'

He was away before she could answer him, and he left her with a head of anxious thoughts as she wondered what the day would bring, and what response that letter would evoke. She had six endless hours to fret away before she knew; and then, as the grey dusk closed on the house, a horseman came quickly from the rising mist—a trim figure in cloak of green and gold, who sat erect, and looked eagerly at door and window as if in search of someone.

Margery was above, in her bedchamber, for it was already time to begin preparing herself for supper. She held her breath as she saw; and then, telling herself that Christmas gave leave for most things, she pushed the lattice open, leaned out, and waved. He saw it on the instant, and she marked his upturned face as his hat gave the answering wave. And then Tom Heber was out of the door in noisy welcome, and Margery left them to it. She called for Anne Sowerbutts and the kirtle of white damask; and with that she grew busy.

She stood at last before the mirror, peered critically, and was modestly satisfied. The damask took a glint from the candles, as she had hoped it would, and the two bands of silver lace that edged the front body made a frame for the cream satin of the stomacher. The damask flared widely at the hip, where the farthingale held it out, and then fell sheer to the ankles. Here was simplicity and no contrast of colour; to keep the simplicity, Margery had rejected the elaborate patterns of lace that were usual, and had left the whole sweep of the damask plain except for some scraps of lace sewn here and there like silver stars.

She gave her attention to the ruff, thin, delicate, and finely pleated. She had not trusted Anne Sowerbutts to set those pleats. She had done them herself, working till her fingers ached with the pleating pins and Mistress Turner's starch; but it had been worth it, for the pleats had set admirably, and the yellow starch was vivid against the damask. A slight frown came upon her as she looked again. The set of the ruff was certainly excellent, but was it level? Pinning a ruff to a kirtle was delicate work if the pins were not to show, and Margery was not satisfied that this one lay evenly. Anne Sowerbutts, hovering behind her, was promptly called to order and told to alter those pins. Margery watched critically, and then turned attention to the high collar that swept stiffly upwards behind the ruff. It was of the same white damask as the kirtle, for once Margery had decided that sweet simplicity would suit her, she had carried it out thoroughly and had been very sparing of her colour-contrasts. But Roger had produced from somewhere a few small pearls, and these she had sewn round the top of the collar, where they gave a fine effect of richness without spoiling the scheme. She looked, and nodded with satisfaction. It would do very well. But she hoped Old Ball would not appear again tonight. If he did, she would have to be careful; last night's kirtle had looked a wreck in the grey light of morning.

Anne brought her the taffeta gown and helped her into it. Once again she looked and was satisfied. The deep orange of the gown brought a glow of warmth to the kirtle it framed, and Margery let it hang open. Then, after setting the furred collar to her liking, and carefully smoothing the long sleeves, she was ready.

She stayed for a last look, and then went quietly to the head of the stair. For a moment she lurked in the shadows, listening to the sounds from the lighted hall below. She was intentionally late, and the pluck of viols and the thump of drums told her that the dancing had begun. Her left hand lifted her kirtle the prescribed six inches, to let the damask fall in flutes, and show the silver stars on her satin petticoat. She made sure of her stance, chin up, shoulders back, right arm straight; and for a moment she stood breathless, summoning her forces. Then, brisk and erect, with a crinkling smile and a roving eye, she went marching down the stair to the lilt of that dancing tune.

At the foot of the stair Roger came from nowhere: Roger in black velvet and arabesques of gold, which made him gay and saturnine together. His eyebrows went up at once.

'What mischief do you brew?' was his greeting, in the old familiar tone.

'Mischief, sir?'

Margery was as innocent as her damask, and Roger nodded affably.

'When a maid brings such fond exactness to her tiring, it's seldom to the sole glory of God.'

He wandered off before she could answer, and left her to pout at his retreating back. Roger invariably knew too much.

Then Frank swooped upon her, darting through the press so that he was the first of them all to greet her. She gave him her hand, thinking that a warmer greeting than a formal curtsey, but to her surprise he bowed over it and carried it to his lips. That meant the curtsey after all, and she was excited as she made it.

'I'm so glad you've come,' she said softly.

'I could do no other,' was his answer, and before she could decide what meaning to put on that, he had swept her into the dance; and she found him as deft in that as he was in other things. She went at it joyously.

'You keep your promise,' he said, when it came to an end.

'Which promise?'

'Of warm welcome. Why did you send it?'

'Was that not natural?'

'I do not know. You bewilder me—aye, and you dazzle me too, as you'd dazzle any man.'

She chose the easier half to answer.

'Do I dazzle?'

'You know it well. As you look tonight . . .' He looked her up and down, and his admiration was obvious. 'As you look tonight you'd light the Great Hall at Lathom—as I once told you you could do.'

She flushed with pleasure.

'I take some pains,' she answered. 'That is all.'

'Not all.' She waited for the further compliment, but it did not come. 'Not all,' he repeated. 'You take pains, but you give them too.'

That was startling, and Margery almost gasped with relief when a surge of people swept them to the wall and the whisper ran that the Mummers were coming. That would at least give her a chance to think, and she felt she needed it. Plainly he had admiration for her; just as plainly, he was not lost in admiration; he had resentments too.

Then the doors were flung wide, and the Mummers came marching two by two in slow procession: rustic fellows these, gay in their home-made finery, and marching slowly with a tramp of their high boots. Then the tramp became louder as it gave the rhythm to their ancient song:

'We've not come to your house to beg or to borrow,
But we've come to your house to drive away sorrow.
Though if when we've ended, we look as if we're dry,
We'd thank you for ale, and a bite of the pie.'

Round the room they went, stiff and wooden, with their deep-chested voices rolling out. Margery, pressed against the wall by the crowd, found Frank somehow at her side, and her hand was in his as the Mummers came round again.

'We come with good will, and a story to play,
To bring you the joy that belongs to this Day.
And God send you grace to give thanks on the morrow,
Who sent One to your house to drive away sorrow.'

The words rang clear, and Margery pressed closely against Frank at her side.

'Shall I have cause to give those thanks?' she whispered.

He let that sink in before he made answer. Then his whisper came in her ear:

'Has God sent grace to you—and me—this night?'

Then Margery knew that the time had come.

'We'll talk of that in private,' she said.

29

The Secret Cold

She led him apart, out of the crowded hall and into the little parlour that was private to Roger Nowell. Margery calmly appropriated it, for Roger was with the Mummers and would scarcely disturb them here.

She sat herself in the elbow-chair and looked up at him steadily as he stood by the tiny hearth.

'You seem,' she told him, 'to have some complaint of me. Certainly we seem at odds over something. Do you care to be precise?'

He chose to remain standing, and when he spoke his words came deliberately.

'When we first met,' he said slowly, 'that day when your horse fell, and you lay among the leaves . . .'

'Yes?' She was half smiling at the memory of it.

'I found in you what I'd never known before. Do not ask me what it was. I'm not skilled with words.'

Margery was avoiding his eye, but the smile was still with her. Memory of her own feeling was helping her to understand his.

'I forgot that papist.' His tone was hardening now. 'I forgot him so that he rode away. I all but forgot him those next three days—till I was reminded, and rode to Lathom. You know why I forgot him?'

Margery looked up and met his eye again, but she did not speak; it seemed as if he hardly expected her to.

'I forgot him because of you,' he went on quietly. 'I forgot him because my head was full of you, and there was no space left for any other. It was so from the moment I found you in the leaves. It was so when we rode in Pendle Forest. It was so when I rode alone to Lathom.'

'Yes?' Margery's voice was hardly a whisper. 'And then?'

'Then there was warmth in you.' His voice was rising a little. 'There was warmth that lit everything—for me. I'd some little conceit of myself then, and perhaps something to ground it on. I could account myself come of a good family and placed in the service of a great one. I'd some share of milord's favour, and some fair hope of rising in the world. And then came you—and we rode in Pendle. I felt your warmth and I dreamed. Was it too much that I should dream?'

He paused and seemed to wait for an answer; but no answer came. Margery was looking down, and clinging tightly to the arms of her chair.

'So it stood,' he went on. 'So it stood that day I rode for Lathom. You came in the dawn to see me go, and your coming warmed the mist. Do you remember that mist?'

She nodded and still said nothing. But the hand kerchief of cambric was crumpled in her hand, and she seemed to be nibbling its corner.

'You stood in the mist,' he said. 'You stood by my stirrup with your hand on mine, and you said it was I that needed to be cared for. Do you remember?'

'Yes. I remember.'

'That was when I rode for Lathom.' A ring was coming into his voice now. 'The next day I rode back. I was no longer in milord's favour. I was scarcely in his service. I was no more than I had always been—a younger son, with neither land nor place. All I had was a worthy name, and a memory of you.'

He waited, as if to give her the chance to speak. Then he went on again.

'A memory of you,' he repeated. 'I made all haste back to you, and again you gave me welcome. You came running down the stair, all gladness. Do you remember?'

'Remember?' Margery stirred at last. 'How could I not remember?'

But he ignored that, and followed his own thoughts.

'There and then, at the foot of the stair, I told you what had passed at Lathom.'

He stopped short, and waited till Margery lifted her eyes to his. Then he spoke bitterly.

'From the hour when you learned how I had fallen, your warmth faded. All was ice.'

'Frank!' The name burst from her in startled protest.

'It faded,' he repeated. 'It faded when I was most in need of it. And only God knows how I needed it.'

'Frank! What are you saying to me?' She was on her feet now in agitation. 'What made you think such . . .'

'Is it not true?' His voice cut her short. 'Is it not true you've shown me naught but coldness since?'

That stopped her. She knew only too well that she had shown him coldness, and she groped wildly for words that could explain.

'What did you suppose?' he asked suddenly. 'That I came to you hunting fortune?'

'Fortune?' This, she thought, was madness, but at least it could be denied. 'Fortune, do you say? What fortune should you find with me, that have none?'

His eye swept over her taffeta and damask, and seemed to linger on the pearls in her collar.

'You're kin to an Esquire of fine estate,' he said slowly. 'And I, a younger son.'

Margery stared wildly, her thoughts all chaos. It was all so plausible, and she had just remembered that even Alice Nutter had made the same mistake. She struggled for control.

'Frank,' she said urgently. 'Understand, if you please, that I'm heir to nobody and nothing. My father's gone, and my family's poor. I've less place in the world than you yourself.'

It was his turn to stand silent, and again he looked her over.

'You're not so attired,' he said doubtfully.

'Nor are you.'

Her retort was instant, and it drew the flicker of a smile from him. Margery saw it, and the sight of it increased her urgency.

'Attire and purse don't always march together,' she told him. 'You should know that.'

'I do.'

'Then listen. You can either give me the lie to my face, or

you can accept it that I did not at any time suppose you to have come to me for fortune. Now which is it?'

She was indignant, and her tone showed it. He had sense enough not to flout her.

'I accept it,' he said at once, and Margery sighed with relief. But at once he returned to his point.

'Then why did you show me such coldness? And so suddenly? You'll hardly deny the fact of it?'

Margery's relief vanished. She had no good answer to that, and she stood silent under his searching eyes.

'Do you deny the fact of it?'

His voice was insistent, and she knew she must answer.

'I deny coldness,' she said at last. 'I can't deny some—some change of manner. There were difficulties.'

'What difficulties?'

That deepened her perplexity. She could hardly tell him she had feared he might learn too much of the Southworth affair. Yet what else could she say?

'May I not be trusted?'

His quiet question went to the root of it. That was precisely what had made her wary. But how could she explain that?

Then he shifted the point of his attack.

'That day I met you,' he said, 'that day I picked you from the leaves and the papist rode away—had you known this Southworth before that day?'

Margery's eyes narrowed. This was coming very near home, and it touched on secrets that were Roger's as much as hers.

'Had you known him before?'

He was very quiet and very firm, and Margery felt she was trapped. This was not to be evaded easily.

'Had you known him before? Look at me.'

There was nothing for it then but the truth.

'Yes,' she said as she lifted her eyes to his. 'But once only.'

He ignored that and pressed his attack.

'Did you know, when you came upon me that day, that it was the papist Southworth who rode beside me?'

Again she was too closely under his eye to evade it.

'I . . . I thought it might be,' she admitted unhappily.

'And did you intend—what followed?'

He waited watchfully, but this time it was Margery who attacked.

'Will you tell me why you put such motives on me? Why do you use me with such uncharity?'

She said it in desperation, and to her surprise and her unspeakable relief, it disconcerted him. He looked at his feet uneasily and when he spoke his tone had changed.

'I have some shame of it,' he said. He looked her over doubtfully, almost as if he were wondering whether he might go on. Margery pounced on it.

'Your name's Frank.'

She said it quickly, and again the half-smile flickered as his memory took the point. It seemed to hearten him.

'You shall have the truth of it then,' he said. 'I've said I've some shame of it, and it's not as I like it. But here it is. I went to Westby knowing you'd be here at Christmas, and having it in mind to visit you and sort these things. But half a week back, there was a vexing tale brought me by Tom Lister. I hated to hear a tale of you, Margery, but . . .'

'What was this tale?'

Her voice rang sharply, and that was by intention. He seemed to be on the defensive now, and she meant to keep him there. But his voice still came steadily.

'The tale was this. There's a woman at Westby, it seems, who has some connections in Pendle. A rustic woman. She swills the dairy and gives some hand in the house. She made a Christmas visit to her folk in Pendle, and being returned to Westby she dropped some gossip by Tom Lister's ear.'

'Gossip, do you say? And of me?'

There was something of anger in Margery's voice now, and apparently it was not lost on him. He was almost diffident when he resumed.

'Aye, of you. Tom Lister told me as a confidence . . .'

'Confidence? Gossip as a confidence? And of me? Here's a fine tale! But pray continue. What was this tale of me?'

'Just this: that you knew this Southworth of old, and that you had given him aid and comfort before; that you spilled from your horse before me with deliberate intent; and that all that followed was deception. That was the tale.'

He ended and stood waiting while icy quiet gripped the little room. Margery stood rigid while the chill crept about her. This tale was wicked. It was too deadly and too exact to be chance. Here was malice, precise, calculated, and informed.

'And did you credit that of me?'

Margery's voice was very clear and steady. The secret cold of Pendle had come into this fire-lit room, and the chill of it had cooled her wits. Her mind was working icily now, and she had remembered young Jennet's tale of Anne Redfern, hidden in the brush and hurrying to the Rough Lee, She was beginning to understand.

'Did you credit that of me?'

She repeated it, and he stirred uneasily, finding it hard to meet her eye.

'It . . . it fitted,' he said at last.

'How?' She almost snapped the question.

'I had thought—I had even told you—that day we met, that you were not so hurt as you made appearance to be. Also . . .'

'Yes?'

'It fitted in another way. You kept me amused. You kept me dreaming—till I was back from Lathom and the papist safe to ground.'

'That's not the tale you told just now.' Margery sounded brisk and confident. 'You say I changed when you were back from Lathom. First it's because you lacked advancement. Now it's because a papist's safe to ground. You leave me giddy.'

But he was hard to put to silence. He was plainly ill at ease, but he persisted.

'At the least,' he said, 'you've admitted some change of manner, and you've not said whence it came. Moreover . . .'

'Yes?'

'You've admitted knowing this Southworth, and guessing it was he who rode beside me. And as I've said, you seemed more hurt than you were. It fits snug to the woman's tale. Am I at fault for raising it? Also . . .'

'Yes? What more?'

'Even from the first, you kept it hid from me that you knew this man and had ridden at me with a guess. There's some dishonesty in that.'

He came to an end, and then he waited quietly. Margery's thoughts ran clearly. She must give him the explanation now. It was all too clear and too dangerous to allow of evasions, and on no account must he detect her in some shifty tale. All that remained was to cling tight to Roger's secrets while letting go her own.

'All that is true.' She said it with a smile, and she hoped her voice was steady. 'It's more true than I like, and you shall hear how it came to be. One question first . . .'

'Yes?'

'Who is this woman who swills Tom Lister's dairy?'

'Jennet Preston's her name. I know no more of her.'

'And her folk in Pendle?'

'That's beyond my knowledge, I never heard their names.'

She nodded and seated herself once more in the elbow-chair. She must seem at ease now, and she went about it calmly. She smoothed her kirtle and examined her finger-tips thoughtfully. When she looked up at him she was smiling, and she spoke clearly and easily.

'As I've said, I had met this Southworth once before, though that was not by my contriving. It's true also that I gave him some comforts then. That was because he was then in some distress of wind and weather, and I . . . I was soft of heart. I saw you and him by chance that afternoon, and it's true I supposed it to be him who rode with you.'

She paused and her eyes searched his face; but it stayed impassive and betrayed nothing.

'I saw you by chance, and I rode into your path with no clear intent at all. But I was hoping . . . hoping for I know not what.'

'For his escape?'

'In some manner, yes. You'll remember that I had not met you then. But I had met this Southworth and had some small esteem of him . . .'

'As had I, escort though I was.'

'You?' She stared at him in surprise. 'You also?'

'I also.' He was half smiling at her surprise. 'And, at the least, drawing's a vile thing . . .'

'It's hideous. But Frank, do you mean you . . . you understand?'

'In some sort, yes. Which is to say I understand that you might have a sympathy for this fellow. But what of your fall from a horse?'

She laughed openly.

'You may acquit me of that. I don't yet know how it

chanced. The beast went from under me, and then—and then you were there, and maltreating me most grievously.'

It was his turn to laugh.

'I did you no hurt. But could you not have told me of these things?'

'Tell you? How could I have told you? You were a stranger to me, and I did not dare. And I've said enough now to be clapped behind bars if you speak it out at Lathom.'

'I'll not do that.'

The ring in his voice put his sincerity past mistake, and Margery, seeing a chance to make an end, went on quickly.

'I'd no thought then of what it would bring to you. I didn't think of that when we rode in Pendle. I didn't think of it in the mist when you rode for Lathom. But when you were back, and I learned what I'd brought upon you—and I knew there was deceit, and I dared not speak of it . . . Oh, don't you see? I could not look you in the face—and you say you marked a coldness!'

She stopped and was staring, moist-eyed, into the fire when he answered quietly:

'I seem to have done you some injustice. Yet one thing more. It's finished now, is it? There'll be no more with this Southworth?'

She turned to him with relief. That, at least, could be answered.

'I have not seen him, nor heard of him, from that day to this. And I neither wish to nor expect to. He came and went and is gone. I'm no papist, Frank, and no deceiver either, when it's not forced upon me.'

His hand was on her shoulder as she came to her feet, her face very close to his. He spoke softly.

'It's ended then. For which, thank God! And now we may be back as when . . .'

'As when we rode in Pendle.'

'Aye. In heart and mind.' He took both her hands in his. 'There's one thing lacking, though.'

'What's that?'

'Advancement. I'm in no good case to wed, nor even to have thought of it.'

'Frank! What matters . . .'

'I'm in no case to wed. So on that I've no more to say—tonight. Let's pray the world will mend.'

His hand was under her chin, and in silence he turned her face to his and drew her close.

Roger Nowell, coming quietly into the parlour he thought private to himself, discovered his mistake and was gone without being heard.

30

East Wind in Pendle

The wind was from the East.

It came with an icy touch, and the track rang hard beneath the horses as they came down the road from Gisburn, down past the Malkin Tower, and so into Pendle Forest. Roger, muffled in his cloak, with his hat pulled low and his chin buried in his scarf, watched warily for ice, and showed no desire for talk. Nor did Margery. She rode at his side, muffled as he was, and she shivered. No cloak was wholly proof against that wind; worse still, her ears were freezing and her nose was dripping; her fingers were too numbed for the proper drying of her nose, and she herself was too chilled to care for dignity. If Christmas led to this, then Christmas was to be deplored.

She had had a surfeit of Christmas. There had been Christmas Eve, and then the Twelve Days of it; and by the seventh night, Margery had had enough, physically and mentally, of eating and drinking, of romping and dancing. By the tenth night she had been longing for the quiet of Pendle and the cool wind on the Hill; now she had got the wind, and she was heartily wishing she had not. This was not at all the return she had pined for.

She had not even got Frank Hilliard at her side. He had ridden for Warwickshire after all, though by no means at his own wish. He had stayed at Marton for three days, and had meant to stay the Twelve; certainly there had been no talk of his returning to Westby. But on the third day there had come a letter from his father, urgently carried by a servant. The news of the trouble Frank had found at Lathom, so his father wrote, had much distressed his mother, who was, moreover, already grieving because her only brother had recently broken his neck from a stumbling horse; and Frank's letter, on top of that, had been too much for her. She was much disordered, and Frank's immediate return might be her best medicine. He was therefore to make all speed home, despite any engagements he might have.

He had brought the letter gloomily to Margery, who had promptly told him he must go; then he had carried it to Roger, who had told him the same, and in more peremptory terms; and he had ridden the next morning, leaving for Margery a void which no junketings could fill. It was, she had told herself, a lot better than it might have been, for suspicions and resentments were gone; but a void it remained, and nothing at Marton could fill it. And now, in this wind, she had forgotten even the void; all she could think of at this moment was shelter, food, and a warm fireside. Only once did her mind stir from present discomforts, and that was when they passed the Malkin Tower; that reminded her that she must see young Jennet again, and as soon as might be; she had a question or two for Jennet.

She had not long to wait. The next day was a Wednesday, and, cold or no cold, Roger thought it his duty to join Nick Banister at Altham. Margery saw to it that he was filled with hot ale before he left, and then she pulled her cloak over her gown and went out on the gravel to see him off. She waved him away and then scampered back to the door, clutching tightly at cloak and gown with freezing fingers; and there was Jennet, sprung from nowhere and leaning against the lintel. Margery did not argue; she was too cold for that; she swept Jennet in front of her and hurried her into the snug warmth of the parlour.

Jennet huddled on the hearth and wriggled herself as close to the fire as she could. Margery, warming outstretched hands, looked the child over and was shocked. Her small body was blue with cold; her face was pinched and drawn, her thin legs were twitching, and there was a glaze in her cheeks that hinted at hunger carried to a far degree. Margery forgot her chilled hands and became busy. She found hot milk, and cake, and the apple tart that Jennet loved; she found honey and spread it on the tart; she found sugar—sugar from the Indies, at a price that kept it under lock and key—and stirred it into the milk. Jennet said nothing; but she flung herself at everything that came, and by the time Margery thought she had had enough for the moment, she was lying flat on the floor and grunting with pleasure.

Margery looked her over and was satisfied. Jennet was certainly looking better, but that might not last when she was out in the wind again. The child was not clothed for such weather; she was barelegged and barefooted, and her rustic smock was of a thin frieze, threadbare with age.

'Jennet.' The child rose to her knees as Margery spoke. 'What do you wear under your smock?'

Jennet said nothing, but she quickly lifted the smock and showed that she had nothing at all under it. Margery shivered. No wonder this child looked blue.

There was in an attic a great chest of painted elm which Roger had shown her when she had been seeking oddments for her kirtles; but it contained more than oddments, for it was mainly a store of old clothes left from the days when there had been children in the house. Roger had told her that she might help herself, and she chose to regard that permission as still valid. She helped herself liberally, and she soon had Jennet clothed with warmth and decency; there was a woollen undersmock, a petticoat, and an oversmock of red serge; and Jennet was almost preening herself when she came down the stair again. Margery gave her more milk and regarded her with a satisfaction qualified by the thought that the clothes were almost certainly damp. But that, she thought, could not be helped, and damp clothes would be better than no clothes; at least, Margery hoped they would. Then she sought an opening for talk.

'You should have had the clothes for Christmas, Jennet.'

'They'd have nicked 'em,' said Jennet darkly.

'Nicked?' This was new to Margery.

'Thieving bitches.'

'Who were?'

'At Christmas.'

Margery paused to think this out. Jennet's thoughts ran quickly, and she was sparing of words; but Margery thought she had the drift of it.

'Who were they, Jennet?'

'Witches.'

'You said bitches just now.'

Jennet nodded vigorously, as if to say that either word would do.

'You mean they came to your house?'

Another nod answered that.

'How many?'

'Two.'

'And who were they?'

'Mouldheels.'

'Who?'

'Mouldheels. She's Hewitt's wife—from Colne.'

'But why Mouldheels?'

'Feet stink.'

And Jennet gave an offhand nod that seemed to dispose of Mistress Mouldheels. Margery thought she had better pass on.

'And who was the other?'

'Jennet.'

'Jennet? But Jennet who?'

'Don't know.' For once the young voice held doubt. 'She came out of Craven, and they called her Jennet.'

'Craven, was it?'

Margery made herself speak steadily. But in her mind was Frank's quiet voice, telling of a woman who swilled a dairy at Westby—a woman who had carried a poisoned tale, and had the name Jennet Preston.

'And what did she come out of Craven for, Jennet?'

'Don't know. She's come before.'

'Has she? But what did she talk about?'

'Don't know. Got put to bed.'

'Who? Oh, you did, you mean? And who put you to bed, Jennet?'

'Greediguts.'

'Jennet! Who do you mean?'

'Alizon. She is.'

But that seemed to remind Jennet of something, and she began to peer hopefully about the room. Margery laughed, and decided she had better let this wait. The child had probably told all she knew, and clearly her young mind had now gone into her stomach again. Margery accepted it and took Jennet to the kitchen.

Roger was home before dusk, and Margery let things

wait till he had thawed. But she told him in the parlour after supper, and he heard her with interest.

'Is it so?' he mused. 'Our Demdikes here, and this Preston crone out of Westby. I did not know our coven linked with Craven. I ask myself whether this Preston came here by chance. Or was she sent for?'

'That's to be guessed.'

'We've no doubt guessed alike. Meantime, do you hear any tale of mischief done in Pendle?'

'I've heard of none.'

'Nor have I. Nevertheless, I think we'll show ourselves at the Newchurch on Sunday. It will let folk know we're back. And there may be some gossip.'

Margery agreed, though when Sunday came she was inclined to regret it. The freezing wind still blew from the East, and the clouds were low in a sullen sky. Roger tightened his cloak and spoke gloomily of coming snow, and Margery wondered if it would hold off till they were home again. Nor was the Service cheerful that morning. The grey light left the grey church dark, and the cold of the week had settled deep into its stones. Margery shivered as she sat, and even Richard Baldwin had for once made a concession; he had forgone the dignity of his gown and appeared in his weekday cloak and jerkin. But he met them at the door and took them to the front pew, where Grace was sitting huddled against her mother, both of them cloaked and gloved. Nor was Master Town impervious to the cold; he hurried through the Service in a style that set even Roger nodding with brisk approval, and he cut his sermon to less than an hour—and not even the Wardens murmured at the indecent brevity of that.

Then they were out in the churchyard, where the wind was as keen as ever, and the clouds seemed even lower; and there was Grace, waiting while her father cleared the church and her mother chatted with a neighbour. Margery took the chance at once.

'We didn't know you were back,' said Grace, as Margery went up to her. 'How's it with your Frank?'

'Well enough.'

'Is that true? You're happy of it?'

'Why yes. But—but why do you put it so?'

'It's . . .' Grace hesitated. 'It's only that we had heard . . .'

'Heard what, Grace?'

'It must have been an idle tale. But we had heard that he'd left you and gone altogether from the North Parts.'

Margery stared at her, wondering what lay behind all this.

'He *has* gone,' she said steadily. 'He's gone to visit his mother, who's ailing and asks for him. It's tedious for me while it lasts, but it's not a thing to be complained of.'

'He's coming back to you then?'

'To be sure, he is. Why should you think otherwise?'

'There's no . . . I'm sorry, Margery.'

'No need for sorrow. I only wonder that you should have thought it.'

'I—I heard the tale so. That is all.'

Margery's eyes were narrowing.

'Who told you that, Grace?'

'It was from Miles.'

'Miles told you Frank was not returning?'

'He did not tell *me*.' Grace smiled sadly. 'I've hardly seen him. But my father chanced to meet him, and had the tale from him.'

'Who had it no doubt from his infernal mother. And but for the trifle that he's coming back, the tale's exactly true.'

No need to mention that even that trifle had come perilously near to being as true as the rest.

'Will you tell me,' she went on, 'how Alice Nutter knows these things?'

'Knows?' Grace sounded bitter. 'I never know how Alice Nutter knows anything, but know she does. And for the most part it's as you say—exactly true.'

'Yes.' Margery seemed to be musing on that. Then her tone changed. 'But what's this of not seeing Miles? I noted that he was not in the church.'

'No. Again I don't know. But it seems he's to hear Service at Whalley these days. His mother so commands. For the rest of it—they were festive at the Rough Lee over Christmas, and she was busied in that, and for all of every day.'

'Which his mother commanded also, no doubt.'

'Yes. He . . . he contrived a letter.'

'I see. And you? You were not invited?'

'What do you suppose?'

'In these days, Grace, I suppose a good deal. And most of it's not pleasant.'

But Grace's comment on that was never heard. Margery caught Roger's eye and saw that he was ready. It was too bitter in that wind to keep him standing, so she made a hurried farewell and ran to join him.

'I've been in talk with Hargreaves,' he said as they rode off. 'He'd not heard we were back, but he's nothing to tell. There seems to be no mischief done—as yet.'

Margery nodded.

'And our Master Baldwin?'

'Scandalized.' Roger laughed shortly. 'But it's not a jest to all. The Rough Lee turned gay, it seems, and held high revel for the Twelve Days—and nights. Half Pendle were there, and they think high of our Alice for it. But not Baldwin. It jars his creed. Besides which, he'd thought Alice to be as prim as himself. Young Miles, by the way, is out of Baldwin's favour.'

'Why?'

'Too deep in the revels. But your question rang sharp. What's behind it?'

She told him of her talk with Grace, and he whistled softly.

'Prettily contrived,' was his comment. 'No bungler this Alice. She pleases half Pendle. Miles can't visit Grace. Grace's father looks askance at Miles. And if Miles should think to turn to you again, he's assured no rival stays. No bad return, that—for a pig or two and a few sheep.'

But his laugh had no echo from Margery.

'I feel for Grace,' she said bitterly.

'And for some others too. And I ask myself what's coming next.'

What came next surprised them both. They got home before the snow, and when they had warmed and dined neither had any inclination to leave the fire. Roger, settled at his ease, was feeling the warmth and growing perceptibly drowsy; Margery was staring gloomily through the glass at the ominous yellow in the surly clouds, and pondering darkly on Alice Nutter. Silence seemed to have settled for the afternoon. And then Margery brought Roger to attention with a sharp whistle of surprise. A horseman was riding quickly up to the house, and the horseman, to her keen surprise, was Tony Nutter.

'What the Devil?' said Roger when he had looked. 'Here's

no weather for visiting. And if it were, he never visits here. There'll be a reason, no doubt.'

There was, but it was not a cause for alarm. Tony came to it quickly, and as soon as decent greetings had been said, he produced a packet done in the brown paper that some people had lately taken to using as wrappings. One of his acquaintance, he said, offered this to Master Nowell. Himself, he had just heard of their return, and had been in haste to carry it for friendship's sake. He put the packet on the table, grew vague as to who his acquaintance was, and evaded further questions.

It was very mysterious, and Margery's curiosity was at boiling-point. But Roger accepted it coolly, and let the packet lie. He spoke some words of thanks and went on to inquire about Mistress Crook.

Tony looked relieved, and at once he became more talkative. Margaret, he said, was well enough in health, though she felt the cold. She was disturbed, though, about Miles, who seemed less happy than he should be. Then Tony turned to Margery and bluntly asked her how Frank Hilliard did.

'Well enough,' she told him, 'though he's with his mother now.'

'Aye?' His tone was doubtful, and it was suddenly clear to Margery that Tony supposed, as Grace had done, that Frank would not return. She hastened to correct him. His face cleared at once, and he would have said more, but Roger interrupted him sharply. He was peering through the window as he spoke.

'Tony,' he said. 'You're welcome here, and I'd not seem inhospitable. And I'm grateful for your kindness in coming. Nevertheless I commend you to get to your horse this present instant and be gone. You're not a man who should ride in blizzards.'

One glance through the window told Margery that Roger was right, for the clouds seemed to touch the trees, and the light was livid. Tony looked once and needed no pressing. He called at once for his horse, and both Roger and Margery braved the cold to see him off. Nor was it too soon, for the first thin flakes were powdering down as he went.

'He was a fool to come,' said Roger bluntly as they hurried back to the parlour. 'He's frail of the lungs and should have kept his house these days. What's he brought?'

That was enough for Margery. She reached for a knife and hastily cut the sealed cord that secured the packet. She parted the paper wrapping and disclosed a book, fat and plump in brown leather with some embossings. She held it for him to see, and then opened its title-page.

'What have we?' asked Roger quietly.

'It's . . . it's in French,' she said.

'French?'

'French it is.' She read slowly from the title-page. *Discours des Sorciers* was its title, which meant, she supposed, that it was a Discourse about Witches.

'Witches, is it?' Roger came across and looked curiously at the page. 'And from papist France. Our Seminary keeps his promises, it seems.'

'Seminary?' Margery gaped at him as the memory came to her of Christopher Southworth sitting in that same chair and regretting that Roger had no work of authority on witches. 'You mean he sent it?'

'Who else? Which will be why Tony was fool enough to ride this day.'

He turned away to the window and left Margery to examine the book further. It had been printed, 'Privilége du Roy', at Lyons nine years ago, and was by one Henri Boguet.

'And who might he be?' asked Roger when she told him.

Margery consulted the book again and then announced that Master Boguet was Chief Judge in the High Court of Burgundy, and might therefore be supposed to write with some authority.

'As the Seminary said,' was Roger's comment. 'Do you read French?'

'I . . . I have some rags of it,' she answered doubtfully, with a memory of the Huguenots who had once been her neighbours.

'Reading that will mend your rags.'

'Read it? All of it?'

'Why not? It will give you employment these coming days—and you'll have no other. Here's no passing shower.'

He had his nose to the window again, and his sober words brought Margery to his side. One look was enough to convince her. Trees and sky alike were lost in a flurry of whirling flakes, and already the gravel was smooth and white. Crystals of ice were sliding down the window-glass; and as she looked they ceased to slide and began to stick.

'God save our Tony,' said Roger softly.

31

Candlemas

The thought of Tony Nutter stayed with Margery in the stormy days that followed, and from this anxiety she found some distraction in the study of the book he had brought. For the storm lasted a full three days; and as the snow settled and the drifts grew deeper, as the shape of the land was changed and thick white branches came cracking from the trees, she sat by the glowing hearth and sank herself in the writings of this judge from Burgundy. Little by little, with much searching of memory and many consultations with Roger, whose French was even worse than hers, she began to get the sense of it; she never achieved, nor even attempted, a full translation, but the general sense and drift of it came slowly into her mind. Yet it was always in the front of her mind; always behind it was a thought of Tony Nutter struggling homewards in the blizzard that had surely overtaken him. And if such exposure had sent Tony to a sickness, Margery could find nothing in this book to compensate for that. The book, in truth, told little that she and Roger had not already discovered for themselves. It was of interest, to be sure; and even Roger agreed that Master Boguet knew his witches. For the book spoke of poison-powders, and of an ointment made from such a powder blended with baby's fat; it told of witches who would act as midwives, especially when the coming child was not wanted; it described how witches habitually kept their eyes to the ground and sometimes muttered; and it had an interesting tale of a sharp-eyed girl of eight, who might have been own sister to Jennet Device, and whose evidence had sent a witch to death. But when it came to practical matters, Master

Boguet had little to recommend but accusation by rumour, followed by torture to get confession—at which Roger muttered something about Richard Baldwin and flung the book across the room; and again Margery asked herself whether Tony Nutter had not shown more zeal than sense in bringing it that day.

On the fourth day, when the storm had passed and the sky was a pale cold blue, she was still kept to the house by the deep piled drifts, and more than a week had gone before she could wring consent from Roger. Then, in the deep cold slush of the melting snow, breeched and booted, on a horse that slipped and stumbled, she fought her way to Goldshaw. The day before, it would have been impossible, and on this day it was barely possible; but she was determined to attempt it; news of Tony Nutter had become urgent to her, and she meant to get it.

She won to the house in the end, and she found it ominous that it was the old servitor who came out to her and Margaret Crook who called her in; and Margaret lost no time in confirming what Margery had guessed. Tony, she said, had won his way home with difficulty that Sunday afternoon. He had been thick with ice when he was helped from his horse, and though he had at once been put to bed, and had since had all he could need of warmth and comfort, the damage had been done. A distemper of the lungs had set in, and he was even now most grievously sick.

Margaret spoke quickly and in a rushing whisper, lest she should disturb the sufferer in his bedchamber above. At once Margery was fervently offering help, and she took it upon herself to pledge Roger's too; but Margaret shook her head regretfully; she was grateful, but what help could be given? She had help enough in the house, and she had food and fuel in plenty; and for the rest, who could help but God?

That was hardly to be disputed, and Margery took a sorrowful leave. She hated the thought of the quiet and friendly Tony lying stricken there, perhaps in peril of his life, and all because of his haste to do service to her and Roger; but there seemed no more to be done than was being done, and she had to content herself with condolences and promises to call again. She struggled home, depressed by the news and irritated by the raw wind and the antics of her horse in the sliding slush; she could have borne it with more content, she told herself, if the book had been worth it.

She told Roger all about it as soon as she was in, and Roger nodded absently and agreed that there was no more to be done. Margery stared at him, decided that he must have something on his mind, and promptly set herself to learn what it was. The task was not difficult. Roger admitted frankly that he was becoming uneasy about Candlemas. He explained that Candlemas, like All Hallows, seemed to be in the Witches' Calendar; the Church, to be sure, no longer celebrated the second day of February, but the witches did, and some disturbance was therefore to be expected on the eve of that ancient Feast. Roger had not forgotten All Hallows, and now, concerned at the thought of what might come, he had it in mind to ride through the Forest on the eve of Candlemas. Then, after talk with Margery, he decided against it; he would let others ride the Forest while he stayed at Read in instant readiness to ride if he should be called.

Margery agreed, but she found it tedious waiting. There was more than a week yet to pass before Candlemas, and Margery had little to do. Roger was in Preston for the Quarter Sessions, held late on account of the snow. Frank was still in Warwickshire. Grace Baldwin was in Colne with her mother, Richard having prudently packed them both off to lodge with his brother there till Cand'emas should be safely past. So Margery had neither work nor company, and she found the time hang heavily; it was not wholly from a sense of duty that she went three times that week to inquire about Tony Nutter. She was beginning to like Margaret Crook, for all her exasperating chatter, and she found her, moreover, a useful well of local gossip. Margaret had plenty to say, and most of it, as usual, was about Miles. Miles was out of Pendle just now; he was at Lathom, staying with his cousin Matthew and hoping to be presented to milord; and Margaret was away in full tongue to the praise of Master Matthew Potter—until something disconcerted her, and she stopped abruptly; it did seem to her that an odd glitter had come into her young guest's eyes. At once she was away about Tony. Tony did very well; the fever had abated, and if all went well she hoped to have him in his elbow-chair before the week was out. Margery heard it with relief which she did not try to conceal.

And then Candlemas was come. Roger had made his plans with care, and two bands of men rode armed through the dark that night while Roger and Margery waited at Read, their boots by the hearth and their cloaks ready on the ingle-shelves. They waited for six long hours, and they waited in vain. Midnight had come and gone before Harry Hargreaves came to report that all had been quiet where he and his men had ridden; and another long hour had ticked away before Richard Baldwin, who had headed the other party, came in with the same tale. Roger nodded with satisfaction; the Devil, he said, must have stayed warm in Hell this night.

He knew better in the morning. He decided, this cool grey Sunday, that the Newchurch might offer gossip more than Whalley, so to the Newchurch he and Margery went; and one look, as they came to the brow of the hill, was enough. Here was not the quiet and seemly service of God, but uproar, unseemly and confused. The churchyard was thronged with people, and here and there in the bustle a woman was in tears.

'The Devil!' said Roger, as he saw it.

'After all,' said Margery dryly, and Roger spared her an appreciative grin. Then his face hardened as Christopher Swyer, white-haired and now white-faced too, came up the path with the curate after him. Farther down, Richard Baldwin was standing in silence with Hargreaves at his side. But Roger ignored them. He saw Swyer, who was a Warden, and that was enough for Roger.

'Whatever's chanced, I'll not watch this,' he snapped. 'Here's the church of God and the day of God. And here's a bawling and a squalling like so many cats. In God's name, man, stir yourself as a Warden and bring these folk to the decencies.'

Swyer turned slowly and looked at the crowd. Then some understanding seemed to come to him.

'Aye,' he muttered. 'Aye. Here's no behaviour.'

He went down into the churchyard, and at once his high voice rang among the stones as he called peremptorily for order. The uproar died away and faces were turned to him as folk recognised the authority of a Warden.

'Profane not the Lord's Day with your chatter,' he told them. 'Get you within His House, and make prayer against what's been done.'

He waited, and Harry Hargreaves moved quietly to his side. That decided it, for it joined the authority of the Constable to that of the Warden, and soon there was a trickle of people moving into the church; then it became a stream, and as it ended Swyer and Hargreaves followed them in, as if to make sure. Master Town was left by the gate, and in the deserted churchyard Richard Baldwin stood alone and silent. Slowly he turned, and he seemed to see Roger for the first time; as slowly he walked to the gate, and as he came nearer Margery was shocked. For Richard Baldwin seemed a man out of touch with Earth, and if she had not known him she might have thought he was drunk; the vigour was gone from him, his face was the white of chalk, and his eyes were dazed and vague. But at the gate he seemed to pull himself together, and he turned suddenly to the silent curate.

'Go you with those folk, Master Town,' he said, 'and set them to the Service of the Lord. And look to it that you preach not from the sectaries this day.'

The curate made no attempt to resist him.

'I'll preach ex tempore, and from Exodus twenty-two eighteen,' was all he said as he hurried off after his flock.

Roger had not dismounted. He was still sitting his horse, rigid as any statue, and Margery was copying his example. But now she leaned across to him, uncertain whether he had grasped the significance of that inflammatory text.

'Thou shalt not suffer a witch to live,' she whispered, and a jerk of her head at Master Town's back completed her meaning. Roger's eyes narrowed, and a faint nod showed that he had understood. Then he dismounted, and Margery followed him through the gate into the churchyard.

Roger spoke quietly.

'You need not tell me that there has been Devil's work, Richard. That's plain. Tell me only what's been done.'

Richard made no answer, but in silence he turned and led them towards the church. Roger looked at Margery, and then, in the same silence, they followed. They passed the church door, and as they did so, Hargreaves and Swyer came out and fell into step behind them. Richard Baldwin led down into the lower part of the churchyard, and at a grave he stopped.

They looked in silence. The turf had been flung back, and the shallow earth disturbed. The body within was in part uncovered; bones showed in the earth, and above ground, by the side of the grave, was a skull, dry and bleached. It was Swyer who pointed, and Margery shivered as she saw what he meant; teeth had been wrenched from their sockets, and chips of white bone lay on the ground to show the force that had been used.

'Teeth for Devil's charms,' said Swyer curtly.

Richard Baldwin led to another grave, and to another. At each the same desecration was to be seen. But the fourth grave he led them to was newer than the others; the body it held had not yet rotted to the bones, and the mouldering flesh was hideously exposed. And here there was no skull to be seen. It had gone completely, and a knife had been used on the blackened neck.

'Not rotted to their purpose yet,' said Swyer, and his short words were enough.

Again Richard moved on. In the same silence Roger went with him, and Margery after. And then Harry Hargreaves suddenly intervened. He slipped past Roger and laid a hand on Richard's shoulder.

'Richard,' he said urgently. 'Let be, man. You've no call to look on that again.'

Richard turned, and for a moment the two men were eye to eye. Roger stood impassive, and Margery was in wonder; for Hargreaves' voice had been soft and kindly, and there was something of gratitude in Richard's face. Yet the puritan Warden and the papist Constable were at odds on most things.

Richard's eyes dropped, and Margery felt a rush of sympathy as she saw the suffering in his face; for once, only for once since she had known him, Richard Baldwin seemed to find a load too great to bear.

He stood aside, and Swyer stayed with him. Harry Hargreaves, white-faced and unhappy, led Roger on, and again Margery followed. Another grave, also a recent one, had been disturbed, and again the torn flesh showed where the head had been hacked away.

'It's the same as the last?' said Roger, and looked inquiringly at the Constable.

'Aye, it's the same,' was the answer. 'But the last wasn't his.'

'His?' Even Roger looked startled. 'Grace of God, Harry! Are you saying . . .'

'I am.' The white-faced Constable spoke grimly. 'Here's his own girl. His Margaret that was.'

'Grace of God!' said Roger again, and Margery gasped with horror. This torn and blackened thing had once been Grace's sister—had played and romped with her, had perhaps swum in the mill pool with her, had roamed in the summer wind with her, had laughed and loved with her. Margery looked again at what showed in the crumbling earth. Then she turned away, sick and white, and walked unsteadily up the path. One more look at That, and she would vomit.

Roger came slowly after her.

'Richard,' he said quietly, 'where's your wife?'

'I thank God she's in Colne—with Grace.'

'Thank God indeed. And get you to Colne and be with her.'

'To Colne?' Richard Baldwin spoke like a dazed man.

'Aye, Richard. To your wife.' Roger was insistent. 'There are times when a man should not be alone to brood. Get you to Co'ne, and swiftly.'

'I'll ride with you, Richard,' said Swyer suddenly, and Roger nodded approvingly.

They went off together, Swyer holding him by the arm and almost seeming to lead him. Roger turned briskly to the Constable.

'How many graves in all?'

'Nine that we've counted.'

'They'll need to be made decent. We've still two Wardens left. You may find them and bid them to that. Meantime . . .'

He turned sharply to Margery.

'Go into the church,' he said curtly, 'and see what that fool's ranting at.'

She obeyed without a word, leaving him in talk with Hargreaves. She went in on tip-toe and stood quietly at the back for long enough to make sure that the curate was keeping to his promise; he had preached himself into a fury, and he was leaning over the front of his pulpit, waving his arms and shouting that the death of a witch was sweet in the understanding of the Lord. And in a congregation that had needed little rousing there was already an ominous buzz and stir; none heeded Margery; they were too intent for that.

She tip-toed out and went in haste to tell Roger.

'That's dangerous,' he said shortly, and Margery nodded. She had thought the same herself.

Roger turned decisively and walked to the church door. Hargreaves and Margery exchanged glances. Then, side by side, they followed him.

He swung the door and walked in. He did not go on tip-toe, and from everywhere folk turned as they heard his firm tread and jingling spurs. He walked half way down the little church, while Margery stayed by the door with Hargreaves. At half way Roger halted, and stared the preacher into silence; the buzz in the church died down, and every eye was on Roger. Then he spoke resonantly.

'Master Town, my regrets that I halt your sermon.' His eyes swept round the church and came back to the preacher. 'The killing of a witch may be as you say—in the understanding of the Lord. If that be Divinity, I'll not dispute it with you. But in the understanding of the King's judges, the killing of a witch is murder—plain murder and no else. Therefore hearken . . .' His eyes swept round the church again. 'He who kills a witch, or heads the rabble that kills a witch, is for Lancaster—and Assize of Oyer and Terminer. And the divine who has preached him to that work shall have Gaol Delivery also. Urging to murder is a hanging crime.'

There was a sigh and a scrape of feet in the silent church. For a trembling curate, Roger had a word more.

'Bring a proven witch before me, and I'll commit her to Assize. Do more, and I'll commit you.'

The silence was deadly. Roger turned on his heel.

32

Cold Comforts

Margery waited most of the week for heads to cool and the Baldwins to return from Colne. Then, on a cold sunlight morning, she rode to Wheathead in a boisterous northerly wind which set her ears tingling and blew her hair into disorder. Black ripples were chasing over the shivering pool as she came round the bend, and the cold spray from the wheel was wetting her face as Richard Baldwin leaned out of the millhouse and waved to her. Grace, he said, was in the house, and he himself would be in it shortly.

Margery went in without ceremony, and found Grace at the great scrubbed table, busy with smoothing irons and a pile of linen. She was newly back from Colne, she said, and this was a consequence. She helped Margery from her cloak and set her a chair by the hearth; then she smiled ruefully as she went back to her work.

'It's ever so,' she said, 'when you've been a-visiting.'

'Need you tell me? Have I not noticed it? But in other ways, how is it since you're back from Colne?'

'Not good.' Grace looked down at the petticoat she was folding. 'What was the truth of it?'

'Truth of what?'

'Of Sunday—at the Newchurch.'

Grace was engrossed in the petticoat, and Margery was looking into the fire as she held her hands to it.

'That? It was less than you might suppose. Some graves had been scratched at, but that's been seen to. They're decent again now.'

'Aye. I've heard so much. But after—in the church?' Grace dropped the petticoat and twisted round. She sat on the edge of the table and faced Margery squarely. 'What did Master Nowell truly say? I've heard . . .'

'Yes? What have you heard?'

'My father says . . .'

'He wasn't there. He'd left.'

'Yes. But there's neighbours' talk.'

'What does it say?'

Grace seemed to steady her breath. Then she spoke firmly.

'It says that Master Nowell gave protection to witches, threatening any who'd move against them.'

Margery sat in thought. She had feared exactly this, and it needed proper answer.

'It's not my cousin that gives protection to witches,' she said carefully. 'It's the law that does that, and my cousin does but insist on the law. What else should a Justice do?'

'Yes. But . . .'

'It's plain enough, Grace. The law promises punishment for witches—punishment of some severity. My cousin has no tenderness for any witch, and he's as eager for their punishment as any. But he does insist that it shall be punishment by the law, and not by a lawless rabble. That's the whole root of it, and that's what he said in the Newchurch—that and no more.'

'I—I think I see it.' Grace seemed hesitant. 'I'll not give you the lie on it, Margery. Never think that. And yet . . .'

'Yet what?'

Grace hesitated again, and then plunged at it.

'My father says the law does no more than promise. In Master Nowell's hands it does not perform. Is there no truth in that?'

And before Margery had found an answer the door had opened, and both the girls turned as Richard Baldwin came in.

'What's this?' he asked quietly. Then he explained himself as he saw them puzzled. 'Mostly you talk of fripperies, as girls will. But today you're solemn.'

'We talk of the law,' said Margery slowly, 'and its way with witches.'

His face hardened at once.

'Has the law a way with witches?' he asked. 'It seems not to have—in Pendle.'

Margery did her best. She told him what she had told Grace. She embroidered it a little, and she added her own earnest assurance that Roger stayed only for proof acceptable to law. Richard heard her courteously, but she had made no impression on him.

'He stays for proof he won't get,' was his crushing answer. 'Proof of the sort he asks may be had only by confession, and that's to be had only by what he won't do. Meantime this brood run free to do the work of Hell.'

'This brood, do you say?' Margery took him up on that. 'Meaning the Demdikes?'

'Aye—that brood. But there's many another within this Forest, and all vowed to the same work. And yourself, this Sunday past, you saw what work it is.'

He stopped, and Margery stood silent as she saw the tumult that was in him.

'I've gratitude for Master Nowell,' he went on slowly. 'He'd kindness for me that day—aye, and wisdom too, and I'd need of both in that hour. You may tell him as much from me. But for these witches, I care nothing whether they're sent to account by a judge or a rabble—so only that they are sent. And you may, if it please you, tell him that also.'

And without staying for an answer he passed through the kitchen and into his own parlour. The latch clicked behind him, and Margery looked helplessly at Grace.

'For sake of sanity,' she said, 'let us speak of some matter else. How is it now with Miles?'

Grace turned back to the petticoat and carefully completed its folding.

'It isn't,' she said quietly, as she began to press a collar. 'It isn't at all.'

'Grace! What do you mean?'

'No more than that.' Grace had her eyes on the point of the iron. 'He's still at Lathom—or so I must suppose. I've no word.'

'No letter even? Does he send nothing?'

'How should he? Who rides here from Lathom?'

Grace turned to the hearth and exchanged her iron for another. Margery tried to sound cheerful.

'That's true,' she said. 'He'd hardly get a letter carried. So perhaps he languishes for you. Absence, they say . . .'

'They don't say it when there's a mother like that.'

Grace sounded vicious as she took another collar from the pile, and Margery abandoned the attempt to be cheerful. She agreed only too thoroughly with Grace.

'You think . . .'

'Don't you?' Grace cut in at once. 'I've told you before what Alice Nutter thinks of me. And now she's got him away, and that will be the end of it.'

'Hardly the end, Grace. She can't keep him away for ever.'

'No. But when he's back she'll have some other slyness ripe. She's as crafty as a Jesuit, and as hard as the millstones yonder. I tell you, Margery, I know Alice Nutter, even if you don't.'

But Margery thought she did know Alice Nutter, perhaps even better than Grace did—and nothing in her knowledge offered any comfort. There was, she thought as she rode home, very little comfort for anybody. Grace was plainly miserable, and Miles was hardly likely to be happy. Roger might expect trouble at any time, and Richard Baldwin might both provoke it and suffer its consequences. And she herself felt some impact from all their troubles. The only person who seemed to have any cause for satisfaction was Alice Nutter.

She had a brush with Alice the next Sunday as they came out of Whalley church. Roger had been kept in talk by a neighbour, and as Margery waited in the churchyard, Alice Nutter, very elegant and very self-assured, rounded on her.

'You seem deserted, mistress,' was her greeting, and Margery's eyes were not friendly as she roused herself for what might follow.

'For the moment only,' she answered, with a quick glance at Roger.

Alice nodded affably.

'And how is Master Hilliard?' she inquired, and thus showed her true meaning. 'Have we seen the last of him here?'

'Who knows, madam?' Margery saw no reason to act as informant to Alice Nutter.

'He was no doubt wise to leave. This Pendle climate can be dangerous.'

Margery gasped. This was almost brazen, and there was a

gleam of triumph in the dark eyes. Margery set herself to quench it.

'Indeed, madam, I have heard of some who died most oddly in this Pendle.'

And Margery nodded in her turn. She was holding firm to her belief that Alice Nutter was best dealt with by prompt counter-attack.

The gleam of triumph faded and something ugly took its place.

'They died oddly, did they? And they were folk bred in Pendle?' There was a hint of menace in the smooth voice now. 'There might be greater hazard for another.'

'Another?'

The nod came again.

'Master Hilliard is wise to flee our climate. He was not bred to it.' The dark eyes gleamed again. 'Nor were you, mistress.'

'Nor you, madam, as I'm told. But perhaps you were fortunate?'

'How, if you please?'

'You were bred, no doubt, in an equally treacherous climate.'

The dark eyes quivered, and Margery watched with satisfaction. That thrust had gone home, and already she was preparing another.

'How is Master Miles?' she asked innocently. 'I'm told he's away.'

'At Lathom, mistress. He's been there these three weeks.'

'You are no doubt prudent, madam. He'll be away from harm there.'

'There's no prudence in it.' The smooth voice was rougher now. 'He's there by invitation.'

The gleam was in Margery's eyes now, and her voice slowed to a drawl that was almost insolent.

'Invitation? Ah, yes. Of one Potter, I'm told.'

Alice Nutter's face twitched. Plainly she was not used to this sort of thing, and she was too angry to see the trap.

'Of Master Matthew Potter, if you please. And pray remember that Master Potter is my nephew.'

'Nephew, is it?'

Margery's eyebrows lifted just sufficiently to point her meaning, and Alice Nutter's temper broke. The dark eyes blazed, and a wave of red flushed her pale cheeks; and before she had recovered her poise Margery had made a curtsey that was insolent in its fullness, and was marching down the path with Roger, who had been standing, she discovered, comfortably within earshot.

'That's barbed by-play,' he remarked as they rode away. 'How did it begin?'

'Begin?' Margery was less calm now than she had been. 'It began with Alice Nutter coming wantonly from her way, to play cat-and-mouse with me.'

'Cat-and-mouse?' Roger laughed. 'A pretty mouse you are! You've claws as sharp as hers, and your aim's better. But she'll remember it, and I'd advise you to have a care when she comes again.'

But Alice Nutter did not come again, and in the days that followed Margery neither saw her nor heard of her. And the days grew tedious. Nothing seemed to Margery to go as she had hoped it would. Harry Hargreaves, industriously seeking for any pointer that might show who had desecrated the graves, had to report complete failure; and Jennet Device, on whom Margery had pinned some hopes, was just as useless. She came regularly, and she chattered freely; but all she could say about Candlemas was that her own folk had not been out that night. Then Margery found another source of anxiety. She went frequently to Goldshaw, to chat with Tony Nutter and do what she could to cheer him as he regained strength; and going there one cold and windy morning she was distressed to find that he was no longer in his elbow-chair by the fire. Sister Margaret explained gloomily that Tony was back in bed. He had made such progress, she said, and had regained such spirits, that he had insisted on going out. The wind had been cold and the result disastrous, as his sister had feared it would be. These lung troubles, she said, were noted for their trick of coming back, and Tony should have had more sense. But there it was! Tony had never had any sense, and there *he* was—back in bed again. Margaret chatted lightly about it, but she could not wholly conceal her anxiety, and Margery went away depressed and anxious too.

Her spirits were not much raised by a letter which Frank contrived to send to her. He wrote cheerfully, and he said that all went well at home; but he had to add that his mother had been more disordered than he had supposed, and her recovery was taking longer—and in short, he would not be able to begin his journey back to Pendle until the end of the month at soonest. Margery pulled a wry face at that. The letter was of cheerful tone, and it had some pleasing sentiments, but the fact remained that Frank had not yet started. Margery went to Roger and plied him with questions about probable travelling-times on winter roads, and her calculation after that was that a return in the first or second week of March was the best she could hope for; and that, in her present humours, seemed a whole weary age away.

But she had to make the best of it, and as February went its windy way she filled in her time with whatever she could. She was at least always welcome at Wheathead, and she was able to give Grace the news, which young Jennet had somehow gleaned from nowhere, that Miles Nutter was expected to be back at the Rough Lee before Lent began. That was how Jennet had put it, and as Ash Wednesday would be the fourth of March, Grace had something to look forward to; Miles might surely be expected to contrive something when he was once back in Pendle.

But Lent brought news of a different sort to Margery. On Ash Wednesday she learned that Tony Nutter was perceptibly weaker; on the Friday he was worse, and on the Saturday his sister was in unconcealed anxiety. And on the Sunday, a grey and windless day of teeming rain, Jennet Device made a surprise appearance when Margery was just into her orange-tawny in readiness for Whalley church. Tony Nutter, said Jennet cheerfully, was a-dying; he might last the day or he might not, but certainly he was a-dying.

Margery sent the rain-soaked child to the kitchen to be dried and fed, and she herself went in blank dismay to Roger. She found him coming down the stair, cloaked and booted for church, and she told him with no waste of words; and could they not, she asked, ride to Goldshaw instead of Whalley?

Slowly Roger shook his head.

'That might give embarrassment,' he said.

'Embarrassment? But surely . . .'

'I'll be better at Whalley.' He did not explain that, but he eyed her strangely. 'But *you* may go to Goldshaw. And when you're there, and have seen the shape of things, you may give such messages from me as you then judge proper.'

At another time that might have set Margery probing for his meaning, but at this moment she was too concerned for Tony. She thanked Roger hastily, took one look at the weather, and spared five minutes to change the orange-tawny for her russets and then she was away.

33

The Bitterness of Death

The Forest lay dark under the pattering rain. It streamed steadily from the low unbroken cloud; it dripped from the trees and ran in rivulets among the grass, its lazy drip and patter loud in the windless air. The track was a squelching sponge, and Margery had to keep her stumbling horse to a slow and cautious walk. She took twice her usual time for the familiar journey, and when at last she came to the house in the pines, her hat and cloak were black, her face was scoured with rain, and a cold trickle from her sodden collar was running down her neck.

The pines were stark in the grey mist, and behind them the house was quiet and still. Margery sat motionless on her weary horse, and a vague dread began to work on her. There was something odd here, something unnatural and therefore ominous; this silent house offered her no welcome; it stood aloof in the trees and the dripping rain, and it ignored her. The door stayed bleak and shut, and the old servitor did not come out to take her horse. And then she saw that at the window above the door, which she knew to be that of Tony's bedchamber, the curtains had been drawn across.

Her alarm grew; she slipped from her horse and made for the door, her boots sliding wetly in the gravel. Some impulse kept her from knocking. Instead she pushed open the door and stepped quietly in.

The low square hall was still and empty; but not perhaps deserted, for at the foot of the stair a candle burned, the tallow guttering untidily. The kitchen door stood open, and revealed nothing of any serving girls. But from above, from somewhere past the bend of the stair, a voice could be heard, faint and indistinct.

Margery stood stiffly, and was tense and disturbed. Then she moved slowly to the stair, and the hush that was on the house persuaded her to go tip-toe. She crept silently up the treads till she could see past the bend to the door she knew to be his bedchamber; and here she stopped abruptly. The door was shut, but it fitted badly, and in the chink was candle-light; and unendingly, uncreasingly, the quiet voice ran on.

The voice stopped, and there were sounds of hushed movement; then a clink, and the voice spoke again; but this time it spoke slowly, and the words were clear. *Hoc est enim Corpus Meum. . . .* She heard the low mutter of the Latin, and she pressed back, startled, against the wainscot, as her puritan upbringing reared in her mind, hinting vaguely at subtle dangers. But at least there could be no doubt of what this meant. A muttered Mass in a curtained room could mean one thing only: Tony Nutter was *in extremis.*

But in her alarm she had moved too quickly. Her wet boot slipped on the smooth boards, and her spurred heel clattered against the wainscot. She stood rigid, half frightened and half irritated, wondering what it would bring. Then, when she was beginning to hope she had not been heard, the door was slowly opened, and Margaret Crook, her face white and anxious, peered out. There was relief in her strained eyes as she saw who it was, and Margery did her best to be reassuring; she contrived a smile, and she touched pursed lips with a finger as a sign that she would keep the secret. Apparently Margaret understood, for she went quickly back into the room, and the door shut softly behind her.

Margery tip-toed down the stair, and after pulling off her gloves, untying her cloak and easing her hat from her wet hair, she went across the hall into the parlour beyond. She mended the fire and laid her wet things before it, and then she moved to the window and stood staring blankly through the glass—staring till the dark clouds faded from her view, and time went back, and it was again a bright September morning with the soft wind blowing through the open lattice; and Tony Nutter was standing in the sunlight, giving her easy talk and a first friendly welcome.

Feet shuffled on the stair, and again the sky was dark with the clouds and the drenching rain. She turned wearily as the old servant came in, and in silence she pointed to her wet and shivering horse, still patient in the rain. The old man nodded, and in a few moments she saw him go out and lead the beast to the stable behind the house. Again there were feet on the stair, a sharp precise tread this time; and Margery turned sharply as Christopher Southworth came into the room.

They looked at each other in silence, and it was Margery who spoke first.

'We owe you thanks,' she said, 'for a book. And I for a Cross.'

It was trivial at this moment, and she knew it, but she could think of nothing better. He inclined his head in acknowledgment.

'I owe you thanks for more than that,' he said. 'And twice. I would that you were of the true Faith.'

'You waste your time at that.'

'And time does not belong to me,' he answered quietly. 'It is lent to me only, and for a purpose. And perhaps the loan is running out. What do you intend?'

'Nothing. You know well enough that I shall not betray you.'

He bowed slightly.

'My debt increases. Then I'll be upon my way. But first, Mistress Crook would be—would be private with me.'

He waited, and for a moment Margery was puzzled. Then she understood.

'She's above?' she asked. 'With him?'

'Yes. She watches.'

'Then I'll watch in her stead, and she may come down. But tell me—how is he?'

'That is with God. I cannot say.'

His tone was grave and Margery made no comment. She went quietly out of the room and up the stair. Without ceremony she went into the bedroom, and Margaret rose from a chair by the bedside. There was a whispered word and she was gone; and Margery was alone with the stricken Tony.

It was a simple room. The bed had the centre of it, and there was a press, a table and a pair of chairs; that was all. A fire burned bright in the hearth, and from that and the candles and the drawn curtains, the heat was stifling. Margery gasped, and asked herself if she might at least draw back the curtains now that the priest was gone from the room. But it was not her house, and she hesitated; and while she hesitated, Tony Nutter spoke urgently.

She spun on her heel, wondering what he had said; for his speech had been thick and she had caught no clear word. She answered, but he did not seem to hear; and she stood unhappily, looking between the half-parted bed-curtains to where his head moved fitfully in the shadows. Again he spoke, and Margery leaned forward, desperate to give what help she could. He turned his face to her and seemed to see her as he spoke again.

'Anne!' His words were clear now. 'Anne, my dear! Oh. Anne!'

And Margery, clinging wet-eyed to the bedpost, knew that he had never seen her.

His words ran on, for a moment thick and blurred, and then for a moment clear before they blurred again; but clear for long enough to tell that he was riding with his Anne on an April morning—and he was happy. Margery clung tight to the bedpost, her lip between her teeth, and her face wet in the sweating heat of the room.

She never knew how long it was before a question from nowhere came shooting through her mind, a question from outside herself, that came with a hideous clarity: a chill of the lungs—could that breed such raving?

Margery recoiled from the bedpost and stood quivering; and suddenly a chill she knew had crept into the stifling room. The heat faded, and she felt her back shiver as the Secret Cold came in; and at once her mind was working icily.

She took a candle from the press and carried it dangerously within the bed-curtains; and holding it so that its light was full on Tony, she looked intently. His face was flushed and red, his mouth open, his lips dry and parched. She put her hand on his forehead and felt it dry and hot. Then she gently eased his head back, and the candle-light fell on the great dark pupils of his staring eyes.

Mistress Crook, making her Confession to Father Southworth, was disturbed by the ring and clatter of boots on the oaken stair, and she had no more than got to her feet when the parlour door was flung rudely open and a termagant of a girl burst in.

'What food's he had?' she snapped. 'These last days?'

Margaret Crook quivered. She was indignant, and she was bewildered. This was not the Margery she had known.

'What food's he had?'

The question came again, and the young voice was savage. That was the end of resistance. Gentle Margaret was no match for this hard-eyed truculence.

'Why, milk,' she answered meekly. 'Milk, and syllabubs, and some barley-water. No more.'

'The milk—from your own cattle?' There was a ring of steel in the voice.

'Why yes, to be sure it was. But . . .'

'The barley water—who made it?'

'I did. But my dear . . .'

'And the syllabubs—from whence?'

'Why, I beat them myself.'

'All of them?'

The steel in the voice had the edge of a razor now.

'Myself? Yes, most of them. Though Alice has been . . .'

'Alice!'

She almost spat the word, and gentle Margaret shrank back as she heard the ring of it. But that was the climax. Margery stood rigid, white-faced and tense as she fought for calm; and gradually her bearing eased. She drew a deep breath, and when she spoke again she was almost her own self.

'I must ask your pardon,' she said slowly. 'I've been most ill mannered.'

'Why yes, my dear. Never mind that. But . . .'

'Please!' Margery interrupted firmly. 'I'll tell you later why it was. Just now there's more urgent matter. These syllabubs—you say Alice Nutter sent some?'

'Indeed yes. She's been most kind.'

'Have you one left—of hers?'

'Part of one. Tony had . . .'

'May I see it, please?'

Margery was polite, but the ring was coming into her voice again, and Margaret was too dazed to resist. She led to the door and Margery went quietly after her. Christopher Southworth followed silently, and his dark eyes had an understanding gleam; he was not ignorant, and he was very far from being a fool.

The old servitor, hovering by the kitchen door with eyes agape, stood aside to let them pass. Margaret opened the cool lime-washed larder and brought out a bowl of crystal —thick fluted glass that could take a glint if the light were bright enough. A soft pink curd filled the bowl, smooth except where a spoon had taken some away.

Margery took the bowl in silence, and scanned it with care. A syllabub was cream beaten up with wine, and she was thinking that it might disguise a flavour—almost if not completely. She put the bowl into the curve of her left arm and dipped a finger of her right hand into it. Cautiously she put the finger to her tongue.

The crystal shivered on the stone-flagged floor as she hurled it from her. Margaret shrieked, and the old servitor jumped back, his breeches splashed with curd. Christopher Southworth moved forward with inquiring eyes, and Margery wiped her tongue and spat. Beyond mistake, the acrid bitterness had been there; it was masked and faint, but it was there—to a clean tongue and a wary mind. But would it have been there to the tongue and mind of a sick and weary man? Tony Nutter, she remembered, had been sick from his ride in the snow before ever this began.

Margaret, dazed and bewildered, looked helplessly at Margery as though asking what she should do. She was promptly told.

'Tony's alone,' said Margery quietly, and Margaret stood vaguely until she grasped the meaning. Then she gave a horrified gasp and went hurrying up the stair. The old man stooped and began to collect the pieces.

'Leave that,' said Margery. 'I'll need my horse. Be pleased to see to it.'

She was quite sure what must be done. The old man, half comprehending, moved slowly away, and Margery led Christopher Southworth back through the hall and into the parlour. But at the parlour door she checked in surprise; the curtains were drawn across, and only a single candle lit the gloom; she had been too distracted before to notice that the priest had taken this precaution, but now the dark shadows repelled her and she turned back into the hall. He followed without protest.

He stood grave and impassive under the candle by the stair, and she met his eyes fairly.

'I'm to suppose there was venom in that bowl?' he said. 'And that this sickness was born of it?'

She nodded.

'If not born of it, at least nourished of it.'

He seemed to accept that easily.

'Witches?' he asked, and again she nodded. There was no need to tell him more.

The dying candle flared smokily, and Margery's irritations flared with it. She blew it viciously and then flung the outer door wide open. She had had enough of shadows and candle-light, and she wanted the bright day and the clean air. But the day was not bright; she had been so engrossed that she had forgotten that, and it was almost a shock to see the dark sky again, and the spattering pools in the rain-soaked gravel. The light was fading now, and the rain was as loud and as steady as ever.

'Can you do what's needed?' Christopher Southworth spoke suddenly. 'There's a life to be saved—and you are young.'

She turned from the door and saw his face grave in the fading light. Behind her a horse clopped on the gravel, and she guessed that the old man had saddled her beast and led it round at last. She tried to speak confidently.

'As to saving life—if it's not too late already . . .'

'That, as I have told you, is with God.'

She nodded.

'I think I hear my horse. We must get him away from here, and I'll ride at once for help. Which is to say, sir, that you'll need to be gone when I return. I think your work is done?'

He made no reply to that. His brooding eyes seemed fixed on the daylight behind her, and suddenly Margery spun round in vague alarm.

Out on the gravel, standing by his horse and watching them both in silence, was Frank Hilliard; and Margery forgot everything as she ran to him.

'Frank!' she called excitedly. 'Where are you from?'

'Home.'

His answer was curt, and at the tone of it her excitement faded and she looked at him in dismay.

'I came as I said I'd come,' he said slowly. 'After a week of March. I came this morning, and they told me you were here. So I followed. I . . . I was eager.'

His eyes turned from her and rested for a moment on the priest in the doorway.

'I was eager to see you,' he went on. 'But hardly eager to see so much.'

Then Margery understood; and at once her mind slipped back to the night at Marton when she had assured him so keenly that she had ended with Master Southworth. Her courage began to fail as she understood.

He turned from her, and walked to the door. He shook the water from his dripping cloak, and went slowly into the hall, Margery followed limply, and Christopher Southworth stood impassive. In unbroken silence the two men faced each other. And then, before either had spoken, a chair scraped in the bedchamber above, and feet moved quickly.

To Margery, those simple sounds, ringing loud in the silence, were charged with meaning. Margaret Crook had moved to see to Tony's needs. It was a sharp reminder to Margery that Tony's needs were the greater; and at once her mind leapt away from her own tangle and became alert in another's cause.

'God's Grace!'

It burst from her without warning, and the men whipped round to her in surprise.

'God's Grace!' she said again, and her voice had something of the ring that had conquered Margaret. 'There's a man dying above, and we linger here like slugs.'

She rounded on Frank, who was plainly startled, and explained herself crisply.

'Tony Nutter—you've heard me speak of him—is above there. He's deadly sick, and like as not he's dying. And just now that comes before all else.'

Frank saw the question in her eyes and he nodded his assent. She had convinced him of urgency, and he would allow that to come before resentments. She hurried on before he could change his mind.

'Master Southworth's coming was not contrived by me. I did not think to see him here, nor he, I'm sure, to see me. This Tony Nutter is a papist, Frank, and had need of a priest. That I take to be the truth of it?'

Christopher Southworth bowed his head in agreement, and Margery paused; her eyes held them both.

'There's a dying man. Will you both do now what shall serve his needs? Master Southworth?'

'I'd refuse that at peril of soul.'

'Frank?'

He spoke for the first time since he had entered the house, and his answer surprised her.

'It's a hundred and thirty miles hither from my home. I've had weather foul and roads worse. But I rode it in four days and a morning, and I did not do that with intent to quarrel when I found you.' He paused, and Margery saw for the first time that his face was strained and his eyes bloodshot. But he had a hint of a smile now. 'You seem to have all this under your hand, and I'll not dispute it with you. What would you have of me?'

But she turned first to the priest.

'Master Southworth; your work here is done, and you linger at your peril—and not your own peril only. I would not seem surly, but we'll breathe more freely when you're gone.'

He nodded, but then he turned to Frank.

'She reasons well,' he said. 'But you, sir, are in some sort concerned in this. Have I your leave to go?'

Frank shrugged lightly.

'Margery has this under command,' he answered, 'and I've said I'll not dispute it with her. You'll be wise to go.' The smile was hovering on his lips again. 'And indeed, sir, I've some liking for you and I wish you better than what's prepared at Lathom. So get you gone while none hinders.'

The priest looked steadily at him.

'You're generous,' he said quietly.

'Not wholly. I've had kin at Douai . . .' He smiled oddly at that. 'And in these days I'm not milord's catchpoll. You'll have a horse?'

'Nearby.'

'Seek it then.'

'My thanks—to you both.'

He pressed at the panelling by the side of the stair; something clicked and a panel turned. From the space within he drew cloak and hat, and the discreet travelling-bag that served for plate and vestments—the bag that would hang him if he were taken with it. In silence he adjusted his cloak and pulled his hat low. Then, by the door, he paused and spoke to Margery.

'I do not think that we shall meet again. I am ordered to another place, and I do not think I can do you any service —except that you shall have my prayers. If I had stayed here . . .'

'You must not stay here.'

'No. But it's my great regret that you are a heretic, for I think you are well disposed. However . . .'

His hand lifted quickly, and before Margery had seen what he was about, the sigil was completed.

'God be with you—both!'

He pulled his cloak tight and went out into the rain. He walked quickly across the soaking gravel till he came to the hedge of leafless thorn that ran between the pines. For a moment he waited there, looking back at them as they stood in the doorway. Then he moved behind the hedge and was gone.

Margery shut the door and signed to Frank to wait. She went quickly up the stair and looked into the bedchamber, where a bewildered Margaret, bubbling with curiosity, loosed a flood of whispered questions. But Margery put her off with a brief assurance that the priest was safe away; all else, she said, must wait. She stayed only long enough to learn that Tony, if no better, was at least no worse; and then she hurried down the stair again. Frank was still standing at its foot, and for a moment Margery allowed herself to relax.

'You've been very—well disposed,' she whispered.

'That's what the Seminary said to you.'

She nodded.

'With a shade of difference, I'm saying it now to you.'

He spoke no answer, but his arms came round her and he kissed her with a quiet assurance. And then she flung her head back and pushed him away.

'That must wait,' she said quickly. 'There's work to do.'

'Yes?'

His tone showed that he accepted a necessity. She marshalled her scattered thoughts, and then spoke lucidly.

'Tony's deadly sick. There's malice in it, and I think there's a venom used. His sister, who has him in charge, is kindness alive, but she's no match for this Devil's work. Also, with fear for him and lack of sleep, she's so worked on that she should be *in* a bed, not beside one. So it's urgent to have them safely lodged at Read—both of them, and the old man too. We can't leave him.'

'What old man?'

'He was leading out my horse when you came. I hope he's not still doing circles on the gravel.'

'More likely he's led mine in.'

'You may look to that. But what's urgent is to have men and horses and a litter . . .'

'Which I'm to contrive?'

'You are.'

'How?'

'That's for your wits. Such things must be at Read if they're rummaged for. Meantime I'll be busied here. His sister's given to wordiness, and how she's to be soothed and persuaded . . .'

'That's for your wits.' He flung the words back at her. Then he opened the door and peered out at the dripping greyness. 'The light fades, and if this is to be done before dark I'd best be moving.'

They found the old man wearily swilling the spilt curd from the kitchen floor, and they let him continue while Frank took the speedier course and saw to his horse himself. Margery watched him ride away, and then, reluctantly, she climbed the stair once more. The news that her young guest had coolly made plans to uproot her from hearth and home might not commend itself to Margaret, and Margery foresaw an argument. But to her deep relief she was wrong, and once she had explained matters she had her way without dispute. Margaret Crook was too tired, and too worn with trouble, to care much what was done, if only somebody else saw to the doing of it.

Margery came down the stair again and went into the parlour that could be so pleasant in the sun. But now there was no sun. The curtains were still drawn across the window; the fire had burned out, and a thread of smoke was flaring from the neglected candle. Margery looked with distaste. She pinched the candle and drew back the curtains; and for a moment she had the lattice open to let the reek from the room. She pulled it close, and in the last light of the waning afternoon she sat on the window-seat, alone with her thoughts, and peering at the unending rain.

The room was quite dark, and the last glimmer of dusk was on the pines, when the lanterns came in sight; and when the horses crunched on the gravel, Roger Nowell was the first to dismount.

34

The Stricken Pedlar

Roger's friendly parlour seemed like a corner in Heaven.

Tony Nutter, quieter now, was in peaceful sleep above, and Margaret had with no great difficulty been persuaded to bed also. Margery, who had missed dinner without a thought of it, had made amends for that at supper; and now, in ease at last, she was telling the tale of the day. She ended it, and then she laughed as she saw Frank's puzzled face; he had not known of the coppice where the purple flowers grew, and he had not been told the half of what was suspected of Alice Nutter; but he was soon enlightened and then he showed a fine indignation, looking at Roger as though in expectation of instant action.

But Roger puffed smoke of tobacco and stayed in his comfortable ease.

'With poisons as with sorceries,' he said lazily, 'it's best to have some evidence. And I'm not fool enough to commit without it.'

'But surely, sir, with this tale . . .'

'What does this tale amount to? That Margery thought she tasted bitterness in a syllabub—no more.'

'Something more, surely?' Margery had come upright in her chair. 'Tony Nutter had all the Herbal said—the fever, the eyes, and the rest.'

'Who'll hang Alice Nutter from a Herbal? That woman's no fool. Tony did in truth take chill from the snow. He did in truth come to fever by that. As like as not, he did in truth bring his fever back by adventuring out too soon. And when he's found all but dying of a fever, is it not the same fever?'

'Yet if other things were sworn to?'

'They'd be disbelieved. Please to remember that Alice Nutter is not a Demdike. She's of substance and good estate, and she stands in good repute. She's reared a son who may be thought a credit, and she's known for fair speech and charitable works. And I say again, she's no fool. Her way, even in this, shows it. She waits till he truly has a fever, and then she uses what brings the look of fever. It's perhaps to be deplored that the old fellow swilled that floor. We might have saved the stuff else, and fed it to a dog. A dead dog's poor proof, but it's better than we've got.'

And with that Roger seemed to dismiss the topic. He turned to Frank and spoke in a different tone.

'This Seminary, Southworth—he's had uncommon fortune. A Massing priest who escapes thrice should indeed believe in miracles. It's well enough in itself, and I don't doubt we can hush it. But what of you? I understood your fortunes at Lathom to wait upon his capture.'

Margery sat stiffly. Her head had been so filled during the day that she had thought of none but Tony; she had never even asked herself what it might have meant to Frank to stand easily while that priest departed; and now, when it was brought to her, she was at once acutely anxious. But Frank still seemed at ease about it.

'That's no matter,' he answered cheerfully. 'I said this afternoon that I'm not milord's catchpoll these days. The truth is, I'm better placed in the world than I was.'

'Why, what's this? You never told me . . .'

He told her with no more delay. His mother, he reminded them, had been distressed partly because her brother had died; but this brother had died childless, and his modest estate had passed to his sister—Frank's mother; and she, considering that her elder son was heir to his father's estate, had at once made her younger son heir to this one, and by so doing she had, as he pointed out, wholly changed his prospects.

'Almost,' he said, 'I may claim the status of an elder son. And in the meantime there are some rents made over to me. Wherefore I have it in mind to ride this week to Lathom and be quitted of milord's service. He may keep his favour for another, since I want it not.'

Roger eyed him shrewdly. Then he had a warning to give.

'Quit milord's service by all means, if you've a mind to. I

think you may be wise in that. But spare your resentments and show him the courtesies.'

'Why sir, I . . .'

'Spare your resentments.' The note of authority was in Roger's voice. 'To provoke his anger might well provoke his inquiry into your doings here. And they will not stand inquiry. Nor will Margery's.'

That settled it, and Frank was firm that he would show no resentments at Lathom. He would be smooth, he said, as any Jesuit.

'One thing more,' said Roger. 'I think you'd waste your time at Lathom. Milord's at Lancaster. He attends the opening of the Lent Assize, and he'll be there all week.'

'Then I'll seek him at Lancaster, sir. And perhaps I may come to a word with Master Covell too.'

'Very like. He seems to have some softness for you.' Roger's smile broadened. 'You say you have some money now?'

'Sufficient, sir. But . . .'

'You'll need it, if you let him lodge you at the *George*.'

And Margery led the laughter as her quick mind recalled what Roger had once said of the ways of Edmund Covell.

Then Roger made an end to talk, telling her roundly that it was high time she was abed; but he did not, this night, take her to the stair to light her candle; instead he stayed by the fire and left that work to Frank. He hastened to it, and Margery stood very still as he lit her candle; she gave no sign that she had seen the tallow spill as his hand shook, but she took the candle from him and then paused.

'My thanks,' she said steadily. 'And for more than this.'

He looked up at her as she stood above him on the stair, and a slow smile was on him.

'These new days,' he said. 'May we once more—ride in Pendle?'

Her forehead took a crinkle, and a gleam of mischief flickered in her tired eyes.

'Yours to command,' she said. And then she was away, leaving him to consider the possible meanings of that; it was, she thought, no bad end to a wet Sunday.

He was in no hurry for Lancaster, and Friday had come before he took his departure; and in the afternoon of that day, Margery being then in the parlour with Roger, Alice Nutter came to Read.

Roger saw her first, and Roger was not pleased. She came most elegant in ash-grey velvet—the new ash-grey, as Margery promptly noted—and she rode a grey mare whose saddle-cloth was black and gold. Roger saw her through the window, and his sniff brought Margery to his side. Together they watched the lady dismount.

'We may suppose,' said Roger, 'that she learned something of Sunday and is here to learn more. I think we'll prick her a little . . .'

Margery nodded hastily, and then salutes were punctilious as their guest was shown in. She addressed herself to Roger.

'I'm told,' she said, 'that my brother is your guest just now?'

'Your husband's brother, ma'am.'

'I count it the same, sir.'

'He doesn't.'

The dark head reared a little, and Margery watched with interest; that had seemed a very promising beginning. Alice Nutter's foot tapped the floor imperiously.

'At the least, sir, I hear poor Tony is with you?'

'You set me to marvel, ma'am.'

'How?' Her eyebrows were arching, but Roger's smile was bland.

'Here's Friday,' he said. 'He came to me on Sunday, and you're but newly told?'

'You, sir, did not tell me at all.'

'I accounted it needless, ma'am. You are at all times so well informed.'

'Not in this, it seems.' The foot was tapping again now. 'I'm here, sir, to pay him my respects.'

'You're gracious, ma'am. I'll convey them to him.'

'By your leave, sir, I'll convey them myself.'

'Alas, ma'am! His condition . . .'

'What of it, sir? What's his condition?'

'Did they not tell you, ma'am, that he was come near to dying?'

The dark eyes flickered suddenly, and the watchful Margery had the ghost of a smile. That hit had gone home.

'Dying?' There was consternation in her voice. 'Then most certainly I must . . .'

'Not so, ma'am. Pray do not fear for him. He's watched most carefully. Yet to one in his state . . .'

'Yes, sir?'

'Visitors could be dangerous.'

There was no doubt about that one. The head reared again, and the narrowed eyes took a glitter. Roger stayed poised and watchful. Margery was almost on her toes. Then Alice relaxed; almost, she took on graciousness.

'If it's so, I must not press. Convey my condolences and my sympathies, if you please. My husband's also.'

'Be assured of it, ma'am.'

His bow was formal as Alice moved to the door. Margery ran to open it for her; if they were playing this to the courtesies, she knew her part, and she went politely out on the gravel to help the lady mount. Alice gathered her bridle comfortably into her hand and then looked down at Margery.

'What ailed Tony?' she asked abruptly.

That gave a chance, and Margery went at it with zest.

'Who's to say, ma'am? But I think it may have been the pine trees. There are so many of them by that house, and there's such an effluxion comes from pines.'

'Pines, indeed!' Alice snorted with contempt.

'Yes, ma'am.' Margery had a sweet little half-curtsey for her. 'Or if not from pines, perhaps from some other plant that grows in Pendle.'

The eyes blazed, and Margery was warily on her toes. It was well for her that she was, for with no warning Alice stiffened her back and her whip hissed viciously. Margery saved her face by sheer speed of movement, and Roger, hurrying out as Alice rode off, was quickly reassured.

'No harm done,' Margery told him. 'She missed hitting me.'

'But barely so. But what a temper the woman has!'

'Aye, sir.' Margery laughed, as much in relief as in mirth. 'But all being said, you set yourself to stir it.'

'An enterprise in which I *did* not note that you were backward. Yet I scarcely thought we'd stir so much. I ask myself what will come next. We'd be prudent, perhaps, to expect some counter-stroke.'

He went thoughtfully within, and Margery went as thoughtfully after him. She was wholly in agreement that it would not be the way of Alice Nutter to pass so much without some counter-stroke, and in the days that followed Margery was watchfully alert for it. Yet no stroke seemed to come. Frank came back from Lancaster, duly freed from his service in the Household, and Margery rode with him in Pendle whenever the windy days of March allowed—which was not often, for there was day after day of wind and driving rain, when riding for pleasure would have been a madness; and then, when they had all but lost their wariness, their peace was broken.

Frank Hilliard went out of Pendle for the last week-end of March. His cousins the Listers, he said, had shown him many kindnesses, and it would scarcely be within the courtesies that he should let them continue in ignorance of his new status and of the events at his home; so off he went, with some grumbles and some reluctance, to make the visit that was called for; and Margery was left with Roger.

That Sunday, the last in March, was a day so foul that even Roger refused to go beyond doors, church or no church. He would stay by the fire, he said, and dine in a decent dryness; and Margery, peering gloomily through the glass, soon agreed with Roger. The wind was out of the north-east, and the driving rain was mixed with a freezing sleet that spattered on the windows and came sliding down the glass in icy stars. Only the nearer trees were sharp; all else was blurred in the swirling grey.

Matters were in this state, Roger blowing smoke of tobacco and Margery beginning to think hopefully about dinner, when a wild-eyed lad tumbled from a sweating horse and ran breathless to the great door. Roger waited for nobody. He pushed the lattice open, called the lad to him, and had his tale from him first hand; and within the minute Roger had pulled at the bell-cord and was shouting urgently for horses while he and Margery ran in haste for their riding clothes. For the lad brought a call for urgent help. The rabble was up, under Richard Baldwin and another. They were swimming a witch in the pool at Wheathead, and Hargreaves, the Constable, was hard pressed.

Then they were away, Margery staying somehow at Roger's side, and Tom Peyton and Joe Rimmer storming along behind them. Margery took a risky glance at them and saw the bulges in their saddle-bags; and these, she guessed, meant pistols. She glanced across at Roger, and for the first time by day in Pendle she saw the sword-sheath pushing through his cloak; and she thought of Richard Baldwin.

They came out into the road, and they buried their faces in their cloaks as they turned into the wind and the stinging sleet. Roger rode like a madman, and all his preachings of safety were far behind him. His big chestnut, given his head and a touch of the spur, was away like a Fury, and Margery's grey went scampering after the chestnut. What followed was a whirl, and she was far too occupied in keeping her seat to be able to think; she was perhaps seventy pounds lighter than Roger, and what might have been riding for him was a wild bounce for her. They went past the Newchurch, and she seemed scarcely to have noted that the place looked deserted, when they were down the hill and splashing through the Pendle Water. Then there was Barley and the lesser stream; and then the bend she knew, where the grey mill stood by the shivering pool.

Here all was familiar, and today so strange. For round the pool that was always so quiet and lonely, there was now a swaying surging rabble, perhaps a hundred of them—men and women, and even some children too. They were all wet, all cold, and all ripe for mischief. In the centre of them the press was thinner and here, bare-headed and commanding, was Richard Baldwin.

The crowd turned as they heard the horses, and those on the fringe pressed back in alarm, leaving a lane into which Roger promptly rode. He was not gentle; he forced his way ruthlessly; but he got through; and Margery, who had kept close, dismounted at his side, watchful and anxious.

Richard Baldwin, tight-lipped and stern, stood by the low stone wall and waited silently for Roger. At his side was a man whom Margery did not know, a chubby fresh-complexioned fellow with the clothes and air of a townsman; at another time he might have looked genial, but now, with his round face puckered, his podgy chin set tight, and his clothes soaked through with rain and mud, he had all the look of an angry and dangerous man. But Margery spared him no more than a glance, for behind him, on the ground, was Alizon Device; and Alizon Device was ready to be swum. She lay naked in the mud, scratched, bruised and bleeding, with the cold rain splashing on her. Her left wrist was tied to her right ankle and her right wrist to her left ankle, and her rolling eyes and twitching lips showed the extremity of her terror. Standing beyond her, muddy and dishevelled, was Harry Hargreaves, and he greeted Roger with unconcealed relief.

Roger nodded to him and turned sharply to Margery.

'Untie that girl,' he said curtly.

Richard Baldwin moved forward quickly, his face set and hard.

'Master Nowell . . .'

'Go to your homes—each one of you, and at once.' Roger's voice went sharply to the crowd, and Baldwin waited. Margery, tense and breathless, heard a stir and a buzz—and that was all. None moved. And Richard Baldwin spoke again.

'You'd best know . . .'

'I mean to know.'

Roger snapped it, and the crackle in his voice won him silence. He glanced sharply at Margery, and she hastily remembered what he had told her to do; at once she pulled the gloves from her frozen fingers and dropped on her knees by the writhing Alizon. Then a fierce hand clapped on her shoulder, and the chubby-faced stranger spun her round and spoke angrily.

'You'll leave that . . .'

He got no further. Roger's sword was out like a striking snake, and the point pricked blood from the fellow's throat. He jumped like a startled goat, and at once Roger was between him and Margery.

'Do you stay your hands, or do I slit your throat?'

It was enough. The fellow pressed back, not a word said, against the wall by the pool; and again Margery knelt and fumbled with the knots in the tough wet cord. All her mind was with Roger, and from somewhere deeper than thought a compulsion was upon her. All hung now on the obedience that Roger could exact, and she, who had an order to obey, had an example to give. Her fingers froze, and the hard rope bruised her nails, but she made herself go on; and from behind her she heard Richard Baldwin again.

'Master Nowell, I do beseech you . . .'

'In the King's name, I do command you that you do depart, all of you, peaceably to your homes.'

This was formal, and Margery knew its meaning. If that was not obeyed, a magistrate might make arrests and at need use force. This was the crisis, and Margery turned with an agonised glance to see what should befall. The movement caught Hargreaves' eye, and he saw her trouble; in a moment he was at her side, knife in hand, to cut the knots. Alizon stretched hopelessly, and Margery hastily pulled off her cloak and flung it over the girl. Then she turned quickly to Roger.

The crowd had not dispersed. They had retreated a little, and that was all. Roger, his back to the low wall, had his eyes on the crowd; on the fringes his two servants sat their horses stiffly, and Margery saw that they had pulled off their gloves and had their hands on their saddle-bags. But the crowd was not looking at them, and only a few were looking at Roger; more and more were turning to Richard Baldwin, and Margery understood. He was their leader, and they waited to see what he would do.

Apparently Roger understood it too. He turned to Baldwin and got his word in first.

'I've commanded all to their homes. You are one, and your home's behind you.'

There was a gasp from the crowd, and then a deadly silence as they waited. Margery, standing stiffly by Alizon, caught the tension and found her breath racing. Here was the climax.

'Aye. You've commanded it.' Richard Baldwin spoke doggedly, and his voice shook from the power that was in him. 'But here's witchcraft and a man maimed . . .'

'It's a lawful command. I'll hear of witchcraft only when it's obeyed.'

Margery caught the note of it, and she knew that Roger's resolution matched Richard's. Open conflict was very near, and with it, like as not, would be bloodshed. Margery shivered at the thought; and again she looked helplessly from the one man to the other, while the thought played in her that she, and she alone of all here, had the goodwill of both. And suddenly the unseen forces gripped her, and she knew what must be done.

She moved forward stiffly, and before either man could speak again she had slipped between them.

'I've loosed the girl, sir—as you commanded.'

'My thanks.'

He was curt and formal, for he had not yet seen where she was going. But from Roger she turned to Richard Baldwin, and faced his frigid disapproval.

'You'll perceive why I loosed her, Master Baldwin?'

'I do not,' came the icy answer.

'I was commanded so to do.' Her eyes were as steady as his. 'And being commanded, I remembered the words of Samuel to Saul. That, sir, is why.'

There was a murmur from the crowd, and at her side Roger stirred suddenly. But Margery paid no heed. She was watching Richard's face intently as he searched his memory for the text. And as he groped, she gave it him.

'For rebellion is as the sin of witchcraft,' she told him quietly, and she saw the doubt flicker in his smouldering eyes.

'You fling that at me?' he brooded.

'I do not fling it, and the words are not mine. But if rebellion and witchcraft be twins, I'd shun the one as I'd shun the other.'

That gave him pause, for it was shrewdly said. Richard Baldwin did not take his Bible lightly, and he would let neither his wishes nor his hates over-ride the commandments of his God, when once he was sure what those commandments were. And now, as he stood in anxious thought, Roger had a word to add. Roger, too, could control resentment to serve duty, and he had seen at last where Margery was driving. He put up his sword and spoke quietly.

'Richard—you spoke just now of a man maimed . . .'

'That I did. And by her arts . . .' He pointed to the girl on the ground, still huddled under Margery's cloak. 'By her hellish arts, John Law lies maimed in Colne . . .'

'That's for me to hear of. I've that duty as a Justice. But not before this rabble. Therefore, Richard, go you to your house. And when you're in, I'll come in also, if you'll give me leave, and hear of this in proper form.'

'May I come too?'

Margery spoke quickly as she saw him still hesitate, and her question turned the scale. Even at this moment, goodwill weighed for something, and Richard inclined his head courteously.

'And welcome, mistress.'

He turned, signing to the stranger to follow him; and together they walked slowly through the crowd and into the house. Margery, looking to the house, saw Grace for the first time; white-faced and anxious, she was with her mother at a window above stair.

There was no more trouble. The muttering crowd had lost their leader, and none dared be first in stubbornness. Roger did not have to repeat his command, for none would meet his eye. In five minutes all were gone, streaming away in muttering groups, sullen and disappointed, but without cohesion enough to make a danger. Then Harry Hargreaves seemed to shake himself.

'Mother of God!' he said. 'That came near it. I've been sweating like a foundered horse.'

Roger laughed.

'It's well ended,' he said. 'And I think we've to give some thanks to my cousin here. That was quick wit and a cool head.'

'Amen to that! But I'll thank you too, sir. I can't mind ever being more pleased to see any. I'd been here but three minutes when you came, and for two of them I'd been praying for hope of help.'

Roger nodded and looked down at Alizon. She was lying still and quiet under Margery's cloak, and he frowned.

'If the girl's not in a faint, she's near it,' he said, 'and small wonder! She'll be best at Read. See to that, and then follow us in.'

He walked to the house with Hargreaves, leaving Margery to devise something. But it was not very difficult. Grace and her mother dared Richard's wrath and passed down a blanket and an old cloak. Margery saw Alizon decently wrapped, and then she and Tom Peyton between them heaved her up in front of Joe Rimmer as he sat his great horse. The big man grinned and then trotted off cheerfully, Margery calling after him that, witch or no witch, Alizon was to be handed to the women and instantly put to bed.

Tom Peyton stayed. Margery had expected him to ride with Joe, but he did not; he believed in missing nothing, and he walked unblushingly to the house with Margery.

Grace was at the door to welcome them, and a quick squeeze of the hand showed her feelings to Margery. Then there was the great kitchen and a leaping fire, and cheer and warmth at last.

There was all that, and there was also what Margery valued more; there was an air of friendliness. Margery sensed it at once, and her respect for Richard Baldwin soared. He had consented, unwillingly and from conscience, to give obedience to the magistrate and receive him into his house. But, consent once given, he would not spoil it with sulkiness, nor show ill manners to his guests. So there was a welcome; there were chairs by the fire, and bread and cheese, and hot spiced ale. Richard Baldwin could be hard and he could be narrow, but he could not be petty.

They found Margery space and a chair. Grace passed her an ale-mug, and she took it thankfully, for she had been without a cloak for long enough to feel the cold. And as Tom Peyton slid into a corner with a brimming mug in his hand, Roger was coming to what Margery wanted to hear. Apparently it had been settled that no more should be heard of the attempt to swim a witch, and now Roger was asking what this was, about a man maimed.

'That,' said Richard, 'is a matter for Abraham Law.'

Eyes turned to the stranger, and Margery, like the others, began to give him serious attention for the first time; and it occurred to her now that something in his plump figure and shining red face was familiar. The truculence he had borrowed from the crowd had quite gone now, and the vicious look had gone with it. He was clearly a fellow of mean station, and to be within doors in the presence of an Esquire, especially one who had just pricked a sword into his neck, was a situation that unnerved him. He had not ventured to sit, and he was standing shyly by the hearth; he shifted unhappily as they turned to him, and he was in haste to set his ale-mug down.

In the end it was Richard Baldwin who had to tell his story for him. This man, he said, was the son of John Law, the petty chapman, whom they would all know; and at once Margery knew what was familiar in this man's looks. She had always thought of John Law as Fat Jack, and she had therefore missed the significance of the name; but the resemblance was plain enough once she was reminded.

Richard went on with the tale. Eight days ago, he said, this Abraham Law, being then in Halifax where his work was, had had word that his father lay grievously stricken in an ale-house at Colne; and hastening there, he had found his father deformed and thick of speech, his head drawn awry and his arms and legs without good movement, especially on one side. And thickly and painfully his father had told of meeting Alizon Device in a field near Colne, of being pestered by her for pins, and of sturdily refusing to open his pack. Alizon had been angry. She had cursed and muttered; and John Law, misliking her looks and knowing her to be a witch, had hurried from her at a greater pace than made for ease. But he had gone no more than a furlong when he was smitten down. What had come to him he did not know; but when he had found his senses again, he had been so stricken that he had been in great distress to get as far as the nearest alehouse; and there he still lay. And who could doubt that here was witchcraft?

Certainly his son had not doubted it. Abraham Law had at once made search for Alizon Device, and he had found her elusive; it had taken him a week to come up with her, but when he had at last done so, he had taken her more or less forcibly to his father's bedside at Colne; and there, in his presence, she had admitted to bewitching his father.

Richard Baldwin got so far with their tale, and then Abraham Law interrupted him. Indignation lent him words, and they came with a rush. His father, he said, had been so starkly mad as to forgive this Alizon, and fury at that had all but driven him, the son, mad too. But when he had recovered his wits he had at once hastened to Pendle, whither Alizon had already flown; he had told his tale at a house he had come to down by the river, and the people there had bidden him carry his tale to Master Baldwin. And the rest they knew.

They did, and Roger had tact enough not to probe into details. He gave his orders crisply. He would formally examine Alizon on the morrow, supposing her to be sufficiently recovered by then, and it would therefore be needful for Abraham Law to attend and give evidence. Harry Hargreaves would naturally be needed, and Richard Baldwin would be welcome if he chose to attend. Ordinary presentments due to be heard on Monday must stand till

Tuesday. And that, said Roger, was all; it was time for him to take his leave.

It was not till they were half way home that an odd thought came upon Margery. It startled her, and without intending it she drew rein and stopped.

'What the Devil?' said Roger, stopping also.

Margery collected her wits and tried to speak simply.

'That lad who brought you the message this morning—he sent you on a perilous mission.'

'No doubt. But what of it?' Roger sounded puzzled.

'And perilous too for Master Baldwin?'

'I'll grant you he stood some chance of hanging. But again, what of it? What teases you?'

'I'm asking who sent that lad with that message.'

'Hargreaves, was it not?'

'That's what I ask. Was it?'

Roger stared at her.

'What's in your mind?' he asked slowly. 'There's something chilling here.'

Margery explained it carefully.

'I supposed from that message that Hargreaves was already at Wheathead and in trouble.'

'And was he not?'

'No. He said he'd been there but three minutes when we came.'

Roger whistled softly.

'God's Grace!' he said quietly. 'What wits you have! Tom!'

'Sir?' Tom Peyton drew close.

'That lad who brought alarm to us this morning—did you know him?'

'Yes, sir. Jack Wharton, sir.'

'And who the Devil may Jack Wharton be?'

'Pig boy, sir. At the Rough Lee.'

35

Easter Duties

The Examination of Alizon Device of the Forest of Pendle in the County of Lancaster, Spinster. Taken at Read in the said County of Lancaster, the xxx day of March, Anno Regni Domini nostri Jacobi, Dei gratiae Angliae Franciae et Hiberniae Regis, Fidei Defensoris, decimo; et Scotiae quadragesimo quinto:

Before Roger Nowell of Read aforesaid; Esquire; one of His Majesty's Justices of the Peace within the said County: Videlicet:

Margery put down her pen and sanded what she had written. She contrived a dry cough as she poured the sand back into the jar. Then she picked up the paper, and in a cold expressionless voice she read it aloud. Alizon Device, standing alone beyond the table, turned a shade whiter, and her eyes flickered nervously from Margery to Roger, and from Roger to Harry Hargeaves sitting stiffly by the door; she found no comfort in that, and her throat was twitching as her eyes came hastily back to Roger.

Margery ended her reading and put her paper down. She had a cold and hostile stare for Alizon, and then she spoke icily.

'Alizon Device: you are here to be examined on oath before a Justice on matters touching the hurts lately done in and upon John Law, a petty chapman of Colne. You will therefore be sworn.'

Richard Baldwin, his eyes smouldering and his face set and hard, rose grimly from his chair and came forward with a Bible; it was his privilege as Churchwarden, and Alizon, meeting his eyes, was stammering as she took the oath. Margery, her face impassive, watched with satisfaction; it looked as if Alizon was not going to give much trouble.

She gave none. By her ordeal yesterday and these deliberately chilling formalities today, she had been so cowed that she surprised everybody by making a full confession, and soon Margery was hard put to it to drive her pen fast enough; and what she wrote was damning. For Alizon declared that Old Demdike, her grandmother, had persuaded her to receive a familiar spirit, which spirit appeared to her from time to time in the guise of a small dog; and when she had pestered Fat Jack for pins and had been refused, she had told this dog to lame him; and the rest had followed swiftly.

Alizon told her tale and then stood silent. Margery scratched to the end of her paper and then sat back, resting her hand and glancing quickly about her. Harry Hargreaves and the chapman's son were plainly pleased and satisfied; beside them Richard Baldwin sat with a face of granite; behind the table Roger sat impassive, showing nothing of his thoughts, and Margery had to guess that he was already probing beyond this in search of what might lead him to Alice Nutter; it would not be like Roger to find pleasure or profit in hanging so poor a thing as Alizon. Then, while she still watched, Roger settled himself back in his chair, and coolly invited Alizon to tell him of any more evil doings she might know of in Pendle. Alizon needed no second invitation, and there was a gleam of the old malice in her eyes as she plunged at it and accused her own grandmother of the murder of Margaret Baldwin; and then, before Richard had been persuaded into his chair again, Alizon was speaking of the Chattox, and had roundly accused the woman of the murder of Anne Nutter.

It all had to be set on paper, and it made hard work for Margery; her hand was stiff and aching before it was done, and then she had to make out the Mittimus that would send Alizon to Lancaster. But she was well content, and she read in Roger's eye as he signed the Mittimus that he was content too; that Alizon should know the dark secrets of Alice Nutter was not to be expected, but she had said enough to entangle those who might; and more might be expected to follow.

It did. With his hand once forced, Roger wasted no time, and in the next three days he made formal and thorough examinations of both the witch-families. Squinting Lizzie and the moon-kissed Jemmy had to be loosed again, she because she was too stubborn, and he because he was too stupid to say anything of note; but by the Thursday night Roger had Old Demdike, Old Chattox, and the shapely Anne Redfern under lock and key at Read; a Mittimus had been signed for each, and all was ready for them to journey with Alizon to the castle at Lancaster. But Roger was not satisfied; he had got enough to hang these women, but he had not got what he wanted. He said as much in his parlour that night, while he leaned against the hearth in his familiar stance. Margery sat at the table, her writings of the week spread before her, and Frank, now back from Westby, was attentive in an elbow-chair.

'It's well enough,' said Roger, 'and it will hang those four. That pleases Baldwin vastly and me not at all. There's nothing that touches Alice Nutter. The Chattox seemed to touch the old grandmother, and that's all.'

'Yes.' Margery shuffled her papers thoughtfully, and then read out what the Chattox had said. Some of it was of Anne Nutter, and went close to being a confession. But most of it was of the young Robert Nutter who had died twenty years before, and it bore out Tony's tale even to the sinister grandmother; this grandmother, according to Chattox, had asked her and Demdike and a long-dead widow Loomshaw to make away with Robert Nutter in order that a woman vaguely called a cousin might have the land. And that had been as much as Chattox seemed to know.

'It's of interest,' said Roger tersely. 'I don't doubt that it's true, and I could guess who that cousin was. But does it help?'

'No . . .' Margery shuffled her papers again. 'But there's the Demdike . . .'

'What of her?'

Roger poured himself wine, and then waited patiently while Margery scanned her closely-written sheets. Demdike had had a lot to say about clay images of people, asserting that as these were dried and crumbled, so would the persons represented waste and die. But in one matter she had departed from this; she had killed Margaret Baldwin, she said, as Alizon had maimed the pedlar, by the help of a spirit that had the form of a dog.

'Just so,' said Roger. 'And it will no doubt hang her. But again I ask, does it help?'

'In itself it does not.' Margery was speaking slowly, and now she was looking at Roger, not at her papers. 'But it's a thing lately done—not twenty years agone. And it seemed to me that when the Demdike had said so much, she closed her mouth most suddenly—and thereafter said no more.'

'Now what's this?' Roger had put his wineglass down, and was looking keenly at her. 'She shut her mouth lest she tell of something *very* lately done? Is that it?'

'That and something more.' Margery paused, and then chose her words with care. 'Of all else she spoke not unwillingly. Why, then, will she not speak of more—if more there be?' Again she paused, and she put down her papers as she turned to face him. 'Could—could the woman be in fear?' she asked quietly.

'God's Grace!' Roger stood rigid as he thought of it. 'What will your wits not cut? So she knows what touches one of whom she has a fear! Even so . . .' He was smiling suddenly, and when he spoke his tone had changed. 'I feel myself beholden to those brothers of yours. If they'd sent me a girl of other sort—the common pudding-wit—I know not how I should have fared. But certainly we must see this Demdike, and at once.'

He moved quickly on that, and Demdike was brought to the room. At first it seemed that she was resigned to everything, and she made no difficulty about his first questions. Margery became hopeful. But the first mention of Alice Nutter brought a startling change in the Demdike; at once she retreated to the wall, her little eyes rolling and blinking, and her whole frame trembling. Soon she was in such a state of open terror that Roger had to abandon his questions; the woman was plainly in no state to be pressed further if she were to keep what little sanity she still had. It was revealing and it was exasperating; but there was plainly nothing to be done but let the matter drop.

Demdike was taken away, and Roger looked grimly at Margery.

'She knows,' he said. 'She knows more than it's comfort able to know. And I ask, how is it to be had from her?'

They looked at each other blankly; and then, for the first time, Frank spoke from his chair by the hearth.

'By your leaves,' he said slowly, 'this is not without hope. There's always Master Covell . . .'

'Covell?' Roger rounded on him sharply, and Frank nodded.

'To be sure. He's a Justice, is he not? And therefore able to make examination of these women?'

'So he can!' Roger whistled softly. 'I had not thought of that. And he may wait till fears are less, and then pick his moment. They're too late now for the Lent Assize, so he'll have them in hold till August.'

'August!' Margery sounded dismayed, and Roger had almost a laugh for her.

'We'll hope for an answer before then. But it will be well to have it in Tom Covell that there's an urgency in this.' He paused in thought for a moment, and then he spoke briskly to Frank. 'It will need some nice explaining, and that's your work. You seem to have Covell's ear, and you know the whole of this. So when these women go to Lancaster tomorrow, you may command the escort.' Again he paused, and suddenly the old sardonic tone was back with him. 'Be pleased not to be far diverted if some sightly wench should spill from a horse . . .'

And Margery was brazen enough to lead the laughter.

But there was no dispute about what was to be done, and Frank was away at first light with the ambling horses that bore the captive women and their guards. This time Margery did not rise to see him go; for him alone she might have made the effort, but she had no wish to look on so sad a cavalcade, and she lay behind her curtains till they were out of sight and sound. Even then there was a melancholy upon her, and it was as much to rid herself of that as to perform a social duty that she chose to ride into Goldshaw that morning. Margaret Crook had her Tony back at home now, and it was no more than proper that Margery should inquire how he fared.

She rode out into an April morning, and April seemed disposed to make amends for March. First there was sunlight between showers, and the arching of a great rainbow; then the showers passed, and when she came to the Sabden brook there were white clouds in a blue sky, and a southerly wind that had the scent of Spring. She halted by the brook, charmed by the ripple of the light on the splashing water, and when she lifted her eyes again there was a horseman coming quickly down from Goldshaw. Margery looked once and had no more doubts; here was Miles Nutter, and Margery sat her horse and waited.

His hat was a-flourish long before he came up to her, and his smile was friendly as he drew rein. Margery was glad to see him.

'You're a stranger, Miles,' she told him cheerfully.

'Not more than you,' he retorted. 'But you know I've been from Pendle?'

'Yes. Grace told me.'

'It's good to be back.' He was chattering lightly, and seemed quite at his ease. 'I suppose you'll be for my uncle's house? You ride early this fine morning.'

'Not so early as you, it seems. My visit's still to make and yours is surely made?'

'Not so.' Suddenly there was embarrassment in his face, and Margery thought he was seeking words. 'The truth is, I'm lodged at my uncle's just now, and I'm on my way to Wheathead.'

'Wheathead?' She said it slowly, and only because she could think of no better answer.

'Aye.' He laughed, and she thought that covered something. 'At the least, I see something of Grace these days.'

'God be with you then. I'll not hold you here.' She had a smile for him now. 'Away with you! And commend me to Grace . . .'

He made no ado about that, and his beaver swept again as he wheeled his horse and went splashing through the stream. Margery waved back gaily, and then she let her horse walk slowly up the slope while she gave her thoughts to this. It might, of course, be nothing; he might merely be putting himself at the service of his aunt while Tony was sick. Margery shook her head at that. Miles, indeed, seemed to be rather at Grace's service than at his aunt's; and he had had not a word to say about his uncle's sickness, which must surely have been in his mind; nor would it have been his mother's way to see him so free to visit Grace. Margery's disbelief hardened, and soon she was asking herself what quarrel had flared between Miles and his mother.

The cool grey stones were aglow as she came through the pines, and the sun was glittering on the windows as she halted before them. The old servitor came out to take her horse as he had always done, and Margery had a smile for him as she dismounted. Then, under the stone lintel of the door, a man appeared, and for a moment she thought that here was the ailing Tony; then her eyes narrowed and she stood very still as she recognised brother Dick.

He came out to greet her, and it seemed that she had not wholly concealed her surprise.

'I'm my brother's guest these days,' he said. 'So is Miles. Did you see him as you came?'

'Yes.' She had collected herself now, and she spoke easily. 'We met by the brook. I was coming to see if any service could be done for Mistress Crook, but it seems I'm behind the times in that.'

He nodded, and accepted that view of things at once.

'Aye, we can do what's needed, Miles and I. But Margaret will be glad to see you, none the less. You'll please Tony too. But come you in . . .'

The little parlour, which had been so grey and still, was vivid now with the sunlight gleaming on brass and shining oak; the low window-seat, where she had sat to stare at the rain, was warm in the sun today, and on it, stretched under blankets and with his shoulders propped on pillows, was a smiling Tony. And then Margaret was in the room; Margaret, welcoming and indignant, hopeful and anxious, pleased and petulant, and pouring it all into a flood of words before her visitor was even seated. Tony, she said, was a fool, and she had known that for years. Everybody knew he ought to be in bed; and now, just because there was a patch of blue in the sky, he must needs be down the stair. Margaret snorted at it. If it had been but Tony alone she could have managed him; she could always manage him. But now he had brother Dick at his side, and of course one man was as stupid as another; they had none of them any sense, and they always took each other's parts. And Margaret snorted again.

Margery nibbled at a cheesecake and made soft answers. She did not even ask *why* Tony had brother Dick at his side, and she took her leave as soon as she decently could; there was something here that should be told to Roger.

She told him of it as soon as she was back, and he heard it gravely. He agreed at once that if father and son had both left home, there must be more to it than appeared; some reason would surely have been given if one could decently have been given.

'Which is to say,' he observed gravely, 'that they've guessed something touching their Alice, and something that has no pleasant face to it . . .'

'It's not certain,' said Margery slowly.

'We'll be wise to treat it as certain. For if it's so, and they've left her in the face of all Pendle, she'll no doubt be preparing something. She may even be alarmed . . .' He laughed without amusement. 'But what a woman she must be, when husband and son go out themselves instead of kicking her through the door. But that's no matter. What's of weight is that we'd best be watchful. Alice alarmed might be Alice dangerous.'

Watchful they were, and to no effect. The week-end passed quietly, and then they were in Easter Week. Frank came back from Lancaster with word that all was well and that Tom Covell would attempt the Demdike when she had had a few days' quiet. But in all Pendle was peace. Even Richard Baldwin was at peace now, and had no more than a low grumble that Elizabeth Device should be still at large. The mild Spring weather held, and Good Friday was a day so brilliant that it seemed a Feast Day rather than a Fast. There were two more days of peace; and then, in the sunlit afternoon of Easter Sunday, Alice Nutter came again to Read.

For once Margery was excluded from the talk; for Alice Nutter, speaking very simply and soberly, formally asked for speech with the Justice; and since neither Margery nor Frank could pretend to any cause for intruding on that, they had to stay outside. Alice was with Roger for a full half-hour, and when she left he went courteously to the gravel to see her mounted. When he returned to his parlour, Margery and Frank were sitting waiting for him, and he did not keep them in suspense.

'I do not see where that woman drives,' he said. 'She comes here in the middle of Sunday afternoon—Easter Sunday, if you please!—and she chooses in that time to lay an information.' Roger propped his shoulders in his favoured way, and then stared gloomily at his listeners. 'She lays information that there's been a grand meeting of the witch-coven on Friday last . . .'

'*Good* Friday!' Margery sounded shocked. 'And the witches? But why? And where?'

'She has it all pat and ready set down for me.' He took a paper from the ingle-shelf. 'It's all here. At the Malkin Tower on Good Friday. Meeting began at noon. Dinner of beef, bacon and roasted mutton—which mutton was of a wether of Christopher Swyer's of Barley, stolen and killed by James Device.'

'James?'

'The moon-kissed Jemmy. It's all here, even to the names. The Devices, the Bulcocks, the Howgates, one Hewitt called Mouldheels, and a half-score more. Cause for the meeting, to plot the death of Tom Covell and the escape of Old Demdike.'

'Are they mad?' asked Frank, as Roger tossed the paper on the table.

'Very like. But Alice isn't.'

Margery shook her wits and tried to grapple with this.

'How,' she asked, 'does Alice Nutter pretend to know so much?'

'She says she went a-riding and chanced to pass that way. She sees folk and a horse or two by the Malkin Tower, so she must needs ride close to see what's doing. Thus she stumbles on it all, and being of a dutiful disposition she very properly lays it before the next Justice . . .'

'Two days late?'

'It took her so long to have the truth of it from the Devices. She has an answer to everything.'

Margery stared blankly at him.

'Is it true?' she asked slowly.

'I'm quite sure it's true. The woman's not a fool, and she knows I'll ask the others. It will turn out to be exactly as she says it is.'

'Then why? Why does she say it?'

'I'd hoped your wits could tell me.'

He began to shred tobacco while she considered that, and she could see that his thoughts were busy.

'Could it be,' she asked slowly, 'that Alice was herself,

for some purpose, at this meeting, and that she now seeks the sunny side of law by informing?'

'It could well be that. Or it could be that she thinks these women would be better for a hanging. Rope has a way with tongues, and they may know too much.'

'Yes.' Margery nodded agreement. 'It could be that.'

'It could even be both things,' said Frank suddenly. 'But what now, sir? Do you commit these women?'

'On the face of it I must. But not at once.'

'Why not, if you please?'

'If Alice schemes that I should, it's no doubt wiser that I shouldn't. Also, if I wait there's hope Tom Covell will have an answer from the Demdike. Meantime . . .' He turned to Margery. 'You may make it your concern to fall in with the Device child . . .'

'Jennet?' Margery nodded as she understood. 'She may know more than a little of this. I'll indeed seek little Jennet.'

'Not in her home if you please.' He was sharp on that. 'But you may ride at large tomorrow and hope to fall in with her.' Then he turned swiftly to Frank. 'Will you be pleased to ride to Altham for me tomorrow?'

'Surely, sir. But why?'

'To bear word of this to Nick Banister. He has a shrewd head, and I'd gladly learn what he says to it. We do not hear presentments at Easter, so he'll not be coming here. Nor do I think it well to leave at this moment, or I'd go myself. So you may ride in my stead, and bring me back what words he speaks.'

There was no argument about that, and Frank rode early in the glow of a sunlit morning. An hour later, Margery took the Forest road, and she roamed at large all day, showing herself where she could; it gave her a pleasant day of sun and wind, but of Jennet she saw nothing. Instead, she had a meeting which she had not sought. She chose to return by way of Barley, on the chance that Jennet might be on that tree-lined road; and as she came to Barley and turned away to take the steep hill to the Newchurch, she saw Miles Nutter cantering briskly down the village street. He had obviously come from Wheathead, and Margery drew rein and waited for him. Together they let their horses plod up the long steep hill, and Margery considered him thoughtfully; then she took him by surprise.

'Miles,' she said suddenly. 'Why are you and your father lodged in Goldshaw?'

'Why . . .' He was plainly in difficulties. 'Why, as to that, it's my uncle Tony. You know he's been sick . . .'

'I *do*.' It was short and significant, and plainly it was not lost on Miles.

'Aye,' he said quickly. 'And I think we owe you some thanks over that.'

She disposed of that with a nod. Then she waited in an unhelpful silence. Miles struggled at it again.

'We do what we can for him now he mends. He . . .'

'I'm not a fool, Miles.'

She looked him fairly in the eye, and there was a long silence. Then, as they came to the crest of the hill he suddenly put evasions aside.

'If you must know,' he said, 'there were some matters that had a reek—and we liked them not, my father and I.'

'Matters?' A lifted eyebrow pointed the question.

'Say a syllabub, if you wish.'

He said it almost defiantly, and at once Margery took pity on him.

'I'm sorry, Miles. Perhaps I should not have asked. But . . .'

'You've done no hurt by asking. To put it truly, you knew it all before.'

'Perhaps I did.' She was trying to turn the topic now. 'But do you stay there long?'

'Like as not—for myself, that is. For my father, he's out of Pendle. He rode this morning.'

'Miles! But whither?' She was genuinely surprised this time.

'I know not whither, and neither does he. He said only that he'd be happier clear of Pendle till the reek had died.'

'But—but has he left you to face it yourself then?'

'Not so.' Miles was quick on that. 'He'd have had me ride with him. But I stay by Grace.'

'Oh! You mean . . .'

'I stay by Grace.' He said it slowly, and his eyes were steady; and for once Margery dropped hers.

'You—you do well, Miles.'

She said it softly, and then she was sunk in silence till they were at the bottom of the hill. Their ways parted here, but as he turned to ride down the Sabden brook, he spoke another word.

'One last thing my father did before he rode—he gave me formal leave for betrothal to Grace, whenever it can be contrived.'

Miles stayed for no answer to that. His beaver was already waving, and before Margery had found a word he had cantered off down the brook towards Goldshaw.

Margery was home at sundown, and she sought Roger with no delay; and while they were yet talking, she still in her riding-clothes, Frank came riding in, and at his side was Nick Banister. Margery went running out, and he gave her his own friendly smile as he said he meant to be at Roger's side till this had cleared.

'Another head may help,' he told her, 'even though it's old and rusty.'

'None so old, sir,' she retorted, 'and very far from rusty, if you please.

'Ravaged by time,' he insisted. 'And addled by Roger's ale.'

'That's enough of squabbling,' said Roger from behind her. 'Nick, I'm more than glad to see you, and you shall help us pour libations to Milady Fortune. Our cares shall stand till morning.'

But Roger spoke too soon. For in the last smoking blue of the dusk, at Daylight Gate as Pendle called it, a weary rider urged a wearier horse over the gravel; and being brought to Roger he presented a letter which he had borne from Lancaster, he said, by command of Master Thomas Covell.

Roger dismissed the fellow to the kitchen, broke the seal, and scanned the single sheet.

'Of Demdike,' he announced briefly. He gave himself to the sprawling script until Margery could sit still no longer.

'Has—has she answered?'

'Perhaps.' Roger looked up soberly. 'But not to Tom Covell. She's dead.'

36

Charity and Silence

Roger rode for Lancaster the next morning, with Margery at his side. Tom Covell's letter had done no more than announce the fact of Demdike's death, and Roger wanted to know more of it than that; he had, he said, an itching feel on this, and Margery, whose curiosity was certainly not less than his, went with him willingly. Nick Banister stayed at Read with all things under his hand and Frank Hilliard as his lieutenant; they seemed on good terms with each other, and Roger had peace of mind as he and Margery rode away.

They took the whole day over the thirty miles, and before they were through the Trough of Bowland Margery knew why. The steep and stony track, in places so narrow that she had to drop behind Roger, called for a watchful care, even though the sky was blue and the bright sun drew colours from the grass and the streams and the smooth grey rock. But Margery, riding here on this April morning, saw the slant of the straggling windbent trees, and asked herself what this place would be like in the wind and rain of a Winter's night. But they gained the top at last, and then they were dropping down to a river which Roger called the Wyre; and then up again, and down once more to a lesser stream; and up from this to a stretch of moorland from which they could at last see the river Lune, and grey old Lancaster lying snug against its banks. And here, up on this windy moorland, the road ran past a great triangle of timber—three uprights, and three crossbars from which ropes could hang.

'It's new,' said Roger grimly. 'And Tom Covell's mighty proud of it. Takes six at a time.'

Margery looked at the thing and had a quick, unhappy thought of Alizon. Then she looked away, and she said no more till they were safely into Lancaster.

The *George* made them welcome, and Edmund Covell, portly, rubicund, and with a professional suavity which his brother lacked, came in person to inquire their needs and see to their comforts. Edmund, said Roger in his most sardonic tone, knew to a nicety the rent-roll of every gentleman in the County, and saw to it that each had a welcome that exactly matched his worth. So they supped amply and in comfort; and then, fortified by that, they went out together into the darkening streets and sought the great stone cross that stood before Tom Covell's house by the church.

He greeted them noisily, and he plied them with wine by his warm fireside. Himself, he stood by his hearth with his feet planted apart and his gown swaying—just as his rain-splashed cloak had done at Marton, so long ago on a Christmas Eve. His face was as red and his laugh as rich as he looked down now at his seated guests.

'Aye,' he said jovially, 'the beldame's gone. That was on Sunday afternoon, and none thought to tell me of it till Monday morning.' He grinned happily at them. 'I hope you could read what I sent you. I couldn't. It's ill work cutting quills on a Monday morning, with the sabbath ale still swilling in your guts.'

Margery spluttered, and her wine splashed on her kirtle. Roger laughed openly.

'Aye,' he said. 'I read it—in the end. But what took this Demdike? Your fever?'

'*My* fever?' There was mock indignation in the jovial voice.

'Say the gaol fever if you wish.'

'What a plague has you? You chatter as though there was naught but fever that empties gaols.'

'Your pardon, Master Gaoler.' Roger's bantering tone fairly matched his. 'How is it then in yours?'

'Indifferent well. We've changed our ways these last years. Now, with clean straw every quarter, and thyme and rosemary fresh each year, a gaol's not what it was. These days there's scarce one in three dies of the fever.'

'Then what do the rest die of?'

'Rope, mostly. Did you mark our new timberwork?'

'We did. But touching this Demdike—what took her?'

'Who's to say? It was not the fever. From what I'm told, she—she wilted, and was gone.'

'Wilted?'

'Like a salted slug. Shrivelled within herself, and with that was gone. And so she looked when they showed her to me.'

'Did she so?' Roger was growing thoughtful. 'Had you seen any before that looked so?'

'None that I call to mind. Those others you sent here say the Devil whistled her soul.'

'Very like.' Roger looked across at Margery, and she saw that his thought was matching hers. Then he turned back to Tom Covell. 'Can I see her tomorrow?'

'You'll need a spade.'

'So soon?'

The big man grinned happily.

'It was that or salting. Not a keeping carcase, that one. And its April.'

'Aye. But . . .'

'I've asked the questions for you.'

Margery sat up sharply, for Tom Covell's voice had wholly changed. It was quiet, and it had lost every trace of banter; and Margery, looking with surprise, saw that the whole man had changed. He was looking steadily at Roger with eyes that were suddenly very bright and shrewd; and his voice was grave when he spoke again.

'In the common run I'd have plagued none with questions on this,' he said. 'All being said, your Demdike had some four score years, and such as she don't last long in any gaol. But I had your message. And if it was of moment to you that she should talk, it must be of moment to some other that she should not.'

'Exactly so. And I could guess a name. But you've learnt something?'

'It might be so. Though what it means . . .' The big shoulders shrugged. 'But on Sunday afternoon she was visited . . .'

'Visited? When it's witchcraft and murder?'

'All men must live. And an honest turnkey's not yet born . . .'

'Bribes, do you mean? Your turnkeys . . .'

'Are like others. They have itching palms. And a silver crown will loose most locks on a Sunday.'

'Why on a Sunday?'

'They know I'm with my wife. And so it was this Sunday. But Monday, when I'd heard of it, I first sent word to you, and then I called for certain of my rabble. They did not bluster long . . .'

There was nothing jovial in the Tom Covell who said that, and Roger was smiling grimly.

'And they told you?'

'In short, this: there was a woman came out of Pendle, and desired to see your Demdike. Who she was, you may perhaps guess. My rogues, who've wits like addled eggs, say she'd the evil eye—a black-visaged slut with a rolling squint and a screech like a moonlit cat.'

'Squinting Lizzie,' said Roger promptly, and Margery nodded agreement. It could be no other.

'And who might she be?' asked Tom Covell.

'Demdike's daughter.'

'Very like. That's what my beauties thought. And she brought, it seems, some comforts for her mother. Small things—but there was an apple tart.'

'What?'

Margery had interrupted quickly, and both men turned to her in surprise; she saw that she must give some explanation.

'It's a family weakness,' she said. 'Young Jennet dotes on apple tart, and she once told me her grandmother had a greed for it too.'

'That's justly said, by what I'm told,' said Covell. 'For it seems the old dame guzzled the whole tart in a couple of minutes. And in another hour she was dead.'

'In an hour, was it?' Roger spoke thoughtfully. 'And how did Lizzie take that?'

'Lizzie wasn't there. She stayed but a few minutes, it seems, and then she was at horse while the Demdike still picked her teeth.'

'Horse? I did not know our Lizzie had a horse.'

'She had one on Sunday—a likely foal, they tell me.'

'I'll remember that. Meantime, I'm in your debt once more. You're supposing there was some poison in this tart?'

Tom Covell shrugged his great shoulders again.

'As to that, who's to say? You may guess as shrewdly as I. Yet it's sure that she'll keep her secrets now. And sure also that I'd seen none before who wilted in just that manner.'

'I believe you. There was none of this tart left? None that could be tried on a dog?'

'Not a crumb. As I've told you, she guzzled. If there was venom used, the thing was shrewdly done.'

'It would be.' Roger rose to his feet. 'There's no more to be done then. But you've been my friend in this. Count me yours at need.'

'I'll remember that when next you're Sheriff.' The rich laugh rolled out again as Tom Covell shed his earnest mood. 'How's young Hilliard? He's delivered no more papists, I hope?'

'You think he did deliver one?'

'At the least he'd a softness for the rogue. You should have seen milord's anger. Like a studding bull.' The laugh came again as Tom Covell pulled the bell-cord. 'I'll give over furnishing milord with gentlemen. Tell him it's time he was wed. Then another may have care for him.'

He saw them jovially from the house, and Roger had no more to say on it till he and Margery were back in the snug comfort of the *George*. Then he showed that he had missed nothing.

'Touching that apple tart,' he said. 'You questioned it sharply. Is there more to it than you then chose to say?'

'Something. Jennet said that her grandmother had this greed for apple tart. But she said also that such things are not to be baked at the Malkin Tower. There's no oven there.'

Roger stared at her.

'Meaning that this Lizzie brought a tart that could not have been of her own?' He nodded. 'It fits neatly.'

'More neatly than that. From the way Demdike guzzled, we may suppose that this apple tart was a good one.'

'What of it?'

'Only that Alice Nutter is known for the rare excellence of her apple tarts. Myself I'll bear witness to it.'

Roger's low whistle was eloquent.

'Then we need not doubt further how Demdike died. Nor whose secrets had to be preserved. But what a breed these

Demdikes are! This Lizzie must have known what it was that she came to do.'

'Or was sent to do.'

'It's all one. Though sent is no doubt the just word. We may even guess what took Alice to the Malkin Tower on Good Friday. If Lizzie had guests there, she could not well go to the Rough Lee. But she must have her orders—and on Saturday she must have started for Lancaster.' He was smiling grimly. 'So Demdike's dead, and Alice prospers still.'

'But could not—could not this be brought home to her?'

'How? There's no tart left. Its excellence made sure of that, so we cannot show that it was hurtful. And even if we could, we could not show that Lizzie knew it to be so. It was not of her baking, remember.'

'Precisely. So if it could be shown that Alice baked it?'

'She'll have foreseen that. As I've said before, she's no fool. It would turn out that others had handled it, and we'd end by hanging some kitchen wench—and Alice would have compliments from the judge on her charity to the aged poor. Roger shook his head decisively. 'All that remains is to get us back to Pendle with what speed we can.'

'For a word with Lizzie, let us hope.'

'If she's there. I've doubts of all things now.'

His doubts were justified the next night, and as soon as they were back in Pendle. They came to Read at Daylight Gate, and Margery was tired enough to be drooping in her saddle; but Frank was out on the gravel to meet her, and behind him, in the arch of the door, she saw Nick Banister framed against the candle-light within. Roger waved in greeting, and he called his question before he was out of the saddle.

'Where's Squinting Lizzie?'

'Run.'

Nick's one word was enough, and Roger stared grimly. Then he held his peace till supper was done; and even then he waited till he had told of the doings in Lancaster and the way of the Demdike's death. Nick Banister listened in silence, but he exchanged an understanding glance with Frank. Then he came to it crisply.

'A haunt of peace, this Pendle,' he said, 'until yesterday, a little before noon. And then, of a sudden, there was a most woebegone child flitting in your shrubbery yonder . . .'

'Child?' Roger was quick on that, and Nick Banister had his slow smile.

'As you've guessed, Roger. A child of this Lizzie's—a little maid called Jennet. She played games with your servants when they would have chased her away, and then Frank here went to her alone. At which the child let herself be taken, and it soon came out that she was in search of Margery.' He laughed softly at the memory of it. 'Woebegone, did I say? When she had last eaten, I do not know. And for dirt—I've cleaner beasts in sties. But soon, when she had bitten something, she had a word to say. She has keen wits for her age . . .'

'So we've noted. But her tale?'

'The child, it seemed, had been near starving these three days, her mother being from home and she being left with a brother she plainly thinks a lack-wit.'

'From home three days?'

'Just so, Roger. It fits, and there's the mark of truth in the child's tale. For her mother, she said, came home Monday night. And the next day—being yesterday—the child was pulled from her bed at dawn and bidden walk to Whalley to beg a loan of butter from some woman there.'

'Butter! From Whalley?' Roger was incredulous, and Nick was smiling at him.

'Again just so. The child did not believe it either. I've said she's sharp-witted. She did not go to Whalley. She made some pretence of so doing, and then she lay hid. And soon she saw mother and brother come forth with shawls and bundles, as if on a journey. They made down towards the river, she said, and after that Mistress Jennet waited for no more. She put aside all thought of Whalley and came marching sturdily here.'

'But now, sir?' Margery spoke urgently. 'Where is she now, if you please?'

'In bed I hope—at her age.' The smile was on Nick's face again. 'I gave her in charge to your own woman, with some round orders for cleansing as well as feeding.'

'But then?' Roger spoke steadily.

'Then I sent for the Constable, and with no needful delay we were all at the Malkin Tower. And I took it upon me to bid him force the door.'

'It's well that you were here, Nick. And within?'

'Silence—as the child had said. All deserted. The hearth cold. No food and no fuel. But Roger . . .' Nick paused, and then his tone became grave. 'It's a mud floor there, and in a corner it had been dug. So we thought we'l to dig there also. And what we found was human teeth—a bagful.'

'God's Grace! That's a foulness to keep beneath one's floor.'

'Hidden in haste by the look of things. And also some small images of folk, wrought in clay and crudely done. You may guess what *they* were for.'

'I can. But what was done with these things?'

'Hargreaves took them to Baldwin. As a Warden he may take order for their burial decent.'

'Of the teeth, that is?'

'The clay as well, Roger. Is not a body clay, when all is said? A prayer said over these may quiet some soul's rest.'

'Ye-es.' Roger nodded thoughtfully. 'I'll not gainsay you in that, Nick. So now?'

'So now the hunt is up. I had indeed no great matter to bring against these Devices, but that, I thought, might well be left. So I drew a Warrant and sent word to all parts. Did I well?'

'Excellent well, Nick. Is there more?'

'Not from me. But Margery looks concerned?'

She almost flushed as she found his shrewd eyes on her. Then she came to her feet.

'I'm concerned for Jennet, sir. I've a softness for the child. Will you give me leave?'

She was away for a quarter-hour, and when she came back to the room Nick Banister eyed her with amusement.

'How's your Jennet?' he asked. 'Is she clean?'

'Clean! She's scrubbed and shining, and she'll not forget it readily.' Then Margery grew serious. 'She was asleep, sir, but she roused for me and she's wide awake now. And it's her wish, I think, to talk.'

'Talk? Of affairs, you mean?' Roger was speaking gravely.

'Yes. The fact is—I'm sorry for it, but the child's bitter. You may guess what treatment she has ever had from that mother.'

'I can. Is she then coming here—tonight?'

'Yes. I've told her she may come down—for just ten minutes. It may be worth it.'

It was, though Jennet took a full twenty minutes before she had done. She spoke in the main of the doings at the Malkin Tower on Good Friday, and her tale bore out all that Alice Nutter had told to Roger; but Jennet chattered on, and soon she came to a detail that Alice had *not* told to Roger. Jennet named all she had known of her mother's guests that day, and the names were those that Alice had given—with one more added. There was a woman, said Jennet, who had come out of Craven, a woman who had been to the Malkin Tower before, and whose name was Jennet Preston.

'Was it so?' Frank leaned forward suddenly, and there was a gleam in his eyes; but he recovered, and then he sat back, silent and interested, while Jennet went on with her tale. Jennet needed little prompting, and soon she was telling of this woman coming from Craven and bawling threats against Master Lister of Westby and Master Heber of Marton—until, to the general consternation, Alice Nutter had arrived. The company had then been at dinner, but Alice had peremptorily called two of them out—this Jennet Preston and little Jennet's own mother. They had stayed out in the sunlight for a full quarter-hour in talk with Alice Nutter; then they had come in again, tight-lipped and silent, and Alice had been heard riding quickly away.

That seemed to be all that Jennet knew, and Anne Sowerbutts was called to give her hot milk and put her to bed again. Then Margery had a word for Frank.

'Jennet Preston,' she said quietly. 'Who swills Tom Lister's dairy and gives some hand in his house. Is not that the woman?'

'It is.' Frank spoke quickly in answer. 'A woman who was in Pendle at Christmas, and rode back to Tom Lister with a hurtful tale of you. But two weeks back, when they were swimming your witch here in Pendle, I was at Westby, as you well know. And that Sunday Tom Lister told me some more of this woman . . .'

'Did he? You never told me of it.'

'When I was back here, I listened—to you. And then I forgot this tale . . .'

'What *was* this tale?

Roger had intervened firmly, and Frank responded at once; he turned to Roger and spoke soberly.

'This Preston,' he said, 'a little after Christmas, fell foul of one Dodgson, being a yeoman hard by Westby. There was some quarrel about I know not what, and Dodgson forbade the woman his land. And in no long time after that, a child of this Dodgson took sick and died—something suddenly, as it was thought. Whereat Dodgson made all haste to the next J.P. and swore witchcraft against this woman.'

'The next J.P.? Meaning whom?'

'Your son-in-law, sir—Tom Heber. Who committed her to Assize at York. From whence she's newly returned—acquitted of this charge, and mighty hot against the Justice who committed her and against Tom Lister, who, she says, urged him to it.'

'So?' Nick Banister nodded thoughtfully. 'That tells us why the woman was bawling against Lister and Heber. But does it help us find this Lizzie?'

'It does not,' said Roger firmly. 'And that's the core of it. We cannot commit Alice Nutter on the word of a child of nine. We must have this Lizzie and her moon-kissed son. And whither did they go?'

'Just so.' Nick nodded again. 'The child said towards the river . . .'

'Which might mean Colne. But does it?'

'By your leave, sir, it does not.' Frank was speaking urgently again. 'By your leave, I do think that this Preston woman, like your Lizzie here, had her orders from Alice Nutter.'

'Very like. And what were those orders?'

'To make all ready to receive and comfort Squinting Lizzie. And no doubt her son as well.'

'God's Grace!' Roger sat stiffly as he thought of it. 'Nick, what say you to that?'

'Shrewd, Roger—uncommon shrewd. And it may well be true.'

'Aye. It could be. At Gisburn, hey?'

'A fitting hide, Roger. It's out of the County, where your Warrant does not run—nor mine.'

'Tom Heber's does.' Roger spoke grimly as he rounded on Frank. 'This is your hare, and you shall have the coursing of it. You may ride at dawn.'

'To command, sir.'

'We'll warn Hargreaves tonight, and he may ride with

you. Arrests, when all is said, are for the Constable. Then to Tom Heber, and persuade him along with you—telling what tale you please. Lister will guide you to where the woman is, and you may see if she has the Devices in hide. Is there more?'

He glanced inquiringly at Nick Banister, and in a moment Nick nodded.

'If the Devices are there,' he said, 'you may tell Tom Heber he may draw a Mittimus on his own account—for the Preston woman. This will hang more than Squinting Lizzie.'

37

Moon-Kissed

Margery did not hear Frank ride in the dawn. She was too deeply sunk in sleep to hear anything at that hour; but when she did wake the sun was gleaming through her curtains, and it tempted her to pull them back. The hour was young and the sun was yet low, and Margery lay back contentedly; and then, while she still lingered, she heard a horse come clopping on the gravel. Curiosity strove with languor, and won. She slipped out of bed and pushed her window open, and at once, as she remembered the proprieties, she hastily withdrew her head; for the rider of that horse was Richard Baldwin.

Languor dropped from her. Richard would not be here at this hour without cause, and Margery wanted to know what it was. She sought clothes and hurriedly got herself to some sort of decency, and then she took the stair at a half-run. For once she was ahead of Roger, and when he appeared, half dressed and wrapped in his furred gown, she had already got Richard into the parlour and was hospitably pouring his ale.

'Pour for me also,' said Roger. 'What news, Richard?'

'James Device,' said Richard briefly.

'The moon-kissed?'

'That one.' Richard drained his ale and looked at them exultantly. 'The lord ordereth a good man's going and maketh his way acceptable to himself. Yesterday I rode to Colne to have speech with my brother there. And as the sun grew low and I came from my brother's house, there was a bellowing in the street like a cow that seeks her calf.

Whereat, knowing that voice, I turned aside and laid hands on him . . .'

'Jemmy?'

'None other. Shaking the peace of the afternoon with his moon-calf bawlings.'

'Most happily met.' Roger caught Margery's eye. 'It may be Milady Fortune's smile.'

'Speak not of the heathen.' Richard was stern and exultant. 'The Lord is known to execute judgment; the ungodly is trapped in the work of his own hands.'

'To be sure, Richard.' Roger spoke soothingly, and Margery was in haste to refill Richard's mug. She thought it might distract him, and she had no taste for Psalms at this hour of the morning.

'And what followed?' asked Roger.

'He journeyed home with me.'

'Willingly?'

'He journeyed. And I've two lads now walking him here.'

'It's very well. You'll breakfast with us, Richard?'

'I have eaten . . .'

'Then you'll eat again.'

They brought Jemmy Device into the Justice Room and stood him before the table. Behind the table Roger and Nick Banister sat in dignity. Margery sat at its end, thoughtfully cutting a quill. Richard sat aside, a watchful spectator.

Roger made no prelude.

'What did you do in Colne?' he asked frostily.

Jemmy's eyes went blinking, and his head rolled on his long neck.

'Hadn't no meat,' he croaked.

It seemed to be his way of saying that he had been begging, and Roger accepted it. His shrewd eyes considered the fellow coldly.

'Where is your mother?'

The idiot face twitched violently and a sullen malice flickered in it. For a moment he stood with his tongue protruding; then he burst into speech, quick, indignant, and all but incoherent. Roger sat patiently, and slowly he pieced it together. On Tuesday morning, Elizabeth Device had first sent Jennet to Whalley, and had then told Jemmy he was to go on a journey with her. They had started as soon as Jennet was out of sight, and had tramped to Colne. Then, as they had no food, they had parted; each was to beg for an hour, and then they were to meet in the market place. Jemmy had done his part, and had duly sought his mother in the market place; but he had not seen her there; he had, in fact, not seen her anywhere, either then or later, and he had been roaming at large ever since, eating what scraps he could beg, and sleeping in what alleys he could find. He had been into every quarter of Colne, but there had been neither sign nor trace of Squinting Lizzie; and the hungry Jemmy was both dazed and bewildered.

Roger accepted the tale without much difficulty. This feeble creature had hardly wit enough to have invented it, and it was, moreover, all of a piece with what was known of Squinting Lizzie; she had certainly abandoned Jennet without scruple, and if she was in flight she must have had at least as great a motive for getting rid of Jemmy. Roger nodded thoughtfully, and turned to another topic.

'Why did you leave your home?' he asked.

Again the gaunt head rolled, and suddenly the idiot laugh came pealing out. It quenched abruptly as Tom Peyton's fist jabbed his ribs, and for a moment Jemmy gasped.

'Cats,' he said suddenly, and Margery sat up in surprise.

'What cats?' Roger's voice was expressionless.

'Daylight Gate.' Jemmy leaned forward, blinking. 'Came home a month back at Daylight Gate, and there were hundreds of 'em, all yelling foul . . .'

'Where?'

'By home it was, and children shrieking too . . .'

'And what of it?'

'I was feared. And one come in, and lay on me an hour.'

'And you were feared of it?'

'I was an' all.'

'It comes of images in clay. Did you know that?'

'Im . . . im. . . .' The fellow gawked, and Richard Baldwin leaned forward in his chair.

'Pictures,' he said to Jemmy, and the twitching face cleared as though that was a word he knew.

'Pictures,' he repeated stupidly. 'Aye, pictures.'

'Pictures in clay,' said Roger softly. 'Pictures of men and women—wrought in clay. You have some in your house, have you not?'

'No. . . . No. . . .' Jemmy was shouting, and Margery watched him keenly. The question had pricked too close for him to bear it. His excitement made that plain, but he stuck to his denial, and Roger turned abruptly to the other thing.

'What of dead men's teeth?' he asked suddenly.

'Teeth? Ha! Ha! Ha!' The laugh was coming again, but Tom Peyton's gesture checked it, and Jemmy stood silent, twitching and rolling.

'Do you keep teeth?' Roger asked again.

'Aye, aye. Got my own,' was the answer, and his mouth popped open to show the truth of it.

Again Roger changed his attack abruptly.

'Who's Jennet Preston?' he asked quietly.

The head shook wildly in denial.

'She came out of Craven,' said Roger coldly. 'On Good Friday she dined at your mother's house on stolen mutton. Do you remember?'

The head shook again, but this time without excitement, and Margery wondered if the denial might not be sincere. Jemmy, after all, might not know Jennet Preston by name.

'Who was at your mother's house that day?'

The question came firmly, and while his loose mind was still groping. It seemed to slip through what caution he had.

'All of 'em,' was his thoughtless answer.

'All of whom?'

Jemmy's mouth shut viciously, as if he realised what he had said. Again his eyes began to roll round the room while his breath came noisily.

'Who was there?'

The question rang steadily, and Jemmy, suddenly meeting Roger's eyes, found something there that held him.

'Friends,' he said sullenly.

Roger nodded.

'Is Alice Nutter a friend of yours?'

Jemmy lurched into Tom Peyton and stood quivering. But Margery spared little heed for him. She had seen Richard Baldwin start at the name, and come half to his feet; he was sitting again now, but Margery knew the thin-lipped hardness that had come upon him. Richard, she remembered, had not heard young Jennet's tale. And Roger, as she now noticed, had also a wary eye on Richard as he persisted with his question.

'Was Alice Nutter at your mother's house on Good Friday?'

Tom Peyton jerked Jemmy upright and spun him round to face Roger. Fear was plain on his twitching face, and a trickle of saliva was running down his chin.

'Was she?'

Roger had lifted his voice for the first time, and at the crack of the question Jemmy recoiled as if he had been hit. Tom Peyton heaved him back stolidly.

'Was she?'

Nick Banister echoed the question, and the cold crackle of his voice matched Roger's. Jemmy's resistance collapsed. He nodded wildly, and began to gesticulate. Then, of a sudden, his wild whooping laugh came again, and when Tom Peyton jabbed him he sagged forward hopelessly. Roger looked with distaste.

'Take him away.'

His icy order was obeyed with swift efficiency. The door shut behind the struggling Jemmy, and they heard his idiot bray come faintly through the oak.

'He's a pretty sight,' said Roger.

'Aye.' Nick Banister nodded. 'You did well not to press him further now. He'll have more to say when he's cooled. Meantime, there's not a doubt he stands in fear of your Alice.'

'Alice? Aye, Alice.' Roger turned slowly. 'Richard, there's a tale here for you to know. A tale of Good Friday and the Malkin Tower—and Alice Nutter.'

'The Malkin Tower? In God's name . . .'

The western sky was a reddening gold when Richard Baldwin at last took his leave and rode away. He went tight-lipped and grim, and in his leave-taking he recited some verses from the fifty-third Psalm. He had heard the whole tale, and he had characteristically found the heart of it in the meeting at the Malkin Tower. To have consorted with known witches in such a place and on such a day would have damned a better than Alice Nutter in the eyes of puritan Richard; and if Alice Nutter was therefore a witch, all else fell in line; she was one among the brood, and that was enough. Had he not always seen witchcraft in the death of his Margaret? And what matter how the work was wrought? Spells or poisons—what did it signify? It was still witchcraft, and now at last he was justified of the Lord. He said it grimly, and he found none to say him nay in it.

The last of the dusk was gone and the candles were bright behind the curtains before Frank came in, haggard, dusty and boisterous.

'We have her,' was his brief announcement. 'Safe taken and secured. But Jemmy—no. Not a sight of the rogue.'

'Jemmy's here,' said Roger briefly. 'Where's Lizzie?'

'Up the Forest, sir, in the house of one James Wilsey.'

'Wilsey? How that, if you please?'

'We walked the woman back, sir. Hargreaves had taken no horse for her. He said a walk would cool her impudence —and so it did. I'll say it for Hargreaves that he knew what he was about. He had her wrists fast to his saddle, and he made her trot as much as walk.'

'Can she trot?'

'When you warm her back parts. But she's something wearied now . . .'

'But not impudent?'

'Not impudent. But we judged it well to spare her the last few miles, and since this Wilsey lives conveniently at the top of the Forest, we lodged her with him. Hargreaves said Wilsey was your last Constable, and would know what was needed.'

'He knows.' Roger nodded with satisfaction. 'That's well done, and we'll see her at Wilsey's—early.'

They rode while the sun was low, Tom Peyton going first with Jemmy in his charge, and Frank riding swiftly and alone to summon Richard Baldwin. Margery rode with Roger and Nick Banister, and her saddlebags held paper and quills and an ink-horn. Jim Wilsey, untidy as ever, gave them a grinning welcome.

'Glad to see you, sir,' he said briskly. 'She's safe and ready. Peyton's brought the lack-wit, and Hargreaves has been here these two hours.'

'Good. And Baldwin?'

'Hell! Is *he* coming, sir?'

Roger laughed.

'Aye, he's coming, Jim. But he'll be no plague this day. There's a warmth come upon our Richard.'

'Lord of Mercy! But come you in—all.'

There was proud welcome from Mistress Wilsey, high of

heart at having two Esquires in her house together, and anxious to prove the worth of her October; and a few minutes more brought the jingle of horses as Frank came cantering in with Richard Baldwin at his side. Then the Wilseys' trim parlour took the semblance of a Justice Room as the table was moved and chairs were set. Roger took the centre, with Nick at his side. Margery took the end of the table, laid out her paper, opened the inkhorn, and took knife to a goose quill. Then all was ready.

'Which first, sir?' asked Tom Peyton.

'Jemmy.'

'Aye aye, sir.'

By the time Margery had her pen trimmed to her liking Jemmy had been set before the table, and she looked at him with surprise and a touch of pity. Something had worked powerfully on Jemmy Device, and such poor strength as he had once had was now quite gone from him. He was sagging limply, and Tom Peyton's arm had to support him; his head was lolling, and only the whites of his eyes could be seen.

'So you bury teeth at your house?'

Roger's crackling tone showed that he meant to make an end. Jemmy twitched and rolled, and Margery had to remind herself that pity for him must not be overtly shown. Jemmy was an unsavoury thing, but the fates of some she cherished might hang upon his words this day.

His head was nodding feebly, and Roger evidently took this for assent.

'Whence came those teeth?'

Jemmy twitched and muttered something about the Newchurch. Across the room a chair creaked where Richard Baldwin sat, and Roger took one fleeting glance at him and hurried on.

'And pictures wrought in clay—whose pictures?'

Jemmy gaped as the question cracked, and then he became incoherent. Roger stopped him and made him start again, and slowly his meaning was made out; some of the pictures had been of Anne Nutter, and some of a certain Robinson. At once Roger was pressing him on that, and soon Jemmy had said that he meant John Robinson, a kinsman of Kit Swyer of Barley. Roger turned to Richard Baldwin.

'The man's dead, is he not?'

'Aye, three years agone. But he was mostly called Swyer.'

Roger nodded and turned on Jemmy again; and in two sharp questions he had it from him that Squinting Lizzie had herself made, and crumbled, these images of the departed Robinson.

'Set that down,' said Roger grimly, and Margery put it down in detail; clearly it promised to be useful.

'What pictures did *you* make?'

Roger was inexorable, and Jemmy was far beyond resistance. In another minute he had admitted to making an image of Mistress Towneley of Carre.

'Who died twelve months agone,' said Roger. 'Set that down also.'

He waited till her pen had finished scratching. Then, coldly and at his ease, he surveyed the twitching saliva-dubbed face before him.

'So you *did* have Jennet Preston at your house on Good Friday?'

His tone had relaxed a little, and Margery stole a glance quick at his face; something of pity, she thought, was blended with its stern authority now. Jemmy was nodding weakly, and at once Roger was pressing him further.

'Did she go outside during dinner?'

Another nod gave assent to that. Soon Jemmy had confirmed all that little Jennet had said; his mother had been called from dinner to speak with Alice Nutter on the grass outside; but more than that, Jemmy did not know. He called Alice Nutter an evil woman, and he was plainly in fear of her; but of facts he had none.

'Take him away,' said Roger at length, and turned thoughtfully to Nick Banister. 'You see how it is? Fingers, fingers and fingers, and they all point to Alice. But of facts there's never a one. Do we commit this Jemmy?'

'We must. He's admitted to making images of Anne Towneley, and they'll call that murder since she died thereafter.'

'Aye. And at the least he meant it so. Make it out so.'

Margery busied herself in doing it. She was getting used to drawing a Mittimus now, and she had the forms by heart. She wrote it quickly, and in silence the two Justices signed.

'Elizabeth Device,' said Roger curtly, and Tom Peyton hurried out. Margery smoothed fresh paper and began the cutting of a new pen.

'Squinting Lizzie!' called Tom Peyton cheerfully, and a sullen scowling woman was hustled in.

She limped to the table and glared at them with one eye while the other rolled its white to the ceiling. But Squinting Lizzie was not the woman she had been. Her walk from Trawden had tamed her, and she had no longer the force that commonly gave sting to her insolence.

Roger's hostile stare seemed to disconcert her, and for once she fidgeted and looked uneasy.

'It's sworn against you that you did murder one John Robinson, at times called Swyer.' Roger's voice rang coldly. 'What do you say to it?'

Elizabeth Device said nothing to it. She stood in a sullen silence, and Roger turned to Margery.

'Read what her son has set against her.'

Margery sorted her papers, found the one she needed, and read from it in dry and formal tones.

'And the next day this Examinate saw his said mother take clay at the west end of her said house, and make a Picture of it after the said Robinson, and she brought it into her house, and dried it some two days; and about two days after the drying thereof, this Examinate's said mother fell on crumbling the said Picture of clay, every day some, for some three weeks together; and within two days after it was all crumbled or mulled away, the said John Robinson died.'

Margery's clear voice stopped, and the woman by the table puckered her face in anger.

'Loose-tongued bastard,' she muttered savagely.

'Since he's your son, we'll suppose you to know . . .'

Her eyes rolled in a streak of white.

'Him!' Her contempt for Jemmy was scorching. 'Who speaks of him?'

'Who else?'

'Jack Swyer it is, and he's in Hell for it.'

'For what?'

'Called me a ditching whore, he did. And him no better than . . .'

'Why did he call you that?' Roger spoke coldly as she grew heated.

'Because of Jack Seller, and he was a better man than . . .'

'Enough. We'll spare your amours. Swyer called you whore, did he? So you wrought him in clay and he died. Is that it?'

'I was meet with him for it.'

'Meaning that you did. Quiet . . .' He turned again to Margery. 'Set that down.'

Again she plied her pen, well knowing that what she wrote would hang this woman. But there was no help for that. And Pendle, she thought, could well spare Squinting Lizzie. Then Roger was at it again.

'You'd guests at your house on Good Friday—feasting while others fasted. And you plotted to kill Master Thomas Covell? Is it so?'

'No.' She was sullen, but the word was clear, and she stuck to it against all Roger's pressure. She admitted the meeting, but she denied the plot. Squinting Lizzie might have lost her impudence, but she was far from pliable, and Roger again changed direction abruptly.

'What of Master Lister of Westby? There was talk of killing him?'

'Not me.'

'Who then?'

'The Preston bitch.'

'She spoke of it, did she? To whom?'

'She bawled it like a crier.'

'To all and sundry? I see. But who was it who spoke with her apart?'

A malignant shadow crept over the scowling face. But no answer came. Then Roger's hand slapped on the table, and the woman jumped nervously.

'Who was it?'

The blaze of anger in his voice was too much for her shaken courage, and suddenly she answered him.

'Alice Nutter.'

She almost spat it out, and there was malice mingled with her compliance. But Roger was impassive again, and at once he was pressing her for details. He had it from her that she, too, had talked apart with Alice Nutter and Jennet Preston, but that was all. Lizzie had recovered her courage, and she was as stubborn as Roger. She stoutly denied all intent to harm her mother, and swore that she had thought the apple tart to be sweet and good. Alice, she said, had chatted to her and Jennet Preston only about the trouble Jennet had been in at the York Assizes; and it was only because of that, said Lizzie, that she had gone to Gisburn to give talk and comfort to the woman. She had almost a leer as she said it, but she stuck stoutly to it till Roger's patience was out.

'It's enough,' he said at last. 'Take her away.'

He pushed his chair back and stretched his long legs as she was hurried out. There was a general stir. Wilsey was pouring ale, and Richard Baldwin had moved to join the Justices. Hargreaves went to join them while Margery busied herself with drafting the inevitable Mittimus.

'Are we any nearer, Nick?' Roger spoke doubtfully.

'No,' came the prompt answer. 'They'll hang Jemmy over Anne Towneley, and Lizzie over this Robinson. But in what might touch Alice Nutter we are no inch nearer.'

'Could they have told no more?' It was Richard Baldwin, and he spoke angrily.

'They've spoken enough to hang themselves. Can we ask more? Which sets me in mind, we'll need a Mittimus for her.'

In silence Margery passed it across, and in the same silence Roger signed it. Nick Banister took the pen; and as he ended his signature there was a clatter of hooves outside and his eyes turned quickly to the window as a slim rider swung from a lathered horse. Then the door swung open, and with neither manners nor ceremony Miles Nutter burst into the room.

'What the Devil!' said Roger, and Miles halted abashed. Richard was the first to find speech.

'What is it, lad?' he asked anxiously. 'Is aught amiss?'

'Aye—or it may be.' Miles halted again, tongue-tied, and remembering perhaps his forgotten manners. Jim Wilsey pushed him into a chair.

'Sit you down,' he said gruffly. 'A sup of ale's what you need.'

Roger nodded permission, and Miles drank thirstily. Then he came to it.

'It's my mother,' he said briefly. 'She came to me at Wheathead—at the mill, where I then was.'

'What's that?' Richard Baldwin sounded startled.

'She came to the mill,' repeated Miles patiently. 'She—she said . . .' He stopped, and Margery felt sharp sorrow for him; the tale he was trying to tell was, after all, of his mother. But he drew himself up and plunged at it. 'She told me I'd be wise to leave my uncle's house and return home directly. Else, she said, it might appear I'd—I'd had some hand in what ailed my Uncle Tony.'

'What's that?' Roger's voice came softly in the stunned silence of the room.

'Aye—and there's worse.' His voice cracked as he stumbled for words. 'She said it was my father who put juice of herbs . . .'

He stopped again, and licked at dry lips. Nick Banister went quietly to him, and his hand was on Miles' shoulder as he spoke.

'It's a foul tale, lad,' he said quietly. 'But you may take heart. You may count us your friends here. There's nothing lies against you or your father. I'll warrant that from all of us.'

There was a murmur of assent in the room, and then Roger's voice came steadily.

'By what reasoning was so much fastened on your father?'

Miles turned to face him. He seemed to have found new courage, and his voice was steady as he explained it.

'There was venom in a syllabub, and I carried it to my uncle the day he was most stricken. But—but it's true my father handled it first.'

'Handled it? How?' Roger spoke very quietly.

'It was a Sunday. My mother rode to the church at Whalley, and she was the first to go. Then my father rode for the Newchurch, but it was he, before he went, who handed the syl'abub to me.'

'But your mother had first handed it to him?'

'That she now denies.'

'The Devil she does!' said Roger. 'So your father handled this, and is now ridden out of Pendle?'

'Aye—as she said.'

'Aye aye,' Roger nodded. 'I think we have it plain.'

He sank into silence; and Margery, looking at Miles, went

suddenly to his side and pressed his hand in her own. Frank came to his other side.

'Count me your friend at need,' he said simply.

Miles looked from the one to the other in mute gratitude; and then, surprisingly, Richard Baldwin spoke softly.

'Get you back to Wheathead, lad. There's matter here to hurt Grace as well as you. Go comfort her.'

Roger, brooding by the window, turned quickly.

'Aye,' he said firmly. 'Do that—just that.'

Miles needed no more persuading. He hurried out, and Frank went with him to see him to his horse. Then, in the silence, Roger spoke icily.

'This woman gets past bearing. And I think we must not be too nice in our ways. Come, Nick—let's to horse.'

'Whither?'

'To the Rough Lee.'

38

The Steward's Room

The Rough Lee was bleakly inhospitable.

For the third time Harry Hargreaves set the knocker thundering, and still the oaken door stayed shut. Margery, sitting her horse among the others, had a side glance at Roger, and saw his nostrils begin to dilate. Roger was not used to being kept waiting.

Then, as Richard Baldwin, with tight lips and lowering brow, slipped from his horse to join the Constable, there was a grind of bolts from within, and slowly and without haste the door was swung open. It disclosed a fellow in the sky-blue that was proper for servants, and Margery disliked him at sight; she thought him a sallow-faced rogue with an insolent lip, and nothing in his manner made her like him better.

'What's here?' he demanded with a grin.

'Here's some gentlemen and a lady,' said Hargreaves curtly. 'For speech with your mistress, and at once.'

The fellow stared impudently.

'I'll go tell her,' he said. He made as though to shut the door in their faces. Then he changed his mind on that, grinned again, and led them in. They trooped after him in silence as he swung another door.

'You can wait in there,' he said.

A black-browed Roger spoke dangerously.

'You'll curb your insolence and stir yourself. And tell your mistress she's required, not requested—and by the King's Justices.'

Richard Baldwin's whip slapped his boot. The fellow looked, saw Richard's face, and quailed; then he took one white-faced glance at Roger, and suddenly his mouth shut. Whatever he had intended was left unsaid, and without a word he went off.

'What's in here?' said Roger.

He strode into the room the lackey had opened, and Nick Banister followed him. Richard Baldwin went after them, and on the threshold he halted, cold anger showing plainly in his face.

'What's this?' he asked. 'Esquires put to the Steward's room?'

It was as he had said. Margery, following him, recognised the room at a glance. Once before, on her first day in Pendle, she had been in this room. Half smiling, she looked at Richard.

'In here I first set eyes on you,' she told him.

'Aye—so it was.' His eyes swept round the room as he remembered. 'A day of September, with Harry Mitton stretched on the table there. And I sat here reading.'

'Reading a Psalter.'

'Was it so? Your eyes were keen.'

'They needed to be. I'd to watch my going—that day.'

His stern face relaxed, and for a moment he smiled.

'Aye,' he said softly; and she guessed that he had remembered his first hostility to her orange-tawny.

'Set chairs to the table,' said Roger suddenly. 'We sit as before.'

They went about it quickly. Roger and Nick Banister, still in their hats, had chairs behind the table. Margery, as usual, sat at its end. There was a single chair left, but as none would take it from his fellows, the men all stood, ranging themselves against the wall. Then, as if on impulse, Richard left them and walked across to the hearth; he brought out flint and tinder and set light to the firing that was stacked there ready for the flame.

'If these folk give no courtesies, we must make them for ourselves,' he said truculently.

He stepped back, and while he watched the dry wood flare and crackle, the door-latch clicked, and Alice Nutter swept into the room. She halted, decorous in black and silver, bright of eye and erect of head, and she was the embodiment of cool dignity as her dark eyes played upon them.

'What's this?' she demanded icily. 'I had almost thought beggars were come to town.'

As the noisiness of beggars was a by-word, this was a plain insult. Roger parried it neatly.

'Not beggars, ma'am, but the King's Justices.'

His voice came calmly. It asserted his authority, and it told nothing of his feelings; and Margery, watching keenly, saw the dark eyes narrow. Alice Nutter was far too wary to take Roger lightly.

'Indeed, sir? You do me honour. May I know why?'

She was still icy, but she was not insolent. It was as if she had recognised that this was too serious for such antics.

'We've some questions to ask.' Roger spoke as calmly as before. 'You'll first be sworn.'

She made no demur, but when it was done she moved quickly to the empty chair and coolly seated herself. Roger ignored that and spoke precisely.

'Lately,' he said, 'you were pleased to lay information before me touching certain persons of ill repute who on Good Friday met at the Malkin Tower and there dined. You did not think fit to mention one Jennet Preston as being among that company—although it seems you had close speech with her.'

'I had speech with her for perhaps a quarter-hour.'

The answer came calmly and at once, and Margery was almost startled at this woman's composure. Then she understood. Alice Nutter was far too astute to deny what could be proved; and while Margery still considered that, Alice spoke again without waiting for another question.

'You've been listening to gossip, sir, and since I don't doubt you've had half a tale, you may fittingly have the other half. This Jennet Preston . . .'

She paused, and her eyes had become very shrewd and searching as though she were appraising the perceptions of the impassive man before her. Then she had almost a smile as she spoke again.

'Jennet Preston and I were girls together in Trawden, and for the sake of that I show her what small kindnesses I can . . .'

'Treasure in Heaven, no doubt.'

The old sardonic note was in Roger's voice, and for a moment Alice seemed disconcerted. Then she recovered.

'I do not jest,' she retorted with dignity. 'This woman came out of Craven and sought my counsel. She was in deep distress . . .'

'Had been,' said Roger, and Alice checked at the interruption.

'Had been?' She was almost querulous.

'She'd been acquitted, had she not—of child-murder?'

'Precisely so.' If Alice had again been disconcerted, she had recovered quickly. 'Such a charge would distress any woman.'

'I rejoice in that assurance, ma'am.'

The dark eyes blinked, and for a moment her temper showed.

'Will you hear me, sir? Or, if not, will you take your leave?'

There was spirit in that, but before Roger could answer it, Richard Baldwin spoke unbidden.

'There's children dead in Pendle too. One of them was mine. And others that were not children.'

She swung round on him, her face pale and vicious. But she did not speak. Whatever was on her tongue stayed unsaid, and her mouth shut tightly. Slowly she turned back to Roger, and once again she was speaking smoothly.

'The woman had harmed no child. And being rightly acquitted at York she came here to Pendle, where she had some small acquaintance with several. Which is how it chanced that when I stumbled across those women, at the Malkin Tower that day, Jennet Preston was among them. Yet she was not of their company or counsels. She had come only to ask that one of them should bring her to me. Which is why I chose to speak with her apart. I could not refuse so small a thing.'

'You were most accommodating, ma'am. And being with her there, you talked of—what?'

'Her distress—and nothing more.'

'Spiritual counsel, as it were? That's odd matter at a feast of witches, and on Good Friday.' Roger's voice was hardening. 'What manner of gull do you take me for?'

Alice Nutter smoothed an imagined crease from her kirtle. She paused again to flick imagined dust from its decent black. Then she looked up, half smiling.

'Should you not beware, sir, lest that be asked of you? I'm not a Demdike.'

Her voice was smooth and bland, and there was a hint of mockery in it that made Margery look sharply at her. Again Alice Nutter flicked, as though she saw dust on the cream satin of her stomacher and on the silver lace that laid the black taffeta. And at once Margery found her meaning plain. Satin and taffeta and silver lace! Assuredly this woman was not a Demdike, and no jury would suppose that she was. That was what she was telling Roger. Suspicion would run off this decorous lady. Sworn testimony would be needed here, and of that there was little or none; and it was hardly to be doubted that she knew that as well as they did.

'For the moment we'll let that pass.' Roger's voice was as steady as before, but the watchful Margery thought him none too hopeful. 'There's another matter, and Richard here has put his finger on it.'

'His child who died?' Alice was almost airy now. 'I thought he'd sworn that against the Demdike.'

'There are some others, as Richard has said. One of them was your own brother-in-law, lately distempered.'

'Poor Tony, you mean? And what of it? He was distempered, as you say. But he's mended and there's no hurt done. Is there need to probe further?'

'There is great need.'

Roger's tone was cold, but it did not disconcert her.

'At your insistence,' she said. 'But I'd hoped to spare some scandal. Is it not enough that my husband's fled?'

'Your husband is not in question, ma'am.'

'He will be, if you probe further.'

The smooth voice had an edge in it now, and the sly threat was plain; but Roger would not be put off.

'You insist on accusing him?'

'That's a harsh word.' The dark eyes were unwavering. 'I'll guess that my son has been to you.'

'He has.'

'Then at least you know the set of things. It may be—though I blush to say it—that my husband did put venom in a syllabub and let my son carry it to Goldshaw.'

'I rejoice that you can blush, ma'am.' Roger's tone had the ice of winter in it. 'And since you pretend so much, may we know why your husband should so conduct himself?'

'Inheritance of land, sir. So also, as I do fear, with his elder brother, who died these twenty years . . .'

'Robert? Do you seek to fasten that also upon your husband?'

'I seek to fasten these on none. I've told you, I'll gladly spare this scandal. It's you that delve and probe, not I.'

'It is indeed.' For the first time Roger's anger was plain in his voice. 'And it's you, madam, whom I accuse. Not your husband but you.'

'Do you so?' Her effrontery was unshaken, and she was returning his hard stare with eyes as steady as his own. 'And what shall follow from that?'

'Your committal to Lancaster—if you can find no better tale than this.'

'I'll need no better tale than this.' The dark eyes were pinpoints now. 'I'll tell it at Assize to judge and jury. And I'll remind you, sir, that I'm not a Demdike and they'll not suppose me one. It's my husband who inherits from his brothers, not I. It's my husband who's fled, not I. It's my husband who'll quake and stammer, not I.'

She rose to her feet, erect and steady.

'Commit me, sir, if you've a mind to—and it may be that you will work my ruin. But it's a deal more likely that you'll hang my husband, and for what you say he has not done.'

She paused, and in the icy silence Margery felt a cold shiver in her back. She glanced at Roger and saw his knuckles white as he grasped the table. And Alice Nutter laughed; a cold tinkle of a laugh that had a leer in it.

'I'll retire, sir, to my parlour. You'll wish to ponder this at leisure.'

Her taffeta rustled. Her head was erect and her shoulders square as she glided to the door, and then, with the door open, she turned for a last insolence; correctly, precisely, deliberately, she curtseyed; and as Roger sent his chair scraping back, she was gone and the door had clicked behind her.

'Grace of God!' said Roger Nowell.

'A woman of parts,' said Nick Banister calmly. 'And I much fear that she's right about the ways of juries. She's a murderess, no doubt, but . . .'

'She's a damned witch,' said Richard Baldwin savagely, 'and should have been so committed.'

'Witch, do you say?' Nick was as calm as before. 'You're very likely right, Master Baldwin, but I doubt our getting proof of it.'

'She was at the Malkin Tower on Good . . .'

'God's Grace!'

They turned on Roger, all of them, as his words cut through their talk; and at the sight of his brooding face they stayed silent and expectant. Slowly he seated himself again.

'Richard,' he said softly, 'do you mind the last day we were in this room together?'

'With Harry Mitton on the table here?'

'Just so. How say you that Mitton died?'

Richard stared in surprise.

'I told you—witchcraft,' he said slowly. 'And you'd have none of it.'

'Would I not? Yet who bewitched the man?'

'Demdike and Device.'

'None other?'

Again the chill shivered in Margery's back, and this time it was Roger who had set it there; and at the soft menace in his tone, Richard stood dumb, and Nick Banister leaned forward.

'Roger,' he whispered. 'What's this?'

Roger turned slowly.

'You've put it squarely, Nick. We dare not commit on poison lest we hang an innocent. But witchcraft—that's different. We can at least prove her at the Malkin Tower.' He paused, and then he spoke briskly. 'Who'll be Judges of Assize this August?'

'Altham and Bromley, from what I've heard.'

'A pretty pair! Either would hang any witch for twopence.'

'Roger!' Roger! Nick was expostulating mildly. 'Even Bromley needs a pair of witnesses.'

'He shall have them. I've said we must not be too nice in our ways. Where's that woman?'

'Alice Nutter, sir?' Hargreaves was alert at once.

'No. The Device.'

'Waits outside, sir.'

'Bring her in—her and her precious son.'

Hargreaves went out, and Wilsey with him. Their footfalls rang across the boards; and then silence gripped the room while Roger sat stiffly, his face set and his eyes smouldering.

The footfalls came again, and Elizabeth Device was pushed into the room; the unhappy Jemmy followed, and Roger stared coldly at them.

'How did Harry Mitton die?' he asked suddenly.

They gaped at him, taken aback by the unexpectedness of it; and then Jemmy went off into his idiot peal.

'She did it,' he crowed. 'She did an' all.'

'Who did?'

'He means his grandmother.' Lizzie had intervened quickly, alert to save herself.

'Demdike was it? And how?'

Again Jemmy whooped.

'He denied her a penny. And her spirit sat on him. Sat on him it did. And all for a penny.'

Roger nodded.

'And your spirit also?'

He spoke to the woman, and when she shook her head in quick denial he leaned forward across the table to her.

'You're committed for a confessed murder,' he told her, 'and that will do your business sufficiently. One more shall scarcely signify. Your spirit and your mother's, both of them, sat on Harry Mitton. But there was another woman whose spirit sat also. Who was that?'

She stared blankly at him, and he leaned forward farther.

'Yesterday you were taken at Westby, where you thought yourself secure. Who was it, think you, that knew where you were, and could tell us where to seek you?'

Her lips moved uncertainly, as though she were on the brink of speech, and a sly smile came on Roger.

'Who was it that came to me with word of your consortings on Good Friday?' Roger paused, and then his words fell slowly in the silence. 'Who was it that would have you put to silence?'

Her eyes widened; and suddenly she understood.

'The goddam bitch!' she burst out. 'The poxy lying trull! She said . . .'

'*Who* said?'

'That goddamned Alice. She said . . .'
'Whose spirit sat with yours?'
Elizabeth Device stood twitching while her eyes rolled madly. Then she steadied one of them on Roger, and Margery saw the hate that flamed in it.
'Hers!' She seemed to spit the word.
'Whose? Let's have it plain.'
'Alice Nutter's.' Malice writhed across her face; and then, for once and once only, Squinting Lizzie laughed. 'And all for a penny,' she shouted. 'All for a penny.'
'A dear penny,' said Roger quietly. 'You swear to this?'
'Swear and be damned.'
'Swear and be damned.' Jemmy whooped with glee. 'That's good, it is. Damned good.'
'Do you swear it too?'
'Me? Aye, I do an' all. Swear and be damned.'
Roger turned to Margery.
'To their depositions, add that.'
'Aye, sir.' She dipped her pen and wrote hastily while Nick Banister looked cryptically at Roger. Roger saw it.
'Say not that I do ill?'
'I'll not gainsay you, Roger.' Nick shook his head. 'And truly I think you do well. This woman needs a hanging, and there's no other way. When a woman has both riches and repute . . .'
'Those don't protect when it's witchcraft.'
'For that thank God,' said Richard Baldwin, and Roger nodded his assent.
'Neither does absence at Lathom,' he added. 'It's all one when there's talk of a spirit sitting.' He looked at Margery and saw that she had finished writing. 'Bring the woman in.'
Hargreaves moved quickly to obey, and Richard Baldwin went zealously with him. Margery looked round her, at Roger and Nick Banister impassive at the table; at Jemmy and his mother, watched warily by Wilsey and Tom Peyton; and at Frank, stiff and silent by the wall. For a moment he had the ghost of a smile for her. Then the door opened, and Alice Nutter came in between the two men; and at sight of Roger her face went chalky; a slower wit than hers would have read the menace in his eyes.
'There's further matter against you,' he said curtly. 'Read it to her.'

Margery obeyed stiffly, and she felt her voice shake as she read the formal sentences.

'Good God! What's here?'

It came savagely, cutting through Margery's level tones like a scream in the night; and smooth and level came Roger's answer.

'Matter to hang a witch,' he said.

'Witch! Are you mad?'

'Ask Sir Edward Bromley. He has a way with witches. Make me the Mittimus.'

'I was not there.' She almost screamed it at him. 'When Mitton died I was . . .'

'Telling tales at Lathom. We've cause to know those tales, and you'll tell no more of them. You've tarried overlong in Pendle. Take her out.'

She shrieked as they closed on her, and there was livid murder in her eyes. But the hard-faced puritan had her by the arm as the papist Constable took the other, and between them they spun her round. Frank moved watchfully behind as they tugged her out.

Margery forced her attention to the Mittimus as she wrote it in the ancient form; and before she had ended, the uproar had died and Jemmy and his mother had been taken after Alice Nutter. She finished, and then looked up at the quiet room. Nick Banister was sitting impassively, and Roger was standing by the hearth.

'What's set against her?'

She sanded the paper and then read it to him slowly:

'. . . she did feloniously practise exercise and use her devilish and wicked arts called witchcrafts enchantments charms and sorceries, in and upon Henry Mitton; and him the said Henry Mitton by force of the same witchcrafts feloniously did kill and murder: contra formam statuti in huic casu nuper edicti et provisi: et contra pacem Domini Regis, Coronam et Dignitatem suas.'

Margery's voice died away, and Roger nodded approval.

'It will serve her need,' he said shortly. 'Nick, I think we should see them horsed.'

'Aye,' said Nick soberly. He went out with Roger, and Margery was left alone.

She came slowly to her feet and stared unseeing at the open door, her mind on the assizes that would come to Lancaster, and on what must follow on a windy moorland there. She stirred uneasily, knowing that for good or ill it was done, and that it might not have been done if she had not come to Pendle. Then her eyes came back to the present, and to the goose-quill in her hand. She looked and shuddered; almost she could see blood on the thing, and she ran to the hearth and thrust it into the fire that Richard had kindled in his anger; and when it scorched and curled and twisted into sizzling black there were faces in the smoke —Demdike and Alizon and Alice Nutter.

Margery turned away, shuddering; and Frank, coming in search of her, found her cling to him as never before. Neither of them heard footsteps in the doorway.

'God's Grace!' said Roger, and stood in staring silence.

His friend's hand was on his shoulder.

'Surely', said Nick Banister.